Praise for Isa

'There are plenty of twists to this compelling and compassionate tale, but it's the sensitivity with which Isabelle Grey handles the legacy of harm that gives the story its beating heart'
Sarah Hilary, author of *Someone Else's Skin*

'An intelligent, sophisticated police procedural with a completely believable central character and a strong moral core. Emotional and hardhitting, highly recommended'
Sinead Crowley, author of *One Bad Turn*

'The sort of book Rendell could have produced . . . the standout crime novel so far of 2017' *Crimesquad*

'Plenty of suspense and gripping, instructive writing about real people facing impossible, often tragic predicaments. This is an excellent crime novel, warmly recommended' *Literary Review*

'Combines attention to detail with compassionate intelligence'
Sunday Times

'Full of well-handled forensics and the brooding atmosphere of the Essex coast' *Mail on Sunday*

Isabelle Grey is a television screenwriter whose credits include Jimmy McGovern's BAFTA award-winning *Accused: Tina's Story* as well as over thirty-five episodes of *Midsomer Murders*, *Casualty*, *Rosemary and Thyme*, *The Bill* and *Wycliffe*. She has also written non-fiction and been a magazine editor and freelance journalist. Isabelle grew up in Manchester and now lives in north London.

Also by Isabelle Grey

Out of Sight
The Bad Mother

The DI Grace Fisher series
Good Girls Don't Die
Shot Through the Heart

The Special Girls

ISABELLE GREY

Quercus

First published in Great Britain in 2017 by Quercus
This paperback edition published in 2017 by

Quercus Editions Ltd
Carmelite House
50 Victoria Embankment
London EC4Y 0DZ

An Hachette UK company

A CIP catalogue record for this book is available
from the British Library

PB ISBN 978 1 78429 285 0
EBOOK ISBN 978 1 78429 284 3

10 9 8 7 6 5 4 3 2 1

Typeset by Jouve (UK), Milton Keynes
Printed and bound in Great Britain by Clays Ltd, St Ives plc

For Jo Strevens

Detective Inspector Grace Fisher heard an owl hoot as she got out of the car. It was somewhere off away in the thick darkness of the woods on the opposite side of the road. The faintest whisper of a breeze in the night air rustled the treetops and brushed her cheek as she inhaled the dry, earthy smell of last winter's leaf litter.

'What genius thought it would be a good idea to stop there?' she asked, shaking her head at the two marked police cars pulled up on the verge beside a five-bar gate. 'Right where the perpetrator might have left a vehicle if they had one.'

'Idiots,' agreed Detective Sergeant Blake Langley.

Although she had invited Blake's comment, it annoyed her, and she reminded herself to leave her own negative thoughts unspoken. Chiding herself for her lapse and trying to undo it, she nodded towards the uniformed constable who stood beside the gate ready to escort them to the body. 'It's probably not his fault,' she said. 'No fun hanging about here for an hour in the dark waiting for us to show up.'

'He must have done something to draw the short straw.'

Grace sighed. Not for the first time since Blake had joined the Major Investigation Team in Colchester three months ago, she missed her familiar wingman, DS Lance Cooper. Still, this was neither the time nor the place for regrets; she would just have to keep in mind that the new sergeant had a good reputation as a thief-taker and was easy enough to get along with as long as she ignored his default-mode scornful attitude.

Taking a forensic suit from the boot of their car, she went ahead to identify herself to the young constable and thank him for what she hoped hadn't been too long a wait. 'So where exactly are we?' she asked him.

'On the northern perimeter of the grounds of Wryford Hall,' he said. 'The village, that's Long Wryford, is off to the west.'

'And this road, where does it go?'

'Nowhere really. It winds around a few farms and a small hamlet about three miles away before joining back up with the main Long Wryford to East Fordholt road. Most people just take that.'

'So you mean we're slap bang in the middle of nowhere,' said Blake, joining them.

'Pretty much,' the constable agreed.

'At least house-to-house won't use up too much manpower then,' said Blake cheerfully.

'There are some people staying at the hall,' said the constable. 'Or camping in the grounds, anyway.'

'OK,' said Grace. 'Lead on.'

It was a week or so before the summer solstice, and even well after midnight some light remained in the sky. Under the canopy of the woodland, however, it quickly became dark, and even with a torch Grace was glad the constable seemed to know where they were heading.

'Have we managed to identify our victim yet?' she asked.

'A Dr Tim Merrick. Mr Thomas, who owns the hall, recognized him. He found him when he took his dog out last thing and called the emergency services. Says that Dr Merrick was here with the party that's camping.'

Ahead of her Grace could see a huddle of officers. Beyond them, wound around a wide ring of tree trunks, her torch picked out blue and white police tape. She greeted the local officers and went forward to look beyond the tape. A white trainer caught the light, and she tracked the beam along khaki chinos and a smeared sweatshirt to short brown hair glistening with what she could only assume was blood. The face lay hidden in the scrubby leaf cover beneath the trees, but the exposed skin of the back of his neck looked hauntingly young.

'Can you give me more light?' she called. Those officers with flashlights illuminated what they could of the body and surrounding area. The ground was dry and hard, but there was enough woodland debris to show signs of disturbance – a scuffle, a sexual assignation, a life-or-death struggle? – and, a few feet from the body, a thick branch that looked as if it had been recently moved – perhaps picked up and then flung aside?

'I want Dr Tripathi to take a look before anyone else touches him,' she told Blake. 'Give him a call and see how soon he can attend. And then get Wendy and a scene-of-crime team down here. Ask them to call me as soon as they arrive.' She turned to the local uniformed sergeant who had summoned her. 'I want proper lighting, and two officers on duty here at all times to keep the scene secure. We don't want any foxes or whatever sniffing around. The rest of you can leave carefully in single file. Can one of you please show me the way to Wryford Hall?'

'I'll take you over there, ma'am,' said the uniformed sergeant.

'But I'd like any spare officers to go over to the campsite. There's kids there.'

'Good idea, thanks.'

He fell into step beside her. The tree cover soon gave way to open parkland. Underfoot the grass felt parched and crunchy, more like mown hay than lawn. After a short walk the meadow ended at a gravel driveway on to which spilled light from a line of tall windows, four on each side of wide steps leading up to a front door topped by a curved transom light. Bathed in moonlight, the hall was a handsome flat-fronted, two-storey house. Outlined against the starry sky, Grace could see a pronounced dip in the roof line where ancient beams had settled over the centuries. Apart from a few large pots planted with geraniums, no attempt appeared to have been made to create a garden.

'They don't really use the front door,' said the sergeant. 'Best to go in through the back.' He led the way around the side of the house. 'My daughter got married in the tithe barn here. I got to know Minnie and Toby Thomas quite well. They're very nice people.'

A low door under a sloping roof led directly into a large kitchen. An elderly chocolate Labrador lying in a frayed tartan dog bed slapped its tail against the tiled floor in greeting. Every surface, including a massive pine table that took up the centre of the room, was covered with an assortment of crockery, pans, food, wine bottles, candlesticks, appliances, books, newspapers, wicker baskets filled with yet more stuff and two sleeping cats. A couple of empty champagne bottles sat among the hurriedly cleared remnants of an evening meal. At the Aga, waiting for a huge kettle to boil, stood a tall slender grey-haired woman in frayed jeans, a man's shirt and flip-flops. As she turned to look at them, Grace was struck by the beauty of her face, especially her eyes, which were dark and lustrous under finely arched brows.

The sergeant made the introductions before excusing himself and disappearing back out into the night as Minnie Thomas leaned across the table to shake hands. 'Is he really dead?' she asked.

'I'm afraid so,' said Grace. 'I'm very sorry.'

'I can't believe it. I've been praying that somehow Toby and the paramedics got it wrong. I took rugs and things down there, just in case, but Toby wouldn't let me anywhere near.'

'A sensible precaution. We haven't formally identified the victim yet, but your husband recognized him. Is that right?'

'Yes. He said it's Tim Merrick.'

'Did you know him well?'

'No, not really. Hardly at all.' Steam emerged vigorously from the kettle and Minnie poured water into a large brown pot. 'Tea?'

'No, thanks,' said Grace. She would have loved a cup but needed to get the measure of the situation first. 'Can you tell me anything about him?'

Minnie shook her head. 'He was young, polite, helpful. His first time here with the summer camp.'

'Summer camp?'

'Ned will explain it better than me. Professor Ned Chesham. He runs the eating disorders unit at St Botolph's Hospital in London. You must have heard of him.'

The name did seem familiar, but Grace couldn't recall a face to go with it. She shook her head.

'Well, he brings a group of them here every summer,' said Minnie. 'They camp for a week. Proper camping with tents and singing around the fire and swimming in the lake.' She shook her head sadly. 'They were due to go home tomorrow. Today,' she added, glancing at the big wall-clock.

'The constable said Tim Merrick was a doctor. Was he also at St Botolph's?'

'I assume so. Ned usually brings a couple of the junior staff to help out. Says it's good training for them. This year it's Tim and Crystal Douglad. She's a nurse, and has been here before.'

'We'll need the names of everyone staying here.'

'Ned will give you those. It's a busy time of year for us. We do weddings and B and B,' she explained. 'Besides, Ned knows the ropes far better than we do. We just let him get on with it really.'

The back door opened, and a rotund apple-cheeked man, about the same age as Minnie but a good head shorter, came in. He wore faded red corduroy trousers and a moth-eaten navy sweater. The Labrador immediately heaved itself out of bed and went to thrust its nose into his hand. Grace liked the way he smiled absently down at the dog. Blake followed, shutting the door behind him.

'Toby Thomas.' The man held out his hand to Grace and gave hers a firm shake. 'Thank you for coming. Dreadful business.'

Grace introduced herself and looked over his shoulder at Blake, lifting her eyebrows in an unspoken question.

'Dr Tripathi and the CSIs are on their way, boss.' He looked at his watch. 'Another half-hour probably.'

'Thanks.'

'I went over to let Ned know what's happening,' Toby told his wife. 'Everything's quiet down there. Ned decided not to wake anyone up until he has to.'

Grace also turned to Minnie. 'If it's OK, I will have that cup of tea while we wait for the pathologist.'

Grace watched Toby and his wife commune quietly by the Aga as Minnie mustered four chipped mugs and a pretty milk jug that looked like a family heirloom. Toby invited them both to sit down, sweeping things aside to make room at the cluttered table.

'If you don't mind, Mr Thomas, could you please talk us through finding the body?'

Blake got ready to take notes as Toby heaved a deep sigh, preparing to relive his earlier shock. 'I was later than usual taking the dog out for her bedtime run. We'd been celebrating.' He smiled for the first time. 'The birthday honours. Ned got a knighthood. Jolly well deserved!'

'Ned and Toby have been friends since Cambridge,' explained Minnie.

'We'd had a fair bit to drink, so I wasn't terribly alert. Would've walked right past him if it hadn't been for Daisy.' Hearing her name, the dog raised her head. 'At first I thought it was an injured animal lying there, a deer or a badger or something, but Daisy kept on whining and wouldn't come when I called. Luckily I had my phone in my pocket, and as soon as I got some light and saw it was a man and how badly hurt he was, I called 999. I was pretty sure he was dead. He felt cold and I couldn't find a pulse. But I rang Minnie to bring down some blankets, and called Ned so he knew to keep an eye out in case some maniac was running around.'

'Did you see anyone else while you were walking the dog?'

'No. It must have been well past eleven. And Ned runs a pretty tight ship down at the camp.'

'Does anyone else live here in the house with you?'

'Only our youngest now, but he's away at university. It's not the end of term yet.'

'And on the estate?'

'There's no estate,' said Toby with a smile. 'Those days are long gone.'

'Where is the campsite?'

'Down by the lake. There's a cricket pavilion nearby with basic bathroom and kitchen facilities. My great-great-grandfather built it and laid out the pitch. It's not much to write home about now, but the village likes to use it, so we keep the place in working order.'

'Where's that in relation to where you found Tim Merrick?'

'In the opposite direction, on the far side of the park. I'll find you a map. We treat the camp as out of bounds while Ned's here.'

'Except for food,' said Minnie as Toby left the room in search of a map. 'Ned pays me to do the shopping and some basic preparation, and the girls are on a rota to come and fetch each day's supplies. It's all part of the treatment.'

'The treatment?' asked Grace.

'The girls are patients at his unit,' said Minnie. 'They all have eating disorders. Anorexia mainly.'

Grace tried to review what she knew about anorexia nervosa. Even though the 'slimmer's disease' was a pervasive illness among girls and young women, she'd never known anyone who suffered from it. Her understanding of the condition was culled solely from articles in magazines and the occasional celebrity story or fashion industry scandal.

'Wouldn't it have been safer to bring them indoors?' she asked.

'They're all fast asleep,' said Blake. 'And there are now at least two officers down there with them.'

'I assume their parents have been called?'

'Ned decided it would be better to wait until dawn,' said Minnie. 'He didn't want to risk a parent turning up in the middle of the night and getting them all hysterical.' She must have seen Grace's expression. 'If you saw them ... Even though the ones here are recovering, they're still so fragile. It's desperately sad.'

'So why bring them camping?' asked Grace.

'They love it,' said Minnie simply. 'He's done it every year, ever since Toby's parents' time. And it always goes well, never even been too unlucky with the weather.'

Toby returned carrying a large framed watercolour. 'This will give you the lie of the land. The map is nearly two hundred years old, I'm afraid, but not much has changed.'

Grace and Blake came to stand beside Toby, who angled the picture so that the overhead light did not reflect off the glass. The antique map, faded but still beautiful, reminded her of an illustration in a Tolkien book. The points of the compass were marked in red in a top corner, and at one side the woods where Tim Merrick's body now lay were washed in pale green with neat rows of individual trees symbolically outlined in ink. On the other side, concentric ripples spread out from a tiny fish jumping in the blue lake. There should be no place in such a bucolic scene for the sharp image that sprang into Grace's mind of the young man sprawled in the darkness with a crushed skull and blood-matted hair. Perhaps, she thought, the edge of the map should be inscribed, *Here be monsters*.

It was dawn before Samit Tripathi, the local Home Office pathologist, had completed his examination of the body and agreed with Grace that it could be moved. The corpse was stiffening but not yet rigid, and combined with its temperature, this suggested that Tim Merrick had been dead for around an hour before he was found. Dr Tripathi's opinion at this stage was that the victim had been floored by a blow or blows from the broken branch found nearby and then hit repeatedly on the head and face once he was on the ground. There were defensive wounds on his forearms and excessive damage around the mouth and jaw, probably inflicted by a blood-stained rock found a few yards away.

Once Samit had gone, Grace left Wendy, the crime scene manager, to direct a fingertip search of the dusty woodland floor. The sun had risen enough for Grace to find her way back to the hall without a torch, yet, despite the chorus of birdsong, the colourless dawn light felt bleak and surreal. Tim Merrick had been in the full bloom of life, handsome and strong-limbed. The attack on him had been savage. What had he been doing out there in the darkness under the trees last night?

Grace had called ahead to ask Blake to have Ned Chesham at the hall ready to speak to her before his young campers began to stir. She found Blake in the kitchen waiting to lead her through to the drawing room, a long, high and narrow chamber into which the unused front door opened directly. Much of the wall opposite the door was taken up by a vast fireplace surmounted by a tarnished mirror in a gilt frame. Two well-worn velvet-covered sofas faced each other in front of the fireplace, one already occupied by the two cats, which had moved from the warmth of the Aga into the first patch of pale sunlight. Chesham was sitting on the other, intent on his phone. Grace could hardly believe he had been at university with Toby. He appeared a good ten years younger, of middle height, slim and athletic, with fair hair and blue eyes that matched the colour of his shirt. He looked weary but jumped up as soon as he saw them.

'I hope you don't mind,' he said, holding up his phone. 'I was texting my secretary to ask her to find the contact details for Tim's next of kin.'

'If you wouldn't mind passing them on to us first,' said Grace, 'we'll send someone to break the news in person.'

'Of course. Whatever I can do to help.'

Grace dislodged a cat so she could sit facing him. Blake positioned himself beside the front door, slightly out of Chesham's line of sight. Chesham sat back, crossing his legs and resting his hands in his lap, ready to listen. Grace imagined that the impression he gave of having all the time in the world must be a valuable professional skill.

'When did you last see Dr Merrick?' she asked.

'About a quarter to eight, when I left to come here for supper.'

'And where was he then? Who was he with?'

Chesham took a moment to remember, a slight frown on his face. 'He was supervising the washing-up in the pavilion. I wouldn't normally leave the camp, but' – he shrugged bashfully – 'Minnie and Toby insisted we celebrate.'

'Yes,' said Grace. 'Congratulations on your knighthood.'

'Thank you. It's an accolade for everyone who works on the unit.' He spoke as if he genuinely meant it. 'Helpful to the hospital too.'

'Did you leave the hall at any time last night? To check on the girls or anything?' Chesham's hosts had already told her that the three of them had spent the entire evening together, with Chesham returning to the campsite only when Toby left to take Daisy for her walk.

Chesham shook his head. 'They were in safe hands with Tim and Crystal. Little did I realize it would be Tim who was at risk.'

'Who else was in the pavilion when you spoke to him?'

'Beth and Meghan were on washing-up duty,' he answered promptly. 'Tim shooed me away, told me to go and have a good time, that the kids would be fine. They were excited for me. I was very touched. So off I went.'

'So how had things been this week? Did everyone get on? Did Tim have any problems with anyone?'

'Life is never going to be problem-free when you're dealing with adolescents, let alone adolescents with eating disorders.' Chesham smiled. 'But aside from the usual dramas, the week has gone well. I always bring some of the younger staff. I'll introduce you to Crystal, one of our specialist mental health nurses, once we're finished here.'

'Does she know what's happened?' asked Grace.

'Not yet. She shares a tent with two of the youngest girls, so I didn't want to wake her in case I disturbed them.'

'But she's definitely there?'

'Yes, don't worry. I did a headcount as soon as Toby called me last night. I share a tent with Tim so was already wondering where he'd got to.'

'He'd not been unexpectedly absent at any other time?'

'No. The week is pretty full-on for the staff who elect to come, but it's good for them to spend 24/7 time with their patients. It helps them understand the kind of pressure the families have to withstand. I was pleased when Tim asked to come. He was a very promising young doctor.' Chesham sighed and bent down absently to stroke the dislodged cat, which was rubbing its arched back against his legs and purring loudly. 'I don't suppose you can tell me what happened to him?'

'Not yet,' said Grace. 'Can you think of a reason why Dr Merrick would have been on the other side of the park?'

'No. None at all. He should never have left the camp.'

'Might he have just gone for a walk – stretch his legs before turning in?'

'No. We have to be on the lookout all the time. A common feature of anorexia is secrecy and deceit, and we usually find at least one girl trying her best to sneak away so she can work off a few extra calories. He was supposed to be on watch.'

'Anything going on between Tim and Crystal?'

Chesham looked surprised. 'I very much doubt it. And they'd both know of the extremely dim view I'd take of anything that might destabilize the patients.' He looked at his watch. 'They'll be waking up soon. I should be there.'

'We'll need to speak to each of the girls before they go home,' said Grace. 'Is that going to be a problem?'

'Yes, of course it is. They're young and their psychological well-being is already precarious.'

'We can wait for their parents to get here before speaking to them separately,' said Grace, 'but I think we need to let them know what's happened before rumours start flying around.'

He nodded reluctantly. 'Once you've seen how they react to the news, maybe you can tell me how you want to play it and I'll do everything I can to assist.'

'Thank you.' She glanced at Blake. Had she overlooked anything?

'What time would the girls have gone to bed?' he asked.

'They have to be ready for bed at nine,' said Chesham. 'Then it's quiet time until lights out at nine thirty. The youngest here with us this year is twelve. And we're all up early.'

'Be great if you could you explain for me the purpose of the camping holiday,' said Blake. 'How exactly does it work?'

'Sure,' said Chesham. 'These are kids who feel like they're being watched all the time, and who also obsessively police themselves. They are world experts in self-denial. They're not used to playing or taking risks. But here they can spend time away from home, swim in the lake, climb trees, toast marsh-mallows on the fire, watch the stars, but in a safe environment alongside the people supervising their treatment. Our aim is to establish a healthy adolescent identity and increase personal autonomy.' Chesham laughed. 'Sorry, that's my little presenta-tion speech! But coming here does seem to work. We've been doing it for nearly twenty years.'

'OK, thanks,' said Blake. He signalled to Grace that he had no more questions.

'Professor Chesham—'

'Ned. Please. Everyone calls me Ned.'

Grace smiled. 'Do you have any thoughts on who might have had a reason to kill Dr Merrick?'

'Absolutely none. He'd only been with us a few months, but he seemed open, pleasant, uncomplicated.'

'What about any of your patients?'

Chesham stiffened. 'They're children.'

'I know,' she said. 'And I'm not suggesting they're capable of murder, but I have to ask.'

'The fact that these kids are psychiatric patients doesn't make them violent,' he said. 'Quite the opposite. Their destructive urges are all turned inwards. That's what we're battling to overcome. You have to understand that anorexia is a life-threatening condition. Ten per cent of anorexics die, and for others it's a lifelong disease. There's no quick fix. These kids and their families really suffer.'

'I didn't realize the outcome was so serious,' Grace said. 'If, later, any of them come to you with information, anything they saw or heard, or if they say anything to their parents, you will let us know?'

'Of course.'

'Thank you. I think that's it for now.'

Chesham stood up, brushing cat hair off his jeans. 'If you don't mind, I'm needed back at the camp.'

'If you could hang on for a minute,' said Grace, 'we'll walk over with you.'

Chesham nodded. 'I'll wait in the kitchen.'

Blake shut his notebook and went to close the door behind him. 'So what do you think, boss?'

The disparagement in his tone made her impatient. 'Why? Do you think he was keeping something back?'

'No, he was fine.' Blake's mouth pinched in disapproval. 'Though you have to admit, it's a pretty odd set-up.'

With the sun higher in the sky the park seemed bigger and more expansive than it had an hour earlier. In the distance, beyond a magnificent spreading cedar, lay the woodland where Tim Merrick's body had been found. Turning in the other direction, Grace and Blake followed Ned Chesham past an ancient barn and down a slight slope. A new vista opened before them of a small lake fringed on the far side by silver birch. Mirroring the curve of the water were four khaki-coloured tents that reminded Grace of an old-fashioned scout camp. Beyond them was an expanse of grass which, in contrast to the parched meadows of the park, was green and neatly cut. Overlooking the cricket pitch stood a white-painted pavilion fronted by a fretwork-decorated veranda, its tiled roof topped by a weathervane. It was, she thought, the kind of classic English scene that Agatha Christie would have loved: idyllic on the surface but with dark emotions seething beneath.

'They're up,' said Chesham, nodding to the young figures flitting between the tents and the pavilion. Keeping an eye on the girls was an older woman in knee-length shorts, flip-flops and a white T-shirt pristine against her black skin. Seeing them approach she came to meet them.

'Ned.' She sounded relieved. 'Do you know where Tim's got to?' Her words carried a slight West Indian lilt.

'Crystal, this is Detective Inspector Fisher and Detective Sergeant Langley,' he replied.

'Good morning,' said Grace.

Crystal's eyes showed natural anxiety that turned to shock as Grace briefly outlined how Tim Merrick had died. Her hand unconsciously grasped the gold cross that hung on a chain around her neck. 'God rest his soul.'

'When did you last see or speak to him?' asked Grace.

Crystal frowned, taking time to remember precisely. 'It must have been a little after nine o'clock, once the girls were all tucked up. I usually stay with the younger ones, reading my book, until they nod off. We do the rounds alternately, so I wouldn't have expected to see him after that. Not until morning.'

'So you check regularly that the girls are in their tents?'

'At least until we're certain they're all fast asleep.'

'Had Tim said anything to you that might explain why he'd leave the camp?'

Crystal shook her head. 'He was fine. Maybe a bit preoccupied, but then we're coming to the end of a pretty exhausting week.'

'OK, thanks.' After her own sleepless night, and despite several cups of Minnie's strong tea, Grace could empathize with tiredness. Noticing that a couple of the girls were casting curious glances in their direction, she turned to Ned. 'If you could gather them together, we'd better break the news.'

She and Blake hung back as doctor and nurse went ahead to herd the eight girls gently into the cricket pavilion. She could see them becoming alarmed and was struck by how each was like a little island. When she'd been that age, she and most of her friends would have linked arms or been draped inseparably around one another, oblivious to the tedious interruptions of the adult world; these kids had vigilant eyes, hands bunched under the long sleeves of extra-baggy tops and shoulders hunched against the outside world. Still, they were not the skeletal wraiths she had feared. Skinny and immature for their age, maybe, children rather than teenagers, but not like some of the stick figures with sunken cheeks and grimacing mouths that she occasionally saw exercising to burn off more calories when she was out running.

'Come on,' she said to Blake. 'And keep your eyes peeled for any behaviour that stands out.'

'Not envisaging a *Lord of the Flies* scenario, are we, boss?'

'Hardly. But I doubt there's much that escapes these kids.'

Blake nodded and strode off towards the pavilion. Grace followed more slowly, dreading the words she would have to say.

In the event she was struck most of all by their self-restraint. As Professor Chesham had said, they did indeed police themselves and their emotions rigorously. Tania and Meghan were the youngest at twelve and thirteen, Beth, Lara, Ali, Kim and Mia were all fourteen, and Reena was the eldest at fifteen. Their eyes grew even wider, Meghan and Lara shrank further into themselves, wrapping their arms around their ribcages, and Beth and Reena wiped away tears with their long sleeves.

Crystal shook her head and appeared to mouth a prayer. Grace had noted earlier that the skin on the nurse's hands and arms was smooth and flawless – no sign of defensive or other wounds – and if she was covering up any knowledge of Tim Merrick's murder then she must be a very fine actor.

Grace explained to the girls that until their parents arrived – which would be soon – they must all remain together in the pavilion and not discuss the events of last night. 'We'll need to ask each of you where and when you last saw Dr Merrick, so that we can piece together his movements,' she said. 'None of you are in any trouble, but we need to gather all the information we can. And if any of you did see or hear anything that might shed light on what took place, however insignificant it might seem, then you can tell us privately.'

Her heart went out to the little group, already so forlorn and marginalized, all of them apparently afraid to grow up and take hold of life. Was Blake right that this was an odd set-up? Or had everyone become so concerned with political correctness and bureaucratic health-and-safety restrictions that going out on a limb and organizing something as unconventional as this camping holiday seemed almost crazy? Yet Chesham had said he'd brought vulnerable kids here for twenty years without incident. Now, like the adults, they would have to describe their movements, submit to showing their hands and arms, account for any fresh marks or scratches, and allow all their clothes to be checked for bloodstains. However unlikely it was that one of them was a killer, each would have to be scrupulously ruled out as a suspect.

4

Later that day, in Colchester, Grace watched as Blake fixed a recent photograph of the twenty-eight-year-old victim to the murder wall alongside the maps and crime scene photographs. Despite all the digital tech now available, she liked to keep the old-fashioned essentials of a case in plain view. The photograph was a holiday snap of Tim Merrick looking happy atop a mountain peak and had been supplied by his parents, who had travelled to Essex that morning and, in a daze of grief, formally identified their son's body. Each time Grace witnessed this process, she felt even more strongly that no one deserved to lose a loved one to violence. All she could do was assure them that she and her team would do everything in their power to identify who had taken Tim away from them and bring them to justice, even though the reality was that so far the Major Investigation Team had precious little to go on.

The essential members of the team had been called away from their various summer Sunday-afternoon activities to attend the briefing, including their boss, Detective Superintendent Colin Pitman. Rangy in black jeans and a box-fresh white shirt, he remained at the edge of the circle, leaning against a desk and listening attentively as Grace, feeling grainy-eyed and over-caffeinated, summarized Samit's preliminary post-mortem report. There was little new to add: Tim had been healthy, showed no sign of recent sexual activity, and had defensive wounds on both forearms.

'Dr Tripathi thinks there was only one attacker,' she said. 'The weapons were a fallen branch and a rock, so it does not appear that the perpetrator came equipped or necessarily expecting to kill. And there's no evidence to suggest that the victim either fought back or was the initial aggressor.'

'I doubt there'd be poachers around at this time of year,' said DC Duncan Gregg, 'but what if Merrick disturbed his killer doing something they shouldn't?'

'It's a possibility,' said Grace. 'The concentration of injuries around the mouth, breaking the jaw and several teeth, were almost certainly inflicted once the victim was already on the ground.'

'Do we think that's significant?' asked Colin Pitman.

'It might be,' said Grace. 'Especially if Tim Merrick stumbled upon the killer doing something they were ashamed of. Blake, can you give us his last known movements?'

'The last sighting was by Crystal Douglad, the clinical nurse specialist, shortly after 9 p.m. Two of the girls confirmed that Crystal checked on them at nine thirty and again around ten,' said Blake. 'Professor Chesham spent the evening at the hall with Mr and Mrs Thomas. They were in each other's company throughout. The only other people we know to have been within the grounds of Wryford Hall last night were the eight young girls who were camping there, who Crystal confirms were all where they should have been.'

'Samit believes it's highly unlikely that an undernourished teenage girl could have overcome a fit and healthy six-foot man,' said Grace.

'Not impossible, though, if she had the element of surprise?' suggested Colin.

'No,' she admitted. Chesham had told her that no dangerously underweight patients were allowed to come on the summer camp and explained that, because starvation robs the brain of the ability to think normally, his first aim was always to get an anorexic patient back to a weight where therapy might actually have some effect. He had also warned, however, that regained weight should never be mistaken for restored psychological health.

'We shouldn't entirely rule them out as suspects,' she said. 'So I want background checks on each of the girls and their families.'

'None had any visible defensive wounds,' said Blake. 'One of the girls had recent scars on her arms – and thighs too, apparently – but Crystal confirmed it was from self-harming.'

'For medical confidentiality we agreed not to record her name,' said Grace.

'We checked everyone's clothing for bloodstains and found nothing,' said Blake. 'Crime scene will be examining the bedding and so on in the tents.'

'For now we should concentrate on the nearby gate that led to the road,' said Grace. 'This could be a random killing by a stranger.'

'Or by someone Tim Merrick had arranged to meet there,' said Blake.

She nodded. 'Absolutely. We'll get on to victimology in a moment. Duncan, what about local inquiries?'

'No record of any similar crimes in the area,' he said. 'Nothing going on locally that seems significant; no one of interest to us living nearby, and no reports of any disagreements between the hall and the village.'

Grace turned to the crime scene manager. 'Wendy, did you find anything to help us?'

Wendy shook her head. 'Afraid not. No rain in the past fortnight. The ground was hard and dry. We found plenty of blood spatter, which we're running for DNA, although no consistent patterns because of disturbance and the nature of the scene. It's highly likely the perpetrator's clothes will be heavily bloodstained, but we found nothing on the ground or, as yet, on the victim's clothes that will give us a lead. There's nothing to indicate how the offender arrived at or left the scene, although, given its relative isolation, I'd expect some means of transport – car, motorbike, bicycle. Sorry not to be of more help.'

'Thanks anyway.'

'One thing to bear in mind,' said Wendy. 'Although the perpetrator left nothing behind, it doesn't mean they took nothing away.'

'OK, we'll remember that.'

'What else do we know about the victim?' asked Colin. Grace could see that he was becoming impatient at the lack of actionable leads.

'Dr Timothy Robert Merrick. No criminal record. Full safeguarding checks. Finances seem in order.' Blake ticked each point off his notebook. 'He joined Professor Chesham's unit at the end of January as a psychotherapy registrar. No steady girlfriend. He didn't have a laptop or tablet with him, and we're waiting on his phone records, although use of all mobile devices was supposedly banned at the camp. Crystal Douglad said Dr Merrick was well-liked, easy-going, would make a good psychiatrist. She's in her mid-thirties, married with two small children, an experienced nurse who's been at St Botolph's for three years.'

'He must have had a good reason to leave the campsite,' said Grace. 'Especially when they were short-handed, with Professor Chesham having dinner at the hall. So had he planned to meet someone? Did he know anyone locally? Had he reported any kind of harassment or threat? And why was he near the gate to the road? Did he know it was there? Had he been there before? How familiar was he with the layout of the park?'

Blake and the rest of the team scribbled notes. Duncan received and read a message on his phone and went over to check something on his computer.

'So what's with this camping business?' said Colin. 'Is it, like, Girl Guiding for anorexics or what?'

Blake smiled in sympathy with the comment. Grace saw Colin glance at him in approval and hoped her boss wouldn't be swayed by the sergeant's cynicism. As Blake folded his arms across his navy polo shirt, making his well-toned biceps bulge beneath the short sleeves, she made a mental note to have a quiet word with him later, point out that, as far as she was concerned, there was no place in this inquiry for such casual scorn.

All the same, there was no hiding the fact that Ned's annual summer camp was not officially sanctioned by the hospital. Toby and Minnie, who had moved into the hall two years previously after the death of Toby's mother had forced his eighty-five-year-old father into sheltered accommodation, had simply accepted the camp's continued existence along with the hall's leaking roof. The set-up was idiosyncratic to say the least, but she supposed that if Professor Chesham had stopped to untangle all the red tape, these breaks from hospital routine would have had to stop for good.

'I spoke to all the parents when they arrived to take their

children home,' she told Colin. 'They'd all been thrilled when their daughters were picked because they'd heard such glowing reports from families whose kids had been before.' She saw the superintendent look again at Blake, who made no attempt to hide his scepticism. 'OK, so it's all a bit Famous Five nostalgic,' she said, 'and I imagine Professor Chesham will now have to take a lot of flak for not jumping through the right hoops, but I think what he's trying to do there seems rather refreshing.'

'I've got a teenage daughter,' said Colin. 'Every time she makes a fuss over some bit of food, I start praying she won't go anorexic on us. It's every parent's worst nightmare. Given Professor Chesham's track record, I'm not surprised that people just let him get on with it.'

Grace hadn't expected such understanding, especially when she knew how Colin had championed Blake's appointment. Aware that her boss still blamed her for Lance Cooper's abrupt departure, she hadn't been in a position to argue too strongly for her own choice of candidate, but it was nevertheless ridiculous for her to hold Colin's approval against the new member of the team. It wasn't Blake's fault that Colin combined being a smart operator as a cop with being an untrustworthy weasel of a man, and having Colin's support did not make Blake in any way suspect. She resolved to try harder not to judge him.

'I want you all to do your best on this,' she told the assembled team. 'Tim Merrick was a promising young doctor with his life before him. He died as a result of a sustained attack by a violent assailant. We're going to get whoever did this and put them behind bars where they belong.'

'Boss?' Duncan looked up from his computer screen. 'We've

just been sent Tim Merrick's phone records. He made only one call from Wryford. It was yesterday, at 6.47 p.m., lasting nearly ten minutes.'

'Find out who the call was to,' said Grace. 'See if we can speak to the person today. Maybe he or she can finally shed some light on what this was all about.'

5

Clive Goodwin drained the pasta and waited for the steam to evaporate. He needed those extra few seconds to prepare himself for the ordeal of another family mealtime and prayed silently to the mound of spaghetti that this brutal murder wasn't going to throw his daughter's treatment off course. He and Gillian had been told that Meghan's recovery would be a slow process. Professor Ned had warned them it wasn't like surgery: there was no quick fix, no magic bullet, not even after she regained enough weight to appear normal again. They had to be prepared for setbacks. And yet life had, almost unbelievably, gradually improved over the few months since Meghan had been accepted as a patient at St Botolph's. He'd almost begun to believe that his perfect, joyful, busy little girl really would come back to them. But now this. What was Dr Merrick's death if not a setback?

Clive knew his attitude to the young doctor's murder was selfish and callous, but he defied any father to think differently if, after watching helplessly as his beautiful child turned into a spitting, suspicious, hateful skeleton, he'd been offered the chance of a miracle. Before Professor Ned he had sometimes wanted to walk away and have nothing more to do with women's bodies ever again. Even his decision to marry had been prompted by Gillian falling pregnant with Meghan. Not that he'd been particularly unhappy about it, and the day Meghan was born he'd fallen instantly in love, but now he had this to deal with and he didn't feel equipped for it. It wasn't what he'd imagined signing up for.

He stood frozen at the sink, afraid to turn and set the meal in motion. If Meghan started again with that business of scraping off every speck of sauce and cutting each single strand of spaghetti into ever smaller and smaller pieces he was afraid his heart would simply break, and that would be the end of him. He'd willingly undergo any physical torture rather than endure more of this agony.

'Come on, darling. You're letting the pasta get cold.'

Gillian's voice cut through his rising panic. Composing his expression he tipped the spaghetti into a dish and carried it to the table. The Bolognese sauce, in another bowl, was already on the table. They had learned to serve salad as a separate course, so that untouched food could not be hidden beneath a lettuce leaf.

'Help yourselves,' he said, aiming for a tone of voice that didn't sound too falsely bright and optimistic. Meghan hesitated – and Clive knew that Gillian too was holding her breath – before reaching for the serving spoons. She took a reasonable amount of both pasta and sauce. As he helped himself, he watched covertly as she ate her first few mouthfuls without any delaying tactics. Allowing himself to drop his guard, he found that he was hungrier than he'd thought.

None of them knew what to say. He and Gillian had agreed not to talk at the table about Dr Merrick or the summer camp, yet it seemed wrong to chat as if nothing had happened. After eating almost half of her food, Meghan put down her fork.

'Would you believe me if I said that I just don't feel like it? I mean, who would?'

'Try another few mouthfuls,' said Gillian before Clive could stop her.

'I'm too sad,' said Meghan, pushing away her plate. 'I liked Doctor Tim. He was sweet.'

'It was a horrible shock,' said Clive. Gillian had not accompanied him on the early-morning drive to Wryford Hall. They'd had to wait their turn to speak to the police, and it had been a couple of hours before they were free to leave. 'It's been an incredibly stressful day,' he said, hoping that his wife would hear his warning tone and back off. Meghan did, for she nodded at him gratefully.

'I understand, darling,' Gillian told Meghan. 'But you know what Ned would say if he was here. Food is medicine. I can see how upset you are, but you still have to eat. Ned wouldn't let you get away with it, now would he?'

'I don't care what Ned would say! Why does no one ever care about what I want?'

'Meghan, we just want you to be well,' said Gillian.

Clive watched as if in slow motion as Meghan picked up her bowl of spaghetti in both hands, held it aloft and then dashed it to the floor. Although this was a scene enacted in this room many times before, he had been lulled by the recent weeks of relative calm. As Meghan ran out and he listened to her footsteps on the stairs and then the slam of her bedroom door he felt as if he was about to collapse or have a stroke or simply lose his wits and go stark staring mad. He reminded himself of what

Ned had said in a family therapy session, that this was the adrenalin coursing through his veins, a fight-or-flight response to the anxiety and frustration of dealing with a dangerously ill child who believed that food would kill her. He must keep breathing and wait for the panic-inducing rush to subside, must remind himself that this behaviour was not his beloved daughter but the anorexia fighting for its survival.

'Shall I go up to her?' asked Gillian.

'Not yet,' said Clive. He drew in a deep breath and sighed it out. 'I hope we didn't make a terrible mistake letting her go to the camp before she was ready.'

'Are you blaming me?' Gillian's voice was shrill. 'Because I was the one who thought it would be so good for her?'

'No, no,' he said wearily. 'Not at all. It's just such a damn shame, when she seemed to be doing so well.'

'I feel so guilty,' she said, going to fetch a cloth and dustpan and brush to start clearing up the mess. 'Just imagine, all last week we were thinking how good it was to be normal again, that it was such a relief to imagine her running about and having fun like an ordinary kid.'

Clive hoped his wife wasn't about to start crying. He wasn't sure he could cope. He thought about going up to talk to Meghan, but he and Gillian would first have to discuss whether or not they were going to try and make her come back down and eat some more pasta. He couldn't face either of those battles. Looking at his own congealed food in despair, he hated Tim Merrick for getting himself killed.

6

Grace and Blake had decided to wait for the worst of the week-ending Sunday traffic to die down before setting off for London. Grace would have liked to nip home first for a quick shower and a change of clothes, but was too eager to gain some momentum on this inquiry. They'd left Duncan to follow up a few local leads around Wryford Hall, but she had little confidence that even his diligent legwork would produce a breakthrough. She crossed her fingers that Helen Fry, whom Duncan had identified as the recipient of the call Tim Merrick had made a few hours before his death, would shed some light on what had happened.

They'd discovered what little they could about her in the time available: she was thirty years old, a clinical nurse specialist in Professor Chesham's unit at St Botolph's with a degree in children's and mental health nursing. She'd been there for nearly four years and was working towards a qualification in family psychotherapy. Although her number was in Tim's phone memory, there was no record of his having made any other call to her, and the few work-related texts they'd exchanged had been brief and practical.

'Given the timing of Tim Merrick's call, is it possible that he went to meet her by the gate to the road?' Grace asked, thinking aloud.

'You suggesting he made a booty call?' Blake laughed.

'Unlikely, given their previous uneventful call history, but the timeline is possible. Wryford Hall is less than two hours' drive from London.'

'There's no car registered in her name,' he said. 'I checked before we left. Though she does have a driving licence.'

'Fair enough. And Duncan spoke to her to arrange our visit. If she was Tim's girlfriend, you'd think she'd have said so.'

'She might have reason to be cagey about that,' said Blake, his eyes on the road. 'The prof said he disapproves of relationships between staff, remember.'

Grace nodded and fell silent. She'd just have to be patient for the remainder of the journey.

The basement door to Helen Fry's flat in a leafy road in Crouch End was opened by a willowy young woman with pale skin and silky light brown hair drawn back into a single plait. She wore jeans and, despite the warmth still lingering in the late-evening air, a pale blue sweatshirt. She welcomed them in with wary politeness. A sliding door stood open to the garden, and glasses and a jug of homemade lemonade had been put out ready on the coffee table. Grace gladly accepted a cool drink and found it delicious.

'Your colleague said on the phone that you wanted to talk to me about Tim,' said Helen once they were settled. She addressed Blake but it was Grace who responded.

'Yes. How did you hear of his death?'

'Ash called me this afternoon,' said Helen. 'Ash Rajani. He's head of Adult Psychiatry. He wanted everyone to know before coming to work tomorrow. People are very upset.'

'When did you last speak to Tim?'

Helen bit her lip, looking from Grace to Blake and back again. 'He rang me.'

'When was this?'

'Yesterday evening.' Helen's gaze was fixed on Blake's pen as he took down notes. 'Saturday, about half-past six.'

'And what did you talk about?'

Helen looked scared. 'Do I have to say?'

Grace smiled reassuringly. 'We'll be as discreet as we can, but Tim was murdered. You need to tell us everything.'

Helen nodded, rubbing her hands together anxiously. 'He said he was having inappropriate thoughts about one of the girls.'

Grace hid her surprise. 'Go on.'

'He rang me because he wanted guidance. He wasn't a bad person, he really wasn't. It was counter-transference, I told him that. It happens. It's not real.'

'You'll have to explain.' Although Grace remembered Freud's theory from her psychology degree, the outlines had dimmed.

'Sometimes a patient will develop feelings for a member of staff. They're young girls, full of hormones, lonely and desperate to feel normal. Or sometimes they'll project their fear about their own sexuality on to one of us. Either way, the other person might unconsciously start to feel what they're feeling. So Tim was probably picking up on a patient's attraction and maybe also their ambivalence, denial and rejection. It's complicated. I said he should discuss it with his clinical supervisor when he got back.'

'Would that be Professor Chesham?'

Helen shook her head. 'We're usually supervised by someone outside the unit, someone who can be more objective. I don't know who Tim's supervisor would be.'

'Did he tell you which patient he was concerned about?' asked Grace.

'No.'

'And you didn't ask?'

'I advised him to take it to his supervisor.'

'You were speaking for nearly ten minutes,' said Blake.

'We're trained to listen,' said Helen. 'To reflect back, to let the other person arrive at their own insights.'

'Do you have any reason to think he might have gone beyond inappropriate thoughts?' asked Grace. 'That he could have said things or made sexual advances to one of the girls?'

'He said it hadn't gone that far. That's why he called me.'

'Do you think this started at the summer camp? Had you noticed anything or discussed his behaviour before they left?'

'No.'

Helen got up, collected the lemonade glasses and took them through to the little kitchen that opened off the living room. Grace and Blake exchanged glances but remained silent. Grace took the opportunity to look around the room. The walls, carpet and curtains were all in neutral colours and everything was neat and spotless. The only personal touches were a vase of irises on the small dining table, a shelving unit crammed with books, and a framed photograph on the mantelpiece above the empty fireplace in which Grace recognized Ned, Crystal and Helen with a group of other people who she assumed were other staff at the unit.

Helen came back into the room, her arms crossed tightly over her chest. 'I'm sorry,' she said. 'I'm finding this very difficult to talk about.'

'Of course,' said Grace. 'Take your time.'

'Do you know if he called anyone else?' Helen asked.

'Did he mention that he might?' Grace wanted to get a better handle on this new information before giving too much away.

'I just thought ... It couldn't have been suicide, could it?' Helen asked abruptly.

'No, definitely not,' said Grace. 'Look, you mustn't worry about where this leads. You just have to tell us everything you know and trust us to get it right.'

'If you're worried about one of your patients,' said Blake with a sensitivity that Grace would not have anticipated, 'then, in my experience, when someone ends up being killed because of a situation that has got out of hand in some way, the person responsible is often only too relieved to have it all resolved and to be offered a chance to face up to what happened.'

Helen stared at him before speaking. 'I'm sure it was all in his head. He said he'd been having these thoughts and feeling like a voyeur. That's all it was.'

'And he never mentioned who it was?'

'No.'

'Were you and he good friends?' asked Grace.

'Not especially, no.'

'Only I wonder why he didn't speak to Crystal Douglad or Professor Chesham.'

'Tim said he couldn't find an opportunity at the camp when he could be sure of speaking privately. And we all work very closely together in the unit.'

'Why didn't you come forward with this information as soon as you heard from Dr Rajani that Dr Merrick had been murdered?' asked Blake. 'You must have realized its implications.'

'I think I was in shock,' said Helen. 'And, you know, why

malign the dead? Tim would never have been violent towards anyone. He was a good, caring doctor.'

'And you've no ideas about who might have killed him?'

'No.'

'Can you think why he might have left the campsite? He was found on the other side of the Wryford estate.'

'I think maybe I suggested that, if he was struggling, it might be an idea to put some distance between himself and the girls,' said Helen. 'I can't really remember. I'm sorry.'

'One last question,' said Blake, responding to Grace's almost imperceptible nod. 'Routine, I'm afraid. Where were you last night?'

'Tim's call upset me,' she said. 'I didn't want to stay in alone, so I went over to Hampstead Heath for a walk.'

'Did you speak to anyone? Other than the call from Tim?'

She shook her head slowly. 'No, I don't think so. I remember that I popped out again later, to post a letter, a birthday card. I don't remember what time that was. Poor Tim. I wish somehow I could have saved him.'

'OK, thank you.' Blake closed his notebook and sat back, waiting for Grace to signal that she was ready to leave.

Helen looked exhausted, and Grace wondered what it was that she wasn't telling them. Had she been in love with Tim? Was she protecting one of the girls? Helen must see them all constantly in the clinic and get to know them well. Their parents too. 'Is there anything useful you could tell us about the eight patients who were chosen this year to go to the summer camp?' she asked. 'There was Beth, Lara, Ali, Meghan, Mia ...' Grace counted the names off on her fingers and then looked to Blake for help with the rest.

'Reena, Tania and Kim,' he finished for her.

'Ned only takes those who are doing well enough to go,' said Helen. 'In some ways the camp is quite tough for them. It's a different routine, not much privacy – some of them get homesick. But they all come back with an enormous sense of achievement. It can be a real turning point.'

'We spoke to all of them this morning, and also to some of their parents, but only to establish when they last saw Dr Merrick and what their movements were last night. Professor Chesham said that hiding things is a symptom of the illness. Would you be able to tell if one of them was keeping a big secret?'

'They're my patients,' said Helen. 'Anything they tell me is confidential.'

'But if one of them was worried or had something on her conscience, it would be your job to help her, wouldn't it?'

'They're just kids,' said Helen.

'Vulnerable kids,' said Grace, wanting to force a more revealing response out of her. 'What if one of them acted in self-defence, or because she was a victim of abuse? I don't want a further tragedy and I'm sure you don't either.'

Helen stared at her, but Grace couldn't fathom what the look meant. She had yet to show any real shock or grief over her colleague's violent death.

'Tim lost his way,' Helen said finally. 'But Ned would never let anything bad happen to one of his patients. He just wouldn't.'

7

'What if Helen Fry was right about Dr Merrick picking up strange vibes from one of his patients?' asked Blake as he and Grace travelled back again from Colchester to London the following morning, this time heading for St Botolph's Hospital, where they had arranged to meet Dr Ash Rajani. 'That might put one of the kids in the frame, right?'

Recalling the frightened young faces around her the previous day, Grace hoped this scenario could be swiftly demolished. 'If that was the case, then Tim was sensible enough to call someone he could talk to about it,' she said. 'It doesn't sound like he'd take the risk of meeting a young girl alone in the woods.'

'She might have followed him,' he said. 'Teenage girls can get pretty intense. Or, if one of them had developed a crush on him, perhaps he planned to explain why any sort of romance was out of the question.'

'And she reacted violently?'

'Well, if you think of how terrifying that age group can be around a favourite boy band . . . She may not have taken no for an answer.'

Grace smiled. 'That's true. But then where are her bloodstained clothes? The search dog sent in yesterday evening found nothing.'

Blake wasn't ready to concede the point. 'Could be at the bottom of the lake.'

'Maybe,' she said. 'I'll mention that to Wendy. But I don't see a kid being capable of such clear thinking, not in those circumstances. Do you?'

'No.' Blake frowned, a sign, perhaps, that he was coming round to disliking the idea of a teenage killer as much as she did.

'Plus, even if she used the old pillow-under-a-blanket trick to make Crystal think she was asleep, she still had to sneak in and out of the camp undetected.'

'Yes, but the prof did say that secrecy and deceit are part of the illness.'

'Maybe we should be looking more closely at Helen Fry instead,' Grace said, knowing that she was merely trying to distract him. 'We only have her word for what the phone call was about, or that she went to Hampstead Heath after the call.'

Blake sniffed. 'Up to you, boss, but it's not like she owns a car we can trace through automatic number-plate recognition. Surely we'd want a more positive marker before using precious resources on verifying her movements?'

Grace sighed. 'Yes, you're right. Let's wait and see what we get at the hospital.'

Duncan had completed all the usual criminal record checks on Tim Merrick, including a request to CEOP, the Child Exploitation and Online Protection Centre, to discover if Tim Merrick's name had ever been flagged up, but neither they nor any other police force held information about him. The hospital had supplied a copy of his CV and references, which were textbook perfect. Duncan had contacted his referees, who were uniformly shocked to hear of his death and warmly supported every good word they had written about him. And a search of his flat had turned up nothing worse than some mouldering sports gear. The only thing they had found so far that seemed out of the ordinary was his call to a work colleague.

The modest eighteenth-century entrance of St Botolph's – an archway flanked by a pair of low gatehouses leading to a cobbled courtyard – was misleading. The state-of-the-art main building turned out to be light and modern with signs leading to specialist departments that Grace never knew existed.

They found Dr Ash Rajani on the fifth floor in a narrow utilitarian office, its walls lined with boxed medical supplies and office equipment that didn't seem to belong there. Even the framed photographs on his desk of his wife and student-age children were all but hidden by bulky files. He was a neat, watchful man in his mid-forties, going grey at the temples, and his concern for a murdered colleague was evident from the moment they introduced themselves.

'This is terrible,' he said. 'Tim did his clinical training here at St Botolph's. He's one of our own, one of the best. Do you know yet what happened?'

'We know how, when and where he died,' said Grace, taking a seat, 'but that's all. We're after a more rounded picture. I believe that as part of his psychotherapy training he'd have had a supervisor. Is that right?'

'I was his supervisor.'

'Good. So you'd know if he'd been concerned about anything recently. Any problems he might be having.'

'I would, yes. Except, apart from the usual clinical issues, things were going well. He enjoyed the work. Got on fine with people.'

'Anyone he was particularly close to?'

'Well, Ned, obviously,' said Ash. 'Tim really admired him. Was over the moon to get a job on his unit.'

'What about other members of staff? The nurses, for instance?'

'If you're asking if there was any romance going on, they'd have kept it very quiet,' said Ash. 'Those kind of undercurrents among staff can destabilize some patients with mental health problems.'

'So he might have had a relationship that you didn't know about?'

'Sure, it happens.' He smiled. 'My wife and I met as junior registrars.'

'Is it possible that there were undercurrents between Tim and any of his patients?' Grace asked the question carefully but immediately caught Ash's injured look. 'I'm sorry, but I have to ask.'

'Of course you do,' he said. 'I'm very aware of my safeguarding responsibilities. And also that an absence of concern isn't necessarily sufficient to believe that all is well. But' – he threw up his hands in a gesture of helplessness – 'Tim was an open book. I wouldn't be concerned about him.'

'What if one of his patients had feelings for him?'

'It's possible. They're adolescents; they act out. And vulnerable patients can be very quick to pick up on vulnerabilities in others.'

'But he never raised anything like that with you, as his supervisor?'

'No, never. He was relatively inexperienced and may have thought he could handle it, but I still just don't see it.'

'If you learned that he'd admitted to someone else that he was having inappropriate thoughts about one of his young patients, would that surprise you?'

'It would, yes,' said Ash. 'But if he spoke to someone about it, then he did the right thing.' He held out his hands. 'Look, medics are no more immune to a bit of flattery than ordinary mortals. Fact is, patients like to please their doctors. I mean, can you honestly say that you've never flirted with a handsome young man in a white coat? There's a kind of alchemy involved in hanging a stethoscope around your neck, and teenage girls who don't have much else going on because they're ill and confined can respond to that. It goes with the job. And Tim knew that.'

'A professional hazard?'

'Yes, in a way. You learn to deal with it.'

Grace recalled how little sympathy Helen Fry had shown for the distraught teenagers at Wryford Hall. Maybe her reticence wasn't merely a matter of patient confidentiality; maybe the nurse also had to keep her distance in order to deal with such turbulence and heightened emotions. 'It must be difficult working with these patients,' she said.

'That's why I stick to adult psychiatry.' Ash laughed. 'Look, I don't mean to be dismissive, and if Tim had kept this sort of thing to himself, then I'd certainly be worried. But if he talked it through with someone, then it's probably no big deal.' He looked at his watch. 'Is there anything else I can help you with? Only . . .'

'You must be busy,' said Grace, standing up. 'Thank you for your time.'

Ash appeared to have second thoughts. 'You don't seriously think the doctor-patient dynamic had anything to do with his death, do you? I didn't mean to be flippant, only that it doesn't seem a very likely hypothesis to me.'

'We're keeping an open mind at this stage,' she said.

'You should talk to Ned.' He lifted his suit jacket from the back of his chair and escorted them to the door. 'His unit's there at the end of the corridor.'

'OK, thanks.'

'I don't want to sound even more callous, but it's a crying shame that the timing of this tragedy has overshadowed Ned's knighthood,' he said over his shoulder as he locked his office door. 'Without his fundraising, this hospital's mental health services would be cut to the bone, so this was a feather in all our caps.'

As soon as Ash had walked away, Blake turned to Grace, making quote marks with his fingers. '"Ordinary mortals"? What's that about?'

She laughed. 'You're telling me you've never met a copper who didn't think he was the dog's bollocks merely because of the uniform?'

'Yes, but he's a shrink,' said Blake. 'He's paid to know better.'

'Sounds like he's spent his whole working life here,' she said. 'I imagine that's enough to send anyone a bit stir-crazy.'

She listened to the background hum and clatter of hospital life going on around them. It was a couple of degrees warmer than she would have liked, and the ubiquitous smell of antibacterial hand gel hung in the air.

At the other end of the empty corridor they found the door to the eating disorders unit locked and had to ring a bell. Crystal, who came to greet them, seemed reluctant to let them in. 'Emotions are running pretty high today,' she said. 'You're only going to kick up more dust.'

'I'm sorry,' said Grace, 'but it can't be helped. We'll be as discreet as we can.'

Crystal took them straight to Ned's office, promising to let him know they were there. The room was no more spacious than Ash's but the style was quite different. A row of plants adorned the windowsill. The desk had been pushed to the side to make room for a two-seater sofa covered in a home-made blanket of brightly coloured knitted squares. On the wall above was a sea of teenagers, photographed singly, in groups or with their families and pets.

Grace's phone rang while she was studying the mosaic of smiling faces. It was Colin, informing her that he'd taken a call to say that one of the deputy assistant commissioners at Scotland Yard wanted a meeting with her the following day in connection with the Merrick murder. Colin could supply no further information, and despite his attempt to keep the irritation out of his voice Grace could guess how annoyed he'd be at being kept out of the loop. She cut the conversation short, promising to be back in Colchester later that afternoon to discuss it.

As she ended the call, speculating on what could possibly make a DAC interested in her inquiry, Ned came in. He was dressed more smartly than at Wryford Hall, yet managed to convey the same sense of informality and of having all the time in the world for their questions.

'How can I help?' he asked, taking a seat on the sofa and inviting them to sit on the visitor chairs.

'How are the girls doing, the ones who were at the camp?' Grace asked.

'As you'd expect. Tim's murder has been traumatic for all of us. Do you have any clearer idea yet of what happened?'

'Not yet, I'm afraid. But it would be helpful to know more about any significant relationships Dr Merrick may have had here in the hospital. Was he close to any particular member of staff, for instance?'

'I'm not aware of anything,' said Ned, taken aback. 'If this is about Crystal, about them being together at Wryford, I can assure you—'

'No,' said Grace. 'It's about everyone who works here. I believe Helen Fry is your other specialist nurse. Were she and Dr Merrick at all close?'

'Crystal and Helen between them have a lot of experience. The junior medics are always glad of their support.'

'So you're not aware that Dr Merrick was friends with anyone in particular?'

'No, sorry.'

'And there's nothing in retrospect you may have noticed?'

Ned shook his head slowly. 'I really can't think of anything.'

'What about the patients?'

'Or their families,' Blake added, looking at the wall of photographs.

'Were any of them especially attached to him?' said Grace.

'Tim was popular, but this is a therapeutic environment. We're trained to be aware of interpersonal dynamics.'

'Had any of your patients said they felt uncomfortable with him or mentioned any type of inappropriate behaviour?'

'Of course not! If they had, it would have been reported immediately to Dr Rajani, who is the trust's assistant medical director.'

'And he would have followed it up?'

'Correct. But I beg you to be careful here. If this sort of speculation reaches my patients or their families, it's not going to be helpful. I mean, what if one of the teenagers had thought he was rather dishy and had scribbled his name in her diary and drawn hearts around it, or whatever? How is she supposed to feel about that now?'

'I understand your concern, but if one of the girls at the camp had any kind of relationship with Tim Merrick, real or imagined, we need to know about it. Or if he singled anyone out more than the rest, intentionally or otherwise.'

'I'm desperately sad about Tim's death,' Ned said. 'But my priority is my patients. You have to realize how seriously ill they are. My job is to protect them.'

'Which is why we're talking to you about this, Professor Chesham, rather than directly to the girls who were at Wryford Hall.' She put it as diplomatically as she could. 'You're the best person to get that information for us.'

He sighed. 'OK, I'll make some discreet inquiries. But – I tell you what – I'm giving a lecture next weekend. It may provide some context for our work here and should help you to understand what goes on. Why don't you come? I'll ask my secretary to set it up and contact you with the details. We can talk again then.' He looked at his watch and then smiled at her apologetically. 'I don't want to rush you, but if that's all for now, I'm supposed to be running my morning clinic.'

As they left his office they almost bumped into Crystal. Leaning on her arm was a gaunt figure in baggy sweatpants and a matching top, making painfully slow progress along the corridor. A brief glimpse of huge upturned eyes and teeth that looked too big for her mouth made Grace think it was someone very old or dying before she realized with a shock that it was a young girl. Beside her, she could feel that Blake too was clearly shaken at the sight of the emaciated teenager.

Ned stopped to speak to the girl, acting quite normally and nodding a farewell to them. His solicitude reminded Grace of how the day before at Wryford he'd made time to say goodbye to each of his young patients in turn and to assure their parents that they had his private number and should call him day or night if they were anxious about their daughters. She found it hard to believe that if he'd seen anything remotely amiss in Tim Merrick's behaviour he'd have turned a blind eye.

Once back outside the locked door to the unit, Grace turned to Blake. 'What do you think? Do we keep digging here or concentrate on the premise of a random stranger?' She found herself glad for once that she could trust him to be the dispassionate, even scathing, voice of reason.

'I've seen women at the gym who look like they could put on a pound or two but are still really going for it on the treadmill,' he said, 'but I've never seen anything as bad as that before.'

'And yet by this time next year that poor kid we just saw might be toasting marshmallows over the campfire at Wryford Hall,' said Grace.

'In which case,' said Blake, 'I take my hat off to Ned Chesham.'

8

Arriving ten minutes late to pick up Meghan from the unit at St Botolph's, Clive found his daughter waiting excitedly for him in the corridor beyond the locked door.

'Guess what, Daddy?' Her fingers closed around his arm. 'You'll never guess where we're going!'

At first he was relieved to find her in such a happy mood, but looking more closely her bright eyes and flushed cheeks seemed hectic and febrile. 'Where are we going then, honey-monkey?'

'Buckingham Palace! Come on. Professor Ned wants to talk to you about it.' She pulled him along to the open door of Ned's office. 'My dad's here.'

Ned sat at his desk, concentrating on the computer screen. Helen had pulled up a chair to sit beside him, a pile of bulging folders holding patient notes on her lap. They were obviously hard at work and Clive doubted they wanted to be disturbed.

'Don't worry,' he said. 'We'll come back another time.'

'If you wouldn't mind,' Helen acknowledged with a smile.

Clive was fond of his sister-in-law – it was entirely thanks to her, after all, that Meghan had been able to join Ned's programme – and he was already backing away when Ned swivelled his chair round and stood up.

'Nonsense,' he said. 'You'll be wanting to get home. Meghan's had a long day.' He turned to Helen. 'We'll finish this later.'

As Helen collected her files together and accepted Clive's greeting of a kiss on the cheek, Meghan took her aunt's place in front of Ned. 'Will we really get to meet the Queen?' she asked.

Helen's face drained of colour as she turned to stare at Ned with a mixture of hurt and accusation. He met her eyes calmly before addressing Clive. 'The birthday honours really couldn't have come at a more inappropriate time. Poor Tim.' He shook his head sadly. 'But at lunch today the trust chief executive came over to congratulate me, and I mentioned that perhaps it would be nice if we could use it to gain some good publicity for the hospital. He suggested we show off one of our success stories.' He laughed and ruffled Meghan's hair. 'This one's not doing too badly, is she, Nurse?'

Helen forced a smile. 'No.'

Clive could imagine what she was feeling: Gillian often teased her younger sister over having a crush on her boss, although from what Helen had once or twice let drop Clive wondered if perhaps it wasn't as one-sided as Gillian seemed to assume. Maybe Helen had good reason to expect Ned to invite her to accompany him to the palace?

'I do hope you and Gillian will come as my guests,' said Ned, 'and won't mind too much if St Botolph's gets a bit of a photo opportunity out of the occasion?'

It wasn't really a question. Clive wasn't at all sure that he wanted Meghan's illness plastered across the newspapers and then have the story remain on some database for ever more, but now wasn't the time to be ungracious. He held out a hand to Ned. 'Congratulations! Sorry, I should have said it before.

Incredibly well deserved. And thank you for thinking of us. But maybe it should be Helen and Crystal who go with you? After all, they're the ones who have earned it. This place wouldn't be the same without them.'

'I can't argue with that,' said Ned pleasantly. 'Our unsung heroines. But I'm afraid that now the chief exec has got hold of the idea, he'll be like a dog with a bone.' He ruffled Meghan's hair again. 'You don't mind a trip to the palace too much, do you?'

'No!' She turned to her father with shining eyes. 'Please, Dad. Imagine going in through the front gates of Buckingham Palace and everybody watching. It'd be awesome!'

Over Meghan's head his eyes met Helen's and he tried to signal an apology. 'Let's see what your mother says,' he told Meghan. 'It would be a fantastic experience. And after all, I don't suppose you're ever going to get to go with me.' It was a lame joke, but the others laughed politely and it seemed to break the tension enough for them to escape. 'Come on, honey-monkey. These people have work to do.'

Although they had never shaken hands before, he found himself holding out his hand again to Ned. 'Thanks,' he said awkwardly.

Ned patted Meghan's shoulder, who then went to give her aunt a goodbye kiss, but Helen chose that moment to turn away and adjust the patchwork blanket on the couch. As she straightened up again Clive intercepted the look that passed between his daughter and her aunt. He'd never understand women!

9

Although Scotland Yard had very recently left its 1960s high-rise after that building had been sold to foreign investors who planned to replace it with yet another luxury development, the Yard's new – and smaller – offices on Victoria Embankment were immediately recognizable from the iconic rotating triangular sign outside the shiny new entrance pavilion. Grace took a seat in a reception area that looked out through curving glass windows at a fountain feature and newly planted trees and speculated how much of the old culture and values of the Met – good and bad – had been left behind in the move.

As the wait to be summoned upstairs to the deputy assistant commissioner's office lengthened, she racked her brains yet again for a possible reason for the meeting. Tim Merrick's death was hardly likely to be terrorist-related, and Sharon Marx, who was responsible for professionalism in the Metropolitan Police Service, was tasked with raising standards and increasing trust and confidence. As such her role was also to oversee the Directorate of Professional Standards, the anti-corruption unit. Grace prayed that this was not about the events of last winter that had led to DS Lance Cooper quitting the force, although she was certain that if it was Colin Pitman would have had wind of it and been unable to suppress evidence of satisfaction at her comeuppance. Mind you, nor could she entirely suppress a flicker of hope that Superintendent Pitman himself might be under investigation.

The DAC turned out to be a petite woman with wavy blonde hair, a pleasant smile and a fearsome handshake. Her black uniform jacket with its silver insignia was beautifully tailored, the cuffs of her white shirt protruding the perfect length. Apprehension made Grace's mind skip about inconsequentially, and she found herself reflecting how easy it must be to get up every morning and not have to think about what to wear. Not that she had any wish to return to uniform. She disliked its assertion of power and hierarchy, the automatic reduction of anyone in civvies to a lower level. She had no doubt that that was precisely what she was intended to feel right now. The realization brought her back to reality, making her take a deep and surreptitious breath to steady her nerves.

'You're here because you're the senior investigating officer in the Timothy Merrick case,' the DAC began with no preamble whatsoever as she seated herself behind her desk and indicated that Grace should take the chair opposite. 'Do you yet have anyone in the frame?'

'No, ma'am. It appears to be an unpremeditated attack, although it is possible that he knew his assailant and may even have arranged to meet them at the crime scene. On the other hand, he may just have been in the wrong place at the wrong time.'

'Suspects?'

'We've time-eliminated the four adults known to have been within the grounds of Wryford Hall that night. Eight young teenage girls were sleeping in three tents in the grounds. There's no evidence as yet to suggest that any of them crept out unnoticed, and the absence of evidence is itself significant. Plus, the pathologist considers it unlikely that any of them would have had the height or strength to overcome the victim.'

'Professor Sir Edward Chesham was present, is that correct?'

Grace was surprised that the DAC was so well informed, but did not let that show. 'Yes. At the time of the murder he was having dinner at the hall with the owners, Minnie and Toby Thomas. The three of them spent the entire evening together.'

'And you're certain of that?'

'Yes.' Grace quickly thought back: had she missed something? She was sure she hadn't. Minnie and Toby had seemed so natural, open and concerned to help that she couldn't believe they had conspired to mislead her.

Sharon Marx nodded, her shoulders relaxing slightly as if some tension had been released. Grace thought about asking what Scotland Yard's interest was in Ned Chesham, but knew she must wait to be told.

'The commissioner is setting up a review of an earlier Met investigation,' said the DAC. 'It will come under the umbrella of Operation Hydrant which, as you know, is already investigating well over two thousand suspects.'

Grace strove to remember what, out of the many current Met operations, Hydrant was concerned with, but failed to place the name.

'It's best practice that we appoint someone from outside this force,' the DAC continued, 'and you have come very highly recommended. We've cleared it with the Essex chief constable, and I'm happy to say that you are to lead Operation Mayfly.'

'Thank you,' said Grace, astounded. 'Although I have to ask why you haven't chosen someone more senior.'

'It is unusual for a detective inspector to lead a review,' Sharon Marx admitted, 'but, given the existing link with the Timothy Merrick case, it makes perfect sense.'

End of argument, thought Grace. 'What earlier investigation am I to review?'

Sharon Marx's fingers twitched over a file on her desk. 'It's a long time ago. Seventeen years. But, as we've learned to our cost, sometimes it takes this long for evidence of child sex abuse to surface.'

Grace's heart sank. Now she remembered. Hydrant was co-ordinating allegations of 'non-recent' child sex abuse. Such historical cases were never easy for a whole host of reasons, and she had no experience of handling them. 'Who was the subject of the investigation?'

'Professor Chesham.'

She closed her eyes and took a deep breath. 'How serious was the original allegation?'

'All allegations are serious,' Sharon Marx said sharply, her fingers playing over the file again. 'It's all in here. It'll be quicker if you read it for yourself. And I'm afraid that speed is an issue.' She pursed her lips as if in apology. 'Professor Chesham's knighthood was awarded in the recent birthday honours. Regrettably, this file had not been brought to the attention of the honours vetting committee.'

Grace's heart sank even further. So this was a bigger salvage job than she feared. No one wanted any unwelcome surprises, and Operation Mayfly was doubtless designed to draw fire away from whoever in the Met hierarchy had messed up. Now she understood why this had ended up on Sharon Marx's desk.

'I believe it's not yet fixed which investiture he will be

attending,' the DAC continued, 'but clearly we do not want the palace to be placed in an awkward situation.'

Grace struggled to hide her fury, but Sharon Marx must have spotted it, for she smiled encouragingly. 'You can see the faith we're placing in you, DI Fisher. It's not everyone who would be up to such a task.'

'Thank you, ma'am.' Grace spoke through gritted teeth. 'So what happens with the Merrick inquiry? His family deserve answers. Will I be able to continue working on that as well?'

'I'm afraid that won't be possible,' said the DAC. 'But Superintendent Pitman will be on hand to oversee the investigation, and we'd like you to keep a watching brief in case the two inquiries turn out to be linked. Do you think they might be?'

It was a fair question, but Grace was unwilling to commit herself until she stood on firmer ground. 'Hard to say until I've read the file,' she said, nodding towards the desk.

'Of course.' The DAC passed it over, dropping her hands back into her lap afterwards as if glad to be rid of it.

'Will I be free to pick my own team?'

'Absolutely. Operation Mayfly is to be entirely independent and free of interference. However, given the time pressures, I'd suggest you stay agile, work with people you know will be responsive. We'll give you a preliminary budget, and I'll be happy to liaise on any requests for additional expenditure.'

So not only am I on my own, thought Grace, especially if it goes belly up, but I'm also expected to do it on the cheap. 'Thank you, ma'am,' she said.

Sharon Marx rose to her feet. 'I need hardly add, I hope, that recent events in terms of the Met's handling of historical child sex abuse cases are going to guarantee both media and political scrutiny. There has been considerable disquiet over the direction of earlier reviews. It's important that we get back to the principle of innocent until proven guilty. Besmirching the reputation of a public figure without evidence is clearly not the right way forward and I would urge the utmost discretion.'

'I appreciate the advice.' Grace got to her feet and was about to take her leave when she thought of a final question. 'By the way, who led the original investigation?'

The DAC's face became a mask. 'Keith Stalgood. I believe he was your SIO in Essex for a short while prior to his retirement.'

'Yes.'

'The terms of your remit are to investigate the extent to which the original allegation was robustly investigated and to establish if there were any police failings.'

'Ma'am.' Grace couldn't wait to escape and breathe in some fresh air.

Emerging from Scotland Yard a few minutes later she crossed the road to the Embankment, deciding to walk for a little way in an attempt to clear her head. Traffic fumes hung in the summer air, but the view across the Thames to the giant wheel of the London Eye offered space to think. She was aware that while some police investigations into historical child sex abuse had resulted in successful prosecutions, many had also exposed years of fudging denial, wilful blindness, cover-ups and incompetence by all manner of people whose job it had been to prevent or expose it. But Keith Stalgood was one of the most decent coppers she knew. Surely he could only have done an exemplary job? There could be no possibility of any gross dereliction of duty there for her to uncover. Surely she wasn't being asked to hang her former boss out to dry?

On the other hand, the Met in particular had taken a real beating, in turn heavily criticized for hounding the innocent and wasting millions of pounds on claims that were found to have no substance, and accused of doing too little, too late. Damned if they did, damned if they didn't. Now she was about to find out exactly what that felt like.

10

Standing on Keith's doorstep the following day Grace wished that she'd got in touch with him in the months since his retirement, as she'd always meant to. But she hadn't, and now any apology would only sound false. She could have parked on the drive of his detached 1930s house – one of a row of near-identical family homes situated in a pleasant street conveniently near the centre of Upminster – but that felt like too much of an encroachment. Being here at all felt like bad faith.

A dog barked dutifully when she rang the bell. She tucked her hair behind her ears and straightened her shoulders. As Keith opened the door an elderly spaniel thrust its head past its master's legs and gave Grace what she could have sworn was a reproachful look. Keith, in jeans and a polo shirt, his iron-grey hair a little more flecked with white than she remembered, leaned down to scratch the dog's head before holding out his hand to her.

'Come in,' he said. 'I don't envy you this job.'

The entrance hall was white, freshly painted and, apart from a set of golf clubs in one corner, orderly and uncluttered. She followed him into a pleasant lounge with French windows standing open to a garden where wooden chairs with striped cushions had been arranged around a table under a big green umbrella.

'Enough shade to sit out, if you'd like to?'

Grace looked out at a newly cut lawn and a couple of gnarled apple trees. The day was cloudless and, even though she'd decided to dress more formally than the weather demanded, the shade under the umbrella did look inviting. 'That would be great, thanks.'

'If it gets too hot, just shout,' he said, leading the way.

She saw that a Thermos jug, mugs, a milk jug and a plate of biscuits had already been laid out, the jug and plate covered by old-fashioned nets with pretty beaded edges to keep off any wasps. 'This is lovely,' she said. 'Are you the gardener?'

'My wife,' he said as the dog settled on the flagstones at his feet. 'More than my life's worth to interfere out here.'

There was no point in spinning out the small talk. She hoped that they'd be able to catch up properly once the rest of it was out of the way. She wouldn't mind running the Merrick case past him as well, in case he could spot whatever it was she'd missed. But all that would have to wait. 'So you know why I'm here, obviously.'

Keith nodded. 'I had a courtesy call from DAC Marx.'

'Good. So you've had time to refresh your memory?'

'Yes. It was a long time ago. Before I went to the murder squad.'

'When you were part of the Met's paedophile unit?'

'You've done your homework,' he said. 'Yes, I'd just joined, still a detective sergeant then. As the newbie, I was probably given the case because no one really thought it would go anywhere.'

'And you didn't either?'

'You've read the file,' he said patiently. 'We had one complainant who said that Chesham had sexually assaulted her six years
earlier when she was thirteen and undergoing treatment for an
eating disorder. She could only name one other possible victim,
but she had recently died as a result of anorexia, so there was no
witness networking available to us. We wrote to some of his former patients or their parents inviting them to provide
information, but without fully spelling out the nature of the
inquiry it went nowhere. Many were underage and fragile, and
the parents didn't want us anywhere near them.'

'So the hospital knew the nature of your investigation?'

'No, we wanted as neutral an approach as possible – not to put
ideas in people's heads. Anyway, no one had a bad word to say
about him. He'd begun to make a name for himself by then, and
as far as everyone was concerned he was a saviour. Got these
girls eating and well again, back to normal lives. Was also a very
effective media spokesman, highlighting the seriousness of the
problem and winning extra funding. He was a hero.'

Grace nodded. 'I've met him.'

'Already?' Keith's voice rose in surprise.

'Not because of this,' she said. 'He's part of a murder inquiry.
A junior doctor, Tim Merrick, was killed in the grounds of an
estate where Ned Chesham runs a summer camp every year for
a few of his patients. Ned was nearby at the time, but I
double-checked his alibi as soon as I heard about that earlier
complaint and he's definitely ruled out.'

'So that's why it's been reopened now,' he said. 'In case there's
going to be any mud flying around. I couldn't work out why
now, when there must be hundreds of other cases like this left
lying on file.'

'You didn't see the birthday honours list?'

It didn't take Keith long to catch on. His mouth curled in contempt. 'They're scared I missed something and the Met will take the flak?'

'Yes,' said Grace. She hesitated over saying more but owed him this much. After all, he had stuck his neck out to give her a second chance when, pushed out of her previous job with the Kent force, she had desperately needed one. 'It also makes me wonder if they've given me the job for reasons other than that I'm the SIO on the Merrick inquiry.'

'They're hoping your loyalty to me might influence how you interpret your findings?'

Grace nodded. 'I can see it makes sense to look at neighbouring forces to keep travel and accommodation costs to a minimum. And no doubt some bright spark reckoned it would be a good idea to get a woman. But that still left them plenty of alternative choices.'

'So what are you going to do?'

Keith was looking at her shrewdly. Grace knew that look. It was one she'd always liked. And trusted. She smiled. 'If I have to, I'll drop you in it.'

'Good!' Keith poured coffee from the Thermos and nudged the milk and biscuits her way. 'So what do you make of Chesham?'

'He's very charismatic,' she said, 'which, as we know, can go both ways, but I liked him. You never interviewed him?'

'No. We submitted the file to the Crown Prosecution Service for early investigative advice. They told us we didn't have enough to charge, so we left the man alone.'

'Did you think that any of what the complainant said stacked up?'

He shook his head. 'We had no corroborating evidence, and you know how low the conviction rate is for sexual offences. Twice as bad in those days. Why drag everyone through the mud for nothing? The reputational damage would have killed his career stone dead. That was the thinking back then, anyhow. And believe me, if I'd been convinced that he'd been up to no good, I'd have fought my corner against the CPS good and hard.'

'But you didn't believe he was?'

'I told them that the complainant believed what she was telling us, but that's not necessarily the same thing, is it? Look, she was a psychiatric patient. I know it's totally un-PC to say so, but she really wasn't well. Downright flaky, if I'm honest. They'd have made mincemeat out of her in the witness box.'

'Choose a victim with zero credibility.'

'You think I didn't consider that?' Keith's anger flared for a second, then he contained it. 'Look, seventeen years ago my daughters were just entering their teens. I wasn't about to be charitable or make allowances. I don't care how many lives someone saves, they don't get to lay a finger on my kid or anyone else's.'

Grace smiled and then had to remind herself that she was here to do a job. She wasn't in a position to make allowances either. 'You didn't think that maybe she was flaky because of what he'd done to her?'

'Of course I did. But we couldn't pick up a single negative whisper about him anywhere. And we did a fair bit of discreet asking around. OK, so maybe we didn't understand as much about grooming then as we do now, but his colleagues, especially his juniors, the people who trained in his department, all sang his praises. Frankly, if my daughter had had an eating disorder, I'd have put my faith in him.'

'Who was your bagman?' asked Grace.

'A detective constable named Sam Villiers. Don't know where he is now. We didn't stay in touch.'

'And he felt the same?'

'You'll have to ask him,' said Keith. 'But he never raised an objection at the time. Have to say, he was a bit of a lightweight.'

The spaniel staggered to his feet and Keith reached out to stroke his silky fur before the dog pottered off down the garden.

'Anything else you can tell me?' she asked.

'Only to keep looking behind you,' he said drily. 'Now is not the time for the Met commissioner to be made a fool of, not with all this talk of bringing in leading industry outsiders to fill the top police jobs.'

'According to the DAC's parting words,' said Grace, 'the Met wishes to avoid any public cynicism about the police service. There's – I think I'm quoting correctly – a strong public interest in ensuring that the correct decision had been made, however long ago.'

Keith shook his head in disgust. 'Have a biscuit.'

'Thanks.'

'How's Lance Cooper?'

Grace felt winded. 'You heard what happened?'

'He came to see me. I tried to talk him out of it.'

'We speak occasionally,' she said, 'but whenever I suggest meeting up, he says maybe another time.'

'He'll come round eventually.'

'The last time I called, he said he'd decided to train as a teacher.'

'I can see that,' he said. 'It'll suit him.'

She hoped so. But Keith's question reignited her fear that

she'd been chosen for this job as payback for rattling a few too many cages in the wake of the Dunholt shootings last Christmas. Digging into the equally nefarious dealings of the Police Federation and the intelligence and security services had won her few friends, and there were plenty who'd be delighted to see her career blighted if such a sensitive investigation as this ran off the rails. Her one hope was to keep Operation Mayfly under the radar for as long as possible, or at least until she had gathered sufficient evidence to get her bearings.

'I've secured Duncan as my wingman,' she said, trying to look on the bright side, 'plus a couple of civilian support staff. It means leaving MIT short-handed, but I reckon the new DS rather relishes being given the space to spread his wings.'

'Duncan will play it straight,' said Keith. 'He doesn't have a political bone in his body. Probably why he never even went for sergeant, although he'd have made a good one.'

She knew that Keith was right. Duncan was thorough and unflappable, and she always enjoyed working with him. While he seldom offered a personal opinion, when he did, it was worth hearing. 'It's the politics I'm worried about,' she said. 'The local stuff is bad enough, but I have no experience of Scotland Yard.'

'Well, you know the bottom line,' said Keith. 'If the bastard's guilty, you nick him. The rest of us can look after ourselves.'

Relieved as she was to hear him say it, she nevertheless dreaded the possibility that if he had missed something in that earlier investigation she'd have little choice but to take him at his word and throw one of her favourite people to the wolves.

11

Ivo Sweatman, veteran chief crime correspondent of the *Daily Courier*, took a mischievous delight in how those public servants who brought him stories in return for cash twisted themselves into such knots over their motivation. You really did have to hand it to some of them for the way they hammed it up like tortured method actors, persuading you of their zeal for openness when all they really wanted was either a few bob to treat their girlfriend to a week in the Caribbean or revenge on some boss who'd refused them promotion.

Back before the phone-hacking scandal had ruined it for everyone, a serving police officer had been able to get away with accepting a bung without much risk; now everyone had to tread a lot more carefully, which was annoying given that the wares they had to peddle so often turned out to be exceptionally rewarding. In truth Ivo found Sam Villiers, who had been a useful if infrequent source, irksome rather than entertaining. In his early forties and still a detective constable, Villiers resented those on a higher pay grade. And his resentment was strong enough for him to consider it fair to augment his income by selling trinkets like the one he was now dangling in front of Ivo.

Trouble was, Ivo wasn't sure he really wanted it. Another VIP paedophile – was that even a story any more?

Since their last meeting, explained Sam, he had left the Metropolitan Police Service to set up on his own account as a corporate security adviser – was indeed ready and willing to make himself available to the *Courier* should that bastion of truth ever care to avail itself of his shadier services. Thus, as a civilian he was at liberty to sell to the highest bidder a choice morsel recently deposited quite legitimately in his lap by no less a benefactor than a Scotland Yard DAC. It concerned a review of a historical allegation of child sex abuse against a whiter-than-white pillar of the medical establishment.

Typically, however, Sam had failed to do his homework and remained blissfully ignorant of the fact that the *Courier* had a chunky investment in Professor Sir Edward Chesham maintaining an untarnished reputation – for the next two weeks, anyway, which admittedly was a pretty long time in tabloid-land. Ivo's paper had recently negotiated expensive serialization rights to the ghostwritten autobiography of a British actress and Hollywood megastar that featured the inspirational story of how 'Professor Ned' had saved her life when she was battling an eating disorder. Next week's exclusive was timed to kick off a new fundraising appeal for Ned Chesham's hospital, and there was no way Ivo's editor was going to thank him for paying top dollar for a spoiler.

On the other hand, if Ivo turned Sam down, then not only would he probably sell the story to a rival paper, but he also might not come straight to Daddy the next time he had something interesting to sell. Ivo resigned himself to hearing the man out, intending to beat down the price as much as he could and then shelve it – if only for the time being.

Ivo had always been in two minds about whipping up public outrage about kiddie-fiddlers for the sole purpose of boosting circulation. Call him old-fashioned, but there was always a frisson of something a little *too* curtain-twitching about that particular national obsession, given how many members of the decent British tabloid-reading public must rank among the hordes known to access underage porn online. He preferred to stick with proper crimes like murder, kidnap, rape or torture. But hey, it was a crowded marketplace, and the last time he looked the tabloid mantra was still 'Give 'em what they want.'

On his own, Ned Chesham wasn't quite a big enough name for his potential disgrace and downfall to make a satisfactory front page – or only on a slow news day – but link him to true stardom and the hounds would be out for the kill. Ivo almost considered putting Sam in his debt for ever by tipping him off that he'd get a better price from one of the *Courier*'s competitors if he also told them about the Jessica Hubbard exclusive the *Courier* would be running across all of next week. But he didn't like the man enough.

If he had any financial nous himself, he'd buy Sam's trinket and sell it to a competitor himself under a different name. On the other hand, he was probably being naive imagining that his own editor wouldn't leap at the chance, once the Hollywood star had told her exclusive story, to turn on her and tear her to pieces if that would sell more copies – which it would. Might even be fun, the more he thought about it. Celebrity-baiting remained a popular blood sport, and the best stories were built around emotion. One day it's brave Jessica sharing her most intimate secrets, the next the *Courier* is demanding to know whether poor Jessica was the gullible dupe of a scheming pervert. Build 'em up so they've got further to fall when you knock 'em down – that's the way to do it.

He began to listen more carefully to what Sam was saying.

To be honest, there still didn't seem to be much to the story: nearly two decades ago, when Sam had been a rookie, he'd helped look into an allegation that Ned Chesham had sexually assaulted a young patient. There'd been nothing in it and it had been mothballed, but now the Yard had appointed a review team – probably, according to Sam, to cover their backs given how many other zombie cases had subsequently taken on a new lease of life. Sam had been informed because the new team might want to talk to him.

Ivo's ears pricked up when Sam said his boss on the original investigation had been Keith Stalgood, then a detective sergeant. Ivo knew and liked Keith. The man had had his fair share of mishaps in a long career with the Met's murder squad, but had taken them on the chin and never held Ivo's reporting against him. He reckoned it was a safe bet that Keith had done a decent job back then and the review would find nothing amiss, in which case there wasn't going to be much of a story. Not that that would bother Ivo's editor much. Still, a lot of other VIP paedophile cover-up stories had recently fizzled out in IPSO-enforced retractions in very small print, so what was it about this one that made Sam think there would be money in it?

OK, so Sam, with his fading good looks and knock-off designer clothes, wasn't the brightest of the bunch, but was there something in this for him other than a spot of ready cash? Perhaps he was afraid that some personal shortcoming, a mistake for which he'd been responsible, might be exposed and stymie his new business venture. Or maybe he felt vindictive towards his old boss, Keith Stalgood. Or maybe someone had put Sam up to leaking the story. If so, who? And why? Recognizing that the idea was prompted entirely by his own deeply ingrained paranoia, Ivo was about to dismiss it when curiosity got the better of him.

'Who's heading up the review team?' he asked.

'A DI from Essex. Not anyone I know.'

'Only a DI?' said Ivo, reflecting that either the review was a foregone conclusion and they didn't want to waste money – a more-than-likely scenario – or someone was being set up to fail. In which case maybe he wasn't being so paranoid after all. 'Got a name?' he asked casually.

'Grace Fisher.'

Given a handy telephone booth, Ivo – the wrong side of fifty, overweight, a man to whom fitness was an alien concept – instantly felt he could have dived in, twirled around and emerged a superhero. As far as he was concerned, Grace Fisher had no need to prove she was on the side of the angels. Plus, if there was one thing guaranteed to raise his hackles, it was the very idea of someone trying to stitch her up, especially someone in a position of authority over her. He thanked the Fates that had led Sam to him and not to some other hack. All that remained was to negotiate a price. Sam didn't know it yet, but this was, after all, his lucky day.

12

Grace spoke to one of the women at the reception desk and then took a seat beside Duncan on the long grey sofa. Without mentioning that she was a police officer, she had asked the receptionist to call up and see if Trudie Bevan could stop for a word on her way out. She had decided not to call in advance to fix a meeting, not wanting Trudie to spend anxious hours or days worrying about what they wanted to talk to her about, time in which she might also decide not to speak to them at all. Nevertheless, Grace dreaded this first approach, and the plan to ambush her as she left work felt mean and unfair.

She was happy to have Duncan alongside, and also grateful for the ease between them after the strain of adjusting to Blake's unfamiliar personality. Although she and Duncan had spent the train journey to London in their usual amicable silence, she hadn't been entirely sure how he'd react to retracing Keith Stalgood's steps, looking to trip him up. Keith had been his boss for a lot longer than he'd been hers, and Duncan was loyal to a fault. She hoped he'd understand that that was precisely the reason she wanted him on board.

She'd also been tempted to ask how he felt about working on a child abuse case, but doubted she'd get much of an answer. No one liked these cases. Maybe it would be easier because – as far as she knew – neither of them had children; perhaps that would give them some objectivity. She realized she knew almost nothing about his private life – except that he was unmarried and carried a torch for Joan, the team's civilian case manager – and felt maybe it was better that way.

She'd left it to him to prepare some notes on the woman they were here to see. Trudie Bevan had been nineteen when she'd added her looping signature at the bottom of the statement she had made to Keith, which meant she was now thirty-six. She'd held the same job in university admin for the past five years, lived alone and, while her online footprint was extremely modest, had recently run a half-marathon for a breast cancer charity. Grace hoped this meant she was doing OK.

Beguiled by the quirkily dressed art and fashion students streaming out into the evening sunshine, she was almost taken by surprise when a woman noiselessly approached them.

'Grace Fisher? I'm Trudie Bevan. You wanted to see me?' Her voice was low yet confident, somewhat at odds with her pale face and hair and the featureless layers of her grey and white clothes. She was slim but not worryingly so, and her bright eyes seemed to show an amused, ironic glint. 'If it's about your son or daughter's application, then I'm afraid I really can't—'

'No, it's not,' said Grace, smiling at the idea that she and Duncan might have a student-age child between them. 'Here, let me give you my card.' She had it ready in her hand, and allowed Trudie time to absorb the Essex Police insignia before introducing Duncan. 'There are plenty of places to sit outside. If you have time, perhaps we might talk out there?'

Trudie silently consented to be walked out to where the view was framed by a skyline of new office blocks, some still under construction. Stone benches faced a wide piazza where rectangular grids of fountains rose and plashed to ever-changing rhythms, and off to one side, under a grid-like grove of low trees, café-style chairs and tables were laid out for anyone who wanted to use them. Grace chose a table at the edge of the trees. Duncan offered to fetch tea or coffee from a nearby café, but Trudie shook her head. Grace marvelled at her self-control as she sat down and waited for one of them to speak first.

'We're not here to deliver bad news,' she said. 'It's nothing like that. Nothing to worry about. But we wanted to ask you some questions about a complaint that you made a very long time ago.'

'I'm sorry, but I don't know what you're talking about.'

For a moment Grace feared they had the wrong person, except that there was something about the way Trudie kept her eyes fixed on the tabletop that dispelled any doubt. 'I'm sorry to have to rake up the past.'

'No.' Trudie shook her head and wrapped her arms tightly around her body. 'You've made a mistake.'

'I should say immediately that we have no new information,' Grace continued quietly. 'The inquiry so far remains precisely where it was seventeen years ago.'

'So why are you here?'

'Attitudes have changed. If the police made a mistake back then, we'd like to put it right.'

'No,' said Trudie firmly. 'I'm not that person any more. I don't want to know.'

'All we need is for you to tell us whether you still stand by the statement you made to DS Stalgood.'

'You had your chance. I'm not going through it all a second time.'

'I understand that you must feel very badly let down, but—' began Grace.

'No, you don't,' Trudie interrupted, meeting Grace's eyes for the first time. 'Do you know what it cost me to go to the police and then not be believed? Do you?'

'No. I'm sorry,' said Grace. 'I don't.'

'It was like it was happening all over again,' Trudie said. 'You have no idea how hard it is to recover from a serious eating disorder, let alone something much, much worse. And I'm one of the lucky ones. I'm still alive.'

Grace recalled the notes Keith had attached to Trudie's statement: her weight when she was nineteen had been not much over forty kilos.

Trudie nodded towards the university building. 'I'll be forty before I know it, and this is my first job. Junior admin support for the college where I once dreamed of being a student. I'm not giving this up.'

'But do you stand by your original statement? That's all we need to know.'

Grace waited as Trudie gazed over at the dancing jets of water, thinking that perhaps she wasn't going to answer. The air was warm, yet Trudie drew her light grey cardigan – one of several layers – across her chest. Her collarbones stood out, and Grace noticed that her fingernails had a bluish tinge.

She had approached the police seventeen years earlier after seeing her former doctor on television. Ned Chesham had been interviewed about the death of a singer who suffered from bulimia. It was not uncommon for people with disordered thinking to connect their disturbed thoughts to TV images. If Trudie's allegations then had been false, the promptings of a confused and unquiet mind, then it was unspeakably cruel to rake them all up again now.

'I've lost enough time already,' Trudie said finally. 'I'm over it now. As much as I'm ever going to be, anyway. I can't afford to go back there. I wish now that I'd never tried to speak out.'

'Was it true?' Grace pressed her gently. 'Did we make a mistake?'

Trudie had been unable to offer Keith any dates or details such as a car or a flat or hotel room that could be independently verified. She had claimed that the sexual contact had taken place either in the hospital or at her home. Her mother had confirmed that Doctor Ned – her name for him – had visited the house and spent time alone with her thirteen-year-old daughter, but she absolutely refused to believe that such a kind and understanding man could possibly exploit their trust in such an unspeakable way. Saddened and alarmed, Mrs Bevan had told Keith that Trudie's allegation was proof that her daughter remained ill and in need of help.

It Trudie's allegations were true, had always been true, and then the police failed a second time to dig up anything new to corroborate them, where would that leave Trudie now? Grace could hardly bear to think about that. *I don't envy you this job*: Keith's typical understatement.

'I hated him touching me, having to touch him,' said Trudie at last, her eyes on the fountains. 'It was repulsive. So horrible that I've never been able to have a physical relationship with anyone since. So you'd think, when he discharged me, and I was eating and back at school, that I'd be relieved. But I sent him letters, gifts. And when I finally realized he was never going to respond, I went back to not eating. I'm the girl who sent presents to the man who raped her. You think I could turn up to work once people here knew that about me?'

'I'm so sorry,' said Grace, hugely moved and impressed by the woman's courage. 'But there's so much more understanding now about the psychological impact of abuse. We can make sure you have proper support.'

Trudie shook her head and reached down to pick up her handbag. 'I have to go now.'

'Please, just two more questions first.'

Trudie nodded reluctantly, keeping her bag on her lap.

'You named one other person in your statement. Do you think there were others? Other victims?'

'I'm sure there were. There must have been. Still are, probably. But I can't think about them. I know it's selfish but I can't. That's your job.'

'Is there anyone else you think we might usefully speak to?'

'Doctor Ned?' Trudie gave a grim laugh and stood up. 'I'm going. You will leave me alone now, won't you?'

'I can't promise that, but I do promise we'll only come back to you if we really think we can move things forward,' said Grace.

'Goodbye.'

Grace watched Trudie walk away and then turned to Duncan. 'So what do you think?'

'He's going to deny the accusation,' he said, 'and then it's her word against his.'

'Back to square one.'

'I see no reason not to believe her,' he said. 'Do you?'

'No. Not at this stage, anyway.' She was relieved. It still seemed so outlandishly difficult to reconcile the positive impression Ned had made on her with the allegations against him. But the fact that Duncan had heard Trudie's account before meeting Ned would supply a corrective counterweight.

'We've got access to the hospital because of the Merrick case,' she said. 'We might be able to go fishing for any history of incidents or other complaints against him without attracting too much obvious attention.'

Duncan nodded thoughtfully. The piazza was filling up with the early-evening crowd heading for the hipster cafés and restaurants. With conflicting and seemingly mutually exclusive impressions battling it out in her brain, Grace was not looking forward to the return journey to Colchester. The thought of staying here for a glass of chilled white wine was far more appealing than cramming herself into a packed commuter train, but she stifled the thought: too early in the inquiry to get into bad habits.

'My godson was sent for specialist care at St Botolph's,' said Duncan unexpectedly. 'He had something wrong with his gut and needed an operation. Anyway, the surgical team was amazing. It meant the world to his parents. It's not only Professor Chesham's reputation we'd be trashing if we get it wrong. It would tarnish the hospital too.'

'I know,' she said, watching an apparently carefree young couple enjoying their drinks at a neighbouring table. The full weight of the task ahead felt crushing. 'It would be so much easier if Ned Chesham somehow looked the part,' she said. 'But he doesn't.'

'They never do,' said Duncan. 'Which is how they get away with it. But then everyone thought Tim Merrick was a lovely young doctor despite what Helen Fry told you.'

Grace frowned. 'Maybe he was. Maybe Ned's one of the good guys too.'

'Perhaps, but I'm in no rush to call Trudie Bevan a liar.'

Watching him survey the piazza as if only just taking note of his surroundings, Grace thought how out of place he looked here, every inch the case-hardened copper in his rumpled grey suit. His shoulders were solid and heavy-looking and his closely shaved hair exposed rolls of reddened skin above his white shirt collar. The young students flitting around them were not to know that his appearance belied his kindness and commitment. She caught his eye and smiled. 'We're not in a hurry to get back, are we?' she asked. 'Fancy a drink?'

13

Clive was dropping off to sleep when he heard the telltale repetitive squeaks from Meghan's bedroom. He was immediately alert, a rush of dread hitting his heart. He forced himself to count to ten, breathing raggedly in and out to calm his panic before surreptitiously sitting up and swinging his feet to the floor. No point in waking Gillian. Better to start by seeing if he could deal with it himself.

There was no light showing under Meghan's door, which was a bad sign, but the muted sound of a bed, desk or chair taking the strain as his daughter levered her weight against it, no doubt counting her way through a hundred sit-ups or dozens of step exercises, was unmistakable. It had been when all attempts to curb her obsessive workouts in the past had failed, and he and Gillian had had to take it in turns to stay on watch throughout the night, that they had finally begged Helen for help. Clive didn't care that they had unfairly leveraged their one bit of personal influence. If Professor Ned hadn't been persuaded to accept Meghan as a patient the whole family would have gone under.

Outside her room he stood up straight and took a deep breath before opening the door and flicking on the overhead light.

Sure enough, Meghan, in her pink pyjama vest and shorts, her face a sheen of sweat, was on the floor, her feet hooked under her bed, a tin of chopped tomatoes in each hand to act as weights. He averted his eyes from her prominent ribcage and swollen joints, too large for her bird-like limbs.

'Go away!' she screamed.

'You know I can't do that, sweetheart.'

'You can! Just leave me alone!'

'Please stop for a second and come and talk to me.'

'No! If I stop, I'll have to start again from the beginning. You know that.'

'No, just stop.' He sat on the single bed, his daughter on the floor at his feet. 'Please, tell me why you're so upset. Is there something about Doctor Tim's death that you're not telling us? Did something else happen at the camp? You know there's nothing you can't talk to me about if you want to.'

'Please, Daddy, just go away. Leave me alone.'

'I can't do that. I won't.' He reached out to take the tins but she rolled them away out of reach and he knew better than to fight her for them. 'I love you, sweetheart.'

Meghan drew her knees into her chest and huddled into herself. 'No, you don't. You hate me. You think I'm a monster, that I'm ruining your life.'

'I hate your illness and what it's doing to you, but I love you. Always have, always will.' This was what Ned had taught them to say. Kids like Meghan were too sharp to be lied to, he'd said, and knew very well that sometimes they were indeed acting like monsters and destroying any chance of a normal family existence.

'Not again.'

Clive looked up to see Gillian standing in the doorway, her face creased from sleep, her expression one of utter hopelessness.

'Go away!' screamed Meghan.

'Go back to bed,' Clive told his wife. 'I'll deal with it.' He turned back to his daughter. 'Climb into bed and I'll sit with you for a while. Would you like me to read to you?'

'No!' Meghan leaped to her feet and lunged towards her little Ikea desk in the corner of the room. Clive couldn't see what she picked up, but as she held her other arm, he caught the glint of metal in her hand. Scissors, probably. She had often threatened to cut herself before, and only once actually done so, but he knew that they were now in for hours of weary negotiation.

'I'm calling Prof Ned,' said Gillian.

'No, don't!' Meghan let her arms fall to her sides.

'This is your last chance,' said Gillian, 'because I really can't do this any more.'

'Just wait a bit,' said Clive.

Gillian shook her head. 'Ned said, after what happened at Wryford Hall, to call him, day or night.'

'But not yet,' pleaded Clive as Meghan returned the scissors to her desk and crossed the narrow space back to her bed. It was too late: Gillian was already halfway across the landing.

'Don't let her call him, Daddy. You don't need him. I'll go to sleep now, I promise.'

He patted her arm. 'Let me see what I can do.'

As Meghan pulled the duvet over her, he followed Gillian into their bedroom where she was already holding the phone to her ear. Clive's gaze fell to the clock display on the bedside radio: it was nearly one in the morning. He shook his head at her, but she stared back determinedly, just as she had when she'd told him there was no way they were turning down Ned's invitation to the palace.

'Ned? It's Gillian Goodwin here. I'm sorry to disturb you so late.'

Clive left her to it and went back to Meghan, who was sobbing into her pillow.

'What's the matter, honey-monkey? If you don't tell me, I can't help make it better.'

'Why doesn't she listen to me? I don't want him here.'

'Mum's worried about you. We both are. You were doing so well. Professor Ned's really been helping you, hasn't he?'

'No!'

'He said you're his success story.'

'Leave me alone!'

She was becoming hysterical, and in spite of himself Clive began to feel relief that help was on its way. There had been so many nights when they had caught her exercising secretly and she had promised to go back to bed and be good, only for them to be woken again an hour later by the faint pulsation through their mattress of her doing endless star jumps. Gillian was probably right not to trust her. The thought released a familiar wave of guilt and grief, and he shut his eyes, waiting for it to subside. Beside him Meghan was clambering down to the end of the bed, her eyes wild, ready for a rampage.

By the time Ned arrived half an hour later, carrying a rolled-up sleeping bag and a small overnight bag, Clive thought he'd never been so glad to see anyone in his life.

'What you two need is a good night's sleep,' Ned told them. 'Go to bed and leave her to me. I'll calm her down and then bunk on the floor so she can't get up to any more tricks. Give me a spare pillow and I'll be fine.'

Too exhausted to argue, Clive was amazed to wake up five hours later and discover that he and Gillian must both have fallen asleep immediately. He found Ned in the kitchen, dressed and making coffee, sunlight streaming over his shoulder from the open window. Ned smiled broadly as Clive came in. 'I hope you like it as strong as I do,' he said, indicating the coffee pot.

Clive didn't feel sufficiently prepared for the weirdness of the situation. He had confided things to this man in family therapy that he would never have said to his oldest friend, but that had been in the neutral space of the hospital, and it was a whole different ball game making small talk over breakfast in his own kitchen. It was as if the events of last night had been some sort of car crash, and now he was expected to offer toast and marmalade to the paramedics amid the wreckage.

'I'm so sorry we dragged you out,' he said. 'We can't thank you enough.'

Ned waved his gratitude aside. 'It's the weekend. Not like either of us have to get off to work early.'

'But it's your big lecture this afternoon.'

Ned smiled. 'Don't worry about it. I give the same lecture every time. And you did absolutely the right thing. It's what I'm here for.'

'She'd been doing so well.'

'It's hardly surprising Meghan's having a blip. What happened to Tim was too much for any of us to handle.' Ned helped himself to two mugs from the cupboard and poured the coffee. 'Have you heard any more from the police?'

Clive shook his head. 'Nothing. Not yet anyway.' Giving in

with relief to his helplessness, he sat down at the table and accepted the coffee Ned handed him. 'Have they told you any more about what happened?'

'No. I'm not sure they have much of a handle on it. But don't worry. We'll get over it. These kids are much more resilient than you think. Milk?'

'In the fridge.' Clive knew he ought to set the table and start making toast, but it was comforting to hand control to someone else, just for a little while. Lost for what else to talk about, he gave thanks that for once he didn't have to navigate the mine-field of family life on his own.

14

Ivo was curious to see what the good doctor would be like in the flesh. He'd done his homework: Ned Chesham was a grammar-school boy from the Midlands who'd gone on to Cambridge and completed his medical training at St Botolph's, where he had risen effortlessly to become a consultant in child and adolescent psychiatry. He had published several books and held visiting professorships abroad. According to *Who's Who*, his hobbies were swimming, cycling and reading; he'd never married and had no children. He had even appeared on *Desert Island Discs*, for Pete's sake. You couldn't get more squeaky-clean than that.

Yet, if there was nothing in the decades-old allegation against him, why on earth had the Met risked opening up a box of snakes? Ivo had been tempted to give Keith Stalgood a ring to get his take on things, but was reluctant to burn his boats before he got a better handle on the political manoeuvring that very likely lay behind the story. In his opinion, the only certainty was that it would all end in tears at bedtime for someone.

Not for Sam Villiers. Ivo had paid him more or less what he wanted, sent him on his way and – as yet – told no one about the transaction. If need be the cost could be split between several expense claims and would never be questioned.

The auditorium of the achingly cool conference facility in Shoreditch was filling up, with heads craning to catch a first glimpse of Jessica Hubbard's arrival. As Ivo surveyed the crowd, spotting various paid-up members of the great and the good, his attention was caught by a familiar lissom figure slipping into a seat at the end of a row in front of him. He doubted that Grace Fisher had noticed him and, even had she been aware that the *Courier* was footing the bill for Jessica Hubbard's appearance, she'd have no reason to expect to see the paper's crime correspondent among the throng. He hadn't really expected to see her either, but was delighted to be handed a legitimate opportunity to approach her.

He watched as she stood to allow people to pass along the row. She wore a tailored pale apricot sleeveless dress with a necklace of jade-like green beads. Her bare arms were lightly tanned, and her straight brown hair had been cut to curve neatly into her neck. He had no idea why the sight of her always made his heart sing, but as long as it did, he was happy to leave the why of it unexamined.

With everyone seated, the lights dimmed and a ripple of excitement flowed around the room as Jessica Hubbard was led to her place in the front row as inconspicuously as an entourage of two black-suited minders, a hatchet-faced PA and the star-struck chief executive of the St Botolph's Hospital Trust could allow. Ivo had been at close quarters with movie stars once or twice before, but Jessica, with her dewy English-rose complexion, seemed even more flawless and shining than he remembered them as being. As she sat down, Professor Chesham made his way to the spotlit podium, the charity's logo appeared on the giant screen behind him, and the audience's murmuring ebbed away.

Ivo was far more interested in the man than in what he had to say. Chesham was neither physically imposing nor conventionally charismatic, yet he seemed to possess a natural confidence that he would be pleasing to his audience, that they would welcome him into their hearts. But just what were they letting in? Was he angel or devil?

He would have been thirty-two when the historical assault had allegedly taken place, not yet a consultant. He was now fifty-five and no further complaints had been made – or at any rate had not ended up on any records Ivo had been able to access. An assiduous online trawl hadn't thrown up a single rumour or dark hint; quite the contrary – the man seemed almost a saint. He appeared to be celibate: there were no images of him with a partner of either sex. Once or twice he had turned up to charity events with a teenage patient on his arm: was that an alarm bell ringing or merely a canny fundraising photo opportunity?

As Chesham's lecture progressed, Ivo looked around at the audience, their expressions engaged and respectful. If the original allegation turned out to be true, possibly even the tip of an iceberg, then hundreds of people like this would have to be staggeringly blind. Was it possible that Chesham had pulled that much wool over so many eyes? Experience over the past few years had certainly proved that it was possible. Yet would Keith have slipped up? Or did every doctor in every field clock up at least one mischievous or delusional complaint over a long career?

Like an old warhorse scenting battle, Ivo's nostrils flared: if this guy *was* a paedophile, then that would actually be quite a story!

As Chesham worked through his final few slides, Ivo paid

closer attention. 'While physically they seek to disappear,' he was saying, 'anorexics also crave attention. They distrust their bodies, their appetites and desires. Confusing need with greed, they feel ashamed of wanting and so exert rigid control. Part of our mission at St Botolph's is to help them feel safe in their bodies, safe with their appetites and desires. It's important to provide lots of healthy opportunities for them to learn how to accept the attention they crave.'

Ivo shivered. Were these words deliberately laced with taunting significance? Was Chesham, so self-deprecating and at ease, secretly shafting everyone here while enjoying the sick joke of his life? Generally Ivo prided himself on his ability to see through bullshit, but this guy was either a seriously good actor or innocent, and Ivo didn't feel ready to place a bet either way. He glanced at the back of DI Fisher's head: he'd give a lot to know what she was thinking right now.

Chesham drew his talk to a close with an appeal for donations to the new St Botolph's campaign to expand its mental health services, in particular to provide an additional ward for acute inpatient care at the eating disorders unit. Jessica Hubbard then made a pretty show of creeping up on stage, a finger to those famous lips in an appeal to the enraptured audience not to give the game away as she 'surprised' Ned at the podium.

The star then waited for the applause to die down before delivering a short speech explaining that she had finally decided to speak out about her own secret battle with anorexia in the hope that her story would help others. She embraced Ned, assuring him with glistening tears in her eyes that without his wisdom and care, she might not even be here today. She then announced that she was donating her fee for some articles that were about to appear in the *Daily Courier* to the charity and, raising her and Ned's linked hands aloft in a kind of victory salute, urged others to give generously.

As the lights came up and people made their way out to the lobby and the free champagne, Ivo timed his exit to slip in beside Grace.

'Inspirational?' he said quietly. 'Or seriously creepy?'

She turned in horrified surprise, her grey eyes searching his face. 'What do you mean?'

He leaned closer. 'The Yard has always leaked like a sieve.' The shock on her face made him regret his words, and he placed a hand lightly on her arm. 'Don't worry. I bought the story. It's safely off the table, for the time being anyway.'

Reaching the lobby area, she drew him away from the main crush. 'Ivo!' She shook her head at him. 'Goodness, you gave me a nasty fright just then! How are you?'

'Much the same.' He could feel himself blushing with pleasure. 'You?'

'It sounds like you'd know more than I do. You'd better tell me what you've been up to.'

He took a look around, but there was no one near enough to overhear and no better disguise for handing over secrets than chatting in the midst of a crowd. 'The name Sam Villiers mean anything to you?'

'Yes.'

He waited, but she did not expand. It was typical of her even now, even after they'd successfully pooled information on more than one occasion, to keep her cards close to her chest. He had never let her down, never would, and had to admit to being a little hurt by her reluctance to acknowledge it.

'Villiers brought it to me,' he told her. 'He claims he wants to raise a bit of cash to get his new business off the ground.'

She reacted with a sound of disgust, her face creasing with distaste. 'So what are you going to do?'

'Whatever you want. Run it or bury it. Just give me the word.'

'That's kind. Thank you.' She gave a slow and solemn nod. 'Sit on it for now, would you?'

'I will. But . . .'

'But?'

'Some sixth sense tells me Villiers wasn't only after the cash. Initially I reckoned he missed something the first time round, messed up in some way, and if he's going down decided to take the whole damn circus with him, but then I started to think maybe he was doing what he'd been told to do.'

'Who by?' It was Grace's turn to check behind them and lower her voice. 'Why would the Yard want to sabotage their own review?'

'It may not be the Yard,' said Ivo. 'Villiers has recently set up on his own account as a private investigator. I checked him out. He spent the last eight years with SO17 as part of the dedicated search wing at the Palace of Westminster. He may have a few chums there he's prepared to run errands for.'

'But why?' she asked. 'The only political ripples this would cause would be over Chesham being given a knighthood.'

'It's probably no more than some local beef between the Yard top brass and the Home Office,' said Ivo. 'All the same, when an idea like that pops uninvited into my head, I tend to give it house room. And I thought you ought to know. If there *is* someone pulling the strings behind Villiers, it doesn't bode well for you or your inquiry.'

'No.'

He let her chew on that for a moment and was content when she gave another little nod, proof that she was prepared to trust his gut instinct. 'So what did you make of the lecture?' he asked.

'I was looking around at his audience. They were lapping it up.' She sighed. 'What does the *Courier* have on him?'

'Nothing. And I mean nothing. Professor Chesham has never even made so much as a threat to sue. And that's our money up there.' He nodded towards where Ned and Jessica, each holding a corner of a giant cheque and illuminated by a barrage of flashes, posed for photographs. 'We're running her story across the whole of next week, and I imagine someone on the paper checked the files pretty thoroughly before shelling out the kind of money her agent will have negotiated.'

'If he's done nothing, there's no reason to leak my investigation.' Grace turned to the glittering crowd. 'Not when it would stop all this charity work dead in its tracks. Do untold damage.'

He watched a slight frown crease the smooth skin of her forehead. Her eyebrows were perfectly arched above the wide, still pools of her eyes. Lovely *and* smart.

'Except,' she said thoughtfully, 'if the media run with the story, other victims might well be encouraged to come forward.'

'That would certainly make your job a whole lot easier,' he said.

'True,' she said. 'Although I can't believe that anyone at the Met is going to take responsibility for naming him. Not after the beating they took over the way other high-profile men were hounded.'

'No,' he agreed. 'But it's not as if I'm about to fly a helicopter over his house and run the footage on the evening news.'

He was pleased that this made Grace laugh.

'On the other hand,' he went on, 'if no one comes forward and Chesham is exonerated, then the Met can say job done, blame the media for its vicious and irresponsible coverage, and come out looking snowy white. It's a win-win.'

'Surely no one would deliberately ruin Chesham's career just to cover their own back?'

'They might if it also meant settling a few old scores with the Met's political lords and masters,' he said. 'I imagine the Yard is still licking its wounds after the casualties inflicted by the hacking scandal.'

'That's over now, surely?'

Ivo shook his head. 'Not much love lost. Which is also why, if someone really wants this story out there, there'll be plenty of other takers. Anyway, it's probably nothing, but I wanted to give you a heads-up.' He was fishing for compliments, but what the hell? 'Thought you deserved to be warned, that's all.'

She smiled. 'Thank you, but I'm just a cog in the machine.'

'Maybe,' he said. 'But remember: if it does all blow up in their faces, who are the Met going to push out front to take the flak?'

She looked serious for a second or two, taking the truth of this on board, then laughed, shaking her head and reaching out to touch his arm. 'No one's going to get me,' she said. 'Not as long as I have you watching my back!'

She'd made his day.

15

Nasir Khan lived in a post-war council block in an area of the East End that was showing early signs of gentrification. On the staircase Grace and Duncan passed both a traditionally dressed Bengali mother with two bright-eyed toddlers and a hipster couple manhandling their designer bicycles down to the street.

It had proved far less complicated than expected to track down Mr Khan thanks to the fact that he had not moved from this flat since his arrival in the UK in 1994. Not long after that he had begun working as a cleaner at St Botolph's where, as the hospital trust's chief executive had explained to Grace at their confidential meeting the previous Friday, Mr Khan had reported hearing something out of place on a ward one night. His concern had led to the only complaint on record against Ned Chesham. The chief executive had assured Grace that the trust had robust safeguarding policies and that all the correct protocols then in place had been followed. Mr Khan had been interviewed by Mr James Gibson, an orthopaedic surgeon who had been the medical director on the trust board at the time, and no further action had been deemed necessary.

Mr Khan, a short, gaunt man who looked much older than fifty, welcomed them into his spotless living room, apologizing that as his wife was out shopping, he was unable to offer them any refreshments. He listened courteously as they explained the reason for their visit and was able to recall the incident almost immediately.

'The doctors very nice people,' he said, nodding his head. 'Very respectful, though then my English very poor. Better now.' His smile revealed a missing tooth.

'Can you remember what you told them?' asked Grace.

'I heard sounds.' He wiggled his hand, frowning and pursing his lips. 'Two people. A bed with curtains. Not good. Not right.'

Grace and Duncan exchanged looks. 'Are those the exact words you used?'

'My English then not very good.'

'They didn't offer to bring in an interpreter?'

Nasir Khan shook his head. 'I told my supervisor, then again to a doctor, Mr Gibson.'

'What had made you think there was something wrong?'

In reply he made little panting and grunting noises. 'Like that,' he said. 'And then she cry out. I make noise to show I was there. It stopped.'

'Did you see who it was?'

'No.'

'No one came out from behind the curtain to speak to you? No member of the medical staff?'

'No. But later Doctor Ned, he came found me. Said it was him, nothing bad. I shouldn't worry. I did right to speak.'

'When was that?'

'After I talk to Mr Gibson. He said it's fine. He spoke to Doctor Ned. All a misunderstanding.'

'And is that what you thought at the time?' asked Grace. 'If you think back to what you heard?'

She recalled the account that the surgeon had given them at their meeting with the trust chief executive. Mr Gibson, who had recently retired, had seemed uncomfortable, as if his training had never equipped him to deal with this kind of situation. According to his memory of the incident, Mr Khan had merely imagined hearing something sexual going on behind the curtains of one of the beds on an inpatient ward. Ned Chesham had explained that a patient had become distressed during the night and he had drawn the curtains in order not to disturb others who were asleep. The patient herself had made no complaint, and they had been reluctant to interrogate her. Her parents had not been informed because Mr Gibson had been fully satisfied there was no substance to the allegation, and the trust too had been happy to draw a line under it. 'If you can't accept the word of a medical colleague,' Gibson had said, 'who can you trust?'

Despite Nasir Khan's eagerness to be helpful, Grace thought he looked concerned. 'I see hunger in Bangladesh,' he said, 'but those girls, they starve themselves!' He shook his head in bewilderment. 'Must be very difficult looking after girls like that.'

'How long did you stay working on that ward after all this took place?' asked Duncan.

Nasir Khan's face brightened. 'I got moved to outpatients. No more nights. Better for me and my family.'

'And what do you think now?' Grace pressed. 'Do you think you misunderstood what you heard?'

'I only hear,' he said. 'Not see anything.'

'But when you heard it, you thought something was going on that wasn't right, wasn't good, is that so?'

'Mr Gibson was very respectful to me, very polite.'

'You were the one who was there,' she said gently. 'You were concerned enough to report it.'

He smiled and shook his head. 'My cousin's daughter is a doctor. Big education. Big training. Very clever people.'

'OK, Mr Khan,' said Grace. 'Thank you very much for your time. I appreciate your help.'

As Duncan got to his feet he held out his hand to the man. 'You did absolutely the right thing all those years ago,' he said. 'I'd like to thank you for that.'

Nasir Khan nodded, his smile suddenly a little less resolute. Grace thought perhaps he was about to have second thoughts, but he led them to his front door, shook their hands and shut it behind them.

'Hardly the best witness,' sighed Grace as they made their way down the stairs.

'Especially not after he'd been railroaded,' said Duncan hotly. 'We need to talk to the girl who was in that bed.'

Emerging on to the sunlit street she thought how easily a pleasant summer's day could transform the mood of even such a run-down part of London as this.

'It's nearly twenty years ago,' she said. 'If we're going to open up old wounds, we'd better make sure first that we've got something to offer her in return.'

Grace found herself unaccountably angry with Ned Chesham. Even if he was wholly innocent, there could only be losers in this investigation, and somehow she felt it was his fault. What had he been doing comforting an underage patient behind closed curtains in the middle of the night? What gave him the right to think it was OK to take young girls away on camping holidays and assume no one would draw inappropriate conclusions? Was he merely, like Mr James Gibson, the last of a generation trained to believe that the doctor always knows best? She wondered how often that attitude had silenced the voices of both his patients and junior staff.

Professor Chesham has every right to expect the trust to defend him vigorously. That's what the chief executive had said, warning her against embarking on a damaging fishing expedition. Agreeing that no one wanted a witch-hunt, she'd accepted that if her investigations were made public the trust would have no option but to suspend Professor Chesham forthwith. The CEO had shaken his head at the idea. 'It would be a personal tragedy and have serious ramifications for the hospital and everyone who works here,' he'd said. 'I'm sure I don't need to remind you of all the good work he's done not only for St Botolph's but also internationally.'

I don't envy you this job. Keith Stalgood's words echoed in her head again.

'No one ever wants to talk themselves into believing this stuff.' The bitterness in Duncan's voice cut through her thoughts. 'All they ever want to do is talk themselves out of it.'

'We're supposed to keep an open mind,' she said mildly.

'Like the hospital, you mean, pursuing a policy of utmost transparency? All that means is, don't ruin a man's career, don't damage the reputation of the hospital. Mr Khan assumed they were entitled to tell him he'd made a mistake. No one gives a damn about the kids who get hurt!'

'We do,' she told him.

'You realize that no one wants us to find anything,' said Duncan. 'And you can be sure no one's going to pin a medal on us if we do.'

Grace nodded, finally grasping what Ivo had been trying to warn her about, and what Duncan had been quicker to see – that the harder she worked this case, the deeper she could end up burying her career. She felt a bitter flare of protest. She told herself this was justice, this was why she was in the Job, that any future promotion was a petty irrelevance in the face of the continued abuse of children. But she had to admit it was a struggle to stifle the thoughts of unfairness. And it was that same sense of unfairness, she realized, that had tinged the CEO's protest that the good name of St Botolph's didn't deserve to be dragged in the mud. Duncan was right: there were far too many good reasons for people not to want to believe this stuff.

16

Clive avoided looking at the clock on the office wall. He ought to have left forty minutes ago, but he was determined to do something properly and at least clear the most urgent tasks on his desk before he went home. Once upon a time he'd prided himself on his efficiency – which was all people really wanted from the solicitor handling their house sale – but nowadays his in-box overflowed with emails begging for progress updates and demanding to know if the chain would get moving again before it broke.

So far his employers had been pretty understanding about letting him have compassionate leave or even extra time off on top of that when there'd been yet another crisis. Fair enough, he'd earned some leeway over the ten years he'd worked here, but their patience had to run out soon. And more than that, he hated feeling that his job was turning into a perpetual muddle, a joke, another burden threatening to topple over and crash to the ground.

God knows, being a lowly conveyancing solicitor in a large firm wasn't exactly glamorous, but he appreciated order and neatness, and loved his clients' relief and happiness when a sale completed and he got to tell them the keys to their new home were theirs. If he couldn't cling to a life raft of sanity at work, he was afraid he'd sink without trace.

Besides, being a grown-up and doing the right thing all the time was exhausting. There were times when he too wanted to smash things on the floor and scream abuse and slam the door behind him. Surely taking an extra hour or so to work late and deal with some of the backlog could hardly count as being selfish and irresponsible? He was forty, beginning to lose his hair, and were it not for the food police at home would likely have a paunch too. There had to be more to life than this.

He should have taken the afternoon off to go with Gillian to the clinic. He'd missed a family therapy session. Black marks all round. And no doubt next week he'd have to atone by listening to some blather about avoidance when all he wanted was to finish one job in his life properly.

He knew it was hard on Gillian, having to give up work, but she earned half what he did. They'd discussed both of them going part-time, but it simply wouldn't have worked. And then they had really, truly believed they were turning a corner with Meghan's eating problems. Until Dr Merrick's death over a week ago had sent them all back to square one. Or worse.

Last night he'd woken from a nightmare in which Meghan and all the other kids at the camp had set upon the young doctor and torn him limb from limb like some mad women from a Greek tragedy. Witnessing the wild, snarling rage that Meghan could muster in response to a simple request to eat a slice of toast, it didn't seem impossible. His once-upon-a-time-darling, happy daughter!

The memory made him close down his computer and head for home.

Entering the house he heard Helen's voice: she must have accompanied Gillian and Meghan home from the clinic. Despite the almost constant undertow of tension between Gillian and her younger sister, maybe with Helen there his wife wouldn't give him such a hard time about skipping therapy. He drew a deep breath and opened the kitchen door.

'Helen's been offered a new job!' Gillian exclaimed as soon as she saw him, turning from where she was chopping green beans and carrots for supper. Helen sat at the table with a glass of wine. Meghan must be watching TV in the other room.

'Well, not offered,' said Helen. 'Invited to apply.'

'Congratulations!' Clive was unspeakably grateful for the distraction. 'Tell me all about it.'

'Well, I'm not sure it's right for me,' said Helen.

'Don't be like that,' said Gillian.

'It's in Newcastle for a start. I don't know a soul up there.'

'But Ash Rajani does. The woman running the department used to be his houseman. Ned told me you're exactly what they're looking for.'

'I'll have to think about it.'

'How were Meghan's tests today?' Clive tried to signal to Gillian to back off, all too aware that she could sometimes be a bit of a bulldozer, especially when acting with the best intentions.

'They were fine,' said Helen, smiling at him gratefully. 'Weight's dipped a bit, but her blood tests were all good. Don't worry, we'll get through this.'

'No news, I suppose, about what happened?'

Helen shook her head. 'Not that we've heard.'

Gillian tipped the chopped vegetables into a pan, ran water over them and put the pan on the stove. Picking up her half-empty wine glass, she took a gulp, nearly finishing it. 'Ned thinks it's a wonderful opportunity,' she told her sister. 'He told me that you're more than ready for a more senior role now you've finished your qualification in family psychotherapy.'

'But what about our work together here?'

'He wants to see you spread your wings. He asked me specially to encourage you.'

Helen laughed and shook her head. 'It's so sweet that he always wants what's best for me. He's afraid of holding me back, but St Botolph's is an international centre of excellence. Why would I want to walk away from the amazing work we do together?'

'There's more to life than work,' said Gillian gently.

'He'd be lost without me! We're the perfect team.'

Clive knew what was coming next. Helen might hope that her feelings for Ned were reciprocated, and maybe they were, but, as Gillian often said, there was no evidence that, unmarried at fifty-five, Ned was about to change his ways.

'You're thirty,' said Gillian. 'Time's running out if you want to have a family. You'll meet new people if you go to Newcastle. A whole new life. It might just be the best thing ever.'

Helen gave the maddening secret smile that was always her final defence when Gillian challenged her on anything to do with Ned. The smile clearly annoyed Gillian now for she spoke more briskly. 'He's spoken to the team up there himself, and they'd love to have you. You should at least apply for it.'

'Let her think about it,' said Clive, suddenly too weary to face more confrontation. 'How about giving me a glass of wine?'

Gillian poured a glass and handed it over. 'Where were you this afternoon?'

'Couldn't get away,' he said. 'I'm really sorry, and I know how important it is, but a big sale would've fallen through if it hadn't happened today. And I needed to get the billing through our system to prove that I'm earning my keep and not slacking with all this time off.'

Gillian clanged the pan lid as she checked on the vegetables. Clive looked to Helen for support.

'Don't beat yourself up,' she said. 'That doesn't help anyone.'

It was scant comfort, but it would have to do.

Gillian sniffed dismissively. 'Can you go and call Meghan for supper?'

'Of course.' He crossed his fingers that Meghan wouldn't pretend she had fallen asleep, or just needed to see the end of her TV show, or any one of a dozen other avoidance tactics.

'Gosh, I've just remembered I've still got some left-over salmon in my fridge,' said Helen, reaching for her bag. 'It'll go off if I don't eat it tonight, so I think I'll head home after all if you don't mind.'

'Sure.' Gillian threw her hands up helplessly. 'Whatever.'

Clive tried desperately to recall the delight with which his client had received the news this afternoon that she could go ahead and confirm with the removal company what time to arrive in the morning. He was almost beginning to forget what delight felt like.

17

Grace unlocked the door of the office allocated to Operation Mayfly. It was hot and stuffy and looked over the car park, making her miss the leafy view from her cubicle downstairs. Even though this top-floor corridor away from the main flow of gossip and information felt almost eerily quiet she knew she'd been lucky that space had been found for her in Colchester, where she could still keep tabs on the Major Investigation Team. The change had however made it impossible to avoid questions about what she was busy doing up here. She was pretty certain that so far she'd managed to keep the lid on Ned Chesham's name, and in any case her biggest fear was that word might spread around the station that her new task involved shafting Detective Superintendent Stalgood.

Although Keith hadn't been in charge of Colchester MIT for all that long – only a year or two – he'd made his mark as an effective copper and a decent man. She hoped that in the event of a leak, her liking and admiration for her former boss would be well enough known to scotch the worst of the rumours, which would no doubt be fanned by Colin Pitman, Keith's less popular successor. Grace knew that while Colin might pretend to be fine about being kept in the dark over the reason for her meeting with DAC Marx, it had really pissed him off. She couldn't help but feel a frisson of pleasure knowing how his enforced ignorance must rankle, yet she simply didn't trust him enough to share Operation Mayfly's remit with him.

She was, however, strongly tempted to take Blake into her confidence, despite the possible imprudence of such a step. Not only did she need to know what his investigation into Tim Merrick's murder was turning up, but the allegations against Chesham might shed useful light on his own thinking. But she dared not disclose confidential information to a detective sergeant without also bringing their boss up to speed: Colin held enough grudges against her already.

What Colin's evident irritation at his enforced ignorance did prove, however, was that he couldn't be the one pulling the strings behind Sam Villiers – if Ivo Sweatman was even remotely right about that, of course. And yet, even though Ivo had said it was only a hunch, past experience had given her no reason to doubt either his judgement or his motives. She'd not had much time to think about why anyone at Scotland Yard or elsewhere, especially given the DAC's warning to her to be discreet, would want a tabloid newspaper to know about Operation Mayfly, and she certainly couldn't imagine why such an agenda would have anything to do with her personally.

Meanwhile St Botolph's had been able to identify the young patient who had been in the hospital bed when Nasir Khan heard sounds of a possibly sexual nature. Her name was Karen Wheeler and she was now thirty-two; the only address they could offer was long out of date, but Duncan was pulling out all the stops to track her down.

Nasir Khan had reported his concerns to the hospital authorities two years before Trudie Bevan made her delayed complaint to the police, meaning Chesham had abused Trudie four years before Karen became a patient. Grace had to assume that Chesham had no knowledge of Keith's investigation, which meant – if he was guilty – that he must believe not only that he'd got away with the incident involving Karen Wheeler but also, when challenged, had succeeded in persuading the safeguarding authority that there was no case to answer. Would such a close call have been enough to scare him off, or merely convince him that he was untouch-able? Either way, his continuing ignorance of Grace's investigation was to her advantage: another reason to hope that Ivo could keep the story under wraps for a while longer. If not, and Chesham's name was released prematurely, then she'd just have to roll with the consequences and hope for the best.

Grace's cynical wish was that Karen Wheeler's account of that long-ago night would be definite enough to clinch Chesh-am's guilt or innocence. Apart from the fact that both girls had been thirteen-year-old patients, there was nothing yet to sug-gest a pattern, and her fear was that any evidence provided by this second potential victim would create a scattergun effect rather than narrow the target. If only she could manage to keep clear in her own mind what kind of man Ned Chesham was!

The phone on her desk rang. It was Blake, calling from the MIT office downstairs. 'Thought you'd like to know, boss, that we've got a possible new suspect in the Merrick killing.'

'I'm on my way.'

Colin, standing in the doorway to his office, gave her a nod as she came in. Blake, at the murder wall, was pointing at a photo-graph of a young soldier in dress uniform.

'This was taken seven years ago,' he said to the assembled

team. 'He doesn't look like this now. He's been living rough in the woods for months, and descriptions of him range from scraggy to unkempt, with long hair and a beard.'

'Who's this?' Grace asked.

'Paul Harrison,' said Blake. 'According to the landlord of the pub in Long Wryford, he's been camping out in the woods the other side of the road from Wryford Hall, not far from the gate into the grounds. He's a loner and – I quote – "a bit mental". We went looking for him as a possible witness but found that he'd packed up in a hurry and gone, pretty much the day after Tim Merrick's murder, as far as we can tell.'

'So he might have seen something that scared him off?' she said.

Blake nodded. 'He's served in Afghanistan, was invalided out with post-traumatic stress, has a history of unpredictable violent outbursts.'

'Maybe he simply couldn't cope with the police nosing around?'

'Either way it would be useful to speak to him,' he said. 'We've put out an urgent alert.'

'We've said from the beginning that a random encounter was a possibility,' said Colin.

'Except it doesn't explain what Dr Merrick was doing over on that side of the park when he was supposed to be on duty at the camp,' said Grace.

'Putting himself out of the way of temptation?' said Blake. 'It's what Helen Fry suggested he do during their phone call.'

Grace nodded. It did all fit together neatly, although the irony of a young psychiatric registrar being the chance victim of an ex-soldier in need of treatment would bring little comfort to Tim Merrick's parents. 'What about the concentration of blows around his mouth?' she asked. 'Is that significant?'

'Could be linked to some paranoid delusion that Harrison was suffering at the time,' said Blake. 'We won't know until we talk to him.'

'OK,' said Grace. 'Good work. Thanks for keeping me in the loop.'

As she turned to leave she found Colin at her side. 'Settling in all right upstairs?' he asked.

'Not too bad.'

'Busy?'

'Early days.'

He grinned at her, but she could see the glint of cold steel in his eyes. 'I can see you're enjoying all this Secret Squirrel stuff,' he said. 'Make the most of it while you can.'

He peeled away to return to his office, leaving her with a distinct sense of threat. She knew it was really only sour grapes and that he could do her no real harm, but she could do without the additional anxiety.

Her disquiet was compounded when she found Duncan in their office upstairs. He had located Karen Wheeler, who now lived in Maidstone, Kent. As Duncan gave her the rest of the details he had gleaned about her, all Grace could think about was how Colin had also been her boss in Maidstone, where he had failed to support her when she was bullied by fellow officers, including her former husband, culminating in a vicious assault by him. She'd not been back since giving evidence against Trev in court. Since then Colin had been forced to accept a formal reprimand for his failure to act, which had not endeared Grace to him. Maidstone was not a place she would ever have chosen to revisit. Nonetheless, the memories it evoked were a salutary reminder of what it felt like not only to be a victim but also to be derided and ignored. If Karen Wheeler had something to say, she was damn well going to listen.

18

Grace was grateful at least that Karen's address was not familiar to her, although on the way to it she and Duncan drove past the end of one street she remembered instantly from her first year as a detective constable. A house on the corner had once been a crack den; having survived repeated arrests and attempts to close it down, eventually a careless customer had set fire to the place. The damaged building remained boarded up, its legal ownership or responsibility for repairs still in dispute. Those early days in the Job had been stressful and challenging as she'd rapidly acquired new skills and learned to survive a few hard knocks, but her pleasure and excitement in her chosen career had grown with her confidence.

She smiled to think that an abandoned crack den should be a welcome reminder of the optimistic younger self that had existed before the misery and helplessness of what followed. She mustn't allow herself to bury the good along with the bad, but nor must she forget, when approaching Ned Chesham's former patients, just how hard it could be to move on from difficult events in the past.

It was barely ten o'clock when Karen, a tiny woman in a T-shirt and faded yoga pants, opened her front door to them, yet the smell of cheap brandy on her breath was unmissable, and she staggered slightly as she led the way inside. Her one-bed flat was on the ground floor of a modern block that backed on to a railway line; the living-room window faced a line of parked cars. It looked as if Karen had made a rudimentary effort to tidy up for their visit, but Grace could see that no actual cleaning had taken place in months.

'Sorry,' said Karen as she waved them towards the scuffed leather three-piece suite that took up most of the room. 'I had a little drink after breakfast to steady my nerves. It's a bit scary getting a visit from the police.'

'We're sorry to spring this on you out of the blue,' said Grace, noticing that Karen's shoulder-length brown hair was damp, as if she was not long out of the shower. Her feet were bare, and the chipped green nail varnish on her toes looked as if it had been applied weeks ago.

'You said on the phone it was about my time as a patient at St Botolph's?'

'Yes,' said Grace. 'How long were you a patient there?'

Karen turned away to lean over the side of her chair. Grace was afraid that she was about to puke, but then saw that she was reaching for a bottle and glass tucked away out of sight on the floor. 'Sorry, I need a top-up if I'm going to talk about this.' Karen's hand shook as she poured the brandy and raised the glass to her lips. 'It's about Doctor Ned, isn't it?'

'Why do you say that?' Grace found she was bracing herself against the leather arm of the couch.

'I always hoped that one day there'd be a knock at the door,' said Karen. 'That someone would get him in the end.'

'Can you tell me what you mean?' Grace asked. 'I know it must be difficult, but get him for what?'

THE SPECIAL GIRLS | 110

'It's not difficult at all. Do you have any idea how long I've been waiting for someone official to come and *ask* me?'

Grace glanced sideways at Duncan. He sat very still but his hands were clenched so tightly in his lap that the knuckles had gone white.

'OK, well, I'm asking now,' Grace said gently. 'Did something happen to you when you were a patient at St Botolph's?'

'Doctor Ned used to touch me, and I had to masturbate him or give him oral sex. That's what you're asking for, isn't it?'

'Are you talking about Edward Chesham?' Grace tried to keep her voice steady. First Trudie, now Karen. How long had their abuser been operating unchecked?

'Yes, I am.' Karen poured herself another drink. 'So why are you here now? Why me?'

'We've been speaking to someone who used to work at the hospital. A Mr Khan.'

'The cleaner? Oh yeah, I remember him.'

'You knew that he had reported a concern?'

Karen nodded. 'Doctor Ned told me. Said I needed to understand the grown-up world and how it worked. That same day he had me smiling at my parents while he had his hand down the back of my knickers. The best hospital in the world, all those wonderful doctors and nurses, and not one of them was going to help me.'

'Did you ever tell anyone?'

'Later, years later – a therapist, several therapists.' She raised her glass. 'Cheers.'

'But you never felt able to report it officially?'

'And shame my parents? That's what they both said. Imagine the fuss, the publicity. I felt responsible, thought it was all my fault, that I'd be letting them down. And even then, what if, after all the fuss and publicity, I wasn't believed? How would the family ever live it down? I was trapped.'

Grace didn't know what to say.

'Don't get me wrong,' said Karen. 'They're not bad people. My mum and dad never actually said I was lying, but they don't talk about sex. And deep down, I don't think they ever really believed that a man like that could *want* to do such gross things. I mean, like, he's a *doctor*! And anyway not with me, not the way I looked back then.' She laughed and waved her glass in the air. 'I was a scarecrow. Nothing like the vision of beauty you see before you now.'

Grace wished she could communicate the insight she'd had earlier in the car – about remembering the person who existed before the damage – but she knew that she was lucky, that for some people the wounds had been inflicted too early and gone too deep ever to mend. 'How would you feel now about making a statement?' she asked instead. 'Would you be prepared to give evidence in court, if it comes to that?'

'I've been drinking since I was fifteen. Who's going to believe me?'

Duncan cleared his throat. 'I do.'

Grace bit back the urge to say that she did too. Duncan's words were unprofessional, but she was glad he'd said them.

Karen looked at each of them in turn, her eyes bright with hope, and then shook her head. 'I can't,' she said, slumping back in her chair. 'It's too fucking complicated. He can go in the witness box and say he never threatened me, that I never told him it made me unhappy, never tried not to be on my own with him. He can call people who were in the room while he was doing stuff to me and say I must've liked it or I'd have cried out.'

'You were a child,' said Grace.

Karen nodded. 'People think abuse is about sex, but it's not – it's how they mess with your head. That's what I can't unscramble, can't get straight – the reason why I can't just be normal and get on with my life.'

'You're doing OK,' said Duncan.

'You think?' She cracked a tiny smile. 'Talk to my liver specialist.'

Grace asked herself what on earth she was doing, coming here and threatening to tear down whatever fragile scaffolding Karen had managed to erect around her life to keep it standing. What did she have to offer in its place? 'We can get you all the help and support you need,' she said, crossing her fingers that this wasn't wishful thinking.

'Talking helps,' said Karen, 'but it doesn't kill the demons in your head, the ones that say it's all your fault, you're fucking useless, you deserved it, it'll always be like this.' She poured more brandy into her glass. 'When it started I didn't say anything because I felt like such an idiot for not realizing what was happening. Then I felt an idiot for not telling anyone straightaway. And then he went on and on telling me how happy it made him and that the reason I kept coming back for more was because I liked it too, because this was how grown-up people showed that they really liked one another. Then it was too late to tell anyone. And the thing is – and this is the hardest part – when he wasn't making me do those things, I did like him. Or thought I did. I don't know. I have no way of knowing any more how I'm supposed to feel.'

'You've given it a lot of thought,' said Duncan.

Karen raised her glass again. 'Not much else to do.'

'We're going to keep investigating,' said Grace. 'If you felt able to give us a statement, that would be an enormous help.'

'Have other people come forward?'

'I can't answer that yet, I'm sorry. But if it gets to court, then I'm sure you won't be alone. Meanwhile our work would go more smoothly if none of this becomes public knowledge before we're ready.'

Karen nodded and examined the bottom of her empty glass. 'You want to look out for the girls in red swimsuits.'

'What?'

'You know, like the yellow jersey in the Tour de France? When he took us to the summer camp, he liked his special girl to have a red swimsuit.'

'You went to one of the summer camps at Wryford Hall?' asked Grace.

'If that's the place with the cricket pavilion, then yes.'

'And you were the special girl?'

Karen grimaced as if resisting a wave of nausea. 'Lucky me.'

19

Ivo had not been able to forget DI Fisher's comment that media exposure might bring other people out of the woodwork. She'd said it more to herself than to him, making him speculate whether it wasn't in fact an unwitting admission that her review had already uncovered new information. In which case Sam Villiers' bauble might be a cracking good story after all.

Not that he would wish to shaft Grace Fisher – not in a million years – but if the scandal was going to break anyway, he most certainly wasn't going to be left at the starting gate. His speculations also made him very much more interested in finding out whether anyone *had* tapped Sam Villiers on the shoulder and told him to get busy, and if so, who? And why?

The possibility that the saintly Ned Chesham really was a devil in disguise widened the field considerably, and made the leak less likely to stem from some turf war between the Met, the tabloids and Westminster in which the good doctor was merely collateral damage. On the other hand it was no coincidence that Sam had spent the past eight years popping in and out of MPs' offices checking for bombs, bugs or terrorists hiding under the desks. He was bound to have made a few chums, and with the Met commissioner's contract up for renewal and the government floating the idea that leadership of the force should be open to outside candidates, some negative publicity would feed nicely into political demands for change. If the Yard were to be the cause of red faces among the grandees on the honours vetting committee, then a sharp swing of mood at Westminster against the Met top brass would probably follow.

A quick chat to a couple of the *Courier*'s political correspondents had, however, poured cold water on that idea: the government was fighting on too many fronts right now to take on the Met as well.

It had then occurred to Ivo that Jessica Hubbard couldn't have been the professor's only A-list patient. There must be plenty of others with eating disorders – supermodels, singers, footballers' wives, athletes, soap stars, minor royalty. What if another high-profile patient had got wind of Operation Mayfly and didn't want the embarrassment of coming forward with an accusation but wanted to be sure that the truth came out?

Reluctant to approach the hyenas who ran the showbiz desk – they had no need to trade with the likes of him and he had no intention of letting them pick up the scent of his story – he tried to puzzle it out for himself.

Sam Villiers had been told officially about Operation Mayfly because he'd been part of the original investigation. It might be that he'd tipped someone off, either to parade his insider knowledge or because he knew an individual who had a special interest in the subject. Or – and this was Ivo's favoured theory – someone already knew about the review and had approached Sam to be their messenger precisely because Sam had the perfect cover story.

So who else would have been informed, or been able to find out, that Operation Mayfly had been set up?

Ivo once again briefly considered giving Keith Stalgood a call, but it was still too soon: he needed more to go on before he blew his cover. It looked like he'd just have to resort to old-fashioned shoe leather to get the job done.

He'd already established that Sam Villiers worked out of a rented office in South Kensington. It was only one room on the top floor above a shop, but enough to supply the reassuringly swanky address such an inherently dodgy business required. Sam's new venture was one of many offering to harvest information on behalf of lawyers, businesses, insurance companies and private individuals, some of them doubtless criminal. His target bread and butter was likely to involve high-net-worth divorces, fraud, tracking down debtors and other absconders and, if he got lucky, takeover deals and corporate dirty tricks. If he'd finessed his Westminster contacts properly, he may already have been entrusted with more sensitive investigations.

The weather was clement and the locale afforded a variety of pavement cafés where Ivo could take cover behind yummy mummies laden with designer shopping while keeping watch on the doorway leading up to Villiers' office. It wasn't long before Sam emerged and headed towards the nearest coffee shop. It was child's play to dodge past some slow-moving foreign tourists and bump into him as he came back out. Expressing appropriate surprise followed by expressions of interest in the discovery that this was where Sam had set up shop, Ivo dropped the bait.

'I'm glad I've seen you, actually,' he said. 'I was about to call to let you know that I don't reckon that tip you gave me is going to fly. Don't know if you've seen this week's papers with the Jessica Hubbard exclusive?'

Ivo was willing to bet that since their meeting a week ago, Sam had scoured every edition of the *Courier* for some sign of the story he'd planted. Nonetheless, when Sam demurred, Ivo smiled blandly and explained about the movie star's endorsement of Ned Chesham. 'Thing is, as I'm sure you can understand, my employers don't want me to derail their investment.'

'So you're not going to print the story?' Sam feigned lack of interest, but his eyes gave him away.

'No,' said Ivo. 'Can't blame them. Maybe if we could get a bit more heat behind the original allegation that you and Keith Stalgood investigated, we might be able to run with it further down the line.'

Ivo watched Sam consider this. From the way he involuntarily bit his lip, Ivo reckoned that not only did Sam mind that his leak had failed to make any impact, but he'd mind even more having to report that failure elsewhere. Ivo suppressed a grin and, with the bait taken, looked at his watch, pleaded an urgent appointment and walked away. Glancing back, he saw Sam ditch his untouched coffee in the nearest bin and take out his phone.

Not long afterwards Sam walked purposefully past the shop doorway in which Ivo had parked himself. Keeping a reasonable distance Ivo followed him along the Old Brompton Road and then down one of the side streets that led towards a leafy square. A further turn took Sam along a road where houses on one side faced the backs of those on the other. Some of the multi-million-pound properties had garage entrances on to the street, others had gardens enclosed by high brick walls. Sam stopped outside one such wall in which was set a solid wooden door with an intercom buzzer beside it. He spoke into the intercom; the door swung open, and without even looking over his shoulder he slipped inside.

Ivo strolled past, giving himself enough time to see that there were no identifying names or numbers on the buzzer panel. He counted carefully as he walked on towards the corner, and continuing around the block, counted carefully again as he made his way along the parallel street where elegant four-storey white stucco houses fronted a private square. There was no passing traffic despite the gleaming cars occupying the residents' parking bays, and the only pedestrian he passed was a bored foreign maid walking some fancy pooch. A quick look provided the number of the house into which Sam had disappeared. The ground-floor window was cleverly screened by foliage planted in the neat front garden, and there was a discreet security camera mounted high on a corner of the pillared portico. Shouldn't be too difficult to discover who lived there.

20

Grace was happy to keep her distance as she watched Blake wrap up his piece to camera in front of the remains of former soldier Paul Harrison's bivouac. It was two days since Wendy and her team of CSIs had finished their forensic sweep, which had provided little of interest other than to confirm the former soldier's identity. And so, as no sightings of him had been reported, the media had been invited to the woods near Wryford Hall to record Blake's appeal to Paul to come forward as a potentially vital witness to the murder of Dr Tim Merrick.

The previous afternoon, on her return from Maidstone, Grace had found a summons to a discreet meeting with Hilary Burnett, communications director for the Essex force. To Grace's surprise, Hilary had explained that she had been put fully in the picture about Operation Mayfly by Scotland Yard's head of communications.

'I can see what you're thinking,' Hilary had said with a wry smile. 'It's a bit rich that while operationally no one is to know, behind the scenes the Met is busy making full-scale preparations for a PR disaster.'

'Thanks for the vote of confidence,' Grace had replied with heavy irony. This was precisely what she'd been thinking. She was mollified, however, when Hilary had gone on to clarify that although Blake was keen on a media appeal to locate Paul Harrison, Hilary was stalling until she'd discovered from Grace whether or not the publicity would be helpful to Mayfly.

Grace had assured her that robust media coverage of the Merrick murder could be useful in flushing out any of Ned Chesham's former patients who were tempted to come forward about other matters. Hilary promised to have a word with Blake to ensure that any such approaches were quietly redirected to Grace. Grace reflected privately that it might then no longer be possible to keep Colin Pitman in the dark, even though life would be much easier without having to worry about his manoeuvring behind her back. Not that it really mattered any more: after speaking to Karen Wheeler, Grace was now certain that only tactical considerations could – or should – prevent Mayfly from becoming public knowledge in due course. She had shared this with Hilary, whose judgement she'd learned to trust, adding that she'd rather convey this news to DAC Marx herself.

Grace listened now as Blake, as tactfully instructed by Hilary, repeated that Tim Merrick had been working with the renowned psychiatrist Professor Sir Ned Chesham. Blake, she thought, would look good on television, projecting the right mixture of competence and compassion while not making it appear he was enjoying the limelight too much. She looked around for Ivo Sweatman and was relieved not to see him among the small crowd of mainly local journalists. She wanted a private word with Blake without Ivo's sharp eyes on them.

As one or two reporters lingered for an extra quote she saw Blake look over at her, and she held up her hands to signal that he should take his time. This was his inquiry, and for the time being she was no longer his boss.

He soon joined her and she asked if he would mind walking over to Wryford Hall: she would explain on the way why she wanted a word with Minnie and Toby Thomas. By tacit agreement they skirted around the area where Tim's body had been found. Once out on the open parkland where she could be sure of privacy, she brought him up to date on Operation Mayfly.

Blake's reaction to Karen Wheeler's testimony about Ned's 'special girls' was to whistle through his teeth. 'That fucking conniving bastard!'

'Do you remember the wall of photographs in his office at St Botolph's?' she asked. 'Can you recall if any of the girls were wearing red swimsuits?'

He shook his head slowly. 'Not really. There were so many. Fuck!' He punched a fist hard into his open palm. 'He's even got them all up on his wall! Jesus, I really hope this guy gets what's coming to him in prison!'

Grace shared his anger but knew how vital it was to channel it, to keep the temperature down and proceed rationally. 'Karen Wheeler said her red swimsuit was bought for the summer camp at Wryford Hall in 1997. She said it wasn't the first summer he'd taken kids camping, but she thought it hadn't been going long.'

'Which must make it twenty years or so,' said Blake.

'Even if he only chooses one girl a year,' she said, 'that's still an awful lot of victims.'

'And this summer?'

The lake had come into view away to their left, and Grace

tried not to think too hard about the imploring faces of the eight young teenagers they'd spoken to in the cricket pavilion that day. 'We're going to have to speak to all the parents,' she said. 'But once it starts, we're going to be overwhelmed – victims, their families, the media, the lawyers, the inevitable time-wasters. We only have one chance to get this right. I have to get a bigger team in place. Specialist officers, telephone response lines, a secure ring-fenced computer system, larger offices – it's going to take a good few days to set up.'

'How can I help?'

'What bearing could Chesham's offending have on Tim Merrick's murder?'

Blake stopped and stood looking over to the site of the camp. 'I had been fancying Paul Harrison for it,' he said, rubbing his chin. 'But the whole set-up here is just too weird for there not to be some connection. Plus, from what I've been told, young medics were queuing up to work with Chesham. Did he choose Tim for a reason? Had he been grooming him?'

'It happens,' she said. 'Sexual offenders often recognize something in one another, seek one another out. Although another possibility is that Tim saw something he shouldn't.'

'Then why would Helen Fry lie about it?'

'I don't know,' she said, 'but I've thought a lot about it. If you were Tim, a junior medic, what would you do if you saw your world-famous boss sexually assaulting a child? No one is going to want to hear it; you'll have to persuade other people to believe you. I mean, Chesham had just received a knighthood for his work with these kids! You'd have to be one hundred per cent sure about what you thought you saw, especially if, like Nasir Khan, you hadn't really seen or heard anything specific. No,

ISABELLE GREY | 123

unless Tim could back up his accusation, he'd have just kiboshed years of training and his entire career for nothing.'

'So, what, he runs up a red flag by saying *he's* the danger?' said Blake. 'That's a bit far-fetched, boss.'

'I know,' she said. 'But maybe Tim hoped that Helen would say something to corroborate his fears, give him enough back-up to blow the whistle.'

'Or raise the alarm herself?' he said. 'Do enough to scare Ned off until everyone got safely home.'

'Which gives Ned a pretty strong motive to kill Tim,' said Grace. She nodded in the direction of the hall. 'We need to test his alibi to destruction. And get his phone records.'

'Or Helen Fry is lying.'

'Tim's call to her lasted nearly ten minutes,' she said. 'Whatever they talked about, it wasn't just idle chit-chat.'

Blake nodded, turning the possibilities over in his mind. They set off again, heading for the hall. Grace realized she was actually glad to have him by her side. Taking charge of the investigation seemed to have dispelled much of his relentlessly disparaging attitude and allowed his intelligence to shine through. Good. She was going to need every bit of help she could get.

Meghan slipped through the gap in the changing-room curtains and turned her back to them, waiting for Gillian to zip up the dress. At least this one fitted, thought Clive. It was a nightmare trying to find something formal for a thirteen-year-old who was small for her age that both looked vaguely age-appropriate and didn't cost a fortune. Apparently she'd need a hat for the palace too. But he supposed he was earning brownie points by being here. Taking an overlong lunch break on a weekday was not ideal, but Gillian had insisted she wasn't prepared to face the shopping trip alone.

'It looks lovely, sweetheart,' he told his daughter.

'It's too long,' Meghan complained.

'We can easily take it up a bit,' said Gillian.

'I'll try the other one.'

Gillian unzipped the dress, and Meghan disappeared back behind the curtain. Her parents retreated so they could speak without being overheard. The constant loud music was getting to Clive – how on earth did the shop assistants cope with it blasting away like that all day? – but he rallied himself and smiled at Gillian.

'I quite liked that one,' he said. 'What do you think?'

She nodded wearily, looking close to tears. 'This was supposed to be a treat,' she said.

Clive wondered if she was having second thoughts about accepting Ned's invitation for Meghan to accompany him to his investiture, but now wasn't the time to say, 'I told you so.' He'd already laid out all the reasons why he didn't think it was a good idea, but his wife had enthused about how thrilling it would be to see the ceremony and rub shoulders with all the other people who'd been honoured. She'd finally clinched the argument by stressing how ungrateful they'd look if after everything Professor Ned was doing for them they refused his invitation. On that point he'd had to accept that she was right.

'Was everything OK at the clinic this morning?' he asked.

'All her tests were fine,' said Gillian. 'She's only put on a tiny bit, but at any rate it's a move back in the right direction. But Helen was in a filthy mood. I think it's about that job in Newcastle. Ned asked me again to have a word, but she just goes all silent and tense. You know what she's like.'

'Well, it's her decision.'

'I wish she'd go. Actually, I wish she'd go into some completely different area of nursing and just make a break with all this.'

'Don't be so hard on her.'

'Well, her being cross all the time isn't helping Meghan. You should have seen the way she jabbed away at her arm to take the blood.'

'Maybe, but I don't want to think about what state Meghan might be in if Helen hadn't intervened.'

'If it wasn't for my darling sister,' said Gillian sarcastically, 'I might even know what a normal family mealtime is like, and we wouldn't be in this situation.'

The changing-room curtain barely moved, but Meghan stood in front of them again. This dress rode up under her arms and made her look like a delinquent five-year-old. Her face was grumpy and her father had to stifle a laugh. 'I prefer the other one,' he said.

'Me too. I look like a turkey in this.' She disappeared again without waiting for her mother's opinion.

'Try the first one on again,' Gillian called through the curtain. 'I think it's by far the best yet, don't you?'

Clive put an arm around his wife's shoulders and pulled her close. 'Don't let's get into the blame game,' he said. 'For all we know it's a faulty gene or bad brain chemistry. And if Helen could get over it, so can Meghan.'

'Bit late for me though,' said Gillian. 'If Helen's illness hadn't turned everything upside down maybe I'd have got good enough exam results to go to university, get a decent job.'

Clive had gone to a lot of trouble to be here and his patience was running out. 'So you wouldn't have had to marry me, you mean?' He spoke lightly, kissing the side of her head, but he knew that she'd know he meant every word.

'Oh, don't start—'

The curtains opened fully this time, and Meghan stood staring at her parents. She was back in her own baggy clothes, the two dresses draped over her arm. 'I don't like either of them,' she said.

22

Grace and Blake found Minnie Thomas in the kitchen stirring a roiling pan of strawberry jam. She invited them in, hiding her alarm behind perfect good manners. The tartan dog bed was empty – Daisy must be out with her master – but one of the cats dozed on a faded cushion on a Windsor chair near the Aga.

'I'd offer you some lunch,' Minnie spoke quickly, as if nervous, 'except I daren't take my eyes off this. It's just about to set.' She dropped a little of the dangerously hot liquid onto a chilled saucer on the work surface beside her and peered at it short-sightedly. 'Another few minutes should do it.' She paused, anxiety finally overcoming politeness. 'Do you have news?'

'Not really,' said Blake. 'You'll see on the news later that we're appealing for a possible witness to come forward.'

'The man who's been living in the woods?'

'Yes. Do you know anything about him?'

'No, sorry. I only ever heard people in the village talking about him. You don't think it was him, do you?'

'We just want to talk to him.'

'We're getting cancellations. Even a wedding, at quite short notice. People are afraid to be here at night in case there's someone still out there.'

'I understand,' said Blake. 'And we're doing everything we can to get whoever did this.'

'We told Ned that whatever happens, we can't have his camp here again. We must have been mad, really, not to think of the sort of risks involved, especially with such young girls.'

'How long has he been running the camp here?' asked Grace.

'It must be twenty years. It's so sad to end it but, you know, in the village people are looking at one another with suspicion. It's horrible how quickly everything can be contaminated.'

'We will find out what happened,' said Grace.

Minnie nodded, and then remembered her jam, which had evidently reached a critical point. While she had her back to them, lifting the heavy pan off the hotplate, Grace nodded towards the crammed shelves of the Welsh dresser that stood against one wall. In among the crockery, cookery books and various keepsakes were holiday postcards and family snapshots, and Blake knew what to look for. Grace turned her own attention to the chipped corkboard on the wall beside the back door. Pinned beneath lists, reminders and messages written on the backs of envelopes were more cards and photos.

Making sure that Minnie was fully occupied with filling a row of assorted jam jars that had been lined up ready, Grace rifled through the layers. She could see nothing that appeared to depict Chesham's campsite, but Blake was luckier. He cleared his throat to draw her attention and held up a snapshot of eight young girls about to launch a blow-up rubber dinghy onto the lake. She went closer. The once glossy paper was coated with grease and dust, but one of the girls, half-hidden behind the rest of the group, wore a red swimsuit. She turned it over. Scrawled on the back was '2003'. Sickened, she handed it back to Blake, who looked as though he'd like to punch a hole in the wall.

'Phew,' said Minnie, pushing her hair out of her eyes with an elegant wrist. 'That's done! Always a tense moment. I can leave it to cool now.' She caught sight of the photo in Blake's hand. 'What's that?'

'It's of a previous summer camp,' said Grace, who had already prepared what she might say. 'We were thinking it might be useful to build a picture of how the camps worked each year, see if anything was different this time. If you have any other pictures, it would be really helpful.'

Minnie looked doubtful. 'We've only lived here ourselves for two years, remember. There's a box somewhere where Toby's parents kept all the family photographs. I can hunt it out. My late mother-in-law tended to be the photographer and I'm not sure she would have taken many pictures of the camp. She never liked Ned much, I don't know why.'

Grace fought the impulse to exchange glances with Blake. 'Would you mind if we took a look at the box?' she asked.

Minnie sighed. 'If I can remember where I last saw it. I'll ask the kids; one of them might know.'

'I don't suppose you could do that now, while we're here?' said Grace. She smiled apologetically. 'It would save a return journey and us getting under your feet another time.'

Minnie arched an eyebrow, revealing a glimpse of the striking beauty she must have been when younger and making Grace think perhaps she'd been a model. 'I'll text them,' she said, picking her phone up from the kitchen table.

As Minnie attended to her messages, Grace thought about how the Thomas family were going to deal with the strong likelihood that Toby's old friend from university had abused their hospitality for two decades. She'd give a lot to know why Toby's mother hadn't liked Ned and yet had still agreed to go along with the summer camp, although she could understand from her own encounters with Chesham how persuasive he could be. After all, if he could charm an anorexic into eating again, what else might he not accomplish?

'Thank you,' said Grace as Minnie finished texting. 'You said that Ned paid you to supply food for the camp, and the girls were on a rota to come up here to collect it each day.'

'That's right.'

'So sometimes you got to speak to them alone?'

'Yes, why?'

'Did any of them ever seem upset, or express any misgivings about any aspect of the camp? I'm just thinking if, say, someone like Paul Harrison, the man who's been living in Long Wryford woods, had been hanging around and had spooked them, one of them might have said something to you.'

'I could see that sometimes they were miserable,' said Minnie. 'It's hardly surprising. Some of them were bound to be homesick. But you know what any kid can be like about playing one adult off against another, and I'm afraid Ned's patients could be manipulative, which is why he warned us not to respond directly, but to let him know so he could deal with anything appropriately. So if they did try to talk, I'm afraid I kind of cut them off really.'

This time Grace failed to resist a glance at Blake, and saw her own deep pity for these vulnerable kids reflected in his eyes.

'This may not seem relevant to you, Mrs Thomas, but did you happen to notice if any girl at the camp wore a red swimsuit?'

Minnie shook her head. 'No, sorry.'

'The night Professor Chesham came for dinner to celebrate

his knighthood,' said Blake, brusqueness masking his emotion, 'did he or you or your husband make or receive any phone calls?'

'I don't remember that we did,' she said, 'but Ned had lots of calls and texts, all from people wanting to congratulate him. He had to turn his phone to silent and put it away.'

'He didn't take any of them?' he asked. 'He didn't maybe slip outside to speak to anyone or reply to any of the texts?'

'No.' She laughed. 'We told him he should, that he deserved all the fuss and attention, and it wouldn't happen every day, but he refused.'

'No one special in his life, then, that he'd want to speak to?' asked Grace.

'Too busy for that, I think,' said Minnie. 'His work always comes first. Ned's always been the cat that walked by himself.'

Minnie's own phone beeped. She read the text and smiled. 'Oh good,' she said. 'My son. The box of family photos is in his bedroom cupboard. I'll go and fetch it for you.'

They waited for her footsteps to retreat along the passageway. 'I'm not sure I can bear to find what we'll be searching for,' said Grace.

'If you're right, he is one hell of a smooth operator,' said Blake.

'We need the photographs from the wall in his office,' she said. 'We have to work out a way to get them – and get them officially, as evidence – without arousing his suspicion. We'll have a much better crack at this if we can get to talk to people privately first.'

'I'll try and come up with an excuse linked to the Merrick inquiry.'

'Good. Although we can't afford to take too long,' she warned. They both realized, without having to say it aloud, that her task was no longer a review of an historical allegation; it was a race to save this year's special girl – whoever she was.

23

The short notice for Grace's early-morning meeting with Sharon Marx gave her a bad feeling about what awaited her. The DAC's office had only contacted her late the previous afternoon while she and Blake were still sorting through Toby Thomas's box of family photographs, and as she gave her name to a receptionist and took a seat in the entrance pavilion she couldn't help recalling Ivo Sweatman's hunch that Sam Villiers' attempt to leak Operation Mayfly might have originated here within Scotland Yard. She had long ago lost any naive belief that all police officers, especially senior staff officers, were on the same side, yet the sense that she was being undermined by her own kind was horribly unnerving. Catching sight of her reflection in the glass, she sat up straight and warned herself not to be paranoid: maybe Sharon Marx had called this unexpected meeting because she had useful new information to share.

The day threatened to be overcast and muggy, making the June weather in London more of an ordeal than a pleasure. The previous afternoon she and Blake had spent hours at Minnie Thomas's dining table watching her parents-in-law get steadily older as they enjoyed various foreign trips, other snaps charting Minnie's three sons' journey from babies to camera-shy teenagers to confident young adults at university during annual summer holidays or Christmas visits to Wryford Hall. Grace had been surprised at the depth of her relief at discovering that Minnie and Toby had no daughters.

As Minnie had predicted, there weren't many photographs of Ned's visits, and none of those they found were dated. Luckily, most of the prints were in the original envelopes from the local chemist's processing lab which meant that some still had dated receipts stapled to the envelopes, while others could be loosely dated by reference to the other images the envelopes contained. There were three group shots from different years – one the same as the photo on the kitchen dresser – and a couple that showed a group of young girls splashing about in the lake. One of those featured a red swimsuit. The elfin child wearing it did not look much older than twelve or thirteen.

Deciding to take no chances, Grace had sealed the box and all its contents in a signed and dated evidence bag before breaking it to Minnie that it might be a while before she got it back. She was struck by how Minnie asked no questions and gave her a look of pain and fear that suggested she didn't want to know what the reason might be. For how long, wondered Grace, might Minnie have had some vague sense of something going on that she'd pushed to the back of her mind because she didn't want to think about it?

Grace snapped back to the present when one of the receptionists came to tell her she could now go upstairs. The deputy assistant commissioner's office was comfortably air-conditioned, and Sharon Marx was once again immaculately uniformed. This time, however, she invited Grace to take a seat on one of the low sofas that faced each other across a coffee table at the side of the room. The windows offered Grace a view over the tops of the plane trees on the Embankment to the river and beyond, a view obviously designed to impress.

'I thought this might be a good time to recap on the progress of your review,' the DAC began in a friendly tone. 'How have you got on?'

Grace had a moment of panic. Once she said the words, there would be no turning back. Her anxiety left her confused. If she no longer harboured any doubts about the need to investigate Ned Chesham, why did she feel such an overwhelming reluctance to be the first to pierce the silence that had cloaked his activities for so long? The human need to look away and pretend it couldn't be true must run very deep. But someone had to be the first to speak. 'Given the vulnerability of the original complainant at the time,' she began, wanting first to exonerate Keith, 'I cannot fault the conclusions of Detective Superintendent Stalgood's original investigation.'

Sharon Marx's expression of relief was immediate.

'However,' Grace continued quickly, 'I have found further evidence to suggest that Professor Chesham was then and continues to be a danger to children. My next task therefore will be to form a strategy for identifying further victims and witnesses.'

The DAC tucked a strand of blonde hair carefully behind each ear before she replied. 'But you have completed the terms of your remit? You have found that the original allegation was robustly investigated and there were no police failings?'

'I think that would be a fair conclusion given the understanding of child sexual offences at the time, yes. However, we now have a second allegation.'

'One that was missed by Superintendent Stalgood?'

Grace had given careful thought to how she would answer this. Even if Keith *had* approached St Botolph's seventeen years ago, would the hospital authorities, given prevailing attitudes at the time, have divulged a complaint they had investigated internally and found to be groundless? And if Keith had got as far as speaking to Karen Wheeler, she was then only fifteen – and already drinking. The CPS advice not to proceed would almost certainly have remained the same.

'Even if it was missed, I believe it made no material difference to the outcome at that time,' she said.

'Your loyalty is commendable,' said the DAC.

Grace decided to ignore the supercilious smile and focus instead on what had to happen next. 'I think there's a way of narrowing down patients who may have been most at risk. I'd like to identify them and then issue a general invitation to provide information to Operation Mayfly.'

'The second allegation – is the person prepared to come forward?'

'She was willing to provide a witness statement but feels unable to support a prosecution.'

'Has any current allegation been made against Professor Chesham? Do you have any evidence that he is committing offences at the present time?

'No direct evidence, no, but I don't think it will be difficult to find.'

Sharon Marx nodded and took time to consider her options. 'The testimony of the second witness, on its own, offers insufficient evidence to provide a realistic prospect of conviction, and with no evidence of ongoing criminal behaviour, there is no reason to proceed in the public interest. I must conclude therefore that the remit of Operation Mayfly is successfully concluded. All that remains is for me to thank you for your diligence.'

The DAC rose to her feet and held out her hand. Grace stayed where she was. 'But the evidence suggests there's a case to answer,' she said.

'And your report will be passed to the appropriate command within the Metropolitan Police. Meanwhile, I'm sure Superintendent Pitman will be happy to have his team in Essex returned to full strength. I believe the Merrick murder remains unsolved?'

Grace stood, glad of her small height advantage. 'I'm making good progress. I'm now familiar with the people involved. With respect, it would seem foolish to abandon the lead that gives us.'

'Last time I looked,' the DAC said lightly, 'St Botolph's Hospital was in central London. Any new inquiry would not be under your jurisdiction.'

Grace was about to argue that Ned Chesham's summer camping trips were in Essex but then thought better of giving away information that, kept to herself, might work to her advantage. 'Ma'am.'

Sharon Marx walked her to the door of her office. 'I applaud your commitment,' she said. 'But here at the Met we've learned a tough lesson about allowing allegations to be made public when there is little or no prospect of a conviction. We're all facing further serious cuts to the Home Office police grants; now is not the time to provoke media criticism of the police service.'

The DAC's hand rested on the door handle, forcing Grace to wait helplessly until she had finished speaking.

'Thank you again for your contribution,' she continued. 'You can rest easy that we will do everything we can to investigate further. And, off the record, I'm personally delighted that Keith Stalgood has been vindicated.' Instead of a formal handshake, she touched Grace's sleeve. 'My door is always open to a bright young woman with a promising career ahead of her.'

The door finally opened and was closed swiftly behind her. The brief lifespan of Operation Mayfly had ended.

24

The Right Honourable Adrian Starling QC MP, a former favourite of the centre-left, had been hotly tipped after the 2010 election to take over as party leader. Indeed, had the future unfolded as everyone expected, he would very probably now be prime minister. But at the crucial moment he had disappeared from the fray and declined to put his name forward for nomination. There were rumours of a breakdown, and when he'd finally reappeared it was as a backbencher.

Ivo dimly remembered some family tragedy, and it had not taken long to discover that six years earlier Starling's only child, Lucy, aged twenty-four, had hanged herself in an outbuilding at the family's constituency home in Derbyshire. That was two years after Sam Villiers had joined SO17 and begun roaming the corridors of power.

Ivo had not been able to find a dicky bird on Lucy's childhood or what might have led her to take her own life. The *Courier*'s political correspondents told him there'd been some ancient gossip about her father being into drugs and paid-for sex – an amusing if unsubstantiated photograph of a phial of cocaine and some bondage gear in a ministerial red box had done the rounds for a while – but it was pretty standard fare and none of it had been solid enough to publish. The gossip had certainly not prevented Starling from rising to a junior ministerial post in the Blair government, which was enough to ensure a security blackout around him and his family. That had broken only briefly for his daughter's suicide, and afterwards silence had descended once again, although Ivo had turfed up a small diary piece about Starling's uncontested divorce a year or so later.

One of Ivo's Westminster colleagues commented that Starling had recently remarried and reckoned that with a much younger second wife, he might be putting out feelers about a political comeback. Whatever the truth of that, he simply didn't appear to have enough skin in any game that would involve shafting the top brass at Scotland Yard – or not in pursuit of some territorial power play, anyway.

Maybe, thought Ivo, if Starling *was* considering a second run at power, then Sam's attempt to expose Operation Mayfly had been with the aim of compromising some old foe on the honours vetting committee who might stand in Starling's way, but it all seemed a lot of effort for a rather uncertain return, and Ivo considered the politician too smart an operator for that.

So why else might Sam Villiers have ditched his hot coffee and jogged along to Starling's back gate immediately after speaking to Ivo?

Ivo had waited a couple of days to see what Sam – with Starling pulling his levers – would do, but it was now Saturday and Sam hadn't got back in touch. Did that mean Starling no longer wanted Operation Mayfly leaked? Ivo didn't like loose ends. He'd more or less spelled out to Sam that the *Courier* was still prepared to run the story if offered a little more encouragement, and it had clearly been of concern to Sam to deliver that message promptly, so why was nothing moving? Something must have happened to make Starling change his mind. Or make alternative plans.

Ivo itched to give Grace Fisher a call to find out what was going on, but knew better than to compromise her unnecessarily, not even if he took the precaution of using a public phone box. After all, he'd been right so far – Sam Villiers had been acting on orders from elsewhere – and if this whole business turned out to be as sensitive as his instincts suggested, he wouldn't put it past the Yard to monitor her communications.

Time finally to speak to his old pal and sparring partner Keith Stalgood. His call was answered almost immediately.

'What do you want?' Keith demanded.

'We can skip the small talk if you like,' said Ivo. 'Retirement suiting you?'

'What do you want?'

'Operation Mayfly.'

There was a tiny hesitation before Keith spoke. 'How did you hear about that?'

'Someone wanted me to know,' said Ivo. 'Sent Sam Villiers along especially to tell me.'

Keith muttered a curse under his breath. 'Doesn't matter now, anyway. It's over.'

'What is?'

'The review. The DAC called me yesterday. We got it right first time, apparently. He gets his knighthood and no red faces at the Met.'

'So it's all tidied away nicely?' Ivo couldn't keep the surprise out of his voice.

Keith must have noticed, for his tone sharpened. 'Yes. Why? Were you led to expect a different result?'

'No,' said Ivo. 'Except I can't help asking myself why someone would go to the trouble of involving Sam Villiers unless they had something to worry about.'

There was another pause, and the background sounds altered as if Keith had walked into a different room. 'Do you know who hired him?'

'Would it make a difference?'

'I don't believe it's a whitewash, if that's what you're getting at,' said Keith. 'If there was something to be found, Mayfly would've dragged it out into the open, I'm certain of that.'

'OK,' said Ivo. Something still niggled. Even though Keith Stalgood was one of the few coppers Ivo was prepared to trust, he was still a copper and so possessed an ingrained reluctance to share anything that he didn't have to with a reporter. 'So, just to be sure,' Ivo asked, 'you're happy for me to stop digging?'

He listened as Keith took a deep breath. 'Yes,' he said. 'It would seem that way. But let me know if you come across any reason to change your mind. I have to go. Bye.'

Ivo was disappointed. Then he reflected that Starling too would have heard by now through Sam Villiers that the review had shut up shop. Maybe he had his own reasons for backing away. Or perhaps his initial approach had simply been an attempt to flush out whether the tabloids were sitting on their own hoard of dirt on Ned Chesham. Whatever it was, the trail had gone cold and the chances of hunting down a decent story were rapidly diminishing. Ivo didn't yet feel ready to give it up entirely, but for now at any rate he'd park it for another day.

25

Grace did not wake until well after eight o'clock on Sunday morning – late for her. For a few moments she luxuriated in the realization that with Mayfly officially over, she could if she wanted turn over and go back to sleep, but then the guilt and anger kicked in and she threw off her duvet and got out of bed. Opening the curtains, she saw a cloudless sky, roses blooming in her neighbours' tightly packed gardens, and a cat already sunning itself on a high wall. She had lived here for a little over six months, and her regular view first thing still filled her with pleasure, although not quite enough to dispel this morning's frustration. She decided to go for a run before it got too hot, and before the Wivenhoe day trippers dawdling along the riverside path became a nuisance.

She did her stretches and jogged from her little house down to the quayside a few streets away, only speeding up as she reached the wider path that ran alongside the river. There was still just enough dew on the distant fields to make the grass glisten, and the foliage on the trees on the far bank looked rich and glossy. She tried to let nature do its work and soothe the outrage with which she'd left Scotland Yard on Friday, but it only grew, making her breathing shallow and ragged and preventing her from finding an easy stride. After her second stumble, she gave up and dropped to a walk.

She still could hardly believe what had happened. Leaving Scotland Yard, she'd felt like she'd been mugged. DAC Marx had been at pains to convey that with no active concern apparently merited about Ned Chesham, the Met's policy would be to leave well alone. Grace understood how his high public profile worked doubly in his favour: to step out of line and denounce a man so widely admired demanded some extra-special level of proof, while if a man so well known *was* guilty, surely someone would have noticed and done something by now? And whatever Sharon Marx might say, it was clear she intended to bury an investigation that could only bring problems to her door. Words would be spoken in the right ears so that Ned was discreetly warned off, but nothing further would be done to protect the children in his care.

Or had Grace overreacted? After all, DAC Marx had no reason to share operational details with an officer from another force. Perhaps Grace had misjudged her, and a thorough Met investigation into Chesham's relationships with his teenage patients was already well under way. But if that was so, why had the DAC not wanted to hear what Grace had already found out?

Grace had spent the previous day catching up on household chores. She had barely been home over the past fortnight and it had felt good to throw open all the windows and the doors to her sunny courtyard patio, to water her plants and have a general tidy-up. But all the while, at the back of her mind, the conviction had grown: nothing further would be done.

Grace thought of Minnie not asking why they wanted to take away her precious family photographs, not wanting to believe what it might mean, and not wanting to challenge her own disinclination to find out. She thought of the surgeon, Mr Gibson: *If you can't accept the word of a medical colleague, who can you trust?*

It had to stop. It would be no good going to Colin Pitman and asking him to open a separate investigation. He would never risk displeasing the top brass at Scotland Yard.

She stopped, deciding to abandon her run and return home. She'd been here before with Colin. It wasn't that he was some Machiavellian operator out to destroy her or anyone else; the way he saw it, he was just doing his job, which these days was to successfully navigate the choppy waters of budgets, PR, branding, statistics, management strategies. Justice came vanishingly low on his list of priorities. It was modern policing, and it was stupid to think she could somehow work outside the system.

Maybe she was just being stupid. And stubborn. The question she had to answer in her own mind before she turned up for work on Monday was whether or not she was stupid and stubborn enough to risk losing her job. After all, what good would it do anyone if she rocked the boat so much that she got fired? She loved her job, and not only that, without it she'd be of no use at all to any of those vulnerable young girls in their red swimsuits.

But wasn't that also a convenient argument for doing nothing, or only the token amount she could accomplish without risking her own career?

She had already done that by sharing her concern with a deputy assistant commissioner at Scotland Yard, no less. What more could she do? Sharon Marx had told Grace she could safely leave the matter with her. Who was she to question the judgement of such a senior officer?

But that was just what Nasir Khan must have thought when a consultant surgeon told him not to worry about what he'd heard on the ward that night. Would Nasir Khan have let it rest so easily if he'd held a senior enough position within the hospital hierarchy to challenge James Gibson's dismissal?

Grace turned the corner into her street of higgledy-piggledy Victorian and Georgian houses. Standing outside the front door of her two-storey terrace was a tall man with broad shoulders and short iron-grey hair. He had his back to her, but she recognized him instantly.

'Keith!'

He turned and smiled, although the smile failed to lift the anxious lines creasing his forehead.

'Hello, Grace. I hope you don't mind me turning up like this, but I need to talk.'

'Of course not. Come in.'

It was slightly strange having her former boss in her home for the first time, and she was glad that she'd tidied up so recently. Putting the kettle on, she went upstairs to change out of her running gear. When she came back down he was standing by the doors to the patio, although he didn't appear to be focusing on her plant pots.

'Have you spoken to Duncan?' he asked abruptly.

'Not since Friday,' she said. 'Why?'

He nodded towards the kettle, which had come to the boil and switched itself off while she was upstairs. 'I'd love a coffee.'

She busied herself with the cafetière, reviewing her call to Duncan from the Embankment pavement a safe distance from Scotland Yard. He'd been as angry as she was to hear that the DAC had closed down Operation Mayfly, but the conversation had ended with her telling him to make the most of a weekend off, as they'd be rejoining the Merrick inquiry first thing Monday morning.

Remembering that Keith liked his coffee black, she handed him a mug and sat down at the kitchen table.

'Duncan came to see me yesterday evening,' said Keith. 'I'd already heard the news from the DAC. I must admit that my first reaction was relief. It felt good that my earlier investigation had been vindicated. But then Duncan told me about Karen Wheeler – that you'd found a second victim I'd missed.' He rubbed his face with his hand. 'Sorry. I barely slept. I should have called you first, but I just found myself driving, and . . .'

'It's fine.' Grace wanted to reach out and touch him. 'It wasn't your fault.'

'But it's true, isn't it?' he asked. 'I missed something. I had the chance to stop him seventeen years ago and I messed up.'

'We've only got two allegations so far, your original complainant and Karen Wheeler, who says she doesn't want to go to court. At this stage we're in the same position you were.'

'How many more girls were hurt because I failed?'

'Keith, you were hardly the only one to fail. We only found Karen Wheeler because an incident was reported to the hospital authorities, who dismissed it. Who knows how many other times he's got away with it?'

'So Duncan's right? You believe the two women?'

Grace took a deep breath. 'Yes.'

'So what are you going to do?'

Grace realized her decision was made – had always been made. 'I've already put DS Blake Langley in the picture. There's good reason to believe that girls were abused at Wryford Hall. That's in Essex. We don't need the Met's permission to investigate. Although maybe Blake, Duncan and I will have to operate under the radar until we get a bit more.'

Keith nodded, his frown finally easing. 'I'd be happy to help in any way I can.'

'Thanks.' She smiled. 'Good to know you're behind us.'

'So why do you think the Met have buried Mayfly?' he asked. 'I can understand them wanting to avoid yet another beating over a sex-abuse witch-hunt, but I worry that Chesham is being protected for some reason.'

Grace thought uncomfortably of Ivo Sweatman and what he'd told her. Even though Keith was now retired, she didn't feel ready to tell her former boss about a conversation that should never have taken place. 'We'll find out soon enough,' she said.

'True.' He ran a hand through his hair, a sure sign that something was bothering him.

'Is there something else I should know?'

'I didn't say anything before in case it sounded like I was making excuses for myself, but the truth is that I always smelled a rat over the CPS advice not to proceed seventeen years ago. Without it, I would have opened my investigation up a bit further, at the very least made an approach to the hospital.'

'Chesham wasn't even a consultant back then,' she said. 'Why would people have pulled strings to help him?'

'I don't know. I'm probably imagining things. But I did argue the decision with the CPS lawyer concerned and came up against a brick wall that just somehow didn't feel right. I remember my guv'nor at the time being surprised by it too.'

'There's usually a bit of give and take between us and the CPS,' Grace agreed.

'And then I heard yesterday that Sam Villiers had leaked news of Mayfly to the press.'

'Why would he do that?' she asked, sure that Ivo wouldn't

have given her away but hoping she wasn't betraying her agitation.

'Oh, just because he could, probably,' said Keith. 'Villiers was always a bit of a scally, couldn't resist stirring things up.'

'But you think it could be linked to your misgivings about the CPS advice you were given?'

'No, not really,' he said with a sigh.

'Was Villiers bent?'

Keith laughed. 'He was little more than a rookie back then and none too bright at that. He had no influence. Anyway, it was a long time ago and I don't go in for conspiracy theories.'

Grace could see that he didn't fully believe his own arguments, but if he now regretted voicing his concerns there was no point pushing him further. 'You did what you could,' she told him. 'There's nothing to beat yourself up over.'

'Time will tell.'

'It'll be a long, slow process.'

'It will,' he said. 'One more thing: I think you should keep an eye on Duncan.'

'Duncan?' She couldn't imagine anyone less in need of supervision. 'In what way?'

Keith toyed with his coffee mug, 'I worked a lot of cases with him, but I've never seen one get under his skin the way this one seems to have done.'

'It's a difficult subject. And any crime is harder when kids are involved.'

'Sure, but . . . Look, maybe it's nothing, but it just wasn't like him to turn up on my doorstep the way he did, that's all.'

'I've felt pretty awful since Friday too,' she said. 'And I'll never forget how hurt I was back in Maidstone when I realized that the very people who were paid to protect me weren't going to do their job. It can shake you to the core. Maybe this is just the first time that Duncan's really experienced that from the police service.'

'Maybe,' said Keith, although he didn't sound convinced. He got to his feet. 'I won't take up any more of your Sunday off,' he said. 'I'm sure you've got better things to do.'

Grace smiled, choosing not to tell him that her weekend social life was minimal. 'It's good to see you,' she said. 'And I truly don't believe that you could have done things differently back then.'

'Just make sure you nail the bastard this time,' he replied grimly.

As Grace closed the door behind Keith her phone rang. She could hear the suppressed excitement in Blake's voice.

'Paul Harrison has handed himself in.'

'And?'

'He claims he left in a hurry because he was scared.'

'Do you believe him?'

'No reason not to. Not yet, at any rate. He says he didn't fancy being the next victim of our mystery killer.'

'Why?' she asked. 'Did he see something that night?'

'Other than all the police activity, you mean? Yes. Earlier on he says there was a car parked by the gate.'

'What time?'

'He doesn't know. But it was still light and quite a while before we pitched up.'

'Make? Colour?'

'Compact, white, and with some kind of sticker. He thought it might have been to do with one of those car clubs.'

Grace's mind whirred. 'Check to see if Helen Fry is a car club member.'

She could almost hear Blake's smile. 'Already on it, boss.'

26

Blake was watching out for Grace and got up from his desk the second she walked into the MIT office early the following morning. She beckoned to Duncan to join them in her cubicle, scrutinizing his face for evidence to bear out Keith's disquiet, but apart from his suit looking even more rumpled than usual he showed every sign of being his familiar level-headed self.

'What have we got?' she asked.

'We started on the biggest car clubs operating in north London,' said Blake. 'Got a hit on the third go. Helen Fry booked a car online about twenty minutes after the call from Tim Merrick. A white Toyota. I've got the registration and asked for data from automatic number-plate recognition cameras on the most obvious routes from Crouch End to Wryford Hall.'

'We're going to need the car,' said Grace. 'If it was driven after the murder, there will almost certainly be bloodstains and perhaps also traces of leaves or soil that we can match to the scene.'

'Dozens of people might have used that car since then,' said Blake.

'I know, but if we can find Tim Merrick's blood in it, she'll have a hard time explaining that away,' she said.

'What on earth did Merrick say in that phone call to make a

nurse, of all people, jump in a car and drive out to Essex to batter him to death?' said Blake.

'That's for a jury to decide,' she said. 'Our job is to put her at the scene. Duncan, can you check out any local CCTV around Helen's flat, see if we can get a picture of what she was wearing that night? We'll need those clothes or, if she's got rid of them, an explanation from her as to why she no longer has them.'

'Will do.'

'Blake, let's exert some pressure on getting the ANPR data. If we can place the car anywhere near Wryford Hall that night, it'll be enough to arrest her and get a warrant so we can also look at her phone and computer.'

Blake nodded and was about to head back to his desk when Duncan reached out to bar his way. 'What about Chesham?' he asked Grace.

She turned to Blake, lowering her voice so she would not be overheard outside the cubicle. 'You heard that Mayfly has been closed down?'

'Duncan told me.' Blake folded his arms and waited, his face giving nothing away.

'If we can show that offences took place in Essex, we can legitimately open up a new and separate investigation.'

'We've already got that,' said Duncan. 'Karen Wheeler told us she was his special girl at the summer camp nineteen years ago.'

'But she's not prepared to attend court,' said Grace. 'We need another victim.'

Duncan shook his head in frustration. 'How many does it take?' he asked in disgust. 'One should be more than enough!'

'I know. I've thought about nothing else all weekend.'

She had also used a catch-up service to listen to Ned Chesham's archived radio appearance on *Desert Island Discs*. His favourite piece of music was Bach's *Prelude in C*, his book *Le Grand Meaulnes*, and his luxury a manual on how to grow vegetables. He came across as funny, wise and self-deprecating, and it was clear that he had charmed his interviewer. Hearing him discuss his musical choices and talk about his work had helped her to make sense of Keith's note in the file about how worried Trudie Bevan's mother had been that Doctor Ned would think them ungrateful and be upset if word reached him of the distasteful things Trudie had said. So many voices had been silenced by fear of disbelief. Charm was indeed, as Grace had once read in a book written by an FBI profiler, a highly effective weapon.

'I reckon it's better for us to keep working under the radar,' she said, 'than risk Superintendent Pitman ordering us to stop. Our best hope is to use the Merrick inquiry as cover for the time being. If Helen Fry *is* in the frame for that, then we'll have access to the hospital and to the families whose daughters were at the camp with Merrick.'

'Meanwhile we just leave this year's special girl to fight him off on her own, is that it?' said Duncan.

'What else can I do? We don't have the evidence to arrest him.'

'There's always a reason to do nothing. After all, she's only a kid. They're resilient, right? They bounce back. Anyway, she probably likes it.' Duncan shouldered past Blake and marched across the main office, all but slamming the door behind him.

'What's got into him?' asked Blake.

'I don't know,' said Grace, wondering if she ought to go after him. 'What's he been like with you?

'Fine,' he said. 'Trouble at home, maybe?'

Grace shook her head. Duncan lived alone and had never mentioned a partner, past or present. It was a running joke in the office that he carried a torch for Joan, the team's civilian case manager, who, Grace thought, probably had rather a soft spot for him too, if only he'd speak up.

'I'll have a word later,' she told Blake, who nodded and went off to his desk.

Grace looked out of her window. The trees were green and a few fluffy white clouds sailed high in a blue sky. What was it that prevented Duncan from wooing Joan? He was undoubtedly shy around women, but Joan was friendly and approachable with a robust sense of humour and, like him, pushing forty and single. She considered how little she knew about the man she worked with. He'd joined the police straight from the army, which had recruited him at sixteen. He'd never gone for promotion, although he would easily have made sergeant and probably inspector. What kept him back? And what was it about the Chesham case that made him so angry? She called his mobile, but he did not pick up. She checked her email account – a backlog was already building up. For the time being at least she'd have to let him sort himself out.

27

Helen Fry took a seat at the interview room table and smoothed her cotton skirt over her knees. She looked pale and frightened but otherwise calm. She had told the custody sergeant that she didn't require a solicitor and didn't wish anyone to be informed of her whereabouts. The sergeant had told Grace that she'd waited quietly in her cell as if her arrest on suspicion of murder was some inconvenient formality that had to be got through.

Although Duncan had reappeared in the office not long after his hasty departure that morning and buckled down to the task of locating CCTV cameras that might have captured Helen leaving or returning to her house on the night of Tim Merrick's murder, Grace had decided it would be prudent to keep him out of the interview room until she'd had the chance to probe further into what lay behind his outburst. Besides, she was discovering to her surprise that she liked working with Blake. Despite his cynicism, he was patient and cleverly unobtrusive, and the fact that he tended to take a different angle to her on people and events could prove useful.

Helen answered his initial questions clearly and calmly, repeating her earlier story that she'd gone up to Hampstead

Heath, elaborating that she'd taken a book, as she often did in summer, and after a walk had sat on a bench reading. It was a lovely warm evening, and it must have been after nine o'clock, when it was beginning to get dark, that she'd made her way home. She couldn't be certain of the time. Until asked directly, she did not mention how she'd got to and from the Heath; then, with only the slightest hesitation, she'd replied that she booked a car through the car club of which she was a member.

'We have the details of the car you booked,' said Blake. 'Would it surprise you to learn that it was picked up on a roadside camera on the A12 just south of Colchester at the time you say you were on Hampstead Heath?'

'It would surprise me, yes.' Helen clasped her hands tightly in her lap while her expression remained one of polite interest.

'A record of the car's mileage on that night tallies exactly with a journey from Crouch End to Long Wryford.'

'That's impossible. The car club must have made a mistake.'

Grace knew this was nonsense. Even though image enhancement had failed to show who was driving, without the correct smartcard and PIN Helen would not have been able to unlock or start the car. In court, however, it was conceivable that a clever barrister could persuade a jury that, while highly unlikely, some kind of computer glitch did raise the possibility of doubt.

'Isn't there a bus you could have taken to the Heath? Wouldn't that have been a fraction of the price?' asked Blake.

'I can get there by public transport, but it's a bit of a performance, especially on a Sunday. Sometimes it's nice just to keep things simple.' She gave a smile that Grace found rather maddening: neither patronizing nor pitying, but nonetheless as if

Helen had access to some private and superior understanding of the world.

'Had there been a previous occasion when there was a mix-up over which car you were actually driving?'

'How would I know? No one's checked up on me before.'

'Can you remember what you were wearing that night?' Blake asked.

Helen laughed. 'Goodness me, no! I'm not very fashion-conscious, as you can see. Jeans probably and a shirt.'

'Which bench did you sit on?'

'By one of the ponds. Kenwood closes at eight thirty,' she added with a tiny glint of triumph, as if she'd avoided a trap they were laying for her.

'Where did you leave the car?'

'It was still busy when I went up there. I can't remember where I managed to park in the end.'

'Did you speak to anyone?'

She shook her head. 'I was lost in my book.'

'You weren't anxious about Tim?'

'Tim? No.'

'I thought you said you were upset by what he'd told you on the phone.'

'Well, I was to begin with, but he never called back so I thought he'd probably pulled himself together and was fine.'

'It didn't concern you that one of the girls in his care might be at risk?'

Helen stared at Blake, her eyes wide and empty. 'Professor Ned was there,' she said. 'They were perfectly safe.'

'Professor Ned was having dinner at the hall that night with his old friends,' said Blake. 'Did Tim not mention that?'

She blinked as if slightly disoriented. 'Yes, he did. I forgot.'

'Are you saying that you can't accurately recall what you talked about for ten minutes?'

'No. Of course I remember. It's just that some details didn't seem important at the time.'

'Even though you had earlier texted Professor Chesham to congratulate him?'

'That had nothing to do with Tim,' she said tartly.

'So you still maintain that Tim called you because he was worried about his feelings for one of his young patients?'

'Yes. We talked it through. He did the right thing.'

'You've been to the summer camps in the past, is that right?'

'Yes.' She said the word proudly, tilting up her chin. 'More than once.'

'Why not this year?'

'Ned said he had to give the others a chance.' Her answer came out pat, as if it was something she'd thought about a lot; perhaps, thought Grace, because it was something she minded.

'So you'll be familiar with the layout of the grounds?'

'Reasonably, yes.'

'Why do you suppose Tim Merrick was over in the woodlands? It was his first time at the camp, so how would he know there was a gate to the road?'

'No idea.'

'You didn't discuss an arrangement to meet during your phone call?'

'No.'

'The kids generally seem to have a really good time at the camp,' said Blake. 'At the hall we saw a few photographs of earlier years. It seems like there was always one girl in a red swimsuit. Was that like some kind of team thing, like being head girl or something?'

'Coincidence.' Helen kneaded her hands in her lap and a faint flush crept up her neck.

Grace decided to speak for the first time and push a little harder. 'It's not a choice that Professor Chesham made?' She kept her voice light but could see that Helen felt the significance of her intervention.

'Of course not! Why would he?'

'So you wouldn't know if anyone had a red swimsuit this summer?' she asked.

'Why would Professor Ned care what colour swimsuits any of them wear?' Helen snapped.

'What about Tim?' asked Blake, taking his cue from Grace. 'Did he say anything about the girl he was attracted to? Anything that marked her out.'

Helen shook her head. 'It was all ridiculous. Ned is the kindest, most wonderful man in the world. He'd never allow Tim or anyone else to hurt one of his patients.'

'So why do you think Tim was killed? Savagely beaten to death.'

'It's dreadful,' she said. 'I feel so awful about it. We all do. But I can't help you. I don't know anything.'

'Because you were on the Heath, reading a book,' said Grace, wondering why Helen's protestations of regret sounded so empty.

'That's right.'

'But you can't remember where you parked, what you were wearing or precisely what time you left.'

'I often go the Heath. There's no reason for that particular evening to stand out.'

'So there were other Sunday evenings when you booked a car?'

For the first time Helen faltered. 'Well, not always. Sometimes.'

'When was the last time you booked a car to go to the Heath?'

'Not that long ago, probably. I don't remember.'

Grace made a show of looking at her notes. 'The last time you booked a car club car was a Saturday six weeks ago, and the mileage suggests you went somewhere more distant than the Heath.'

Helen said nothing.

'So it had been six weeks or more since you might have last driven to the Heath, yet you don't remember where you parked this time because all the occasions merge into one?'

'I don't know what you want me to say.'

'The truth would be nice,' said Blake.

28

Clive studied the other parents crammed in around the table in
the budget hotel meeting room near St Botolph's that the police
must have rented for this hastily arranged get-together. All of
them were wondering why they were there. Whatever the reason, he hoped DI Fisher wasn't going to spin it out too long.
Unappetizing croissants, orange juice and coffee had been provided, but he couldn't afford to be late for work yet again. Gillian
had stayed at home with Meghan.

It seemed they were waiting for one more person to arrive. He
couldn't help thinking that DI Fisher looked very young to be in
charge of a murder inquiry: neither she nor DS Langley, both of
whom had been around on that awful morning at Wryford Hall,
could be much over thirty. The third detective here today, DC
Gregg, was older and seemed a bit more solid, yet he was of
lower rank.

Reena's mother finally arrived, and to Clive's relief DI Fisher
immediately got down to business. She thanked them all for
coming at such short notice and explained that an individual
had been arrested in connection with Dr Merrick's murder.

'I must stress that the individual has not yet been charged,' she went on, 'but the arrest has raised some troubling issues that I want to discuss with you all face to face.'

Clive looked once more around the table, as did most of the other parents, exchanging glances of alarm and, with tiny shrugs and shakes of the head, signalling that they knew no more than he did.

'For operational reasons,' the detective continued, 'it would be extremely helpful if you don't discuss any of what I'm about to say with anyone beyond your immediate families. I hope the reason for this will become clear.' She paused and also looked around the table, making eye contact with each of them in turn. 'You're here because your daughters took part in the camp at Wryford Hall this year. Although there's nothing so far to suggest he acted on them, an allegation has been made that Dr Merrick may have had inappropriate sexual thoughts about one of your daughters.'

'Is that why he was killed?' asked Reena's mother.

'Who is it that's been arrested?' demanded Kim's father. He was a nice man, a plumber, to whom Clive had chatted a few times in the clinic. Sometimes Clive had envied his down-to-earth attitude towards his daughter's refusal to eat – no browbeating, no guilt, no sense of failure over his inability to make sense of this infuriating illness – but now he could see the man's hands clench into fists, ready to deal with something he understood.

'Investigations are ongoing and we're not yet releasing a name to the media,' said DI Fisher, 'although I imagine you will find out soon enough at the hospital. The trust chief executive has confirmed that the person under arrest will be temporarily suspended pending the outcome of our investigations. Nonetheless,

I beg you to keep this confidential. It's Helen Fry, the specialist mental health nurse at the eating disorders unit.'

'Helen?' Clive laughed. 'That's ridiculous!' He felt the attention focus on him; most of the other parents would know that Helen was Meghan's aunt. 'She's my sister-in-law,' he told the detectives. 'She's not a murderer! I mean, she wasn't even there!'

He nearly missed the startled look that DI Fisher gave DS Langley but then realized that they hadn't known about the family relationship. If they couldn't even find that out for themselves, what else had they overlooked?

'As I say, investigations are ongoing,' DI Fisher said, 'and Helen strenuously denies the accusation. Be that as it may . . .' She held up her hands to quell the hubbub that had spread around the table. 'The issue I wish to address today is about safeguarding.'

'No, wait,' said Clive. 'You can't just accuse Helen like that and move on. Where is she now? Is she in custody?'

'For the time being, yes. We can hold her for up to forty-eight hours and then she'll either be charged or released on police bail.'

'Why on earth would she kill Dr Merrick? They most certainly weren't having an affair or anything like that, if that's what you think.'

'Please, Mr Goodwin. I understand your anxiety. We can speak later, but I can't discuss this right now.'

'But you *are* saying that Dr Merrick might have interfered with one of our girls?' asked Mia's mother, her face white.

DI Fisher placed her hands flat on the table in front of her. 'I must stress that we have nothing so far to corroborate the allegation against Dr Merrick. It may have no foundation whatsoever. However, if any of you has any reason to suppose that your child has been at risk, we'd like you to tell us. You don't have to speak here in front of everyone, but if you have any concerns or doubts, however small, please bring them to us. Even if it's not about Dr Merrick, even if it seems irrelevant or is about another member of staff or someone else's child, please let us know.'

People were shaking their heads, looking at one another with wide eyes. Had they missed something? Clive felt sick. Had *he* missed something? Was Meghan OK? He wanted to get up and leave, to run home and hold his daughter in his arms, to feel her, look at her, have her tell him that he hadn't let her down.

The thought of telling Gillian about Helen's arrest was inconceivable. How come no one had informed them? Surely Helen would have been allowed a phone call? Or did Gillian already know but had chosen for some reason not to tell him?

In any case, there must be a mistake. Whatever Helen's funny ways, her blind spots and stubborn no-go areas, she wasn't violent. And Dr Merrick had seemed such a pleasant and unassuming young man. Clive had only dealt with him a few times, but could not possibly imagine what fear or grudge or fury Helen could have experienced to spur her into beating her colleague – or anyone – to death.

His mind was whirring, on fire, too distracted to follow what DI Fisher was saying. Something about thanking them for their time and the three detectives being available in separate rooms for the next hour if anyone wanted to speak privately or ask further questions. She could understand how upsetting all this must be. Upsetting! She had no idea. She couldn't possibly have children of her own. As if it wasn't already bad enough that Meghan was making herself suffer so much with this crazy disease, the thought that anyone else would harm a hair of her head—

'Was Helen protecting someone at the camp?' he blurted out, interrupting whatever the detective was saying. 'Is that why you think she killed Dr Merrick? Was it Meghan? Is Meghan OK?'

'Why don't you come with me? There's a room next door where we can speak privately.'

In a daze Clive allowed himself to be guided along the corridor and into a poky little office space furnished with a desk, a phone and a couple of chairs. A net-curtained window looked out on to a brick wall.

'Helen wasn't at the camp,' he said as DI Fisher closed the door behind them.

'We were unaware of the relationship between you and Helen Fry,' she said. 'I apologize for springing it on you like that. I would have handled it very differently if we'd known. I'm sorry.'

'Doesn't matter. Is there something you're not telling me about Meghan? Is she OK?'

'The issue of a doctor's sexual interest in one of his patients was raised,' she said, clearly picking her words carefully. 'At the moment it's no more than that. But if you have any concerns, if there's anything that doesn't feel right to you, anything you might have overlooked at the time but that now maybe, if you look back, seems significant, then please share it with us.'

He shook his head. 'It doesn't take much for Meghan to get upset. I'm not sure I'd know what's caused by this blasted disease and what isn't.'

'I understand. She's never had problems with any member of the hospital staff?'

'She doesn't like it when they make her eat, when they tell her that her weight's gone up. She's hated all of them at one time or another.' Clive felt frighteningly out of his depth. He needed someone to tell him what to do and appealed to the young woman before him. 'Should we take her out of Professor Ned's programme?'

'I can't answer that. I'm sorry.'

'It was Helen who got her in. Thanks to her, we jumped the queue. The waiting list can be a year or more otherwise. If Meghan relapses again, she'll . . .' He sighed helplessly, not able to look at her. 'What do I do?'

'I have a question that we're asking everyone,' said the detective, sounding brisk all of a sudden. 'It may seem random, but it would be helpful to us to know. Does Meghan have a red swimsuit? Did she buy one to wear at the summer camp?'

'Yes,' he said, making an effort to pull himself together and accurately recall the pointless argument Gillian and her sister had had over a shopping bag. 'I think Helen took her to get one. Trips to buy clothes are part of the therapy. There was a bit of a row over it. No idea what that was about – my wife, Gillian, was cross with Helen for upsetting Meghan, but it's why I remember about the swimsuit. I'm fairly certain it was red.'

'Thank you.' DI Fisher paused and then cleared her throat. 'I'm sorry I have to ask you this, but where were you on the night that Dr Merrick was killed?'

Clive laughed bitterly at the remembered moment of fleeting happiness and well-being. 'Out with my wife, catching up with some old friends, celebrating our last night of freedom before Meghan came home and we had to go back to being the food police.'

29

Grace compared notes with Blake and Duncan on the half-empty mid-morning train back to Colchester.

'So how does the family relationship between Helen and Meghan alter our picture of the Merrick murder?' she asked. 'Especially if Karen Wheeler is right about the significance of a red swimsuit.'

'It provides a motive,' said Duncan. 'Helen could have been protecting her niece.'

'Then why didn't Helen warn Crystal Douglad?' asked Grace.

'She might not have been able to get hold of her,' said Blake.

'Then why not tell Meghan's parents?' she said. 'Why drive up there herself?'

'We've assumed so far that she went alone,' said Duncan. 'Perhaps we should rethink that.'

'Although Helen booked the car, someone else could have been driving,' agreed Blake. 'She could even mount a defence that she booked it under duress.'

'We need to get confirmation that Clive Goodwin and his wife were out with friends that night,' she said. 'But if Meghan was Chesham's special girl, why kill Tim Merrick?'

'Maybe Chesham had been grooming him,' said Blake, 'and then Merrick got cold feet.'

'None of the parents I spoke to just now could believe that Tim Merrick had been hiding anything, let alone depraved ideas about their kids,' said Duncan.

'But then no one expressed any apprehension about Chesham either,' said Blake, 'not even when more or less invited to do so.'

'They didn't seem very warm towards Helen,' said Duncan. 'A couple of them said their daughters complained she could be impatient and irritable. They didn't seem to trust her as much as they did Crystal.'

'Helen seems to rather hero-worship Chesham,' said Grace. 'He did her a favour, wangling a place for Meghan in the unit. Is that what made Meghan the perfect target, because, right under the eyes of her aunt, he could hide his abuse in plain sight? As long as Helen was happy, people would be more likely to discount any misgivings they might have?'

'Did you warn Meghan's father?' asked Duncan.

Grace sighed and shook her head. 'I can't risk that when we haven't got enough to arrest Chesham.'

Blake agreed. 'Two allegations from twenty-odd years ago, with neither woman prepared to go to court. Until we're in a position to interview Chesham under caution, the longer we can keep this under wraps the better.'

'She's thirteen years old,' said Duncan.

'I know,' said Grace. 'But I can't go making accusations I can't back up or tip him off that we're trying to gather evidence against him when we don't have to.'

'We should be interviewing Meghan,' said Duncan, 'calling in Social Services.'

'And we will as soon as we have something more concrete to offer. The fact that she has a red swimsuit isn't enough.'

'You're not going to do anything to protect her?'

'Clive Goodwin asked me just now if he should take her out of the programme, a programme that seems to be working for her. What should I have said? She could die if she stops eating again. They all could. I can't alarm them for nothing. We can't afford to be wrong.'

'But we're not!' Duncan was getting irate.

'Then let's prove it,' she said. 'Let's start by working out what impact the fact that Helen is Meghan's aunt has on the Merrick case.'

'I'd like to know why Helen never mentioned it to us,' said Blake. 'Is it significant that she didn't?'

'Tim Merrick presumably knew that Meghan is Helen's niece,' she said. 'The other parents all seemed aware, and Chesham obviously knows. So how does that factor in to why Merrick called Helen that night?'

'He's hardly going to call up and admit he's having sexual fantasies about her thirteen-year-old niece,' said Blake.

'No,' said Grace, 'unless he'd already said or done something to Meghan and wanted to plead with Helen to save his skin.'

'Which would give her a motive to jump in a car and hot-rod it up there.'

'Duncan?' she asked. 'What do you think?'

The older man turned his head slowly from where he had been staring out at the passing countryside. 'Merrick's dead. Whatever he did or didn't do, it's not him but Ned Chesham who still poses a risk.'

'I know,' said Grace, trying not to lose patience. 'But say that Helen did kill Merrick because he was either complicit with or covering up for Chesham, then surely there's no way she would have allowed Meghan to go on attending the unit.'

Duncan looked at her blankly and turned back to the view beyond the grimy window. Grace frowned. His concern for the victims was commendable, but she needed him to focus on what next steps they *could* take.

'What if it's Chesham she's covering up for?'

Blake's words took Grace by surprise. 'She's hardly going to stand by and allow him to sexually assault her own niece!' she exclaimed.

'Might have little or nothing to do with Meghan,' said Blake. 'You said she hero-worships him. He's her boss; he's charismatic, influential, important. She bathes in his reflected glory. She's got a lot to lose in terms of her own credibility if it turns out she's been playing devoted handmaiden to a monster.'

'You're suggesting that she killed Merrick because he accused Ned?'

'People can be very invested in refusing to see something that would turn into a disaster if they did see it,' said Blake. 'And Dr Tripathi did say that a lot of the blows were around the mouth, as if someone wanted to shut Merrick up.'

'Beating him to death with a rock is quite some investment,' Grace said. 'And that's putting aside Helen's disregard for her niece's safety.'

'End of the day, it doesn't matter why she did it,' he said. 'Bottom line is that right after Merrick called her, she booked a car which we can show heading towards Wryford Hall, and within the next hour he's dead.'

'We've been granted another twenty-four hours to question

her,' said Grace. 'Maybe telling her that we know her niece was at the camp will make a difference.'

But when, two hours later, Helen Fry sat opposite Grace and Blake in an interview room for the second time, she remained as blank and composed as before and continued to deny that she had any connection to the car she had booked online which had been photographed by a roadside camera on the ring road south of Colchester.

The rest of Grace's team had been busy while she'd been in London and had collated evidence around Helen's account of that night. Forensics had found blood on the Toyota's driver's seat and were awaiting DNA results to see if it was a match to Tim Merrick. Clothes taken from the search of Helen's flat were still being examined. No CCTV or ANPR cameras close to Hampstead Heath had recorded either her or the car. There were no other calls to or from her phone that night but, interestingly, the browser history on her computer showed that it was only early the next morning that she had checked what time the grounds at Kenwood were shut.

Yet in the interview room, nothing disturbed the calm of her demeanour until Blake asked why she'd failed to mention earlier that one of the girls camping at Wryford Hall was her niece.

'Why should I?' she said. 'That's got nothing to do with anything.'

Grace was pleased to see that Blake waited – she was learning that he had good instincts – but Helen said nothing more, although she glared at each of them in turn.

'But you must feel more protective of your own family,' Blake said mildly. 'She's what – your sister's daughter?'

'Yes. But as far as the unit is concerned, she's just another patient. Everyone is treated the same.'

'You weren't afraid that Meghan was the girl Tim Merrick was having sexual thoughts about?'

She looked momentarily perplexed before firmly denying it.

'Did you take Meghan clothes shopping in preparation for the camping trip?' he asked. 'I believe it's considered part of the therapy.'

'Yes,' said Helen. 'Anything to do with body image is important. It's an opportunity to challenge some of the distorted thinking that accompanies the disease.'

'So did you take Meghan shopping?'

'I often take patients to try on or buy clothes.'

'Did you take Meghan?'

'Probably.'

'You don't remember precisely?'

'What is it you want to know?'

'Can you recall what sort of clothes she bought for the camping trip? Did she need anything special for sports, for instance?'

'I think we looked at shorts and trainers, that sort of thing.'

'And swimwear?'

'Yes, possibly.'

'Can you describe the swimsuit she bought?'

'Just an ordinary swimsuit.'

'Anything significant about it?'

Helen's breathing was becoming almost laboured. 'Like what?'

'The colour?'

'A sort of cherry pink, I think. Look, you asked me about this before and I told you, no one could care less what swimsuits they wear!'

Blake looked at Grace, who nodded and leaned across the table to Helen. 'We want to protect Meghan and the other children as much as you do,' she said. 'Whatever happened in the woods at Wryford Hall that night, you need to tell us the truth. We have strong circumstantial evidence to place you at or near the scene. We believe that either you killed Tim Merrick or you know who did. It's not too late to call in a solicitor to represent you, if you'd like one, but it's time to tell us the truth.'

'I don't need a solicitor,' Helen said. 'And I've told you the truth. The car club records are wrong. I spent the evening on a bench on Hampstead Heath, reading a book.'

'The best way to protect Meghan from anything she might have done is to tell us what happened, help us to understand.'

'Nothing happened. I wasn't there.'

'Very well,' said Grace. 'We'll take a break here. I'll ask someone to bring you a cup of tea. I hope you'll use the time to think things over. But I want you to understand that this isn't simply going to go away. A young man is dead, and we will bring his killer to justice. Please remember too that when an action is taken in defence of a child, justice can show some mercy.'

Helen merely stared at the wall between Grace and Blake. They waited for her to be taken back to her cell and then went slowly upstairs.

'She's not going to face it,' he said.

'A lot of ordinary people who have never been violent until the day they kill someone simply blank it out,' she said, 'sometimes for ever. It's like a fugue state, as if they can't believe it ever happened, so their brain decides that it didn't, that it never took place, and just shuts down. They know logically what must have occurred, but they genuinely don't remember.'

'Seems to me like she's making a pretty big effort of will not to remember,' said Blake.

'Maybe,' said Grace. 'But when the effects of remembering would be so catastrophic, maybe the brain just can't cope with the reality.'

'All sounds like convenient mumbo-jumbo to me,' he said. 'You don't forget picking up a rock and smashing in a man's head with it.'

Grace smiled, better able now to tolerate his black-or-white attitude. 'She knows something about the red swimsuit, though,' she said. 'Couldn't even bring herself to name the colour.'

'You don't think we're reading too much into that, boss? I mean, just because Karen Wheeler thought it was significant back before Meghan was even born, doesn't necessarily mean anything now. Karen has no way of knowing whether it's something that Chesham still cares about.'

'If it's part of his compulsion to offend, it will be,' she said.

'But red must be a popular colour,' he said. 'It's even used to advertise that slimmers' cereal.'

'Eight kids on each camping trip, and in the photos we've seen so far one of them each time – and only one – in a red swimsuit,' she said. 'Those odds feel like more than coincidence. Besides, you saw how Helen reacted. That's not nothing either.'

'I still don't see how it ties in with why Tim Merrick is dead,' he said. 'None of it makes any sense to me.'

'Not yet, maybe,' she said. 'But Helen has lied to us from the start. The big question is why. What it is she won't tell us?'

'Maybe we need to blow the whole thing out of the water,' said Blake.

'What do you mean?'

'Arrest Ned Chesham.'

'We barely have enough to charge Helen Fry!'

'Duncan's right, though,' he said. 'Someone has to be the first to come out and say that the emperor has no clothes. Might as well be us.'

Grace felt a rush of gratitude. For too long she had been looking over her shoulder, wary of unseen consequences, lacking enough support to speak her mind. Blake's courage might be politically naive, might even be counter-productive, but it was courage nonetheless. Too many abusers relied on people being fair and balanced, worrying about what others might think or simply too nice to make irresponsible accusations. It was time to stop being sensible and to trust her instincts. It felt good to have Blake ready to back her up.

30

Detective Superintendent Pitman, however, had other ideas. He was philosophical when told that, following CPS advice that there was as yet insufficient evidence to charge, Helen Fry had been released on police bail, although he readily accepted their belief that Helen had been, at the very least, party to murder. As they had agreed beforehand, Blake then left Grace to speak to their boss alone, quietly closing the door to Colin's office behind him.

'There's another, related, matter that I need to discuss with you, sir. As I'm sure you're aware,' she said, happy to offer a fig leaf for his ego if it would ease her path, 'Operation Mayfly was a review of a non-recent allegation of sexual abuse against Professor Sir Ned Chesham. Although DAC Marx is happy that Mayfly's precise remit has been concluded, there are outstanding matters for the Essex force regarding his annual camping trips at Wryford Hall.'

Colin did an admirable job of nodding sagely and pretending that he had always known but discreetly not mentioned the subject of Operation Mayfly. If he was surprised by Chesham's name, he hid it well. 'You had better bring me up to speed.'

'We spoke to a complainant who had not come to the

attention of the original inquiry,' Grace explained. 'She alleges that, at thirteen, she was sexually assaulted by Ned Chesham at Wryford Hall. According to her, he would choose a "special girl" and ask her to wear a red swimsuit. We found group photographs of two other years where there's been one child in a red swimsuit. Four weeks ago Meghan Goodwin, who is Helen Fry's niece, was taken to buy one. That's four potential victims out of a possible twenty.'

'Have you spoken to the others?'

'The photographs are unidentified and there's no record of which patients went camping. The whole set-up was unofficial, organized by Chesham himself.'

'What about Meghan Goodwin?' asked Colin.

'I'd like a specially trained officer to speak to her,' she said. 'And I'd like to seize photographs on the wall in Chesham's office at St Botolph's which may show other years and other children.'

'The complainant you have spoken to, she's made a statement and is willing to give evidence in court?'

This was the issue that Grace needed to play down. 'It's the usual catch-22,' she said. 'I think she'll go to court if there are others, but we need her evidence if we're to appeal for them to come forward. I'd hope that the woman who made the original complaint investigated by the Met would support a prosecution if she knew she wasn't going to be a lone voice. I'd like to ask St Botolph's to supply a list of all former patients so we can write and invite them to provide information.'

'You can't name Chesham,' said Colin. 'If you go trawling for testimony as blatantly as that, his defence counsel will simply dismiss it as leading any witnesses who come forward as a result.'

'We'll follow the witness approach protocols and make it as general as possible,' she said, 'but we have to start somewhere. And there's a safeguarding issue regarding Meghan Goodwin. I think we have to speak to her as soon as possible.'

'Investigative interviews should only take place when they're in a child's best interests,' he said.

'I'm aware of that, sir, but until we can arrest Professor Chesham I believe she remains at risk of significant harm.'

'Very well, but follow formal ABE guidance and get it properly videoed.'

Achieving best evidence. *Tell me something I don't know*, she thought. 'Yes, sir. Of course.'

'Are you planning to tell the hospital authorities what you're up to?'

'I'd like to, yes. We need to speak to any staff who went on earlier camping trips.'

'The complainant you do have, does her account bear the hallmarks of credibility?'

'She's had, let's say, a chequered history,' said Grace, aware that there was little point in pretending otherwise. 'But that's as a direct result of the abuse.'

'Can you independently corroborate her story so that it stands up to scrutiny?'

'We can't effectively interview his colleagues or fellow patients and their parents without naming him. We need to search his flat, his computers, find out at what addresses offences may have taken place, note any letters or cards or gifts given to him or that he gave to his victims. We need to arrest him.'

Colin leaned back in his leather chair and, elbows on the arms, placed his fingertips together. Grace could see him calculating how best to extricate himself while still appearing to be supportive and politically correct.

'Once you name him, there'll be no getting the genie back in the bottle,' he said, frowning in order to demonstrate the effort he was making to assist her.

'I realize that. I'd still like to question him under caution.'

'You feel you have a reasonable enough threshold of certainty to bring proceedings against him?'

'Not yet, no. But nor do I believe that doing nothing is any longer a viable option.'

'I admire your commitment,' said Colin.

In other words, thought Grace, *no*.

'But the case isn't ready. You've more or less said so yourself.'

'I'm saying that it'll never be ready unless we're prepared to stick our necks out in the hope of opening up new lines of inquiry.'

'And if you fail to bring the CPS on board, Chesham will end up winning so much public sympathy that it'll take an even higher threshold of proof to go after him a second time.'

'We can seize the photographs on his office wall as part of the Merrick inquiry,' she argued. 'If we can identify any former patients ourselves, through Facebook or whatever, at least let me write to them.'

Colin shook his head. 'Bring me more and we'll discuss it further.' He reached for a file on his desk and pulled it towards him. The subject was closed.

Grace rose reluctantly and left his office. Both Blake and Duncan were waiting expectantly. She shook her head and walked towards her cubicle, not trusting herself to speak. Duncan got up from his desk and followed her.

'You're not letting the bastard get away with it?' he demanded.

'We won't let it drop, I promise you. But we will—'

'What are worried about? Your career?'

'I beg your pardon?'

'You're all the same. None of you really give a damn, not if it's going to rock the boat, not if it's going to look bad on your record.'

'That's not fair! I won't be spoken to like that!'

'Whatever you say, ma'am. It's a waste of breath trying to talk to you anyway.'

Duncan turned on his heel and walked out of the office. Watching him go, Grace caught Blake's eye. He held up his hands in a 'What's that about?' gesture. She shook her head, wishing she knew the answer.

31

Blake had worked miracles and at short notice secured not only the use of an ABE suite in a London police station near the Goodwins' home but also the services of a trained social worker who would conduct the interview. The local child protection officers were proud of their recently updated facilities, which had both state-of-the-art digital recording equipment and new, comfortable soft furnishings donated by a local department store. Red cushions and a striped rug brightened the muted tones of the carpet, curtains and upholstery, making the room look reassuringly as much like an ordinary sitting room as possible.

Meghan's parents had been shown to a comfortable waiting room, and Grace now sat beside Blake in the viewing room, ready to watch the video feed. Meghan entered the room and, casting a disdainful look at the colourful pile of children's toys in one corner, took a seat on the couch. She barely made a dent in its surface, and it was hard to make out the shape of her body under her baggy clothes. Her young face was sharp and pointy, in need of soft flesh to fill it out, but she bore a strong resemblance to her mother, whom Grace had just met for the first time, and had the same pale skin and silky light brown hair as her aunt. Pulling the long sleeves of her cotton top down over her thin wrists, she hunched into herself as if she felt the cold. Outside it was a beautiful hot June day.

The social worker, Judith Eames, was a plump, practical woman of around forty who looked as if she ought to be judging a jam-making competition for the Women's Institute. She glided effortlessly into the initial 'establishing a rapport' phase of the interview. Chatting with a reserved and anxious young teenager about nothing in particular took great skill, and Grace relaxed, confident that they were in good hands.

Once Meghan, too, relaxed enough to sit back against her cushions, Judith got down to business. 'We're here because of what happened at Wryford Hall,' she said, 'when you went on your camping trip with Professor Ned. That's what you call him, I think. Is that right?'

Meghan nodded, tugging at her sleeves.

'I'd like you to tell me about the week you spent there. Maybe begin with when you arrived. Can you describe for me what it was like?'

'Daddy took me there in the car. I got upset and didn't want him to leave, but he said it would be like staying at Hogwarts, that we'd all have fun together. And Beth and Lara were already there, and said I could share their tent, and Crystal came and showed us where to put our things and stuff, so it wasn't too bad after that, though I cried a bit at night to begin with.'

'What made you cry?'

'Crystal said it was homesickness, that everyone got it.'

'So what did you do the first day?'

'We went exploring. We were allowed to go by ourselves so long as we stayed together and didn't go out of the park.'

'Tell me about that.'

'We followed Reena. She's the oldest, and she pretended that we were in like a fantasy land and there might be elves or vampires or something. I thought it was silly but the others liked it. We didn't go very far, just to the other side of the lake, into the trees, and back around.'

'What else did you do?'

'One afternoon we picked strawberries for Mrs Thomas. She said we could eat as many as we liked, but I expect she knew we wouldn't.'

Grace felt a pang of sadness at the matter-of-fact way that the child referred to her illness. She seemed like a bright kid, polite and helpful, which only made it more of a mystery why she should inflict such suffering on herself.

As Judith slowly continued to draw Meghan out, the girl talked about playing rounders and hide-and-seek, described how she and her friends launched themselves, screaming, into the chilly waters of the lake in order to avoid the horrid feeling of the squishy mud oozing between their toes, and shared the magic of hearing an owl hoot as she fell asleep under canvas.

'You didn't have jelly shoes for paddling in the lake?' Judith asked.

'No, we should've thought of that!'

'But you'd remembered to bring a swimsuit?'

Gillian had earlier confirmed what Clive had already told them, that Meghan did have a red swimming costume, bought specially for the camping trip on a shopping expedition with her aunt. However, it had been agreed between Grace and the social worker only to raise the subject enough to observe Meghan's reaction.

Meghan nodded.

'Pretty or sporty?'

Meghan shrugged and looked at the floor.

Judith quickly moved on, asking friendly questions about the camp's routine.

Meghan spoke warmly of Crystal and, after some initial hesitation, recounted how Doctor Tim had teased everyone and made them laugh, how he'd pretended to be naughty, encouraging them to plan a 'secret' midnight feast and offering to go into the village to buy clandestine supplies. She didn't appear to be badly upset by what had happened to him, although when Judith pressed her gently she shed a few tears over how much they all missed him at the clinic. It was clear, however, that she had only a sketchy and immature notion of what death really meant. Not once, in any of her stories about the week she spent in Essex, had she yet mentioned Ned Chesham.

Reminding Meghan that she could ask for a break at any time, and mindful of the clock – an hour of such intensity could be exhausting for a child – Judith asked Meghan to describe what part Professor Ned had played in their activities.

Grace saw Meghan immediately tense up, her bony shoulders rising towards her ears. 'He joined in with the rest of us.' She paused to pick again at her sleeves. 'He was always in charge of washing-up.' She then seemed to become aware of where she was, and her eyes flicked around the room. 'Are Mummy and Daddy watching?'

'No,' said Judith imperturbably. 'But they're just next door if you want them.'

Meghan shook her head quickly and stared silently down at the striped rug.

'Did anything else happen at the camp that you want to talk about?' asked the social worker.

'No.' The single word was barely more than a murmur.

'Can you describe washing-up with Professor Ned for me?'

'We took the dirty plates and cutlery and mugs to the cricket pavilion. We took it in turns, in pairs, after each meal. One washed and one dried. Only he said it was better to leave everything to dry in the air because there were more germs on a tea towel than in the air.'

'So what did the person who was on drying duty do?' asked Judith lightly.

'She didn't have to stay.'

'That doesn't sound fair somehow! So which job did you get?'

'Washing.'

'And when you'd finished the washing-up, what happened next?'

Meghan wiped at her cheek with the back of her hand. 'Nothing.'

'You talked about being homesick at the camp. Did anything else happen that upset you or made you unhappy?'

Another shake of the head. Sitting hunched in front of the screen beside Grace, Blake muttered to himself, 'Come on, come on. Spit it out. Just say it.'

But Meghan raised her chin and straightened her back. 'I had a lovely week.' It was as if she was saying thank you at the end of a birthday party. 'It was a really special place to visit. We were lucky to go there.' She tipped herself forward off the couch and stood up. 'Can I see my mummy and daddy now, please?'

'Of course,' said Judith. 'Thank you very much for talking to me. It's been helpful to understand a little more about your week at the camp. If you think of anything else you'd like to add, then your parents know how to get in touch.'

Grace watched Meghan leave the room. How could anyone bear to inflict further harm on such a frail child?

'If I was her dad,' Blake said through gritted teeth, 'I'd kill the bastard with my bare hands.'

They watched Meghan leave with her parents. Grace was glad to see her father place a protective arm around her shoulders and pull her close, although she resisted his hug. Grace felt like she had failed. She didn't believe Meghan's denials and was more than ever convinced that Ned Chesham had deliberately engineered time alone with her in the cricket pavilion, yet Meghan's parents would go away from here thinking that their daughter had been questioned about Tim Merrick. But without some stronger indication from Meghan about what might have taken place, Grace was helpless and unable to warn them against Chesham. Recalling Karen Wheeler's words, Grace felt she was beginning to see for herself how the psychological hold that the psychiatrist exerted over his young victims could be even more sinister than his sexual assaults.

32

Duncan's apartment block was one of those building projects that had been sideswiped by the credit crunch of the previous decade. While buyers might have got a bargain at the time, even discounting the cheap and hastily finished kitchens and bathrooms, the current peppering of FOR SALE signs suggested the flats were not desirable. The internal corridors were featureless and unloved, and she located his third-floor flat on the side of the building with the dullest view.

Grace had phoned him the night before after he failed to return to his desk, and again twice after she got back from London and discovered he had not turned up for work and sent no word as to why. He'd buzzed her in only after she had pressed the street bell three times and now opened his door looking bleary-eyed and unshaven and without meeting her eye. She couldn't be sure, but she suspected he was still wearing yesterday's clothes. Her first impression was that he must be recovering from an epic drinking session, but there was no lingering smell of booze, the living room was clean and tidy, and a glimpse into the galley kitchen revealed no telltale empty cans or bottles. She examined him more closely: had he been *crying*?

'What do you want?' he asked.

Recalling Keith Stalgood's concern, she chose to ignore his surly tone.

'You didn't turn up for work. I got worried.'

'Well, you can see I'm fine, so just leave me alone.'

'Look, Duncan, I can be here either as your friend or your boss – you choose.'

He made a sound of derision and shook his head, turning away.

'Do you want me to give you a formal warning?' she asked. 'Make this the start of disciplinary action?'

'Suit yourself.'

She decided to try another approach. 'Is it this case?' she asked. 'Keith said he didn't understand why it had got under your skin so much. Do you want to try and explain it to me?'

'So you can tut-tut and be awfully sorry about it and do nothing?'

Duncan was still half-turned away from her but she saw him lift a hand to his face. Was he brushing away a tear? She moved to where she could see his face properly. He *was* crying. He was trying hard not to, but suddenly he couldn't stop and dropped onto the cheap leather sofa, his face in his hands, broad shoulders heaving.

She sat down beside him and put an arm around him. 'Duncan. I'm so sorry. Whatever it is, I'm here. Talk to me. Tell me what's wrong.'

He leaned away from her, trying to shrug off her touch, but she kept a hand on his back. 'Tell me,' she said gently.

'I can't.'

'Duncan, whatever's happened, you have to tell someone.'

'No, never. I can't.'

His hands were wet with tears, and more were dripping off his chin. She dug in her bag for some tissues and handed them to him. He wiped his face, taking deep hiccoughing breaths as he tried to stop the sobs. Finally he nodded his head, indicating that the worst was over.

'What's wrong? Please, talk to me. Has someone died? Are you ill?'

He put his face in his hands again and let out a long shuddering sigh. 'I don't know what's happening to me. I feel like I'm falling off the edge of a cliff or something.'

'Is it this case?' she asked again.

He nodded.

'But why? After all the terrible cases you've dealt with, why has this one got to you so badly?'

'Just leave me alone. I'll be all right.'

'Look, I know you're angry that we don't seem to be doing anything to protect the girls who may be at risk from Ned Chesham,' she said, 'but you know the law as well as I do. We can't act when we don't have the evidence. If we can't arrest him, he doesn't have to talk to us. But we won't give up, I promise you that.'

He nodded again but spoke to the floor. 'I don't think I can face coming back to work. In fact, I think it's best that I don't.'

'Why ever not? What are you talking about? You're one of the best detectives in my team.'

His head bowed deeper and he whispered something that she couldn't hear.

'What did you say?' she asked softly. 'Please, say it again. I want to know what's wrong.'

'I can't.'

'I'm not leaving until you do.'

'It happened to me.'

He lurched to his feet and stumbled out of the room. Grace heard him retching in the bathroom across the narrow hall. She sat back, taking time to fully understand what he meant. How had she been so blind? So stupid and so blind? A man who had joined the army at sixteen and never to her knowledge had a romantic relationship; someone who clung to his chosen 'family' of the police yet never sought promotion; a colleague about whom not even Keith seemed to know very much and with whom she had never spent any real time outside work.

She looked around the shipshape flat. No photographs, few personal items, a lot of books and films on DVD.

A man abused as a child.

The retching stopped, and she heard a flush and then the sound of water running. Soon afterwards he came to stand in the doorway, his head hanging. He looked ashamed, and her heart went out to him.

'Thank you for telling me,' she said. 'It must have taken real guts to do that.'

He gave a tiny nod, not looking at her.

'How can I help?' she asked, not feeling as if there was anything she could do to make a difference. 'Have you eaten today? Why don't I start by making a cup of tea?'

Slowly over the next couple of hours, as if, having finally spoken the truth aloud, he wanted no more secrets, Duncan told his story. A father who walked out on his family when Duncan was five, a stepfather who came on the scene when he was nine, four years of sexual abuse that began when he was twelve and ended when he persuaded his mother to sign the papers so he could join up. It was that, he said, or suicide.

Later he saw service in Bosnia, where he hoped he might be killed. He wasn't, but one good friend was, and Duncan decided he owed it to his comrade to make the best of his life. He'd never gone home, not even to visit his mother, but he found he liked service life and, leaving in his twenties, had joined the police, hoping to recreate that feeling of safety and belonging. Gradually he'd begun to believe that he could leave the abuse behind, pretend it never happened. Recently he'd really thought he could, until listening to Trudie and Karen talk about their experiences had brought it all rushing in on him again, and he'd felt like he was drowning.

'It felt like I was right back there,' he said. 'Helpless, in pain, humiliated. All the feelings I'd buried.'

'I'm so sorry,' said Grace. 'So sorry you've had to be alone with it all these years.'

'I was so ashamed.'

'It wasn't your fault.'

'I missed my dad. I wanted my stepfather to love me.'

'That what every child wants. It doesn't make it your fault.'

'He said I seduced him, that he'd never done anything like that before, that it was me that wanted it.'

'You were only twelve, Duncan. How old was he?'

He shook his head. 'It's so hard, so hard not to believe all the things he said.'

'Whatever they were, he only said them to protect himself, to shut you up, to keep you afraid. You're free of him now. You don't have to think those things.'

'I can't come back to work.'

'What are you talking about? Of course you can. You must. We need you – you're the heart of the team.'

'I'm not good enough.'

'Listen, we'll get you a counsellor, a therapist,' she said. 'The force will pay. No one need know. Only me, if that's the way you want it. But you're not giving up on us. I won't let you!'

'It doesn't matter what happens to me.'

'It matters to me, and I'm still your boss. You'll do what I say, and I'm telling you that the team needs you, that you're the best detective we've got, and there isn't a single person in that office who wouldn't be proud to call you a friend. Especially me.'

As she said it, Grace knew that she'd taken Duncan's unstinting kindness and support too much for granted. She simply hadn't bothered to find out what made him tick, what he did with his weekends or holidays, what floated his boat. She could think of dozens of occasions when he'd given her a reassuring smile or a nod of approval just when it really counted, and it had been all too easy and convenient to assume that he didn't expect the same sort of support because he didn't need it. It seemed it was as simple for the victims of abuse to hide in plain sight as the perpetrators.

She squeezed his arm. 'I haven't shown myself to be much of a friend,' she said, 'but I can't tell you how much I appreciate the friendship you've shown me, and I'd do anything to return it. I'll do whatever I can to help – other than let you quit work.'

He gave her a wan smile. 'You won't tell anyone else?'

'Not a soul.'

'I'll come in tomorrow.'

'Promise? If you don't, I'll come looking for you again.'

'I promise.'

Duncan stood up and she could see that now he just wanted her to go. 'Get some sleep,' she told him. 'You look bushed.'

'I am.'

After the intense intimacy of the past hours they felt suddenly shy of one another, and after an awkward attempt at a hug, Grace left. She felt awful, all shaky and tearful. She recalled what Helen Fry had said about counter-transference and thought that if she was experiencing even a pale shadow of Duncan's agony, then no wonder he had cried all night and not turned up for work.

How must Trudie Bevan and Karen Wheeler have felt after she and Duncan had visited them? How were they both doing now? Who was there to support them, to believe in what they said and to fight for justice? How was young Meghan Goodwin managing to survive?

Suddenly she knew what had to be done.

33

Ivo had received the call around lunchtime, which left him plenty of time to write the copy and badger his editor into running it. Nothing he loved more than a tight deadline. It gave him a shot of adrenalin, which since he'd given up booze was like nothing else. Besides, he now realized that drink had only ever helped dull the edge of the flat, empty feeling he always had *after* an edition had gone to bed and he was left alone with the come-down. He supposed actors or singers or stand-up comedians must feel the same when the curtain fell and the lights went out.

But not tonight. Tonight he could go to sleep with the lovely wired excitement of knowing that for an awful lot of people, tomorrow's *Courier* was really going to spoil their day.

The paper's in-house lawyers, whose eminent counsel had spent billable hours poring over the finished copy, had advised the editor to expect trouble, even though Ivo's final story merely reported the all-too-brief existence of Operation Mayfly and had taken great care not to accuse Professor Sir Ned Chesham directly of any wrongdoing.

All the same, the celebrated trick cyclist was about to experience that weightless moment before his life took a new and distinctly unpleasant turn. Tomorrow's *Courier* and the media doorstepping that would inevitably follow would be just the beginning. Chehsam wouldn't be able to use his phone because every time he put it on standby a dozen calls would come in. He'd be vilified on social media. Every detail of his past would be raked over. And he'd be suspended from St Botolph's – albeit with a carefully worded statement of neutral support and on full consultant's pay.

The shit storm that Ivo was about to release was going to offer Ned Chesham a whole new meaning for the word relentless. Even if it turned out he'd been dragged off his pedestal for nothing, this would never go away. The tag of paedophile would remain, and smear and innuendo would be attached to him for ever. Life as he knew it tonight was over.

Did that bother Ivo? Not one bit. He'd once read a brilliant book in which a neurosurgeon made the point that if he worried too much about the potential negative consequences of his actions, he'd end up never daring to operate at all. That was the stance that the fourth estate also had to take. Except that for a tabloid journalist there was of course nothing remotely equivalent to the Hippocratic oath. Instead, there was little that most red-top editors liked better than a bit of gratuitous hooliganism, trashing reputations in the same mindless fashion that louts smashed up their local high streets on a Saturday night. All part of a great British tradition, innit?

The hospital's crisis management team would swing into action, especially once it became clear that the chief executive of the St Botolph's Hospital Trust would be forced to admit that the internal investigation of an earlier complaint had failed to reach as far as actually speaking to the underage patient concerned. This nugget, not in tomorrow's paper, had been kept for later, but the information DI Fisher had given him was more than enough to convince the in-house lawyers that his story had legs. By the time tomorrow's lunchtime news went on air, the trust chief executive would doubtless have put out a statement supporting anyone who might have been hurt by the actions of the hospital or its staff while at the same time expressing full confidence in Professor Chesham – at least until the time came to throw him to the wolves in the best interests of the hospital's future.

The only person so far contacted for comment was Jessica Hubbard – or her various agents, at any rate. Through them she had declined to issue a statement echoing the warm words of praise she had heaped upon her saviour only the previous week – words that would now appear in a separate box below a photograph of her with Professor Ned at his recent fundraising lecture. And lo, brave Jessica would be effortlessly transformed into poor Jessica, the dupe of a child molester.

Ivo's editor had wanted to get a comment from Scotland Yard, but Ivo had persuaded him to leave that for tomorrow's follow-up story, arguing that the Yard might tip Ned off, buying him or St Botolph's an opportunity to seek a last-minute injunction. The Yard's likely reaction was the only aspect that Ivo wasn't happy about: if they were swamped with evidence against Ned, then the Met would pin the blame for previous shortcomings on Grace Fisher, insisting that their hands were clean and it was her review that had failed to find sufficient evidence to mount a prosecution.

Grace had insisted over the phone – a call made from a public call box in Colchester – that this needn't concern him, that the only option left to her was to go public and pray that other victims then came forward. What happened to her afterwards didn't matter. He'd warned her that even if she was proved right, the Met would never forgive or forget. She'd end up like so many of those who tried to expose wrongdoing within institutions with powerful vested interests: dubbed a traitor and forced out. But she had refused to budge, insisting that she owed it to the victims to do all in her power to get this man locked up.

Fair enough. If that was what she wanted, that was what she'd get. Ivo fell asleep relishing the prospect of a galloping good story.

He was woken early by the first phone call of the day. He didn't recognize the number and cleared his throat before saying hello, hoping that he'd sound alert and not ready to be caught out.

It was Sam Villiers. 'Why the hell didn't you tell me you were running a story?' he demanded.

'Wasn't too sure whose side you're on, old bean.'

'Why do it now? What made you change your mind?'

'I told you before,' Ivo lied. 'It's the Jessica Hubbard angle. The timing had to be right.'

'But what's the deal? Is he guilty or not?'

'Don't you know?'

'I wouldn't be asking.'

'What about your client? Does he take a view?'

'What client?' Villiers blustered.

'Adrian Starling.'

There were a few seconds of shocked silence. 'Don't know what you're talking about.'

'Look, I've got a busy day,' said Ivo. 'And you're a very poor liar.'

'Forget it.' Villiers ended the call.

Ivo rubbed his face, feeling the stubble on his chin. He already had quite enough to get on with today, but at some later point he intended to ferret out precisely why the Right Honourable Adrian Starling QC MP took such an interest in the good doctor's moral fibre.

34

The morning had begun quite well. Meghan had been compliant at breakfast, if a little subdued, but that was only to be expected after the ordeal of being questioned the day before about Wryford Hall and poor Tim Merrick. Except, *was* he poor Tim Merrick? Clive and Gillian had never spent much time with him, so how were they to know if there'd been something wrong? They'd tried several times since to have coded conversations with Meghan about whether he'd upset either her or any of the other girls, or made them feel uncomfortable, and she'd always insisted that they all really liked him and were really sad about what happened, and they'd believed her.

So why then had he been killed? And why on earth did the police think Helen was involved? That was just crazy.

Gillian had rushed round to see her sister as soon as the police let her go. Her arrest hadn't made any sense to Clive at all until Gillian reported that it was all some stupid mix-up over a car Helen had booked online to go up to Hampstead Heath that Sunday night. She hadn't fully got to the bottom of it because Helen had been exhausted and wanted a shower and sent Gillian home. Clive tried to imagine what it must have been like for Helen to sleep in a grubby police cell. She was so fastidious, liked everything to be in the right order – and *clean*. She wasn't very resilient at the best of times, and the experience must have been everything she most hated.

Gillian had wanted to ask Helen to stay with them the night before but had reluctantly accepted Clive's decision that Meghan had to come first, and with everything going on, a quiet family evening would be best. Gillian had texted – Helen was as usual ignoring her calls – to say she'd go over to Crouch End if her sister wanted her to, but Helen texted back to say that she was fine. Clive supposed they should be grateful that at least Helen's name had not – or not yet – been released to the media.

Gillian was about to go upstairs to hurry Meghan along to get ready for the clinic when a call appeared on Clive's mobile from one of the secretaries at work. Before he picked up he racked his brains to recall which of the many things he had left undone was urgent enough for her to call so early.

'Have you seen this morning's *Courier*?' she asked instead.

'No. Why?'

'Your daughter's under the care of Professor Chesham, isn't she?' Clive said that she was, and she continued. 'There's a big article about him. I think you ought to read it. If you need me to tell them at work why you might not come in today, I will.'

She insisted that he read the article for himself and rang off. She sounded sorry and embarrassed and he assumed it must be something to do with the weird nightmare of Helen's arrest. Clive caught Gillian on the stairs and whispered to her not to leave for the hospital until he came back with a copy of the paper.

There was a newsagent at the bottom of the street. Clive couldn't recall when he had last read the *Courier* – it wasn't his kind of paper. He meant to carry it home before looking, but anxiety got the better of him. He'd thought he'd prepared himself for the worst there was likely to be about Helen, but that wasn't what it was about at all, and there was no preparation he could have made for what he now read.

For an absurd moment he had the idea that if he didn't actually take the newspaper indoors, if he ditched it behind a hedge or something, then they wouldn't have to face it. He found his mind latching on to the least dreadful of the consequences of what he'd just read, which was that he'd have to miss work yet again and sooner or later his line manager was going to tell him they were letting him go.

Gillian was waiting for him in the kitchen. Meghan, thankfully, was still upstairs. He handed the newspaper to his wife. 'Better read it for yourself.'

Blind panic had set in. He scarcely knew where he was. But then he forced himself to think. It was just a tabloid newspaper. Everybody knew they made up any old rubbish they thought they could get away with. It didn't make it true. Besides, the article had said – hadn't it? – the allegations against Professor Ned had been dismissed. And it was years and years ago. There was nothing in it. Of course there was nothing in it.

The detective in charge of looking into this was the same young woman who'd set up the interview with the social worker. The one who'd arrested Helen. Who'd asked if any of them feared their daughters might have been abused by someone at the summer camp. He and all the other parents had assumed she meant Dr Merrick. Had they misunderstood? Had her agenda been about Professor Ned all along?

Gillian finished reading the article. Beneath her make-up her skin had gone white, and her hands trembled as she tried to fold the newspaper. 'It can't be true,' she said. 'This police review, Mayfly, said it wasn't. We *know* Prof Ned!'

'I don't think we can take any chances,' Clive said. 'Doesn't matter what we think or believe, we have to protect Meghan, just in case.'

'Look, they accused Helen,' she said, 'and we know that's nonsense.'

What could he say? So far he'd kept his own misgivings about his sister-in-law to himself – after all, the police don't arrest people for no reason – but now?

Gillian avoided his eye. 'Come on, I mean for goodness' sake, they even asked where *we* were the night Dr Merrick was killed. This stupid story doesn't mean a thing. It can't.'

'What if that's why they wanted to interview Meghan yesterday?' he asked, feeling ice-cold and shivery all of a sudden. 'We don't know what she told them.'

Gillian threw the *Courier* down on the table. 'This allegation they're talking about was years ago. If he was like that, it would've come out by now. We'd know!'

'We still ought to talk to Meghan,' he said. 'Make sure she's OK.'

'And put what kind of ideas in her head?' Gillian's voice rose dangerously. 'Give her reasons to stop listening to a word we say? To stop eating again? Is that what you want?'

All too aware of what sharp ears Meghan had, Clive made soothing noises to calm her down. Besides, part of him wanted to agree. These past two or three weeks had been unreal. They simply weren't his life. Nothing like this had ever happened to him before, and he had to believe that any moment now it would all stop and he could go back to worrying about the mortgage. And then, if Meghan continued to respond to treatment, she could probably go back to school in the autumn. She'd have to repeat a year, but maybe they could get her into a different school, a place where no one knew her history, where life could get back on track. Even though it seemed like an impossible dream, did he really want to sabotage it by admitting these events could be real?

The urge to believe that nothing had fundamentally changed was overwhelming. It coursed through his veins like some highly addictive drug taking hold of his mind and willpower.

Gillian brought her voice back under control. 'It says right here that the police investigated years ago and found nothing. And now this latest review has also found nothing. We know Ned. It's fine.'

'I don't like thinking badly of him,' he said, forcing himself to think clearly, to face the impending catastrophe, if that's what it was, 'but nor am I prepared to give him the benefit of the doubt. Not until all this has been cleared up.'

'But it has been!' Gillian tapped the newspaper. 'That's exactly what the article says.'

'Then why run the story, if there's no smoke without fire?' He didn't add that Tim Merrick's murder seemed to him like an awfully big smoke signal.

'Look. Meghan mentioned last weekend about getting Ned something as a present when we go to the palace,' she said. 'She'd hardly do that if there was a problem.'

'A problem?' he echoed in disbelief.

'They've just awarded him a knighthood!'

'I don't care,' he said doggedly. 'Meghan comes first.'

'I am putting her first!' She struggled to hold back tears. 'Have you forgotten how ill she was until we got her in to see the prof? Are we really going to throw away all the progress she's made because of some tittle-tattle in a scandal sheet like the *Courier*?' She grabbed the paper from the table, rolled it up tightly and thrust it deep into the rubbish bin.

Clive was glad to see it go. For a fleeting second the pressure lifted as if the issue had been magically resolved. Then it returned and hit him like a truck. He longed not to believe that Ned was an abuser, but for Meghan's sake he had at least to make himself act as if it might be true.

He and Gillian looked at one another across the kitchen table. There had been too many rows in this room about the best way forward with Meghan. They were both too worn out and weary of failure to start another one.

The doorbell rang.

Afraid it was the media, already somehow in possession of Meghan's name and their address or perhaps on Helen's trail, he opened the door on the security chain and peered through the gap. It was Ned, and for a second Clive felt a rush of familiar relief at recognizing the man who had so often made things right for them before. He fleetingly considered simply closing the door in the professor's face, but Ned looked just the same as he always did. He hadn't grown horns or a tail, he wasn't leering or drooling. He looked relaxed but concerned: his usual self. Clive undid the chain and opened the door, keeping hold of the door with his other hand braced protectively against the wall, ready if necessary to bar entry.

'How are you?' Chesham asked. 'You must be so upset about Helen. Is there anything I can do?'

Clive licked his lips. 'We've seen the story in today's paper.'

'Oh, don't worry about me,' said Chesham with a wave of his hand. 'The hospital has lawyers to deal with that kind of thing. And I've told them I'll take leave of absence while they sort it out. Much easier for them that way. But some tabloid getting itself hot under the collar over nothing doesn't mean I'm about to let my patients down.'

'I don't know if it's a good idea for you to come in right now,' said Clive.

'No, that's fine. I just wanted to make sure you and Gillian are OK.'

'Not really, but we'll manage.'

Chesham shook his head angrily. 'The thought that patients might suffer because some celebrity-obsessed tabloid wants an extra bang for its buck on the Jessica Hubbard story makes my blood boil,' he said. 'I'm so sorry you have to deal with this when the two of you must already be beside yourselves with worry over Helen. I heard they haven't charged her yet. That's something, I suppose. Just tell me how Meghan is. She must be so confused. Are you sure it wouldn't help for me to come in and have a quick chat?'

Somehow, he was never entirely sure how or why, Clive found himself standing aside to let Ned walk into his house.

35

Grace had tossed and turned for hours before falling asleep, wondering who would be the first to alert her to Ivo's revelations and trying to rehearse how best to feign shock and ignorance. She was terrified at the thought of how badly her impulsive action might backfire yet deep down couldn't regret it. Duncan's story and the pain with which he had brought it to light after so many years of trying to make it go away had devastated her. No, that wasn't true. What had been devastating was that she had always so blithely assumed he was fine. A bit shy or repressed perhaps, but never that he was carrying such a burden. And if Duncan, how many others? People who couldn't speak, couldn't accuse, couldn't demand justice?

Every new police recruit is taught that the power he or she is given is real. It matters. The Job is to police without fear or favour and never let anyone down. The power given to officers is there to keep people safe. After finding no shelter at home, Duncan had sought his safety in a uniform – first the army and then the police – and she wasn't about to let him down, let alone any of Ned Chesham's potential victims.

A call from Blake woke her. 'Hello,' she said, glad that the exhaustion in her voice at least was genuine. She'd anticipated the inevitable call would come from Colin or Hilary and had been pretty certain she could fake it convincingly with them; lying to Blake felt harder than expected.

'Sorry to bother you so early, boss,' he said, 'but I thought you should know.'

'What?'

'Operation Mayfly is all over the front page of the *Courier*.'

'Shit!' Her reaction wasn't entirely false. As she sat up in bed, she experienced an unexpected jolt of reality: it was true, Ivo had actually managed to persuade his editor to do what she asked, and even faster than she'd expected. 'What does it say?'

'At least it's only about Mayfly. They don't seem to have found out about our investigation yet. Although I bet it's only a matter of time before they do. How do you think they got the story?'

'Could've come from anyone.'

'It's by a reporter called Ivo Sweatman. Ever come across him?'

'He's a crime correspondent,' she said with deliberate vagueness, relieved that no rumours of a closer relationship with Ivo had reached Blake. 'I've seen him a few times at media briefings.'

'Do you think the Yard leaked it?' he asked.

'Anything's possible,' she said. 'The DAC knows I wanted to follow up on Karen Wheeler's allegation, so the Yard might see this as a good way to cover its back.'

'Bastards!'

'Let's not go pointing fingers,' she warned, although she couldn't help a small smile of pleasure at his support. 'It won't get us anywhere, and certainly won't make us any friends.' A second incoming call flashed up. 'It's Hilary Burnett,' she said. 'I'll see you later in the office.'

She took Hilary's call, thankful that she could say honestly that she'd already heard about the article.

'Let's not discuss it on the phone,' said Hilary. 'My office, as soon as you can.'

The reason for Hilary's curtness was explained when Grace arrived forty minutes later and found Colin already there. It was swiftly made clear that while the communications director's office offered greater privacy than the superintendent's, he intended to own the meeting.

'We need to contain this,' he said before Grace had even taken a seat.

Hilary caught her eye and gave a tiny but encouraging nod, and Grace supposed she should be grateful that Colin had not begun by accusing her of being responsible for the leak. Even if he had, she felt reasonably shielded by her secret knowledge that if a scapegoat had to be found, she could hide behind the fact that Sam Villiers had already sold the story to the *Courier*. Villiers had placed the dynamite; Grace was merely the detonator.

'As you can imagine,' said Colin, 'Deputy Assistant Commissioner Marx is pretty incandescent. She's told me, off the record, that they'll be putting out a statement to the effect that while they have every confidence in you, perhaps in retrospect they underestimated the extent to which you might have been blinded by your loyalty to Keith Stalgood.'

Grace shook her head in contempt.

'It could have been worse,' Hilary said gently.

'The Yard has also had St Botolph's on the phone,' Colin continued. 'They want to know if any offences took place on hospital premises. They're keen to understand the extent of their liability.'

'No one's going to come out of this well,' said Grace.

'The trust chief executive expects to be kept updated,' he said. 'DAC Marx has handed that responsibility over to us. I suggest we appoint a liaison officer as soon as possible. Perhaps Duncan would be good for that role.'

'No.' Grace spoke without thinking and had to backtrack quickly. 'No, I need him at the heart of the inquiry. Perhaps we could attach someone from outside the team? Ruth Woods is a family liaison officer. She did a very good job after the Dunholt shootings.'

Colin raised his eyebrows and gave her a hard look. 'I wasn't aware that I had sanctioned an ongoing investigation,' he said with deliberate coldness.

'I fully expect this publicity to bring forward fresh allegations,' she said.

'That's handy for you,' he said acidly. 'An eminent psychiatrist becomes human flypaper for your investigation, is that it?'

'If he's guilty, then yes.'

'I do not intend to condone using a witch-hunt as a means of enforcing the law,' he said. 'I thought I'd made that clear.'

'You could see it as a matter of presentation,' said Hilary. 'A decision to take no further action would leave a very uncomfortable question mark hanging over Professor Chesham's name and reputation. We could portray any further investigation as seeking unequivocally to clear his name.'

Colin thought it over. 'Well, it's one avenue for damage limitation, I suppose.'

Grace struggled to restrain herself from arguing that the only issue at stake here was child protection, but Hilary cut across her. 'The Met has been heavily criticized for its failure to investigate allegations against VIPs properly in the past. We don't want to risk Essex Police becoming tarred with the same brush.'

'So what do you suggest?' Colin asked.

'A statement to the effect that while it would be inappropriate to comment on decisions made by another force, Essex Police is conducting its own investigation into a historical complaint, and that Essex Police remains absolutely committed to bringing the perpetrators of abuse to justice regardless of the passage of time.'

'I suppose it's enough to hold the dyke for now,' Colin said grudgingly. He turned to Grace. 'But you are not to go digging unnecessarily into any matters where you do not have a credible complainant ready and willing to go to court, do you understand?'

'Sir.'

'Right then. So for now that only leaves the question of where the leak actually came from.'

'Thank goodness that's not our problem,' said Hilary briskly. 'We can leave the Met to deal with that.'

'Unless they start accusing one of us,' said Colin with an unfriendly look at Grace.

Hilary shook her head firmly. 'The Met has always leaked like a sieve. Besides, I've had a word with their head of communications and we're agreed that the last thing anybody wants is to get into a firefight over this.'

'Very well,' Colin agreed. 'Let's wait and see where we are when the merry-go-round stops.' From the way he glared at her, Grace could see that he was spoiling for a fight. 'Don't let us keep you from getting back to work, DI Fisher.'

Although Grace would have appreciated a private word with Hilary, she was glad to escape.

As she made her way downstairs to the MIT office she thought about how easy it would be to stop struggling and fall in with the norms of an institution that said that image was more important than action and corporate survival came first. Yet she had to face Duncan. She had to face Trudie Bevan and Karen Wheeler. Sharon Marx no longer had to face any victim in person and had probably forgotten what that was like. To those caught up in a world of palace intrigue and ambition, the simple values of the service in which officers like Duncan had put their faith looked naive and irrelevant. No doubt Colin and DAC Marx sincerely believed that the correct priority really was safeguarding the future of the Met, so that anyone challenging it became a problem to be resented and brushed aside. Or worse.

The first thing that struck her as she entered the large open-plan office was that the phones were ringing even more than usual and there was an infectious energy in the room. She was relieved to see Duncan in his usual place, engaged in a call. He spotted her and stuck up a thumb. Blake, also with a phone to his ear, looked over and smiled. She relaxed: she would not be doing this alone.

Blake ended his call and came over. 'How did it go upstairs?'

'Not too bad. What's happening here?'

He grinned. 'Plenty. The DNA results are back on the blood found on the driver's seat in the car club Toyota. It's a match for Tim Merrick.'

'Yes!' Grace punched the air.

'The leaf matter on the floor is a match with the ground where he was found too,' Blake said. 'Whoever drove the car had to be present when he was killed. I can't see any jury buying Helen Fry's story that she wasn't there.'

'No,' said Grace. 'And hopefully the CPS will now see it that way too.'

'They'll want motive,' he said doubtfully. 'And I for one still don't get why she did it.'

'Has to be something to do with Chesham,' she said. 'She'll tell us in the end. We'll get there.'

Blake raised an eyebrow. 'If you say so, boss.'

She laughed. She was getting used to his scepticism and no longer found it so grating. 'What are we getting in response to the *Courier* story?' she asked.

'Endless people calling in. One or two of the usual crazies and time-wasters, and an awful lot of worried parents, but also a few former patients. None so far alleging that anything happened to them – mainly wanting to talk about how the unit was run.'

'Good,' she said. 'Anyone who went on a summer camp?'

'Not yet. We're still collating the information.'

'Fine. I want a statement from every patient, whatever they can remember – places, dates, people. It'll help us build up a picture.'

'Sure, boss.' Blake leaned over and pulled a yellow Post-it off his desk. 'And Karen Wheeler wants you to call her. She says she'll only speak to you.'

Grace took the note. She had agonized over whether there was some way she could have prepared Trudie and Karen for Ivo's story but had failed to come up with a way of doing so that wouldn't give away her advance knowledge. She also wanted a word with Duncan, to check how he was, but knew she mustn't keep Karen waiting any longer than she could help. With a glance at Duncan, busy on the phone, she went to her cubicle and dialled the Maidstone number.

She could tell from Karen's first words that her breakfast had included a lot of cheap brandy. 'I'll do it,' she slurred. 'I'll give evidence. I want to stand up in court and tell everyone exactly what that bastard did to me.'

Grace knew she should advise Karen to take more time to think it over, but this was the 'Open Sesame' she so desperately needed. If she could tell Colin she had a victim willing to testify he would have no choice but to green-light a wider investigation.

Above all, if she got moving before Karen sobered up and had a change of heart, she could arrest Ned Chesham.

36

Grace had expected that, advised by his expensive London solicitor, Ned Chesham would give a 'No comment' interview, but from the minute they had arrived at his 1930s mansion flat at six o'clock in the morning he had remained courteous and cooperative. The media, already camped outside, had called out questions to her as they went in, to which she gave no response. Ned was clearly shocked at the formality of his arrest and appropriately anxious about what would happen to him, but he dressed swiftly in a suit and pale blue shirt, matched with a dark red tie woven with what looked like a professional insignia, and even thanked them for their discretion in managing their exit via a back entrance to a private courtyard where the police vehicle was ready and waiting.

Sitting beside him in the back during the journey to Colchester – he was under caution, so they barely spoke – Grace speculated as to why such an amiable and successful man would ever have allowed himself to indulge sexually with children. Was it a tragic flaw, some faulty wiring in his sexual make-up, an obsessive compulsion he couldn't withstand, or something more predatory, to do with manipulation and control not only of his victims but of everyone around him? And if so, was that just more faulty wiring, or because someone had done something to him as a child that had sent his personality off down such a dark track? The hardest thing of all for Grace to understand was how easy it would be to go on liking him.

Once the interview began, Chesham expressed concern for his patients, for his colleagues on the unit, and for the hospital fundraising that would suffer because of this unfortunate situation. When Grace named Trudie Bevan and Karen Wheeler, he instantly remembered them, saying he never forgot a patient and how appalled he'd been to learn from the *Courier* that Keith Stalgood had missed an opportunity years ago to speak to him about Trudie's allegation. He blamed no one and listened attentively to Grace's questions.

Compared to the heinous figure that had filled her thoughts over the past two weeks, the man who sat across from her in the interview room struck her as flat and insubstantial. She had experienced this sense of diminution before when finally faced with a suspect. Even after a murder hunt, a perpetrator seldom possessed the physical or psychological power attributed to him over a long and painstaking investigation. But in those cases, by the time the police had someone in custody there would be forensic evidence and clear and contemporaneous witness statements to justify the arrest. Here they had nothing so tangible. Hit by a sudden wave of vertigo, Grace gripped the sides of her chair. *I am right about this, aren't I?*

She glanced sideways at Blake, who returned her look with an imperceptible nod and a gleam of quiet triumph in his eyes. She reminded herself of a story she'd once heard about a young officer having to question his old head teacher over a particularly nasty domestic assault and finding the reversal of power so unnerving that he had apologized to the man for having to hold him in custody. She asked herself if Keith Stalgood's reluctance to approach Chesham directly seventeen years ago and the eagerness of the hospital trust's medical director to disregard Nasir Khan's inconclusive complaint had both come from the sense of unreality she was experiencing now.

But this was a police interview room. Chesham had been formally cautioned and had his solicitor present. Every word they said was being recorded and could be used in evidence. In this setting his courtesy and respectful deference to her authority were not about politeness; they were more likely to be a conscious strategy. He was depending on her liking and approval in order to get away with his crimes.

Testing this insight, she offered him a friendly smile, and he immediately smiled back. In her experience the anxiety of an innocent person falsely accused was not so easily dissipated. She watched his shoulders drop slightly and, as he straightened his shirt cuffs, imagined him calculating that his charisma had successfully undermined her initial defences, as it must have done before in other tricky situations. Fine. If charm was his chosen weapon, she could wield it too.

'I'm sure you can understand that I carry a heavy burden here,' she said to him. 'We've spoken to the parents of some of your patients, and they've told us how you've worked miracles with their children.'

Out of the corner of her eye she was pleased to notice Blake, who was sitting beside her, relax his body language and nod sympathetically in order to mirror her change of tactic. He'd been surprised – and pleased – when she had asked him, not Duncan, to partner her, expecting instead to be the one to monitor the interview remotely, ready to chase up any potential new leads or feed back any insights. If he'd also been surprised at Duncan's failure to dispute her decision, he'd kept it to himself.

'My patients are my life,' said Chesham. 'The tragedy is that there are some I'm unable to help. I'm not saying I'm infallible, far from it, but with a few of these kids the damage runs too deep.'

'Could you give me an example?' asked Grace.

Ned leaned over and spoke discreetly into the ear of his solicitor, who nodded. 'Professor Chesham is concerned about the issue of patient confidentiality,' said the solicitor. 'On the other hand it's difficult for my client to adequately defend himself without divulging his clinical judgement on former patients. Can we agree not to reveal such information unless absolutely necessary?'

'I understand,' said Grace, addressing Ned directly, 'and my feeling is that we're here to establish the truth, so you should feel able to speak freely. If, down the line, there should be a problem with disclosure to a jury, it can be decided by a judge.'

She suspected that this freedom to speak was exactly what Chesham wanted, that he would have no qualms at all about using his authority as a consultant psychiatrist to damage and undermine his victims.

He sighed to display his reluctance. 'I'm afraid that Trudie Bevan was one of those very vulnerable patients. Her anorexia was merely one part of a much more complex personality disorder. Her sense of self was notably porous, making her highly suggestible. How long after she left treatment did you say she made up the allegation against me?'

'Six years,' said Grace. 'Not long, compared to many abuse victims.' She was pierced by the image of Duncan, red-eyed and shame-faced, admitting for the first time to acts that had taken place nearly three decades earlier. She tamped down her anger, forcing her expression into one of pleasant neutrality.

'And she made the allegation after seeing me on television, is that right?' Ned asked.

'Yes. It's not uncommon for victims to have flashbacks,' she said. 'Seeing you again, if only on screen, may well have been traumatic.'

Ned rubbed his chin thoughtfully. 'I wonder if she's had a more up-to-date psychiatric evaluation?' He turned to his solicitor. 'Would we be able to ascertain that?'

Below the table Blake clenched his fists.

'I believe that you don't normally discharge patients until they've reached a survivable weight,' said Grace. 'Is that right?'

'If then,' he said. 'We prefer to keep them with us until they're fully functioning, socially and emotionally.'

'Until they can trust their bodies again?' she said. 'That's what you talked about in your lecture, wasn't it? That you want them to feel safe with their appetites and desires.'

'Exactly so.' Ned betrayed no discomfort at his earlier choice of words.

'So why did you discharge Karen Wheeler before she had reached the target weight you yourself had set in her notes?'

Ned frowned. 'Did I?'

'Yes.' She waited for him to fill the silence.

'I don't remember.'

'Yet you never forget a patient?'

'I haven't forgotten her,' he said. 'I merely don't recall the precise circumstances of her finishing treatment with us.'

'Her hospital discharge had nothing to do with what a cleaner suspected was going on behind closed curtains on an inpatient ward one night?'

'Of course not. And all that was perfectly properly dealt with at the time. In fact I seem to recall thanking the cleaner afterwards for his vigilance.'

'Indeed you did. Mr Khan also remembers that.'

Ned's solicitor leaned forward. 'DI Fisher, if your case is going to hang on a misunderstanding that was fully elucidated at the time, I must ask that you either produce new evidence or release my client immediately.'

Grace ignored him, keeping her gaze fixed on Ned. 'What can you tell me about red swimsuits?'

She saw the tiny muscles in his face stiffen involuntarily and a faint flush creep up from his neck. Then he laughed. 'Nothing! What should I tell you?'

'When you take your chosen patients camping each summer at Wryford Hall, do any of them wear red swimsuits?'

'I've no idea!'

'What about this year? It was only three weeks ago. You must remember if one of the girls was running around in a red swimsuit.'

He held up his hands. 'Sorry. Maybe I'm colour-blind!'

'Are you?'

She could see him make the calculation about whether to lie. 'No,' he answered.

'When Helen Fry took one of the girls shopping, a red swimsuit was bought in preparation for the camp. These shopping trips are part of the therapy, aren't they? Are the purchases discussed in advance? Have you ever specified that a particular patient should have a red swimsuit?'

'I don't know what Helen Fry has said, but she is hardly a reliable source of information,' said Ned.

'Why is that?'

'Well, for a start, I believe you've arrested her for murder.'

'Until which point she was a trusted member of your team,' said Grace. 'What changed, other than her arrest?'

'She's been having issues,' he said.

'Can you elaborate?'

Ned turned to his solicitor, who shook his head.

'Are these questions relevant to my client's arrest?' the solicitor asked.

'As Professor Chesham is already aware,' she said, 'Dr Merrick's death may be linked to the possibility of sexual abuse taking place during the camping trip at Wryford Hall.'

The solicitor whispered in Chesham's ear. He nodded before turning to Grace. 'I'm not prepared to say anything further about Helen Fry at this time,' he said. 'I owe her that.'

'Very well.' Grace opened the folder she had brought with her and removed six colour photographs in individual evidence bags. She laid them out on the table. Two were from the family box at Wryford Hall and the other four retrieved, thanks to a search warrant, from the wall in Ned's office at St Botolph's. They had shown them to Crystal Douglad, who had only been able to identify one of her former patients as the other camping trips had taken place before she joined the unit. 'I am showing Professor Chesham six photographs, labelled exhibits one to six,' said Grace. 'Are you able to identify any of these young people?'

As Ned studied the photographs, each of which featured a different teenage girl in a red swimsuit, Grace could all but hear the cogs in his mind spinning.

'Can you tell us who they are?' she said.

He took a deep breath and pointed to one of the prints from his wall. 'This was a couple of years ago. That's Shelley Palmer.'

'Thank you. And the others?'

'I don't remember.'

'You're sure about that?'

'Yes.'

'Even though another three of these snapshots were on the wall of your office at the hospital?'

'When I said I never forget a patient, I meant their treatment, their psychological well-being.'

'Not what they look like? Not whether you spent a week on a camping trip with them, playing rounders or doing the washing-up?'

She watched him carefully, but Ned merely gave a wry smile. 'I'm afraid I just don't have a very good memory for faces. Or clothes.'

Grace sat back, unable to resist an exchange of glances with Blake. It didn't matter that Chesham wouldn't give them any more names; they'd be able eventually to identify all the girls in the photographs. Maybe one of them had already spoken on the phone to one of the team and was waiting to be interviewed. Maybe one of them would talk about what had happened when she'd been alone with Ned in the cricket pavilion. What was far more important was that he was now on tape claiming not to recognize five former patients whom he had picked to attend his annual summer camp. He might have a bad memory, but she was certain that those girls, however old they were now, would each harbour very significant recollections of him.

37

While the detainee enjoyed his statutory forty-five-minute meal break, Grace went looking for Duncan. She found Colin instead.

'I thought I'd monitor the interview,' he told her, 'so that I can feed something back to DAC Marx. Purely as a courtesy, of course,' he added in response to her angry look. 'It's no good ignoring the politics, Grace. You have to believe that I'm just trying to watch your back. If the Yard finds any reason to suppose you had anything to do with those headlines in the *Courier*, they'll be out for blood.'

'Thank you, sir. We're already following up on Shelley Palmer. One of the nurses at the unit had identified her before we interviewed Chesham. She's now fifteen and was a patient three years ago.'

'Good. Anything from the search team at his flat yet?'

'Not so far,' she said. 'And it'll be a day or so before we can see what's on his computer and other electronic devices.'

'Let's hope he has an interesting browsing history,' he said drolly. She responded with a tight smile, but he was already looking over her shoulder into the MIT office. 'Duncan was watching the video link with me. He was very quiet. I'd have thought he'd be cock-a-hoop at being able to reel in your man.'

'He's been a bit under the weather,' she said. 'Maybe a virus or something.'

Colin held the door open for Grace to precede him, an old-fashioned courtesy that was second nature, not calculated for effect like so many of his actions. Phones were ringing and several members of the team immediately waved their hands, beckoning to her that they had something. Duncan had his back to her, his shoulders hunched over his keyboard. She was about to approach him when Blake stepped forward, a sheaf of print-outs in his hand.

'We've got names and contact details for two former patients who want to share specific information with us,' he said. 'Eileen Hendrick and Gail Roberts. Neither felt able to go into detail on the phone, but both made a point of saying that they'd been to a summer camp.'

'In the same year?'

'No.'

'Did either of them mention swimsuits?' she asked eagerly.

'No, and, given what that could signify, I didn't go into it on the phone.'

'Absolutely right,' she said, recalling the agony with which Duncan had torn his story out of himself. 'Set up interviews with both of them as soon as you can. Let's not leave them hanging about now they've come this far.'

'Will do, boss. We've also got dozens of concerned parents worried that their daughters might have been abused while under Chesham's care. They all want advice on how to talk to them. Several are beside themselves, worried that they failed to spot something or that their kids didn't trust them enough to say what was going on. We have to offer some kind of support.'

'We're going to need help on this,' said Grace. She turned to Colin. This was the kind of thing he was good at. 'Do you think you could have a word with Social Services and maybe a couple of the charities who have experience in dealing with this? Request them to provide some back-up?'

'Absolutely.'

To her relief, Colin went straight to his office. 'Someone needs to speak to Meghan Goodwin's parents again,' she said. 'Chesham has been suspended from the hospital, but if they're still in any way resistant to the idea that she's at risk, we may need to get a protection order in place. We may also at some point have to discuss the possibility of a medical examination.'

Blake nodded. 'I'll get right on it, boss.'

He handed her the printouts of the calls that had come in during the morning, and she flicked through them as she walked over to her cubicle. She felt someone behind her and turned to find Duncan at her heels.

'Can I have a word, boss?'

'Of course.'

Once in the relative privacy of her cubicle, she turned to him. 'How are you?'

'I'm fine,' he said. 'Which is why I'd rather you didn't keep shutting me out.'

'I'm sorry,' she said. 'I just didn't think that being in the same room as a child sex abuser was what you needed right now.'

'Maybe not, but I don't need wrapping in cotton wool. I still want to work the case.'

Grace studied him carefully, trying to decide the right way forward. She blamed herself for missing the warning signs and didn't want to slip up and leave him vulnerable again. Standing before her now, he looked strained and paler than usual, but otherwise it was hard not to see the same dependable detective he'd always been. But was he really in a fit state to know what was best for him?

'I ought to refer you to Welfare,' she said. 'They have very good specialist counsellors.'

'Don't put me on the bench, boss, please. Or not yet, anyway. I want to help put this one away.'

'I know, and I understand – I'd feel the same – but what you told me is no small thing.'

Duncan shuffled his feet and looked anywhere but at her. 'I told you as a friend. I'm asking you not to make it official.'

She was touched by his sincerity. 'Very well. And actually I can't help thinking you would be the best person to be a point of contact with some of the victims. How would you feel about that?'

'Fine.'

'Good. But I still advise you to talk to Welfare. It'd be totally off the record; you'd remain operational, and it might help lay some ghosts.' She hoped she wouldn't regret her decision.

'Thanks, boss. I'll bear it in mind.'

She saw she wasn't going to shift him further so got down to business. 'OK then. First off I'd like you to call Karen Wheeler to keep her updated. She may have sobered up enough to regret her offer to testify, in which case, fair enough. But if she doesn't mention it then I don't want you to either. At least not until we've finished questioning Chesham. Are you OK with that?'

'Yes, boss.' He saw her scrutiny and smiled at her. 'That article in the *Courier* was a real stroke of luck, by the way,' he said. 'Genius, even.'

Grace hid her alarm. Surely Duncan didn't suspect her of the leak? 'If it gives more witnesses the courage to come forward, then for once the press are on our side,' she said carefully. 'Have you spoken to Shelley Palmer's parents yet?'

'Yes. But they moved away to give her a fresh start after her illness. Cornwall. Do you want to ask the locals to step in?'

'No, I think one of us should go. Meanwhile, I want you to write to Trudie Bevan. We need to inform her of Ned Chesham's arrest but respect her wish to be left alone. A letter will be less intrusive.'

'No problem. You want to see a draft before I send it?'

'No, thanks. I trust your judgement.'

'Ma'am?' A uniformed constable tapped on the edge of her cubicle.

Grace looked at Duncan first. 'We're finished here?'

'Yes, boss. And thank you.'

Duncan left.

'There's a Minnie Thomas downstairs, ma'am,' said the PC. 'Wants to know if you have time to see her. She'd rather not speak to anyone else.'

Grace glanced at her watch. They could only keep Chesham in custody for twenty-four hours, or until they had sufficient evidence to charge him, and she really didn't need the distraction, but her instinct told her that Minnie wasn't a time-waster; she wouldn't have come unless she had something pertinent to say.

'I'll come now,' she told him.

Minnie had been asked to wait in one of the soft interview rooms downstairs. She unfolded herself from a chair and stood up when Grace entered, an anxious smile accentuating the fine bones of her face. Dressed in a faded but perfectly cut lavender linen dress and flat sandals, she seemed to fill the box-like room, the air of which was now tinged by the old-fashioned perfume she wore.

'Thank you for seeing me,' Minnie said. 'I heard on the news that you'd arrested Ned.'

Grace smiled back. 'You understand that I can't discuss that with you?'

'Of course.'

'Please sit down.'

Minnie sat back down, crossing her long bare legs and stroking one veined hand over the other. 'I went to see my father-in-law,' she began abruptly. 'He lives in sheltered accommodation in the village. His choice. He couldn't bear the hall without Margaret, his late wife. He's physically frail but perfectly fine otherwise.' She sighed and looked down at her hands and then up again at Grace. 'I asked him why Margaret never liked Ned.'

'And?' Grace prompted when Minnie fell silent.

'He said she always thought he had a whiff of something nasty in the woodshed about him.'

'I see.'

'We should have known.'

'What makes you say that?' asked Grace. 'Have you remembered something we ought to know? Or did your mother-in-law witness something specific?'

Minnie shook her head. 'Toby's beside himself. He can't handle it.'

'His mother never said anything to him?'

'I imagine she thought that would be unfair. Toby and Ned were such old friends.'

'But now Toby is afraid she was right?'

Minnie nodded. 'We all of us just let Ned get on with it, didn't we? We never questioned why he wanted to spend his holiday time with eight young girls every summer, and we should have. I'm not sure Toby will ever forgive himself.'

'You must feel very betrayed,' said Grace, trying to imagine how she'd react if one of her good friends from university was accused of child abuse. She could understand how the brain would just push away the suggestion, be unable to think the unthinkable about someone you'd liked and trusted for years.

'Betrayed?' Minnie gave an angry laugh. 'Us? Thank goodness we never had a daughter. Our three are boys. Ned is godfather to the eldest. We thought he was a good role model. I recommended him once to help the daughter of an old friend. And the girl did recover from an eating disorder, although she still ended up killing herself years later. It makes you wonder, doesn't it?'

'Whatever happened, you're not to blame,' said Grace.

'We should have known. We'll always worry now whether, deep, deep down, we didn't always suspect that something wasn't right.'

'Can either of you think of an incident you now feel you should have reported?'

Minnie shook her head. 'No. Honestly, I never saw him put a foot wrong. But that means nothing. I had a career as a model, started when I was fifteen. I saw plenty then. Looks, touches, suggestions. It's not like I'm naive about what goes on.'

Grace took a discreet look at her watch. 'You won't be the only people feeling like this, Mrs Thomas.'

'That's not going to stop us asking ourselves what we missed, what we should have seen.'

Grace rose to her feet. Minnie took the hint and also stood. 'What about Tim Merrick?' she asked. 'We've gone over and over that evening, but Ned was with us the whole time. He couldn't have killed Dr Merrick. He didn't, did he?'

Grace hesitated. Helen Fry's arrest had so far been kept under wraps, but might Minnie shed some light on Helen's past visits to Wryford Hall?

'You've met Helen Fry?' she asked. 'One of the nurses who sometimes accompanied Ned on the summer camps.'

'Yes,' said Minnie, taken aback by the change of direction. 'Why?'

'Dr Merrick called her that night and they spoke for about ten minutes. I just wondered if there was anything you could tell us about her?'

'Not really. Well, only that she'd been one of Ned's patients herself.'

'What?' Grace didn't try to hide her shock.

'Yes, she told me once it was the reason she went into nursing. In fact I think she said she was on one of the very first summer camps. It's why she loved coming back so much.'

Grace mentally reviewed the images of unidentified teen-agers in red swimsuits. When they'd found the snap of a skinny kid in a baggy red swimsuit in Minnie's box of family photo-graphs Grace had quickly dismissed a fleeting impression that the young face seemed vaguely familiar. Then she'd had no rea-son to make the connection, but now she realized that the immature teenager – and one of the five girls whom Ned had claimed not to be able to identify – was the nurse he worked with every day, Helen Fry.

38

As Grace waited for the return of the car she'd sent to pick up Helen, a line from a poem by W. B. Yeats, *Tread softly because you tread on my dreams*, repeated itself on a loop in her head. She wasn't sure how Minnie's revelation about the nurse fitted into Tim Merrick's murder, but it made her feel some pity for Helen Fry, whose life had become so deeply entangled with Ned Chesham's that escape appeared impossible.

Grace used the time to catch up by phone with the search team, who were still working through Chesham's flat. Although the team had not yet found anything incriminating, their feedback offered some interesting insights. Chesham's professional certificates and awards had been framed and hung on the wall above his desk in the narrow second bedroom he used as an office. In an old shoebox in his bedroom cupboard were similar tokens of achievement dating back to his schooldays. He had carefully preserved several decades' worth of letters, cards and Christmas greetings from grateful patients, their families and former colleagues along with programmes from all the conferences at which he'd spoken. These seemed to be the only personal tokens he had kept. There were no family photographs or letters. When Chesham had been asked by the custody sergeant whether he wanted someone informed that he was in Colchester nick, he'd said there was no one. What had been Minnie's description of her husband's friend of thirty-five years? *The cat that walked by himself.*

The team also described finding a strange assortment of items, each individually wrapped in tissue paper, in a hinged wooden case that bore the ivory plaque of a Victorian maker of medical instruments. The case, displayed on a sideboard in his living room, was, they said, one of the very few decorative objects in the room that seemed personally chosen. She asked them to email her photographs of each of the items and then called Duncan into her cubicle.

'Did you send that letter to Trudie Bevan yet?'

Duncan turned to look back at his desk. 'Still in the out-tray.'

She nodded. 'Do you recall her saying that after she was discharged and back at school, she sent Chesham letters and gifts?'

'Yes.'

'The search team have found a wooden box which I think is where he stored any presents he was given. There aren't that many, and they're preserved like treasures even though some are worthless in themselves. He must receive hundreds of gifts from patients – most doctors do – so why did he keep these?'

'You reckon they're from his special girls?'

'It's only a hunch,' she said. 'Could you bear to approach Trudie, ask her if she recognizes anything from the box?'

Duncan looked over his shoulder at the wall clock in the main office. 'How much longer have we got him?'

'Unless we ask for an extension, only until early tomorrow morning. Just about long enough for you to get to London. How do you feel about calling her to find out if she'll see you?'

Duncan stared past Grace, out of the window at the view of Colchester. She waited, wondering what painful places he had to revisit before he could make a decision about what it was fair to ask of another abuse victim. Finally he nodded. 'I'll call her. See how it goes. No promises.'

'Thanks.'

She watched him return to his desk and sit heavily in his chair, remaining motionless for a few moments before tapping at his keyboard to pull up Trudie's contact details.

She thought about Helen Fry. Had she, like Karen and Trudie, been a victim of Chesham's abuse but chosen to deal with it differently? Although *choice* was hardly the correct way to describe how a vulnerable thirteen-year-old psychologically processed repeated sexual assaults. But why else, facing the possibility of a life sentence for murder, had Helen failed to tell them firstly that Meghan was her niece and secondly that she herself had been anorexic and a patient of the man she appeared to hero-worship?

It seemed to Grace that Helen was besotted with Ned. He wasn't simply her charismatic boss – he'd been her psychiatrist and had invited her to one of his earliest summer camps, where she'd worn a red swimsuit. Had she, like a hostage suffering from Stockholm syndrome, sought some kind of psychological safety by becoming emotionally dependent on her abuser?

Grace had assumed that Helen had claimed her niece's swimsuit was pink rather than red in order to steer them away from what Meghan might have done to Tim Merrick, but perhaps Grace had got it wrong. What if it had been Helen's desperate attempt to maintain her own state of denial that Ned was anything other than wonderful and kind?

Half an hour later an officer buzzed up to say that Helen had arrived, had been formally reminded that she was still under caution, and was waiting in an interview room. As Grace and Blake made their way downstairs, she could see that he was hyped and excited, certain now that they'd break through Helen's defences. Grace had forgotten that during the brief time she'd been in charge of Operation Mayfly, he'd regarded the Merrick case as his. He wanted to crack it and clearly felt no sentimentality towards their prime suspect. And he was right: whatever sympathy she felt for Helen, this was an investigation into a brutal murder.

Helen looked up as soon as the door opened. Her hair was unwashed, and she had dark rings under her eyes, but she sat upright in the chair, poised and apparently confident. 'When is this going to be over?' she asked. 'I want to go back to work.'

Grace ignored the question, holding up the file she brought with her. 'You've been brought back for further questioning because we have new information that we'd like to put to you.'

'Yes, but I need to work. I need to get back to the hospital.'

'The more you cooperate, the sooner we'll be done.'

Helen nodded as if she really believed that she would be freed, that St Botolph's would welcome her back and that life would go on as normal.

As Blake set up the recording equipment, Grace sat down and took the bagged photograph from Minnie's box out of the file. She placed it in front of Helen.

'This is exhibit two,' she said, when Blake was ready. 'Can you identify the girl in this photograph?'

Helen picked up the evidence bag. 'It's me. At the summer camp.'

'Why did you not mention that you had been one of Professor Chesham's patients?'

'I didn't see that it was relevant.' Helen smiled down at the image of her younger self.

A chill ran down Grace's spine. 'Happy memories?'

Helen nodded. 'He couldn't have done it without me.'

'Done what?'

'Developed his method,' she said proudly, meeting Grace's gaze with a clear and direct look of her own. 'I was part of it. Always. Right from the very beginning. And now it's world famous. That's why I need to get back to work, you see. He needs me.'

Blake glanced at Grace. Helen clearly had no idea that they had Chesham in custody along the corridor.

'Did Tim Merrick know you'd once been a patient?' Grace asked.

'I suppose so.' Her tone was dismissive as she returned her attention to the photograph.

Grace gently took it out of her hands and placed it on the table between them.

'Might that be a reason why Tim chose to speak to you rather than to Crystal?'

Helen frowned as if not understanding the question. 'When?'

'I'm talking about the night that Tim Merrick was killed.' Grace wondered for an instant if they ought to have had Helen medically assessed as fit for questioning. 'You're here because you've been arrested on suspicion of the murder of Tim Merrick.'

'Tim never fully appreciated the nature of Ned's work,' she said.

'What was it he missed?'

'That Ned gets results because he knows when to disregard conventional rules.' Helen emphasized the last word as if it should have contemptuous quote marks around it. 'Sometimes the best treatment, the only treatment, is love.'

Grace could almost feel Blake's disgust as he shifted in the chair beside her. 'Professor Chesham spoke about that in a lecture I attended,' she said. 'That's partly what the summer camp was about, wasn't it? An opportunity for patients with eating disorders to learn to trust their bodies, to accept attention, to feel safe with their desires.'

'That's right!' exclaimed Helen. 'It's wonderful for a teenager to be told she's loved, especially by someone she admires.'

'By the doctor who is treating her?'

'Yes.'

'Is that what you told Dr Merrick when he called you that night?'

'What? No. I told you. Tim didn't understand.'

'He didn't understand that it's OK for a doctor to show a patient that she's loved?'

'Not any doctor,' said Helen impatiently. 'One who genuinely cares.'

'Like Professor Chesham?'

'Yes.'

'When you were his patient, did you ever give him presents? Little gifts or tokens?'

Helen gave the smile Grace had seen before, as if she possessed some private and superior understanding. 'If I did, it was between us.'

'Let me guess.' Grace mentally reviewed the odd assortment of objects the search team had photographed for her. Her mind pounced randomly on a pine cone, two shrivelled acorns and a small feather shot with iridescent blue that had been wrapped up together. 'Little treasures found when you were camping, like a feather or a pine cone.'

The smile slid off Helen's face. Almost immediately she rallied. 'Reminders of a special time together.' Her voice was not as steady as it had been a minute before. 'Anyway, how would you know?'

'Did you give them to him?'

'He told you!' she said victoriously, as if suddenly working it out. 'He must have. He remembered!'

Helen's eyes glittered, making Grace think she was about to cry. With happiness? The idea was intolerable. She couldn't bear to collude with Helen's delusions a second longer. 'Professor Chesham was arrested this morning following an accusation of sexual assault.'

Helen stared back at her for a moment, her eyes wide with shock. 'No, that's ridiculous!'

'You didn't see the story in the newspapers about an earlier allegation?'

'It's nonsense.'

'He's taken a leave of absence. If he hadn't, the hospital trust would have suspended him.'

'But he saves so many lives! He saved mine. I know him better than anyone. That's not what he's like.' She sounded genuinely distressed.

'You were his special girl?'

'Yes.'

'In a red swimsuit?'

Whatever Helen had been about to say, she clamped her mouth shut and stared at Grace with furious hatred.

'We've found six girls in red swimsuits so far, including you,' Grace said, taking the other photographs out of her file and spreading them across the table. 'Only one each year.'

'It's coincidence!' Helen almost spat the words.

'A different special girl each year.'

'No!'

'We showed these pictures to Professor Chesham. He claimed not to recognize you. Why would he do that?'

'He's protecting me!'

'From what?'

Helen did not reply.

'Did he ask you to buy a red swimsuit for your niece?'

No answer.

'Was Meghan his special girl this summer?'

Helen said nothing, but the curl of her lip and a dismissive shake of her head conveyed her attitude to the question.

'Is he abusing your niece?'

'That's disgusting!'

'Yes, it is,' said Grace. 'Which doesn't mean it's not true. Is that what Tim Merrick wanted to speak to you about?'

'Of course not.'

'You had a bit of a row with Meghan over buying the swim-suit. Your sister was cross with you for upsetting her. What was that about?'

'She's nothing,' said Helen, unable to hide the viciousness in her voice. 'She's just another patient. He didn't single her out. Why would he?'

Grace was taken aback. 'You sound almost jealous.'

The mask snapped back into place along with the strange smile. Helen tossed her head. 'Ridiculous.'

At last Grace understood the full tragedy of the ongoing legacy of Ned's abuse – the waste of life, not only for young Dr Merrick but also for Helen. Together with the DNA evidence, this was the final piece of the jigsaw that the CPS would require to charge her with murder.

'Is that why you killed Dr Merrick?' Grace asked. 'Not because you wanted to protect your niece but because Tim told you that Meghan was Ned's special girl and you were jealous?'

'You have some very strange ideas, DI Fisher.'

'Professor Chesham wanted you to apply for a better job in Newcastle, is that correct?'

'He didn't want me to leave. He was just thinking of what might be best for me.'

'He wanted you to stay with him in London?'

'Everyone needs to be loved, DI Fisher. Even you, I imagine. He needs someone to support him in his work.'

'So why did he take Crystal with him to this year's summer camp instead of you?'

'He has to be seen to be fair.' There was anger in Helen's eyes and a stubborn set to her mouth.

'It wasn't that he wanted you out of the way while he enjoyed himself with your niece?'

'No. I told you, she's nothing. She'll never see the real him.'

'Like you do?'

Helen shook her head with contempt. 'How would someone like you ever understand?'

'Because I'm not special?'

The strange smile returned. 'If you say so.'

Grace looked down at the photograph of Helen as a child, her immature body covered only by the baggy red swimsuit, her eyes peering anxiously into the camera as if craving reassurance. Grace could delicately remove as many playing cards as she liked from the precarious structure that Helen had constructed piece by piece since she was a child and it would make no difference: her delusion would remain intact.

'I believe that Tim Merrick phoned you to say that he knew or believed Professor Chesham had sexually assaulted your niece, and that you killed him either in a fit of anger or to stop him telling anyone else.'

'Complete rubbish.'

'I'd like to inform you that we now have the results of forensic and DNA tests. They were on blood and leaf matter found in the car that was booked using your credit card and that we have evidence to prove travelled from near your home to Wryford Hall and back that night.'

'They made a mistake with my online booking.'

'I can confirm that the blood was Tim Merrick's and the organic material came from the woodland floor where he was killed. If you were not the driver, can you suggest how else it might have come to be there?'

'No idea!' Helen's laugh was brittle and without mirth – what Grace knew her stepmother would call a 'cocktail-party laugh'.

Repelled, Grace had to remind herself that anorexia was about a need to control, that denying oneself food was not about being thin or attractive, it was about exerting rigid self-discipline. Helen might no longer be underweight, but that was nonetheless the tragedy Grace was witnessing here: a rigid and absolute refusal to accept that what was unbearable could be true.

39

'I was afraid it would come to this.' Ned Chesham sighed and shook his head with sorrow when Grace showed him the photograph of Helen in her red swimsuit and put it to him that he had previously failed to identify the thirteen-year-old patient who, as an adult, he had now worked alongside for four years. 'This is what I didn't want to have to speak about this morning.'

'Well, here's your opportunity to explain,' she said.

'I've been concerned about Helen for some time. I discussed the situation with Dr Rajani. He tried to persuade her to apply for a job in Newcastle to give her some distance, some perspective.'

'You wanted to get rid of her?'

'Not at all. It's my mistake. Vanity, really.' He smiled ruefully. 'Originally I thought it would be helpful to have a specialist nurse on the team who had herself recovered from anorexia. I should have taken action as soon as I realized that her earlier dependence on me as her physician was developing into this kind of fixation, but I wanted to give her a chance. I thought if I could keep her under my eye in the unit, perhaps . . .' He held up his hands. 'I felt responsible, but in retrospect it would have been kinder to have lodged a formal complaint and terminated her employment.'

'What kind of fixation?' Grace asked.

He gave a self-deprecating shrug. 'An escalating morbid infatuation. Erotomania.'

It had given Grace no satisfaction to stand beside Helen as the custody sergeant read out the formal charge of murder and informed her that she would be remanded to police custody until she could appear before the magistrates on Monday morning. And now to hear this man, who had trained as a healer and taken an oath to do no harm, be utterly and shamelessly ruthless about using the authority of his medical training to undermine a former patient heedless of the further damage he would inflict, sickened her.

Pulling herself together, Grace glanced at Blake, who looked as if he'd like to grab hold of Chesham and throttle him.

'Ask her sister if you don't believe me,' said Chesham. 'Gillian has also been worried that Helen's crush has been getting out of hand.'

Grace reflected that Ned must be very sure of the hold he had over Meghan and her family if he felt confident enough to drag Gillian Goodwin into it. The memory of Meghan's politeness in claiming that she'd been lucky to have been invited to the camp made Grace feel sick.

'I don't want to make too much of this,' he went on, 'but I feel partly to blame for poor Tim Merrick's death. Ash Rajani told me about a surgeon who had an ex-patient who was so delusional that she ended up vandalizing his car when he didn't reply to her letters.' He sighed again. 'I can't say I wasn't warned.'

'What exactly are you saying?'

'I fear that you're probably right to suspect poor Helen of killing Tim. She was probably in the grip of a psychotic delusion. I hope she's been properly evaluated by a decent psychiatrist. If not, I'm sure I can recommend someone.'

'Professor Chesham, you seem to forget the reason *you* are here.'

'I'm here because I treat people who act out,' he said. 'They say things that aren't true.'

Grace tried to imagine the reassuring effect that his certainty and composure would have on a jury, and then tried not to think about the inevitable contrast with the prosecution's sole witness – if Karen even got as far as a courtroom. And yet the very fact of Karen's alcoholism was itself evidence of the legacy of his abuse. If Karen and Helen and so many others were damaged it was because of him.

So everyone is lying except you? She was tempted to say it aloud, but it was a question for a trial barrister. Her job was to offer that barrister evidence, or at the very least a build-up of nitty-gritty discrepancies and holes in Chesham's account of what took place, where and when. It was time to take a different tack.

Until now the antique medical instrument case from his flat had remained concealed inside the large carrier bag Blake had brought with him into the interview room. Grace nodded to Blake now to remove it and place it on the table. It had been emptied and each of the items it contained had been bagged and stored separately, ready to be produced one by one.

Taken by surprise, Ned lurched forward as if he wanted to snatch it, but then recovered and sat back.

'I imagine your work is very much your life, Professor

Chesham,' she said, pretending to ignore the object between them.

'Yes, it is,' he said, eyeing the wooden box uneasily.

'Not much time to see family or friends?'

'Regretfully, no. Although I don't have much family.'

'Do you socialize with colleagues?'

'Of course. Sometimes.'

'What holidays did you take last year?'

Ned turned to his solicitor. 'Is this relevant?'

'Bear with me,' said Grace. She did not repeat the question, but deliberately waited for him to answer.

'Actually, none,' he said at last. 'I did a great deal of travelling to various conferences and meetings and had seen quite enough of airport departure lounges.'

'Do you go walking at weekends, visit friends, play sports?'

'What is it you're trying to say, Detective Inspector Fisher?'

'The annual camping trips at Wryford Hall. Are they a holiday for you too?'

'They're for the benefit of my patients.'

'But a break from routine for you as well? You must put a lot of time and effort into organizing them.'

His gaze flicked to the box and away again, then he shifted slightly in his chair, settling into his familiar professional listening position. He gave a slight smile. 'I suppose so, yes.'

'So they're also a chance to recharge your batteries, so to speak.'

'Indeed.'

He was humouring her, but she didn't mind at all. She wanted him to assume that he was in charge, that a consultant psychiatrist could surely outwit a police detective.

'You told me before that the summer camp is about self-esteem, finding physical confidence and lifting self-imposed restrictions and rules, is that correct?'

'Yes.'

'It must make you happy to see the girls flourish and blossom.'

'Yes.'

'It must raise your self-esteem too, leave you feeling good about yourself and the work you do.'

'It's not about me.' He frowned as if finding the suggestion disagreeable.

'But you don't have much family; you don't socialize a great deal with colleagues; you don't take holidays. Everybody needs some kind of appreciation – to feel loved – you said so yourself. You must enjoy running the camp every summer. Why do it otherwise?'

'It's a therapeutic environment.'

It was his pat answer. Grace laid her right hand on the polished wooden lid of the box. 'Tell me about the things you keep in here,' she said. 'For the tape, I am showing Professor Chesham exhibit number fourteen.'

Under his skin she saw the muscles tighten as he clenched his jaw. But then he made himself laugh, his professional demeanour back in place. 'Some of my patients like to make me little presents. They ask me to promise to keep them. And I like to keep my promises.'

She turned to Blake. 'May I please have exhibits fourteen A to C?'

Blake handed her the acorns, pine cone and feather, still nestled within their tissue paper in a see-through evidence bag.

'These must be nearly twenty years old,' she said. 'That's quite some promise.'

'So I'm sentimental.' He held up his hands. 'You've caught me out!'

'Do you remember who gave them to you?'

Ned shook his head.

'Can you answer for the tape, please.'

'No, I don't remember.'

Grace turned to Blake, knowing he would follow the strategy they had discussed before the interview. He handed her the photograph of the thirteen-year-old Helen in its evidence bag.

'Exhibit two. Are you now able to identify the person in this photograph?'

'You already told me. It's Helen.'

'Helen Fry aged thirteen, wearing a red swimsuit. Helen Fry, the nurse you now claim suffers from a morbid infatuation with you. Did she give you these items as gifts when she was your patient and attended the summer camp?'

'I've no idea. And if she's behind this rigmarole, it's more than likely because she's been suspended and is out to sue the hospital and make a bid for compensation. Or to mount some kind of desperate defence against killing poor Tim Merrick.'

Grace turned again to Blake, who was ready with the next two evidence bags.

'I am showing Professor Chesham exhibits fourteen D and E, a tie pin and a man's linen handkerchief with an N embroidered in one corner.' True to his word, Duncan had managed to call from London just in time with the news that he had persuaded Trudie Bevan to help their investigation. 'Are you able to recall who gave you these?'

'Sorry, but I have no recollection.'

'A former patient has identified them from photographs as presents she sent you after she had been discharged.'

'What can I tell you?' he said. 'They were all sweet kids.'

'Sweet enough to go to the police six years later and allege that you had raped her when she was thirteen and under your care at St Botolph's Hospital?'

'These are from Trudie Bevan?' he asked with apparent surprise.

'You knew that Trudie went to the police?'

He nodded. 'Her mother called me to apologize. I assured her it wasn't Trudie's fault and wouldn't be a problem, which, as we know, it wasn't.'

Certain he was faking his lack of concern, Grace moved the box to one side of the table, making room for Blake to spread out the remainder of its contents.

'Are you able to tell us who gave you *any* of these gifts?'

She could see him thinking rapidly before dipping his head to listen to the advice whispered into his ear by his solicitor.

'On the advice of my solicitor, no comment.'

'You have a collection of thirty-two small and random objects, all wrapped in tissue paper and stored in an antique box displayed in your living room, but you're unable to tell us anything more about them other than that they are presents from young female patients.'

'On the advice of my solicitor, no comment.'

'We intend to do our best to match every item to the individual who gave it to you. It will be interesting to see how many of them took part in one of your annual summer camps, whether the gifts in this box represent only one girl each year, and how many of them can recall wearing a red swimsuit. Do you have anything to say about that scenario?'

'On the advice of my solicitor, no comment.'

'Has Meghan Goodwin given you anything that is in this box?'

'On the advice of my solicitor, no comment.'

'What about Eileen Hendrick or Gail Roberts?' This was a long shot, but Grace thought it was worth testing the names of the two women who had called in and with whom interviews had been set up for early the following week.

He showed no reaction to the growing list of names. 'On the advice of my solicitor, no comment.'

'I suggest that you have kept these otherwise largely valueless gifts for twenty years or more,' she continued, 'not because of any promise you made, but because they are of great value and significance to you. Do you have anything to say about that?'

'On the advice of my solicitor, no comment.'

'Apart from documentation charting your professional achieve-ments, this box would appear to be the only item of emotional or psychological value we found in your home. Would you care to comment on the significance of the objects we found in it?'

He shifted in his seat and met her eyes. 'On the advice of my solicitor,' he repeated, his gaze steady and utterly vacant, 'no comment.'

40

Adrian Starling's drawing room was exactly how Ivo had imagined it when he'd tried unsuccessfully to peer in through the strategically placed foliage in the manicured front garden. It was like a film set or an artfully accessorized luxury hotel room. Occasional chairs upholstered in Regency stripes picked out the colours of the looped chintz curtains; antique rugs lay on top of fitted carpet; above the marble fireplace hung an abstract painting in the post-war St Ives style that had shot up astronomically in value over the past decade; and the mantelpiece itself was thick with 'Sloane braille' engraved invitation cards. The over-stuffed cushions would be impossible to bash into comfort and the glossy coffee-table books looked untouched. There was not a speck of dust anywhere, and a kind of expensive hush hung in the air. The only personal objects in the room were the three mobile phones on the polished mahogany table beside the arm of Starling's chair. Ivo looked down at the visual affront of his own crumpled linen jacket and scuffed shoes and suppressed a smile.

Starling himself, in jeans, loafers and a pink Jermyn Street shirt with the sleeves rolled up, had opened the front door and led Ivo into the room, where table lamps had been lit regardless of the evening sun streaming through the tall windows. He was an average-looking bloke, Ivo thought, but with a lively energy that at a pinch could pass for charisma. Starling offered his guest a choice of drink, and when Ivo chose water went to the door to call down to someone in the basement kitchen – a uniformed Malaysian maid who appeared soon afterwards with an unopened bottle of mineral water and two glasses on a tray. Ivo was obviously not going to be introduced to Starling's new wife.

Ivo took his glass and, sinking awkwardly into a sofa, was amused to recall a coincidence he'd come across in his background research: that he and Adrian Starling, albeit several years apart – Ivo was younger – had attended the same prep school. From such an unpromising start, Starling had certainly done well for himself as a commercial barrister before entering Parliament, although to be fair family money had also given him a bit of a leg-up.

'Thank you for coming,' Starling began, fixing Ivo with a piercing look. 'As I explained on the phone, I'd very much appreciate an off-the-record briefing about the story you broke in yesterday's *Courier*.'

'Whether or not this meeting remains off the record rather depends on what you want to know,' countered Ivo. 'And why you wanted the Met review leaked in the first place.'

'I'm willing to bet you're not that interested in party politics,' Starling answered easily with what looked like genuine amusement. 'Shall we just say that my reasons are private. However, as I'm sure you're aware, or you wouldn't be here, I'm not without influence. It may be that we can help one another.'

'What do you want to know?'

'Is Ned Chesham guilty or not?'

'He probably is.' Ivo could see no reason to lie, and was happy to rely on Grace Fisher's certitude. She would never have asked him to run his story without good reason. 'Proving it is another matter.'

'Would the Met prefer a whitewash?'

'I'd hoped you'd be able to tell me that.' Ivo's background research suggested that with Starling's experience as a member of the Home Affairs Select Committee during the later stages of the phone-hacking scandal, he was unlikely to expect transparency from the Met's upper echelons. Ivo decided to prod a little. 'If they do,' he said, 'it won't be out of any great concern for the professor. They won't give a damn about his reputation so long as they come out of this squeaky clean.'

'I wouldn't be too sure,' said Starling. 'It's not only Chesham's career that's at stake. The company currently providing crisis management to St Botolph's Hospital Trust is owned by a former colleague and close friend of a Met deputy commissioner. One of the deputy commissioner's sons recently enjoyed a sixth-form work experience placement at the hospital.'

Handshakes, thought Ivo. *You scratch my back and I'll watch yours.* 'That's useful to know,' he said.

'Your career, on the other hand ...' Starling left the end of the sentence hanging. 'No doubt the *Courier*'s political journalists have already made you aware that rival papers are busy briefing MPs that you can't back up your claims. With a Commons Media Select Committee imminent, I expect your invitation to appear before it will already be in the post.'

Ivo shuddered, less from fear than from the futility of imagining that any kind of truth would survive once a global media giant decided – for whatever feckless reason of its own – to demolish his story. It would annihilate it, using any means at its disposal, fair or foul, and leave nothing but desolation in its wake. Ivo had a certain sneaking admiration for the sheer blitz-krieg effectiveness of such an all-powerful machine – although he'd never been tempted to write for any of its titles.

He found Starling observing him astutely. 'Tell me what you know,' said the MP. 'When did Chesham's offending behaviour begin?'

'Roughly twenty years ago,' said Ivo.

'That long ago? You're sure?'

'Looks that way.'

'And has continued since?'

'It would seem so.'

'Why do you think the original Met investigation reviewed by Operation Mayfly failed?'

'It was never followed through,' said Ivo.

'Is there any suggestion that the original investigation deliberately looked the other way?'

'Not that I've heard,' said Ivo. 'Just a different mindset then, probably. Except of course the Met hoped Mayfly would go the same way.' He watched Starling nod slowly, his thoughts clearly elsewhere. 'They've already spent millions on child abuse inquiries,' Ivo continued, 'and from their perspective far too much of what they've achieved has been a humiliating sham-bles. You can see why they might have preferred to pass by on the other side on this one.'

Starling stared out of the window, barely listening. Ivo experi-enced a flash of insight: what if all this talk of scheming and conspiracy was a smokescreen? The Right Honourable Adrian Starling MP had remained a backbencher since his daughter's suicide, hadn't even accepted a seat in the Lords, something that would surely have been his for the asking. Maybe this wasn't political at all, maybe it was personal.

'Worst of all,' said Ivo, blatantly fishing for a reaction, 'Ned Chesham has been enabled to go on abusing the young girls in his care.'

Starling's head jerked up and Ivo saw the flash of pure hatred in his eyes. *Bingo!* he thought. *Pay dirt!* There was no better thrill than hitting the target. He decided to go for the jugular. Starling had gone to a great deal of trouble, hiring Sam Villiers in an attempt to force the Met's hand and now entertaining a tabloid hack in his elegant drawing room: surely he must realise he'd started a hare and left it too late to get the dogs back in the traps?

'I have a daughter,' said Ivo. 'Emily. She'll be twenty-two now. I haven't seen her since she was little. She wouldn't know me if she stood next to me in a queue. Long story. But for all I know, she could've been one of Chesham's patients.'

All of a sudden – and too late – Ivo realized he wasn't just baiting the hook. It wasn't often that he let himself dwell on being a father – a totally absent one following his second divorce when he was drinking heavily and had hit rock bottom – and now he knew why: it fucking hurt. Which meant that if he was right about what Starling wasn't telling him, then a tragedy had occurred.

'When you've lost the right to protect your own child,' Ivo went on, clearing his throat, 'you'd bloody well hope that the people who are supposed to step in and take your place are doing their jobs properly. We're all helpless otherwise.' He eyed Starling. The man appeared to be examining the patterns in his

Bokhara rug, but Ivo was sure he had his attention. 'I don't care who the commissioner's best buddies are, or what favours are owed,' he said. 'If the Met had missed a chance to protect my kid, I'd want to go and break them into tiny little pieces and then stamp on them extremely hard.'

Starling nodded. He let out a long sigh and lifted his head. The haunted look in his eyes was terrible. 'My daughter, Lucy, was anorexic,' he said. 'Ned treated her. Successfully, we thought. It was all kept highly confidential. I was a junior minister at the time, solicitor general, so I don't need to tell *you* what the tabloids would have done with the story if it had got out. But she was never ... She didn't ...' He sighed once more. 'She killed herself six years ago. We never really understood why. Then I heard some gossip last month from the honours vetting committee that the Met was panicking in case they'd slipped up. Some minor royal had also been a patient, which would have made it doubly embarrassing. Suddenly Lucy's untouchable unhappiness began to make some sense.'

'Why didn't you simply go to the police?' asked Ivo, amazed. 'You could have spoken privately to Operation Mayfly. Given your clout, the Met would have kept you informed.'

Starling laughed contemptuously. 'There was a time when I was tipped to lead the party, maybe even become prime minister. You really think I'd trust the police with my private business?'

But Ivo wasn't really listening. He was thinking about Emily. Starting's bitter words had torn open an old wound and now all he wanted was to get out of there before bled all over the expensive upholstery.

41

Clive woke from a nightmare in which he was screaming, his hands and arms hot and red with blood, kneeling on the mangled and reeking pulp of the body of a man he had battered and torn to pieces. Yet the house was calm. It was barely light outside, the dawn chorus in full swing. Gillian lay sleeping beside him. He knew he wouldn't go back to sleep. Didn't want to, not if it meant returning to a realm of such terrifyingly violent images.

It was Saturday. He didn't know how the three of them would get through the day together, never mind the entire weekend, not with Helen in custody and this new fact of Ned Chesham's arrest solid and real and locked inside the house with them.

He had failed as a father. His one job was to protect Meghan, and he had not only failed, he had opened the door to evil and welcomed it in. He wanted to die, except that would only cause more trouble and distress. He had to step up, he had to deal with this and somehow win back his daughter's trust so that he could keep her safe.

Soon after they'd spoken to DS Langley yesterday, the hospital had emailed. It was typical legalese, the same text sent to all parents and guardians who may have already heard or read stories in the media about a police investigation into Professor Sir Edward Chesham. He has been arrested on suspicion of offences against children. As the police inquiry is ongoing, the chief executive is unable to go into the details of the case. The trust is working very closely with the police as they continue their investigation. Professor Chesham, at his own request, stepped down from his post as soon as concerns were raised and is no longer working at the trust.

The chief executive was sorry to have to write about a situation that would cause distress but wanted to reassure all parents and guardians that the trust was there to support them through this difficult time. Various phone numbers were listed in case Clive and Gillian had any questions.

Clive had plenty, but he didn't think Blake Langley, the hospital helpline or even the NSPCC could answer them. Why hadn't he demanded immediately to know what lay behind DI Fisher's questions about Meghan having a red swimsuit and why they had wanted to carry out a formal interview with her? Why had he allowed Gillian to talk him out of his alarm? Why, after he'd read the *Courier* story about a long-ago allegation made against Ned, had he still allowed the man to enter his home? What was wrong with him that he'd put some weird notion of politeness or deference or loyalty before the rage he'd just experienced in his nightmare against anyone who laid a finger on his precious daughter?

And other questions he wasn't sure he'd ever want truthful answers to. *Had* Ned laid a finger on Meghan? And if so, why hadn't she run to her dad? Was it something to do with Helen?

If Helen really had killed Tim Merrick, was Meghan trying to protect her for some reason? Or was she afraid, too afraid even to tell her daddy? Or had he simply failed completely as a father?

He slipped out of bed, grabbed last night's jeans and T-shirt from the chair and crept out to the silent landing, where he pulled them on. He tiptoed over to Meghan's bedroom and pushed the door open enough to look in at her in her single bed. He thought his heart would burst with the pain of having let her down. She was so young and small and tender, her mouth slightly open in sleep like when she was a baby. It felt like yesterday that she used to nestle her head into his neck, when he felt like even the brush of his unshaven chin was too rough for her delicate existence.

If something had happened, why hadn't she told him? Why hadn't he pressed her harder about the camping trip, about Dr Merrick's death? Why didn't she trust him enough to come to him for help?

They would have to talk. He would have to find the words to ask. He was desperate to hold her, to scoop her into his arms and hug her and tell her that he would make everything all right, that Daddy would chase away all the nasty monsters. But the sharpest pain was the fear that if he touched her, he'd remind her of Ned. Would she think that *he* was like that? How would he ever know?

He pulled her door to and went downstairs, his bare feet making no noise on the carpeted treads. The kitchen would provide a temporary refuge until his wife and child woke up. It couldn't be true. Ned hadn't touched their daughter. They'd have noticed *something*, either in him or in her. Some instinct would have kicked in, and they'd have known not to trust him. And if she'd been . . . been *hurt* in any way, they'd have felt her distress. How could they not?

But that was the heart of the trouble: that instinct to look away, to pretend nothing had happened, that Meghan could not have been harmed, that they could not have got it so wrong. It was that psychological survival mechanism that they now had to guard against. It was time to confront what could not be faced.

Clive sat down at the table, staring sightlessly at some coloured mugs on a row of hooks. He felt helpless. He had never imagined that helplessness could feel so overwhelming, so frightening. It would be easier if he could fix on a target, someone to blame: the hospital, Gillian, Helen. His mind shied away from blaming Ned. If he did that, he'd be back in the reeking, bloody world of his nightmare. If he blamed Ned, he'd have to let himself think about what Ned might have done to Meghan, about the cricket pavilion at Wryford Hall or some shady corner behind some outbuildings, or his hands under the water as Meghan splashed in the lake in her red swimsuit. That way madness lay. Such thoughts would crack his skull in two. He couldn't go there.

He understood better now why Gillian had sworn that there couldn't be a word of truth in the *Courier* story. She'd known Ned since she was at school, when Helen was anorexic and her parents had been at their wits' end – just as he and Gillian had been with Meghan – and Ned had taken Helen's illness off *their* hands just as he had taken Meghan's illness off theirs. Ned would come to their house, Gillian said, just like he turned up here, and take Helen out for the day.

After reading the email from the hospital, Gillian had

explained how ashamed she'd been at the time when she'd felt such relief at Ned carrying Helen off to Wryford Hall for a week and she'd been able to have her parents to herself, how deeply she'd resented her sister for always being the centre of attention while she just had to get on with it. Yesterday she'd admitted for the first time how jealous she'd been that Ned had never taken any notice of her and how, when he agreed to take Meghan on as a patient, and seemed to care about her so much, she'd felt validated at last.

It was a sick, toxic mess that he'd elected to ignore. He'd chosen to go off to work, where he could grumble safely about having to make a living. In reality he'd walked away and left the door wide open for Ned to come and go as he pleased.

Yesterday Gillian had tried to convince herself that it could still turn out OK. Her parents, both sensible people, had trusted Ned just as they had. If he had abused Helen, why would she have worked so hard to get a job in his unit? How could she possibly have worked alongside him for the past four years and not noticed anything at all? Surely, if she'd had the slightest doubt, she'd never have pulled strings to have Meghan admitted to Ned's care?

With only a little shame Clive realized that he no longer cared about Helen. All that mattered was Meghan. Yet the question remained: why was Helen accused of doing to Tim Merrick exactly what Clive in his nightmare had just done to Ned?

42

Grace was surprised when Blake walked into the office late on Saturday afternoon. With Helen Fry in custody and Ned Chesham released on police bail pending further inquiries, there was no special reason for either of them to come into work over the weekend.

'What are you doing here?' She found herself idly speculating whether his appearance meant there was no one at home to miss him on a summer evening, but then dismissed the thought as none of her business.

He raised an eyebrow. 'I could ask the same of you, boss.'

She smiled, reluctant to admit that she was checking through the calls and emails that had been received since Thursday: she'd hate Blake or anyone else on her team to assume she was duplicating their work because she didn't trust them to do it properly. The truth was that, finding no peace at home, it had been less stressful to come in to join the duty staff in the almost-empty office and keep busy. 'Couldn't sit at home and twiddle my thumbs any longer,' she told him.

'Nor me,' he said. 'Anything from Duncan?'

'Not yet.' He had stayed the night in London so he could travel down to Cornwall to speak to Shelley Palmer's family. Blake knew as well as she did that Duncan's conversation with them might crack open the case against Chesham.

'Found anything?' he asked, glancing at the mound of paperwork on her desk.

'There are the usual screeds that almost certainly have nothing to do with our case. Then there are several women who say they were former patients and claim they always had their suspicions about Chesham, although nothing happened to them and they can't name anyone they thought for certain was a victim. The four names they give will need to be checked out thoroughly before we can make any kind of approach, although one name is mentioned twice, which is interesting.'

'Any dates given?' asked Blake. 'Any other corroboration?'

'Not everyone gives dates, but we can follow that up. What's interesting is that the dates we do have continue to suggest that he chose only one girl a year. If so, there's a pattern to his behaviour, and that gives us something to build on. A critical mass of evidence, even if it's largely circumstantial, may be enough to sway a jury.'

'Similar details will make each personal testimony all the more effective.'

'Exactly,' she said. 'It also means we can concentrate our resources on the eight patients he took to the summer camp each year. His annual special girl is very likely to be among them.'

'We've got interviews lined up on Monday morning with Eileen Hendrick and Gail Roberts,' he said. 'If they tell us they were abused and corroborate the accounts we already have, then this becomes a major inquiry.'

'St Botolph's has agreed to help contact former members of staff who worked on the unit. Their recollections will all help add to the jigsaw.' Grace turned her head from side to side, jiggling her neck to free the stiffness in her shoulders. 'I so hated letting him walk out of here this morning.'

'Don't worry, boss. We'll nail him.'

Grace smiled. It was what Keith Stalgood had said to her that sunny morning in his back garden. It seemed a long time ago, although in reality little more than a fortnight had passed.

'I mean it,' Blake said. 'It's only a matter of time. You were right not to give up. He's a serial rapist. He's going to get banged up and discover all the joys of a segregation unit.'

'I hope so.'

He looked at his watch. 'Look, what say we get out of here? Go get a drink or something.'

She hesitated. If it had been Duncan asking, or Lance Cooper, Blake's predecessor, she would have agreed without a second thought. The true reason for her indecision – that she was beginning to find him attractive – made her awkward, although he didn't appear to notice.

'Yes.' She hoped she wasn't making a mistake. 'That would be nice.'

Blake took her to a bar in Colchester she'd not discovered. A wooden counter stretched to the far end of a long narrow space with an attractive display of bottles and glasses on the wall behind the bar. Some laid-back Motown was playing in the background. They slipped into one of the few unoccupied booths with brown leather banquettes that lined the other wall. Despite the daylight outside, a candle on the table glowed in an orange glass holder. Looking around she saw a mainly youngish crowd talking and laughing at a noise level that felt pleasant and relaxed.

'They do good cocktails here,' he said as a waitress with braided hair and purple lipstick came to take their order. 'I'll have a Tom Collins.'

'And a Manhattan,' said Grace.

'Good choice.' He smiled at her. She'd been noticing for a while now that she liked his smile. He had nice eyes too. She reminded herself sternly that this was not a date and Detective Sergeant Langley was oblivious to her thoughts.

Three Manhattans later she didn't care. Blake was good company. What she'd taken for scorn hid a droll, clever sense of humour, and he chatted easily about topics that steered clear of work or office gossip. She soon realized she was enjoying herself in a way she had never really done since she'd come to Colchester. The last time she'd kicked back like this had been during the good days of her marriage, when she and Trev had regularly hung out with their police colleagues and she'd felt anchored to something solid and supportive. But, she told herself, the fact that that illusion had been destroyed and she'd found herself outside the magic circle was no reason to fear history would repeat itself, and so when Blake said he knew a club nearby that played good dance music she went along happily.

He had good moves and they danced together easily. It was bliss to empty her mind, to laugh and sway to the different rhythms. It was impossible to hear themselves speak so they communicated by touch: her hand on his arm, his on her shoulder or the small of her back, his hand taking hers as, both tiring, he pulled her outside into the fresh air of the street. The night was balmy, the sky velvety and awash with stars. It took no conscious decision for them to start kissing. The vague thought that this wasn't a good idea was banished when Blake hailed a taxi and they tumbled into it. He held her hand during the drive to Wivenhoe, turning to kiss her only once, and she felt her whole body thrum with anticipation. As soon as her front door closed behind them, they began to pull off each other's clothes.

Grace woke in the morning to the buzz of her phone, which seemed to be coming from the landing outside her bedroom. Her eyelids were heavy as she struggled up out of a deep and refreshing sleep. She turned to see Blake's shoulder rise from the pillow. A line above his biceps marked where the short sleeve of his polo shirt protected his skin from the sun, and – as she had discovered last night – he had the delicate tracery of a tree inked on his shoulder. She smiled to herself. However unwise their actions, right now she didn't care and had no regrets.

Naked, she slipped out from under the duvet and located her phone, which was on the floor beside the last of their discarded clothes. Two missed calls. She didn't recognize the number, but the code was familiar – Maidstone. She grabbed her robe from the back of the bathroom door and, going downstairs, pressed redial.

'Grace Fisher?' The woman's voice was also familiar, but she couldn't immediately place it. 'This is DS Margie Lowe.'

Margie! Of course she knew the voice. Margie had been her best friend, a witness at her wedding to Trev Haynes. It had been Margie's choice to side with the group that had vilified her as a whistleblower that had cut the deepest.

'Hello, Margie,' she said as neutrally as she could manage. 'How can I help you?'

'I'm calling about Karen Wheeler,' said Margie, also keeping it formal. 'Does the name mean anything to you?'

'Yes,' said Grace, alarm bells beginning to ring. 'She's a witness in a current inquiry.'

'Then it's bad news, I'm afraid. She was found dead in her flat early this morning.'

'How?' She looked up at the wall clock – they had slept late. 'What happened?'

'There'll be a coroner's post mortem, but it seems simple enough. A neighbour complained about loud music playing all night, looked in through her window and saw her on the floor. Empty brandy and vodka bottles beside her. Cause of death appears to be suffocation following inhalation of vomit.'

'How did you know to get hold of me?'

'She was writing something addressed to you.'

'A suicide note?' Grace breathed in sharply.

'More like a kind of witness statement. We'll send you a copy.'

'Thank you.' Grace was too busy thinking about Karen, about whether Ned Chesham could have got to her in some way, to hear what Margie was saying. She apologized and asked her to repeat it.

'She'd been doorstepped, apparently,' Margie said with obvious distaste, as if this must all be Grace's fault. 'Had a couple of journalists banging on her door all day yesterday.'

'Poor woman,' Grace said with a sigh, wondering how on earth the press could have obtained Karen's name. Behind her she heard Blake descending the stairs. 'Will you keep me informed?'

'Yes.' There was a pause. 'How are you?'

'Very well.' Grace no longer smarted too painfully at Margie's disloyalty, but neither did she feel responsible for any regrets her former friend might have. Besides, Blake was standing close behind her. 'I have to go,' she said. 'Goodbye, DS Lowe.'

The other woman hung up without saying goodbye. Grace realized with relief that she no longer cared about the events of two years ago.

'Trouble?' asked Blake.

She turned to him. He had pulled on jeans but was barefoot and bare-chested.

'Yes,' she said as he reached out to her. 'Karen Wheeler's dead. Looks like she went off on one binge too many.'

'So we've lost our witness.'

It wasn't how Grace wanted to think about a young woman's messy and unnecessary death, but he was right. 'I'd like to hear how Duncan's got on,' she said.

'Too early to call him?'

'No.'

Before she could connect to his number Blake took the phone out of her hands and placed it on the kitchen table. He put his hands around her waist and pulled her into a kiss. Grace let herself relax, enjoying the memory of last night's sensations. Eventually he let her go.

'I'll put the kettle on while you call Duncan,' he told her, dropping an extra kiss on her forehead.

After several rings Duncan's phone went to voicemail. She felt bad about leaving such news in a message, but Blake would think it odd if she didn't share this latest development. She briefly explained about Karen and asked Duncan to call her back, then turned to Blake. 'Never mind,' she said, keeping her tone light. 'I'll try him again later.'

43

If the story hadn't been big before, it was now. Ivo found the media pack tightly corralled on the pavement either side of the portico entrance to the 1930s apartment block where Ned Chesham had lived and died. Invoking the unspoken privilege bestowed by the more long-standing crime hacks on the reporter who had broken the initial story, he was able to jostle his way to the front of the scrum without too many sharp elbows bruising his ribs. He doubted that the sports master at his minor public school would ever have foreseen the true benefits derived from all those cheerless afternoons spent on a waterlogged rugby pitch.

So Ned Chesham was dead, and they'd all been cheated out of a good trial and all that satisfying post-verdict gloating and poring over the most salacious details. At least it wasn't suicide, which would have been disappointing. He'd been killed, which was a turn-up for the books. Robbed of a trial, you couldn't beat a good murder for pulling in readers and keeping your editor happy.

Ivo had already overheard enough to learn that Ned's body had been discovered at nine that Monday morning when his cleaner had let herself into the fourth-floor flat and tripped over it. Since then, it was unlikely that anyone had been allowed inside the building other than those invited by the Met's Homicide Command. Their forensic van, parked right outside on double yellow lines, was difficult to miss. He also saw that two TV satellite vans had bagged the nearest metered spaces further down the street. The networks concerned would pay as many parking fines as it took to remain there for days if that was what was required to shut out the competition.

All eyes turned to the main entrance as DCI Harry Desai emerged through the curlicued art deco wrought-iron and glass doors wearing a white forensic suit. The entire pack surged forward, taking Ivo with it. The senior investigating officer caught Ivo's eye but did not acknowledge him, then waved his hands dismissively and shook his head, not even bothering with 'No comment.'

'Can you confirm it's Edward Chesham?' shouted one of the TV reporters.

'Is his murder linked to Operation Mayfly?' called another.

'How was he killed?'

'How long has he been dead?'

The rear doors of the forensic van opened long enough to admit the detective and closed behind him as decisively as the entrance to a stone tomb in an adventure movie.

Ivo approved of Harry Desai. He was smart and a good enough thief-taker to have ridden out the behind-his-back whispers that he'd been fast-tracked only because it was good PR for the Met to be seen to promote ethnic-minority officers. Whatever his rank, Desai must know he'd always remain an outsider, which Ivo reckoned had to be a good thing: if he wasn't going to be invited to play golf, then the only way to keep afloat in the rough waters of the Met was to keep his nose clean and stay honest.

Ivo became aware of another groundswell of attention behind him, this time directed towards a red-faced young man panting with exertion and excitement. He was dressed in khaki with the strap of his leather satchel slung across his chest like a bandolier – clearly some media outlet's latest work-experience kid, who seemed to think his next assignment would be a war zone.

'I tracked down the cleaning agency,' he was telling all and sundry, oblivious to his mentor, who was desperately trying to shut him up. 'She told them there'd been a lot of blood and a big knife on the floor.'

Too late the kid's mentor hustled him away, all but shoving a hand over his mouth. The unfortunate intern's eagerness had just blown out of the water any hope of being rewarded for his scoop with a paid job. It was tough, but some people just had to learn the hard way.

So the professor had been knifed to death – Ivo assumed, given that he must have opened his door and let the person in willingly, by someone he knew. Well, there would be no shortage of suspects if all the unpleasantness was true, as Ivo had little doubt it was. Although that didn't necessarily mean that other media outlets would choose to take the same line. Ned Chesham's guilt or innocence could still be made to go either way. Ivo smiled at the image of the obituary writers busy scratching their heads and ransacking their arsenals of euphemisms just so their title didn't get caught out on the wrong side of the fence.

On the other hand, with Chesham dead all sorts of people could now say whatever they liked about him without fear of expensive libel suits. Yet Ivo was far from sure that the great British public could stomach another frenzy like the one that had followed Jimmy Savile's death. High-profile parents wouldn't want their daughters plastered over the front pages as victims of yet another child sex abuser who got away with it for years, and there was no lack of vested interests that would far rather see the whole mess swept under the carpet, not least the NHS hospital for whom Chesham had acted as a goodwill ambassador.

It was Grace Fisher he most wanted to speak to, but this wasn't her turf and he didn't expect her to put in an appearance. He hoped Ned's death wouldn't find a way to rebound badly on her.

His phone buzzed in his pocket. He took it out and looked at the screen, then shouldered his way out of the scrum to where he could speak without being overheard.

'I just heard the news,' Adrian Starling said without preamble. 'I'm outside his flat.'

'What are they saying?'

'Not yet officially confirmed, but knifed to death. No sign of forced entry. Care to give me a comment?'

'I thought our discussion had been off the record?'

'This is different. Don't suppose you have any kind of handle on who did this?'

Starling ended the call. *Typical politician*, thought Ivo. Couldn't bring himself to answer a straight question.

44

Clive walked out of his line manager's office knowing that this time the firm would find a way to fire him for sure. He had arrived late this morning because he'd had to stay at home to look after Meghan while his wife went to the magistrates' court, where as expected Helen had been remanded and her case sent to the crown court. Now he'd just told his line manager that he'd have to leave early too. He no longer cared about losing his job. There was only so much he could care about at any one time, and unemployment seemed the least of his worries.

Gillian had come home distraught that Helen had been refused bail and taken away to prison. Helen wasn't exactly high on his list of priorities right now, but it was as though Gillian still hadn't grasped that her sister had quite probably killed someone.

By the end of the weekend Clive could not look at his wife without imagining her with her eyes shut, fingers in her ears, loudly singing, 'La-la-la!'. She had made sure it was impossible for him to speak properly with Meghan. Gillian was always there, policing him, refusing to mention her sister or the police or the email from the hospital about Professor Ned. Instead she'd found pointless jobs and errands for Meghan to do all weekend – helping to reorganize the kitchen cupboards, getting her hair trimmed, going into town on Sunday to a museum shop to buy Meghan's grandmother a scarf linked to an exhibition that she'd enjoyed on a day trip to London, even though her birthday wasn't for months yet, and Clive reckoned his mother-in-law was going to be more concerned about Helen's murder trial than a birthday present.

He should have put his foot down, but how could he, with Meghan standing between them, pale and miserable, her long sleeves pulled down even though it was a beautiful summer's day? In the end, Gillian was always so ruthless about insisting there was no elephant in the room that her refusal to confront the issue became the battleground, which meant she always won. And if upholding that denial also meant shutting out their daughter's emotions, then, as far as Gillian was concerned, so be it.

He'd tried to broach the subject of Ned with Meghan this morning while her mother was at the magistrates' court, but after Meghan had taken an hour and a half to eat a bowl of cereal, he'd been glad to escape to work when Gillian returned. All that had been before one of his colleagues had come to tell him that it was on the news that Professor Ned had been murdered. Then he'd seen clearly just how crazy Gillian's constant sidestepping of reality really was. It wasn't as though the truth could make Meghan any more upset than she already was. And if this latest bombshell couldn't clear the air, then nothing ever would.

When his colleague told him, for a moment Clive thought she must know how many times he had killed Ned, hacking and bludgeoning and tearing, until he woke up in his dark bedroom with a dry mouth and his heart pounding. As the moment of shock passed, and he realized he wasn't responsible, he felt diminished. Someone else had done the job for him, the job he ought to have done to keep his family safe but had been too cowardly to contemplate outside his nightmares.

Now Meghan had to be told, and Clive wanted to be the one to tell her. If Ned had been more than her doctor, then her reaction would surely reveal it. If Ned had hurt her, then Clive wanted to be there to promise that she was now safe and could finally tell him the truth.

When he got home, Gillian, who had only just heard the news on the radio, was only concerned for Helen and had not yet said anything to Meghan. He persuaded his wife to find some jobs to do in the garden, and closing the back door behind her, went to find his daughter.

Meghan was curled up on the couch in the sitting room. He sat in the armchair at right angles to where she lay.

'Something's happened, honey-monkey, and I'd like to talk to you about it.'

She put her book aside, dug her elbows into the seat cushions to push herself up, wrapping her thin arms around her legs so her knees were under her chin. She regarded him warily. 'OK.'

'Something's happened to Professor Ned. He's died.'

Her eyes grew huge. 'He's dead?'

'Yes.'

'Really dead?'

'Yes.'

Her shoulders slumped – with relief, he hoped – and then she burst into tears. He moved to sit beside her on the couch, placing an arm around her. He still had to force himself not to recoil whenever he felt the bony shoulders and jagged shoulder blades beneath her cotton sweatshirt.

'Do you mind, honey-monkey? Does it make you sad?'

She shook her head, but the sobs intensified.

'I don't know what kind of man he really was,' Clive said carefully. 'I don't know how to feel about him being dead.'

Meghan dragged the back of her hand under her nose and sniffed back the tears. 'What happened to him?' She sounded scared.

'He was at home in his flat,' he said. 'Someone killed him. They don't know who.'

'Like Doctor Tim?'

'Not quite.'

'It's to do with me, isn't it? I'm to blame.'

'No! None of this is your fault.'

'You don't know.' She rested her head on her bunched-up knees, hiding her face.

Clive took a deep breath. 'I think maybe I do, honey-monkey. I've not been sure, and I didn't know what to do, whether or not to speak to you about it. But now he's dead, you can tell me anything you want. And whatever it is, it is absolutely not your fault.'

'Doctor Tim got killed because of me.'

He had to strain to hear, her words muffled into her joggers. 'What makes you think that?'

'He saw.'

Clive's skin crawled, and his blood turned to ice. Was he about to hear the thing he had longed not to be true? The thing that, if he were honest, he'd avoided just as much as his wife. 'What did he see, sweetheart?'

Meghan shook her head. Her face remained hidden, but the tips of her ears turned red.

'Did Dr Merrick see something Professor Ned was doing?'

'Yes.'

'Were you there with Professor Ned?'

'Yes.'

'Did Professor Ned hurt you?'

She began to cry again, but this time it was different, full of pain and shame and emotions no thirteen-year-old should have to experience.

'I'm so sorry,' he said. 'But he can't ever hurt you again. You're safe now.'

She clung to him in a way that she hadn't since she first stopped eating. *I should have known*, he said to himself. *I failed her. I'm guiltier than he is.*

'When the social worker talked to you last week, did you tell her what happened?' He tried to subdue his rising anger that the police could have refused to share knowledge that would have shielded her from further harm.

She shook her head. 'I was too scared.'

'But you're safe now,' he said. 'You can tell me anything you want. I'm so sorry I let you down, but I'm here now, my darling, I promise.'

'But what if they come for me?' She raised her head to look at him with frightened eyes. 'The people who killed Doctor Tim and Professor Ned. What if they want to kill me too?'

45

Grace and Blake were about to leave the office when Colin summoned them back. Someone in DAC Marx's office had just called to inform him that Ned Chesham was dead. Colin did not hide his relief – this was one political hot potato he'd no longer have to juggle – but Grace felt an unpleasant mix of emotions at the news, with anger and frustration that Chesham had escaped justice uppermost.

She and Blake had been heading out with the intention of first driving to St Albans to speak to Gail Roberts before travelling on around the M25 to High Wycombe, where Eileen Hendrick lived. Calling to postpone both meetings also meant breaking the news to both women of the death of the man who, after so many years, they had finally been ready to unmask. Neither was an easy conversation.

It seemed so horribly ironic that on her way into work that morning Grace had been so confident that, within days, they'd have enough to charge Ned Chesham. Now there would be no trial, no closure or vindication for his victims – or for her and her team either. She felt cheated.

She realized she must also tell Trudie Bevan before she heard it on the news and ask Duncan to inform Shelley Palmer's parents. He hadn't yet come in to work. He had emailed the day before to say that he was on a slow Sunday train back from Cornwall, where he'd been unable to persuade Mr and Mrs Palmer to let him to speak to their teenage daughter. Although her weight had stabilized since they'd moved to their Cornish smallholding, she remained fragile, and her continued well-being had to come first. They had, however, confirmed that it was Shelley wearing a red swimsuit in the photograph taken from Ned's office wall, and that while they couldn't recall her giving Professor Ned any gifts, she had gone through a phase of making friendship bracelets for everyone. Three plaits of coloured cotton thread had been found carefully wrapped in Ned's box of treasures, but identification could wait until the team had gathered further evidence. Grace had suggested in her quick reply to Duncan's email that he take his time coming into work the next day after his long journey, but if he didn't appear soon she'd have to give him a call and bring him up to speed.

Not long after Duncan's delayed arrival a DCI Desai followed up the initial call from the DAC's office in London. Grace had not met or spoken to him before and was relieved when he explained diplomatically that as Chesham's murder might well be linked to her investigation, he was hoping to pool resources and would welcome her initial input into his investigative strategy. He was ready to leave London now, if she was free to see him?

Grace made sure she went down personally to greet DCI Desai in the front lobby when he arrived a couple of hours later. Although she'd been grateful not to have to make yet another time-consuming trip to London, she was anxious to avoid any appearance of pointless power play: there was no sense now in going to war with the Met.

Harry Desai was five or six years her senior, broad-shouldered, about her height and with quick, attentive eyes. They shook hands, their appraisal of one another equally frank, both smiling at the realization that they were doing the same thing.

'I've organized a debrief for you with the case managers, sir,' she said. 'Detective Superintendent Pitman will also sit in. But I thought an informal preliminary chat might be helpful.'

'Sounds good to me.'

He declined her offer of coffee, and they settled in one of the soft interview rooms.

'I'm here,' he began, 'because I'm working on the reasonable hypothesis that some of the possible suspects may already be known to you.'

'That's my thinking too,' she said.

'Good.'

Harry Desai inspected his fingernails for rather a long moment. They looked fine to Grace, and she braced herself for whatever was coming next.

'Before we get to that,' he said, 'we should also touch on a joint media strategy.'

'Of course, sir,' she said, glad that he didn't intend to pussyfoot around the issue. 'I can see it's going to be a sensitive issue for the Met.'

He flashed her a smile, relieved maybe that she wasn't going to be difficult either.

'I'm sure our respective communications directors will already have spoken,' he said. 'There's a fear at the Yard that certain newspapers might choose to take the line that British

justice is no longer based on evidence, but on rumour and accusation, and that both St Botolph's and Professor Sir Edward
Chesham's legacy should be protected from those seeking to
jump on a bandwagon of unproven speculation.' He flashed her
another smile. 'I think I've got that right.'

She laughed. 'The message is loud and clear, thank you. What
DAC Marx wants is either clear and irrefutable evidence of his
guilt as a child abuser or for me to shut up.'

'In a nutshell.'

'Well, when we go upstairs the team will take you through
everything we've got so far and you can decide for yourself. How
does that sound?'

'Fine, thank you.' He reached over for the attaché case that
he'd placed on the chair beside him and snapped it open, taking
out a file. 'I understand that as part of your inquiry you carried
out a search of the victim's London flat.'

'That's right, yes.'

'We'll need a list of everyone from your team who entered the
flat so we can identify and eliminate them forensically.'

'I anticipated that,' she said. 'Joan, our case manager, has
everything ready for you.'

'You have Chesham's home computer?'

'It's still with the forensic analysts. Nothing flagged up so far.'

He nodded. 'Although the weapon, a knife we believe came
from his kitchen, suggests a spontaneous act, there may also
have been an element of planning to the event. The perpetrator
knew where he lived and Chesham almost certainly let him in.
He or she must been contaminated by the victim's blood, yet
evaded detection when leaving the flat and so far appears to
have left no forensic trace.'

'Do you have anyone in mind?'

'We're wondering if there's a connection with the Merrick murder.'

Grace shook her head. 'We charged Helen Fry on Friday night, and she remained in police custody until remanded by the magistrates this morning.'

'And you're certain it's her?'

'Our evidence is circumstantial,' she admitted, 'but it's also pretty compelling. Plus there's no one else in the frame. Helen's a nurse in his unit and was also a patient of Chesham's when she was a teenager. We're pretty certain she was one of his victims, but suffers from a kind of Stockholm syndrome and I'm not sure will ever admit that it was abuse. She won't hear a word against him. He accused her of erotomania, and in a way he's right.'

'The damage can run very deep,' said Desai. 'Everyone in the family can be affected by it. It's why we have to consider the possibility that Chesham's murder is linked to potential past offences.'

'We're gradually identifying more victims, but they are victims,' Grace said firmly, 'not suspects.'

'I understand. I have some photographs I'd like to show you.' He opened his file and handed her a number of prints.

In the first one she recognized the background as the distinctive entrance to Chesham's apartment block. She looked at DCI Desai with annoyance. 'What are these?'

He regarded her steadily. 'They're from a surveillance team set up by DAC Marx.'

'But I'd been led to believe there was no Met inquiry into Chesham,' she said indignantly. 'Was the DAC shadowing my investigation?'

'She wanted an insurance policy, I suppose, and to gain some kind of handle on Chesham's lifestyle and relationships so the Yard wouldn't be too badly caught out.'

Grace was appalled. 'She had police officers spy on a British citizen in order to minimize the risk of a public relations fiasco?'

'She didn't confide her reasons to me,' he said drily.

'No, sir, I don't suppose she did.' Grace had a sudden suspicion that Sharon Marx's surveillance might have gone further: had *her* movements been recorded, even her phone tapped?

'Still,' he said, 'she did hand them over. She might have chosen not to do so.'

Grace dismissed her unease and stared down again at the first image before shuffling through the next few. 'When were these taken?'

'On Sunday night. We don't know who among them was visiting Chesham – there are thirty-seven flats in the block – but it's possible our killer was caught on camera. House-to-house is under way, but with people who were at home on Sunday night now out at work, it may take a while.'

Harry Desai waited while she worked her way through the small pile of prints, mainly faces caught as they came out through the doors, looking down at the steps or sideways along the street, some lighting cigarettes. Both men and women, some alone, some in couples or groups. None was familiar to Grace except one she recognized instantly. She swallowed, asking herself for a few foolish seconds if she could pretend not to have seen it, but then realized such a course was idiocy.

Striving to sound casual, she handed the photograph to DCI Desai. 'That's DC Duncan Gregg,' she said, praying that the news of Karen Wheeler's death hadn't shaken Duncan so hard that he had set off to confront the man he'd hold responsible. 'One of my team.'

Harry Desai was waiting for her to explain what one of her detectives had been doing there, and, if it was official business, why she hadn't mentioned it sooner.

Grace felt the blood drain from her face as she remained silent. *Stick to facts*, she told herself. *Don't rush in and say things that will only dig a deeper hole.*

'Why was he there?' he asked.

'I don't know, sir. You'll have to ask him.'

'Any idea what's in the bag he's carrying?' There was a clear hint of suspicion in his tone, and she could understand why. If Duncan had gone there intending to kill Ned Chesham, he would have known better than anyone how best to go prepared.

'I expect it's an overnight bag. He was on his way back from Cornwall, speaking to a potential witness.'

DCI Desai looked at his watch. 'Perhaps I could grab five minutes with him before the briefing?'

'Of course. Let me text and ask him to come down here.'

As she did so, willing her fingers not to tremble, she racked her brains, trying to recall precisely how Duncan had seemed when he'd come into the office.

His shock at the news of Ned's death had seemed genuine, and he'd asked all the obvious questions. He'd looked tired, and she had asked him how he was. He'd said he was fine – it had been a long journey – and she'd thought no more of it. But what if the resurgence of traumatic memories had . . . *Had what?* Made him flip? Unleashed an anger he couldn't control? Turned him into a murderer? Did she seriously consider him capable of that?

Yet ruling him out wasn't her decision to make. She had none of the available intelligence, and it was her duty to offer a fellow SIO all information relevant to his inquiry, even though she entertained no doubt that if DCI Desai were to be made aware of Duncan's history and psychological state, he would be forced to consider him a suspect.

Now was the moment to speak. She froze, and the words she knew she ought to say simply refused to leave her mouth.

46

Grace wished there was a way to manage a word alone with Blake before Desai's briefing with the case managers, but it was impossible. The DCI, now talking to Duncan in the soft interview room downstairs, was likely to return at any moment. Besides, did she have the right to share the secret of Duncan's past with Blake? On the other hand, did she still have the right not to, even though it was not Blake the detective sergeant in whom she wished to confide, but her friend, her lover, a man whose judgement and discretion she was learning to trust?

She had spent most of Sunday with Blake. A lingering morning in bed followed by a long walk along the river, filling each other in on the things that new lovers want to know – family and childhood, first loves and heartbreaks. They had even managed to grab seats for a late lunch outside the thronged pub on the quayside. However, a sombre mood had descended once they began to discuss the coming week and the ramifications of Karen Wheeler's death and, back in work mode, they'd agreed to part. As she'd waved him off on the little train back into Colchester, where they'd left their cars the previous night, should she instead have been thinking about Duncan? Should she have kept better tabs on him, or invited him over for supper when he returned from Cornwall?

She supposed it was possible that Duncan might himself tell DCI Desai about the nature of his personal investment in this case, but she knew it was unlikely. The best she could hope for was that he didn't lie. That he had nothing to lie about.

Did she seriously think Duncan capable of premeditated murder? Too agitated to think straight, she'd give a lot right now to know what Blake's answer to that question would be, ready to welcome the clear-eyed attitude that once she'd spurned as trite and scornful.

As the team gathered around the conference table, with Colin in the chair, Blake, sitting opposite, caught her eye and gave her an encouraging smile. Duncan and Harry Desai were the last to arrive, and she covertly scrutinized Duncan for any sign of how their chat might have gone. He looked a little strained but otherwise his usual self – no one else would guess the toll this investigation had taken on him.

Colin was in his element and, to be fair, he was good at chairing meetings, making sure that everyone felt heard yet slicing efficiently through an agenda. Most of the team who'd worked the case were present, signalling both professional courtesy to their visitor from the Met and a willingness to cooperate as openly as possible. Dealing swiftly with introductions and opening remarks, Colin invited Blake, whom Grace had tasked with presenting the case they had built thus far against Ned Chesham, to begin.

'We believe that Edward Chesham committed a range of offences as defined under the 2003 Act,' he began, 'including sexual assault, sexual assault by penetration, causing a child to engage in sexual activity and rape. These offences took place over a twenty-year period, if not longer, and we have so far identified five potential victims and had been due to speak to two more today. We believe there will be far more.

'We are confident that his offences followed a fairly set pattern of behaviour. There's no intelligence so far to suggest other crimes, although obviously we don't rule that out.

'It would appear that each year he singled out one victim from among his patients. Their stage of development was an important factor. He chose girls who were on the cusp of puberty, with twelve to thirteen being the average age. It's below the average age for the onset of severe anorexia, but he made that cohort his speciality. He would groom his young patients within the hospital setting, getting to know their families and winning their trust.

'The "special girl" would then be invited to go camping for a week in the grounds of a country house in Essex, usually with seven other female patients and accompanied by one or two other members of staff. We believe that sexual activity usually commenced during these holidays. He organized the trips himself, with no official sanction from St Botolph's. Each victim had bought for her, or was encouraged to buy, a red swimsuit. We also believe that any gift, however small, given to him by one of his victims was carefully preserved in a special box he kept in his flat.'

'There are photographs in the file in front of you,' said Joan.

'The sexual offences continued after the return from the camping holiday, sometimes on hospital premises, sometimes on visits to a victim's home,' Blake continued as DCI Desai flicked through the contents of the file. 'We have no reports so far of offences taking place elsewhere. The abuse generally continued for a few months, after which the patient would be discharged from his medical care.'

'You said five *potential* victims,' said DCI Desai. 'Do you have statements?'

'Not yet, sir, but these things take time.' Blake answered with an assurance that Grace privately did not feel. She tried to view her investigation through the Met's eyes: it was clear that she had given DAC Marx plenty of scope to spin it that Grace's decision to widen her inquiry after the conclusion of Operation Mayfly had been wilful and reckless.

'Two of them have independently described to us how they were raped or sexually assaulted by Edward Chesham,' Blake went on. 'Their accounts fit directly into the pattern I've described, including the limited number of keepsakes that he preserved.

'And we are in the process of identifying photographs taken of four other former patients wearing red swimsuits at the annual camping trip. We are also tracking down all medical staff who previously worked on Professor Chesham's unit, and have already received calls from some former staff members as well as patients, all citing moments of unease and/or anxieties that support the pattern of offending behaviour I've outlined. It's only a matter of time before we speak to someone able to identify the four girls in the photographs.'

'Playing devil's advocate for a moment,' said Colin, 'it's only fair to add that nearly half the calls we've received were full of praise and support for Professor Chesham.'

Seated beside Blake, Duncan tensed and shot a glance of pure hatred at the superintendent.

'Nevertheless, it's a compelling pattern,' said DCI Desai, patting the file of photographs.

'The fact remains,' said Colin, 'that if Professor Chesham were still alive, the CPS would almost certainly conclude that there was still insufficient evidence to proceed with charges against him.'

'If he'd lived,' said Grace, 'we'd have had time to build a water-tight case.'

'So you've no other evidence?' asked DCI Desai.

'We have a witness who overheard sexual noises, but the vic-tim in that incident – who was willing to make a formal statement and give evidence in court – was sadly found dead on Saturday. She left some notes in the form of a statement, but they weren't signed, dated or witnessed.'

'That's unfortunate.'

'We also believe that Helen Fry, the defendant in the Merrick murder and a nurse at the eating disorders unit, was a victim when she herself was a patient. Her niece, Meghan Goodwin, wore the red swimsuit this year at the camp where Dr Merrick was killed. At the moment Helen denies the charge, but Ches-ham's death may change that.'

'His death may also encourage other victims to speak,' said Blake with a reassuring look across the table at Grace. 'Women who couldn't bear the idea of facing him in court may now come forward.'

'And I can only assume that any institutions that failed to pro-tect his victims will now hold their own inquiries,' she added.

Harry Desai nodded, but she could see from his expression that his confidence was draining away. 'It certainly widens our net of possible suspects for his murder.' He held up the file of photographs. 'I appreciate the sensitivity required of such an approach, but my team will need to trace and eliminate all the previous patients and their families who fit into your pattern.'

'We'll do everything we can to assist,' Grace assured him.

'Right,' said Colin. 'If you're happy, Chief Inspector, then I think that pretty much wraps things up.' He nodded to the others around the table. 'Thank you all. I don't want to keep you from your work.'

Colin, signalling to Grace to stay, waited for everyone except Desai to file out. At the door Blake caught her eye and, with a smile, lifted his head as if to say *Chin up!*

Once the door had closed, Colin stood up and stretched his back and shoulders. 'Off the record,' he said, 'I'd like to clarify that the Essex force is not going to make any public accusation of child abuse against Chesham without solid evidence.'

'I understand, sir,' said DCI Desai. 'Nevertheless, the circumstances suggest that he was killed by someone he knew, which makes the motive personal too.'

'And with respect, sir,' said Grace, trying to keep the heat out of her voice, 'I am not prepared to doubt the credibility of those we've spoken to.'

'That's all very fine and honourable,' said Colin, 'but it's one thing to put minutiae like swimwear or an embroidered handkerchief and friendship bracelets in front of a jury, and quite another to pretend that they'll carry any weight against a hostile media.'

'If it looks as if we've simply dropped our investigation without offering his victims any kind of conclusion, what kind of message does that send to them?' Grace turned to appeal to the Met detective. 'One of them is already dead, an accidental suicide. DCI Desai has said that he needs our cooperation to trace the others. The history of Chesham's offending and the search for his killer are inextricably linked.'

'Fine,' said Colin, throwing up his hands, 'then it's a Met operation. Nothing to do with us. Although I suspect that the Met too would rather look to the future.'

Desai frowned. 'The future, sir?'

'The Yard has been more mired in controversy over historical child abuse allegations than any of us. I can quite see why DAC Marx feels it's time to move on and not be seen to be getting into the business of further victimizing the dead. Part of her role, after all, is to increase trust and confidence in the Metropolitan Police Service, and I'm aware that the chief constable of Essex has undertaken to support that aim.'

Grace could almost hear the echo of the chief constable's words in her boss's voice. She'd realized some time ago that he had set his sights on a corner office, and it was clear that from now on he was only going to offer operational support when it was politic to do so.

DCI Desai got to his feet, looking ostentatiously at his watch. 'This has been an extremely helpful meeting, thank you, sir.' He turned to Grace. 'Perhaps you wouldn't mind showing me the way out?'

'Of course.'

The two men shook hands, and Harry Desai held the door for Grace, following her out. She walked in silence, not trusting herself to speak.

As she tapped in the code to open the internal door to the entrance lobby, he said quietly, 'No need to wait around, DI Fisher. The front desk will call me a cab for the station.' He shook her hand briefly. 'Don't worry – we'll keep in touch.'

He disappeared.

Grace stood in the corridor behind the door and closed her eyes for a few moments. How had an organization become so divorced from its original purpose that its internal welfare had become a higher priority than murder or the rape and sexual assault of children? And on which side of the fence would Harry Desai choose to stand?

47

Duncan looked up as she came back into the MIT office. 'I've updated the policy file, boss.'

'About Shelley Palmer?' she asked, puzzled. Duncan's visit to Cornwall had already been entered in the file that recorded all strategic and tactical decisions made in the management of an investigation, so what was he talking about?

'No, boss. A line of inquiry. It went nowhere, but I realize I should have written it up.'

'Come and talk to me at my desk.'

She waited for him to join her and then checked over his shoulder that no one was paying them undue attention.

'Why didn't you tell me you'd gone to Chesham's flat?' she demanded.

'It was a spur-of-the-moment idea,' he said. 'I had to get from Paddington across to Liverpool Street station and wanted to stretch my legs so I went to see if Chesham's apartment block had a porter.'

'Was there a porter?'

'Yes.'

'And that's what you told DCI Desai?'

'Yes. He asked me to make a statement so it's covered, and I realized I should have added it to the policy file too.'

'So did you actually speak to this porter?'

'Yes. He'd never seen any kids coming or going with Chesham. Rarely saw Chesham with anyone, come to that. Well, you saw his flat when we arrested him. Didn't look like he did much entertaining.'

'Did DCI Desai caution you?'

'Sure,' he said. 'It's routine. Did you know they had Chesham under surveillance?'

'No. Why didn't you tell me you'd gone there?'

'Didn't see the point of disturbing you again on a Sunday for a lead that had gone nowhere.'

'And when Colin told everyone that Chesham had been murdered?' she asked. 'That didn't remind you that you'd been in his apartment block that same evening? You didn't think to mention it?'

'I'm sorry, boss.'

'Why didn't you tell me?'

'I don't know. It was a dead end. I'd forgotten.'

It was too glib. Duncan didn't forget things. He was one of the most thorough detectives she'd ever worked with. 'Would you ever have said anything,' she asked, 'if DCI Desai hadn't shown me that photograph?'

Duncan's expression changed and he drew back. 'Are you accusing me of something?'

Grace's heart beat faster. She couldn't do this, couldn't risk losing another friend, and one who needed her support, yet nor could she afford to be naive. Duncan's visit to the porter could be a cover story, part of a carefully prepared plan to rid the world of a man who had ruined so many lives. 'If you were me,' she said carefully, 'and had been placed on the spot by the SIO investigating the murder of a child abuser, would you have told him what I know about you?'

'Did you?' The question shot out angrily.

'No,' she said. 'But should I? That's what I'm asking you, Duncan, as a police officer. Did I do right not to tell him?'

He sank into the chair next to her desk and shook his head, more in sorrow, it seemed to her, than anger. 'So what happened to me as a kid makes me a potential killer, is that it? Capable of stabbing an unarmed man to death in his own home?'

'If DCI Desai knew your background, that you'd come from speaking to other abuse victims, knew that Helen Fry, also a victim, had been charged with murder, and had just heard that Karen had been found dead, what do you think he would've made of it?' Grace said. 'Add in that you were seen right around the time Ned was killed and that your own SIO had no idea you were even there, and you have to see how it looks.'

Duncan hunched into himself, his misery plain on his face. 'Damaged goods,' he said. 'That's all I'll ever be.'

'No, no, that's not what I'm saying!' Her heart went out to him. This had to be a cock-up, not a conspiracy.

Over his shoulder, Grace saw people in the office packing up for the day, some already leaving. Blake caught her eye and with an inquiring smile waggled his open hand: *Go for a drink?*

She gave a tiny shake of her head, hoping he'd read from her face that she was having more than a routine chat with Duncan. He seemed to get it, for he mimed *Ring me*, slung his jacket over his shoulder and headed off.

'You do see that given all the recent pressures on you, Desai could argue that events in your childhood might suggest a motivating factor, don't you?' she asked gently. It struck her suddenly and with force that this – tacitly accusing Duncan of a violent murder – was also precisely what Desai's officers would be doing in approaching each of Ned's victims.

'If you want to tell him,' said Duncan, 'go ahead.'

'It's you I want to help, not him.'

'Look, I know what you did for me, boss, and I'm grateful.' He must have seen her flare of alarm, for he raised his hands as if in surrender. 'No one's going to hear it from me, I promise.'

'I've no idea what you're talking about,' she said stiffly.

'Sure, of course. If it hadn't been for the timing, and that guy you know on the *Courier* who broke the story, I wouldn't have thought anything of it.'

'No, you've got it all wrong.'

'That's fine. I get it,' he said. 'But look, I didn't kill Ned Chesham. I bet an awful lot of people will be very happy he's dead, but not me. I wanted to put him in the witness box, watch him squirm, see him humiliated and called a liar and a filthy pervert, no longer able to hide behind his titles and position. I wanted every one of his victims to spit in his eye and walk out of court with their head held high.'

'That's what I wanted too,' she said. 'Except maybe not the spit in the eye.'

He barely smiled at her weak joke, but a little of his tension eased.

Grace leaned forward across her desk. 'Have you ever thought about reporting your own abuser?'

A frightened look crossed his face and he shook his head

firmly. 'No way. I'm not going back there. I'm not making it real.'

'Is he still alive?'

'No idea.'

'Duncan, I know it's not a fair question for you to deal with right now, but could he still be a risk to other children?'

He shook his head in pain. 'Don't, please.'

'If it's what you want for Ned Chesham's victims, then why not for yourself?'

He shook his head again. 'It's no good. I can't. Who's going to believe me?'

'I do.'

'I can't,' he repeated. 'Anyway, I have my mother to consider. It'd break her heart.'

Grace was about to go to him, to touch his shoulder and offer comfort, when she saw Joan walking purposely towards her cubicle. The case manager tapped politely on the open partition and smiled. 'I'm ready to email the log of information received over to the Met,' she said. 'Do you want to check through it first or shall I go ahead?'

Duncan did not look round. Instead he dropped his head to his chest, his face reddening. Grace felt for him: no one in the office could understand why he didn't simply invite Joan out on a date. It was pretty obvious to everyone but him that she'd accept.

'Thanks,' said Grace. 'Send it now. I'm sure it's all fine.'

Joan glanced at Duncan, tactfully pretending not to notice that something was wrong, and then walked back to her desk. Grace was at a loss for what to say. Feeling it was such a waste, she wished she could wave a magic wand and let two such decent, kind people toddle off together to the fairy-tale ball. If only life was that simple.

Duncan looked up at her. 'Are you going to tell Desai?'

'I ought to,' she said.

'If you do, it'll all come out. Everyone will know what happened to me.'

'Not necessarily.'

'I'd be arrested immediately. He'd have no choice.'

She knew what she had to say, what she had to do. She closed her eyes for a second, and an image of Karen Wheeler on the floor surrounded by empty brandy bottles filled her mind. 'Let's give it twenty-four hours,' she heard herself say. 'Wait and see how things develop.'

48

Grace was shocked by Toby Thomas's appearance when he opened the back door at Wryford Hall later that evening and welcomed her and Blake into the cluttered kitchen. He had lost weight, especially from his face; his bottom eyelids sagged, and even his handshake seemed less purposeful. The Labrador raised her grizzled muzzle and slapped her tail once or twice against the floor before settling back to a watchful doze. The cats, curled on the chairs nearest the Aga, ignored them.

'Come through to the drawing room,' he said. 'The girls are in there.'

Minnie was seated on one of the velvet sofas beside a woman who could almost have been her twin. The last rays of the sun streamed in through the tall windows opposite the empty fireplace, throwing their high cheekbones and long, elegant necks into greater relief.

Toby began the introductions. 'Annabel, this is Detective Inspector Grace Fisher and ...' He ground to a halt, unable to recall Blake's name.

Minnie stepped in. 'Detective Sergeant Blake Langley. This is Annabel Starling, an old friend from our modelling days together. I explained on the phone why she'd like to talk to you.'

Minnie's call had come as Grace was leaving the office, just in time to catch Blake on his mobile as he was driving out of the car park and ask him to return to work.

'Please sit down.' Toby's manners remained impeccable, despite the lapse of memory.

Grace sat on the opposite sofa while Blake selected an upright chair off to one side where he could take notes less obtrusively.

'Well, I've leave you to it,' said Toby, bouncing anxiously on his toes. He hurried back through to the kitchen.

'It's hit him very hard,' said Minnie as her husband closed the door behind him. 'Shaken his faith in everything.'

'I can imagine,' said Grace. 'The news must have been a terrible shock.'

'I appreciate you coming,' said Minnie. 'You must be having a rather long day.'

'Well, the Met are handling the investigation and we're doing all we can to assist.' Grace addressed Annabel Starling. 'I believe you knew Ned Chesham?'

Minnie reached out and grasped her friend's hand. 'We recommended Ned to Annabel and Adrian. Now we're asking ourselves just what a terrible train of events we unleashed.'

Annabel Starling squeezed Minnie's hand and let it go. 'He blinded us all,' she said.

'Can you tell me your story?' Grace asked simply. Minnie had told her on the phone that the Starlings' daughter had committed suicide six years earlier, and she wanted to tread carefully.

Annabel nodded, taking a moment to compose herself before looking up again. Her eyes, of a deep violet blue, were even more beautiful than Minnie's, and Grace suddenly recognized her as

Annabel van Velsen, a model whose face had once graced the covers of *Vogue* and other international magazines.

'We had a daughter, Lucy,' she began. 'We sent her to boarding school at thirteen. She was young for her age, but she wanted to go. She was our only child, and with her father's political career really starting to take off I was afraid she'd be lonely at home. We thought it would give her privacy and stability.' She paused to take a deep breath. 'She stopped eating. We took her away and got her into the same day school in London as some of her friends, but it just got worse. Then Minnie suggested we take her to see Ned Chesham. We went privately. Adrian didn't want anything finding its way into the newspapers.'

'Did she come here on one of the camping trips?' asked Grace, hoping for Toby and Minnie's sake that the answer would be in the negative.

'No,' said Annabel. 'Ned invited her, but she thought it would be too weird, after she'd stayed here with us once or twice and already knew the place quite well.'

Grace breathed out a silent sigh of relief. 'Around that time did she have a red swimsuit?'

Annabel frowned and shook her head. 'Not that I can remember. I doubt she'd have wanted to be seen in a swimsuit, not when she was so ill.'

'Did she recover from the anorexia?'

'She seemed to. Eventually she put on enough weight to go back to school. She went on to university and got a good degree. But she was never happy, never happy with herself, never found a proper boyfriend or a job she liked.'

'And you're concerned that her unhappiness had something to do with Ned Chesham?'

'I always blamed Adrian,' she said. 'My ex-husband was very ambitious. And, for several years, very successful.'

'I remember that he was expected to become party leader when they lost power after the general election defeat,' said Grace.

Annabel nodded. 'That's when Lucy killed herself. And he had to stand down.'

'I'm sorry.'

'Not as sorry as he was,' Annabel said tartly, allowing an ancient and deep bitterness to reveal itself. 'We divorced soon afterwards.' The violet eyes met Grace's fiercely. 'Not many couples manage to stay together after the death of a child, especially suicide. If it was actually Ned Chesham who derailed her, then I'd like to know. I'd like at least to stop hating Lucy's father.'

'I'm sorry to make you revisit painful memories,' said Grace, 'but did Lucy leave any kind of explanation, or a diary – anything that might shed light on her relationship with Professor Chesham?'

'There was no note or anything to explain why she did it. She hanged herself. She was found by the gardener.'

'Can you remember if Lucy ever gave Chesham a present?'

'No. I imagine we sent him something, a case of wine probably, but to Lucy he was merely another doctor. She never raved about him but she certainly never seemed scared of him either.'

'It's impossible to say for certain,' said Grace, 'but there's nothing in what you've told me to lead me to believe that your daughter was abused.'

Annabel leaned back into the faded cushions of the sofa, a veined hand to her forehead, as if crushed by the thought that she would after all have to go on blaming her former husband for contributing to Lucy's death.

'But Ned was definitely an abuser?' asked Minnie.

'We have several credible witnesses to that effect.'

'And you will go on investigating? You will find out for sure, won't you?' Minnie asked urgently.

'We will do our best.' Grace was appalled at her own weasel words, but she refused to make a promise she could not keep.

'Do you know if there's going to be a funeral?'

She was taken aback by Minnie's question. 'His body won't have been released yet by the coroner.'

'Toby can't decide whether he ought to organize it. He doesn't think there'll be anyone else to do it. Says he can't just watch his oldest friend tipped on a dump with no one to say a few words over him. He doesn't know what to do for the best. Condemn the sin and not the sinner, all that sort of thing.'

Behind her, Blake cleared his throat, and Grace wondered if he had just been struck by the same awful idea as her, that they ought to ask Toby to account for his movements on Sunday night. Even in death Ned Chesham was still managing to poison the lives of all the good, decent people around him.

49

Grace watched Blake as he went to the bar to order their drinks. It was a village pub, fairly quiet so late on a Monday evening. Dusk had fallen so they'd elected to sit inside where open windows looked on to a garden with picnic tables and hanging baskets, leading to fields and dark trees beyond. The day had been hot, and a couple of tiny bats skimmed the heavy air. Grace was exhausted but had been glad when Blake suggested they stop off on their way home. He said he'd been before and had liked it. It was a good choice.

He stood with his back to her at the bar and she let herself enjoy the idea of his body beneath his dark grey suit trousers and white shirt. He turned, catching her eye and smiling as if he'd guessed her thoughts. She blushed slightly as he returned to the table with a glass of white wine for her and a soft drink for himself. Now they were off duty he'd removed his tie and undone a couple of shirt buttons.

'I got you a large glass,' he said, chucking down a couple of packets of crisps. 'I reckon you could do with it.'

'Thanks. I'm sorry you can't join me.'

He waved it aside, opening a bag of crisps and digging in. 'They do food, if you want it.'

'Maybe later.'

Grace knew it had been unwise to start a relationship with a junior member of her team, but didn't think she'd made a mistake in acting on her feelings for Blake. He had shown himself to be organized, discreet and supportive, and with the invitation to this pub he had confirmed that he would like to continue what they had started – had confirmed that something *had* begun.

Her divorce from Trev Haynes had been finalized a few months earlier, and she'd expected that when she finally plucked up courage to get involved with someone else she'd be nervous, anxious about her judgement, unfamiliar with the rules of dating. But somehow it just didn't feel like that with Blake, which had to be a good sign. And after all, she'd started out not particularly liking him, so it wasn't as if she'd been bowled off her feet, her usual prudence cast aside.

'When I first met you,' he began, as if again reading her thoughts, 'I was all prepared for you to be a stickler, prissy and uptight.'

She laughed. 'Well, maybe I am a bit.'

'Nah, not at all. You're precise and careful, not sloppy on the detail, but you're all heart.'

She laughed and let the chilled wine loosen her up. 'I thought you were snippy.'

'But now you get the true depth of my subtle humour, is that it?'

She leaned over and kissed him lightly on the lips. 'Something like that.'

He smiled. 'That'll do.'

They rested in companionable silence, letting the events of a long day settle into place.

'Imagine if I turned out to be a kiddie-fiddler,' he said after a reflective pause, 'and I'd successfully misled you and everyone around you for years. Must be even worse than discovering your wife's had a secret lover for decades.'

'Toby Thomas, you mean?'

'Yes. Poor bloke. You almost wouldn't blame him if he had killed Ned.'

Grace's longing to seek Blake's advice about Duncan returned more strongly than ever, but it wouldn't be fair: Blake was a police officer, and it would be his duty to report what she told him.

'I did ask Toby where he was on Sunday,' Blake continued. 'You were talking to Minnie when they walked us out to the car. He spent the evening at the care home with his father, who wasn't well.'

'Did he realize why you were asking?'

'He's not stupid. He said Ned's death meant that now he'd never get answers to all the questions that are plaguing him. He told me he got up one night to go out and torch the cricket pavilion that his great-great-grandfather built – wanted to burn it to the ground because of what must have happened there. Minnie had to stop him.'

'It was Toby who found Tim Merrick's body too,' said Grace. 'You don't forget something like that in a hurry.'

Blake crumpled up his empty crisp packet. 'Will Helen Fry be fit to stand trial, do you think?'

'I don't know. And she's never going to brief her defence team to use the fact that Ned abused her as a child as a mitigating factor. Perhaps we should make sure it's in our disclosure documents.'

'Not our job to make excuses for her.'

'No, but getting to the bottom of what Tim Merrick said in that phone call and why she reacted the way she did is a major part of our case.'

'You saw his body,' he said. 'Whoever did that was no shrinking violet.'

'I know,' she said. 'But Helen Fry is still one of Chesham's victims, and I want to finish building the case against him. We should at least wrap up what we started.'

'You want to talk to the two women we were meant to see today?'

'Yes,' she said. 'It might be of assistance to DCI Desai's investigation as well.'

'You don't have to convince me,' he said. 'Although of course you do realize what the worst-case scenario is?'

'What?'

'That Chesham was knifed by some complete stranger whipped into a frenzy by reports of his arrest and our investigation.'

'The urban myth of the idiot who lynched a paediatrician instead of a paedophile?'

'Except in this case,' he said, 'Chesham was both. Another drink?'

'No,' she said. 'Let's go home.'

Blake grinned. 'I was hoping you'd say that.'

50

Grace's morning began with an early call from Hilary Burnett. 'Brace yourself,' said the communications director. 'Some papers have run with the line that Ned Chesham was falsely accused.'

At the sound of Grace's expletive, Blake rolled over in bed beside her and raised himself onto one elbow. She held a warning finger to her lips. 'Read me the worst,' she asked Hilary, her eyes meeting his.

'"An innocent man hounded to his death. An inevitable tragedy waiting to happen as a result of continued police vilification of public figures."' Grace could hear the rustle of newsprint in the background. '"A senseless tragedy provoked by a gung-ho and irresponsible police investigation. Self-righteous victimization of a distinguished medical man. A tragedy for his colleagues and abandoned patients."'

'What about the other papers?' asked Grace.

'Mainly a good excuse to run an array of celebrity photos,' said Hilary. 'Lots of Jessica Hubbard, as you can imagine. Most of them hedge their bets while suggesting there's no smoke without fire. Only the *Courier* led with whether the Met closed down Operation Mayfly prematurely.'

'DAC Marx won't like that,' said Grace.

'No. She's widely quoted as saying that she stands by the operation's original conclusions. You can be sure that if any fur starts flying, the Yard will spin it off in our direction.'

'Do I need to come in?' Grace asked. 'I've got two interviews lined up and wasn't planning to be in the office until the afternoon.'

'May be best for you to stay off the radar today,' said Hilary. 'Let the dust settle and leave me to do my job.'

'Thank you.'

'If you have anything cast iron I can use to refute, you will let me know, won't you?'

'Of course.'

'Not that some of the papers let the truth interfere with a good story. Stay in touch. I'll let you know if anything changes.'

'Thanks. Bye, Hilary.'

Grace ended the call and briefly explained the media reaction to Blake.

'It's not about you,' he said comfortingly. 'The papers just want a stick to beat someone with. They'll be after the Met commissioner or the home secretary or have someone else in their sights. Bigger fish than you.'

'Meanwhile I'm self-righteous and vindictive.'

'Tomorrow's fish-and-chip paper.'

'It's not going to make our interviews with Gail Roberts and Eileen Hendrick any easier,' she said.

'They might not read that trash.'

She laughed. 'You're usually the cynical one who's down on everything!'

He raised an eyebrow. 'You didn't seem to mind last night.'

'Stop it! I'm going to make coffee and then have a shower.'

'I might join you.'

'We have to be in St Albans by ten.'

'Plenty of time.'

Less than an hour later Blake was driving them down the A12 heading for the M25 orbital north-east of London. Grace's phone buzzed – an unfamiliar number. She picked up in case it was one of the women they were going to see.

'Can you talk?' asked Ivo Sweatman.

Grace looked over at Blake, who showed no sign of interest in the call. 'Sorry,' she said casually, 'I think you must have the wrong number.'

Grace put away her phone. She hated having to lie in front of Blake, but there was no way she could compromise either of them by admitting that she'd been about to commit a serious disciplinary offence by sharing unauthorized information with a journalist.

Blake glanced at her and smiled. Did she detect a flicker of curiosity over the wrong number, or was that just her guilty conscience? She wanted to know why Ivo had called, whether or not it was anything more than support in the face of the hostile press coverage. She would have to find an opportunity later to ring him back, which would mean slipping out to a public pay-phone. Blake would have to sleep at his own place tonight. Whatever Ivo wanted, it had better be good!

Gail Roberts was twenty years old and lived at home with her mother in St Albans while completing a business degree at a nearby college. One of the college counsellors had won her trust and enabled her to speak for the first time about the six months of slow grooming and then accelerating sexual abuse that Ned Chesham had inflicted on her when she was twelve and recovering from severe anorexia. Since then her weight had gone the other way as she kept eating as insurance against ever being sent back to see him again. With her counsellor's support, she had telephoned the police after seeing the *Courier*'s story about Operation Mayfly, believing that if she told her story and saw her abuser punished she would finally be able to get her life back on track.

His death, she felt, had liberated her. (She only said his name once, when pressed by Grace to identify her abuser.) He could no longer hurt her physically or interfere with her thinking and emotions in order to manipulate her back into all the self-doubt and self-blame that had kept her quiet for so long. She was eager to tell her story and would be happy to sign a formal statement.

She had been twelve years old. She'd stopped eating around the time her parents split up. She thought the divorce was her fault, while her mother, who became depressed, blamed herself for Gail's illness and saw Professor Ned as an angel sent from heaven to help them. Looking back, Gail could now see how the psychiatrist had exploited her mother's vulnerability, offering lifts or shopping trips or even to 'babysit' so that Gail's mother had the opportunity to rediscover her old life and friends from before the divorce. And if ever Gail tried to stop what he was doing to her, he'd ask if she wanted to make her mum unhappy again, and of course she didn't. On one of their days out he'd taken her to a museum, where in the gift shop he'd hinted that he'd like her to buy him something. Grace recognized the pocket address book Gail described as among the items in Chesham's wooden instrument case.

Until the summer camp, for which he had helped Gail choose

a red swimsuit, there had only been hugs, tickles and stroking of her hair or arms. Then, splashing about in the lake, his hands, unseen underwater, had 'accidentally' brushed her thighs and probed between her legs. In the cricket pavilion, over the course of the week, it went further. He told her that they did the things they did because they loved each other, and that these had to be kept secret because other people were too ordinary to understand the very special kind of love they shared.

Gail had been very frightened and confused – until then she'd never seen a male in an aroused state and had been totally ignorant of oral sex – and his penetration had hurt and made her bleed. Yet at the same time – and this was what the counsellor had finally helped her to unravel – she'd found the attention and the secrecy exciting. She missed her dad, who hardly ever came to see her, and had liked being made to feel special.

He had made a point, Gail said, when they got back to the hospital, of managing to touch her intimately when her mother or other members of staff were in the room, so certain was he that she'd smile and pretend that she liked it. And then, in front of her mother or a nurse, he'd give her that look of triumph as if to say, *Just you try complaining now that you don't like our secret!* How would she ever have been able to explain away the fact that she'd actually chatted with her mother when, behind the examination drapes, he had his finger inside her?

Mrs Roberts, who waited in the kitchen while they spoke, came out to see them to the door. 'I don't want to hear the details,' she said. 'I can't. She's so brave. So brave. I never knew. Never even suspected.'

Grace thought that she looked even more harrowed than her daughter.

As she and Blake drove in silence along the motorway to their next appointment, Grace recalled her first meeting with Ned Chesham at Wryford Hall. She had liked him. There was no getting away from it: she'd been perfectly ready to admire and trust him. So had all those people who had been in such desperate need of his professional expertise.

They stopped at a service station to buy water, and Blake went to look at the display of red tops with their insinuating black banner headlines. Why were they leaping to the defence of the man Gail had just described? The truth of course was that it made money. Plus an opportunity for some tawdry political point-scoring and maybe the settling of some ancient grudge against the police.

They found Eileen Hendrick's flat above a shop in the centre of High Wycombe. She was twenty-eight and also ready to speak on the record. She held hands with her girlfriend throughout the hour-long interview in which she told a similar story to Gail's. She spoke levelly, almost eloquently, while her girlfriend stared angrily up at the ceiling. At the end Grace asked Eileen what had made her decide to come forward now.

'I never thought I would get away with it before,' she said. 'It was only when I read in the paper that you were going on with your investigation even though the Met wanted to close you down that I thought maybe it was safe after all.'

'Safe?' Grace asked, puzzled.

'I threatened him once with telling someone at the hospital if he didn't stop. He laughed. He said, go ahead and try it. He said if I became a problem then he had friends who knew how to make problems go away. It scared the shit out of me. I never dared say anything after that, just went along with it. Especially later, after I read all the stuff about the other powerful men who got away with it for years, like those entertainers and MPs. Maybe, even years later, he really could carry out his threat.'

Grace looked at Blake before turning back to Eileen. 'Do you think he was telling the truth about being able to carry out his threat?' she asked.

'The truth?' Eileen gripped her girlfriend's hand tighter. 'My mum will tell you how many lies he told, but then I guess there's a first time for everything.'

51

It was nine o'clock and the out-of-town superstore did not close until ten. Ivo had imagined it would be quiet at this time of night, yet it was still busy, even though it must be way past the bedtime of half the kids being dragged around by their desperate-looking parents. It had seemed blackly appropriate to arrange to meet Grace in the children's furnishings department, but he reckoned an old hack could be forgiven the small pleasure of a bit of irony.

He was looking forward to seeing her. They hadn't met since Ned Chesham's fundraising lecture, and although in the meantime they had communicated by phone he had a lot to tell her. She announced herself with a light tap on his shoulder, and he spun round to greet her. She wore green chinos that ended above her bare ankles. Her sandals were a stronger pink than her loose T-shirt, and her straight brown hair was tucked behind her ears, from which dangled pretty gold earrings.

'Hello,' she said, smiling.

'Aren't we supposed to exchange passwords like "The tall man rides by moonlight" or something?'

'That'd give the surveillance team a laugh.'

'You're being watched?' he asked, immediately serious. He had to stop himself looking over his shoulder.

'We can get on to that later.' She looked around at the pink princess duvet covers and bunk-bed pirates' dens as if only now taking in her surroundings, and shook her head sorrowfully. 'If only childhood really was as simple as this.'

'It's only adults who believe that,' he said. 'Kids know better.'

She nodded. 'So why are we here?'

'There *was* someone pulling the strings behind Sam Villiers,' he said. 'But it wasn't anything sinister after all, just the father of another of Chesham's victims wanting to keep tabs on your investigation.'

'Who is it?' asked Grace.

'An MP called Adrian Starling.'

'Starling?' She looked surprised.

'Remember, he was solicitor general a good few years back?'

'Yes,' she said. 'It's only that I met his ex-wife yesterday. She asked to meet and didn't feel the need to resort to any cloak-and-dagger stuff. So what stopped him approaching us directly?'

'Doesn't make a lot of sense to me either,' said Ivo. 'He said he wanted Operation Mayfly leaked to make sure that the Met did a proper job this time.'

She still looked doubtful. 'There's nothing to suggest that Lucy Starling was one of Chesham's victims.'

'He told me he needed to be sure,' said Ivo. 'He lost everything because of Chesham. If you've met his ex-wife then you know that their daughter committed suicide – it was the end of both his glittering career and his marriage.'

'Annabel Starling said she'd always blamed him for Lucy's death.'

'Did she say why?'

'I had no reason to pry into their marriage.'

Making way for a young couple wanting to measure the height of a bunk bed, they wandered on along the painted line that led customers ever deeper into the maze. Ivo stopped in front of a display of brightly coloured miniature chairs and tables. The wall behind was painted with giant stylized flowers and butterflies that looked to him like the artist had scored some very cheap drugs. 'There was gossip about Starling when he was a junior minister,' he said. 'Cocaine and prostitutes. But that's pretty much par for the course for an MP these days. Maybe that's what his ex-wife meant.'

'Unlikely to impress his family,' Grace said with the glimmer of a smile.

Ivo thought of his own daughter, Emily. He'd never been tempted to pay for sex, and luckily his few snorts of the white powder had never proved exciting enough to lure him away from his love affair with alcohol. If he had taken to cocaine, he'd be bankrupt by now as well as twice divorced. Ivo's own failings as a father cut deep, and it made perfect sense to him that Starling had hired Sam Villiers to assuage his guilt.

'When I asked why he wanted your operation leaked,' said Ivo again, 'he claimed it was because he didn't trust the Met to see it through. According to him, the deputy commissioner is best mates with some top brass at St Botolph's.'

'He was afraid of some kind of cover-up, is that what you're saying?' she asked.

'He certainly didn't want it all swept back under the rug. He wanted to know what, if anything, happened to his daughter.'

'We told his ex-wife everything we know,' said Grace. 'I assume she'll have told him.'

'If they're on speaking terms,' he said. 'There's also a pushy new wife on the scene. The political hacks are taking bets on Starling mounting a comeback. Maybe this is all a cynical move to put him back in the public eye, get a groundswell of sympathy going before he lines up a new leadership bid.'

'Sounds a bit far-fetched to me,' said Grace, 'but then I'm not that interested in party politics. What about his association with Sam Villiers: how far back does it go? Did they know one another at the time of the original inquiry?'

'I don't think so,' said Ivo. 'Starling's version is that he heard about Mayfly from some chum on the honours vetting committee. He would have come across Villiers in the Palace of Westminster and then probably heard that he'd just set up his own PI business. Perfect timing, I admit, but no more than that.'

She shook her head, still not buying it. Ivo reflected that DI Fisher looked pretty even when she frowned.

'It also occurred to me,' he said, 'that Starling might be in a position to help you a bit by calling off the attack dogs.'

Her eyes widened in alarm. 'Which attack dogs? What have you heard?'

'I meant the unfriendly tabloids,' he said soothingly, but then remembered her earlier comment. 'Do you really think you're under surveillance?' Her hesitation as she considered her reply cut him to the quick. 'I am on your side, you know.' Hearing his own wounded tone, he cursed himself. *Sentimental old fool.* Nearly twenty years between them, and him looking pretty frayed at the edges even on a good day. Still, he couldn't help being pleased when she smiled and reached out to touch his arm.

'I know,' she said. 'And I'm always grateful.'

'So who's watching you?' This time he did take a good look around. It was impossible to say who was a genuine shopper and who wasn't, although if Grace was being watched someone was sparing no expense tailing her all the way out to this land without hope.

'No one, probably,' she said. 'But Deputy Assistant Commissioner Marx omitted to tell me that she had Chesham under surveillance. Or why. No reason why she should, but today a young woman who had been abused by Chesham said that he'd threatened her once, claiming he knew people who could make problems go away. It doesn't mean he did. It's the kind of thing an abuser would say to an impressionable child taught to obey authority.'

'Except that it fits with what the Right Honourable Adrian Starling MP also happens to think,' said Ivo. 'And he didn't strike me as the impressionable type.'

'But why would anyone at the Met cover up for a child abuser?'

'Because they're in it too?'

She shook her head. 'There's nothing to suggest that Chesham was part of any kind of paedophile ring. The pattern we've established is that he chose one girl each year, always one of his patients. The pattern itself seemed important to him. And he didn't appear to keep or share images or access illicit online sites. His special girls were private to him.'

'Like Lewis Carroll and the little girls he photographed?' Ivo suggested.

'No, don't say that! I loved *Alice in Wonderland*.'

He gave her a look.

'I know,' she said ruefully. 'But some illusions are precious.'

'Maybe you should simply have a chat with Starling,' he said. 'I could set it up, if you like.'

'No,' she said, pushing a lock of hair firmly back behind an ear. 'I have to do this by the book. Which would mean giving his name to DCI Desai at the Met. It's his investigation now.'

'Your call,' he said, 'although I'd be grateful if you could leave my name out of it for the time being at least. It might be useful for me to keep Starling's door open, and he won't approve of me blabbing.'

'Fine. Besides,' she said with a smile, 'I'm not keen on explaining what I was doing talking off the record to a reporter either.'

'Anonymous tip-off?'

'We both know it wouldn't end there.'

'No, I guess not.'

'What I can tell Desai is that Starling's daughter was a patient and that Starling's probably someone who keeps his ear to the ground. It'll be up to the DCI to decide whether to take it further.'

'I'll keep digging meanwhile,' Ivo said.

'That would be great.'

He didn't say aloud that he'd happily blast off to the moon if she thought it would help.

52

When Clive first heard that some of the papers were shrieking with outrage about the supposed smears and defamation levelled against a man who had saved so many lives he wanted to go straight to their offices and reduce them to a pile of smouldering ash. He had once thought that his daughter refusing to eat was as much stress as he could bear; that was a picnic compared to this. But then Gillian came off the phone to her grief-stricken sister and not only started spouting about how Helen felt helpless that she had not been there for Ned when he needed her but also seemed to expect him to echo her sister's faith that Ned had been grotesquely and unjustly accused.

He knew it was his fault for not sharing with his wife what Meghan had told him. He couldn't account for it rationally. Maybe it was that saying it aloud would make it real. And if he spelled out the insanity of Helen's delusions, he'd have to cope with Gillian's questions, with her anger and distress. For the past few days it had been easier to postpone the moment, to give himself time to process his own reactions, and to focus on Meghan.

He had emailed work to say that he had no idea when he would be back and then ignored all calls and emails from the office. Preoccupied with her sister's plight, Gillian barely seemed to notice. Determined not to leave Meghan unprotected, Clive had cancelled her clinic sessions and refused to leave the house. He knew he couldn't go on like this for much longer, but even the thought of a strange man passing Meghan in the street was more than he could bear.

He was pretty sure that he'd worked out what had happened at Wryford Hall. Meghan had told him that Tim Merrick had seen Ned doing something to her when they were supposed to be washing up in the cricket pavilion. She must have noticed Dr Merrick watching them together. But now the only person left alive who could explain what had happened was Meghan. If she wanted to tell him, then he'd listen, but he didn't yet feel up to the task of asking her those kind of questions.

In his mind Clive had gone over and over why Merrick hadn't immediately intervened. But Merrick had done something: he'd called Helen. Helen had given Clive and Gillian permission to speak to her solicitor, who had explained the evidence against her – evidence she still flatly denied – so he had a rough idea of events. The police were saying that Helen had driven to meet Merrick, who must have told her what he'd seen. Refusing to hear a word against Ned, Helen had killed the messenger. Her fixation on Ned had proved stronger – far stronger – than love and loyalty to her niece. How was Clive supposed to get Gillian to believe that?

Clive himself couldn't begin to understand what Helen had done. She wasn't so dysfunctional that she'd not been able to hold down a job. Gillian said she'd dealt calmly with the police and the court procedures. She was sufficiently sane to stick to her story of having gone to Hampstead Heath. Yet she had displayed no sign of being traumatized by taking the life of a conscientious young doctor.

Had she already known what Ned was like? Had she turned a blind eye or even been complicit? A nurse, someone who was supposed to protect the young patients in her care! OK, so she'd been anorexic as a kid, but—

And then it struck him: Helen's pathological attachment to Ned must have begun when she was Meghan's age. Had Ned fooled Clive's parents-in-law in precisely the same way that he had wormed his way into this house? Just what kind of perverted history had Clive married into? He instantly regretted the thought; it was selfish and unworthy of Gillian and her parents – even of Helen – yet he could not help it. It was as if he'd suddenly discovered that he'd built his house on top of a tar pit in which lay the remains of ancient but lethal monsters which were now stirring and rising up to suck Clive and his family into the black depths.

He looked out of the kitchen window at his bright garden with its rectangle of lawn and tangled flower beds. Here in this very kitchen Helen had offered to speak to Ned, to ask if he'd take Meghan on as a patient as a special favour to her. Had she understood then that she was delivering her sister's child into the hands of a rapist? Surely, if he was right, and Helen had herself been molested by Ned as a child, she had to have realized. Perhaps it was even what she had intended all along.

Clive couldn't think about that possibility without going insane. He was intensely glad that Helen was safely locked away from him in prison.

He tried to remember how his in-laws – decent, unassuming people – had reacted when told that Professor Ned had accepted

Meghan as a patient. They'd brought up their two daughters in a pleasant semi-detached house in Surrey – Gillian had taken him there once, long after they'd moved away. It still had the cherry tree in the back garden that she remembered, and they caught a glimpse over the fence of some other child's swing and paddling pool.

His in-laws never spoke of Helen's anorexia and had been inordinately proud when she became a nurse at such a presti-gious hospital. When Meghan first showed signs of an eating disorder they'd skirted around the issue, although – he was sure he remembered correctly – they had expressed relief that Meghan would be in such good hands. Yes, in good hands, those were their very words! Surely they couldn't have suspected for an instant how Ned had groomed two generations of their fam-ily? How would Clive ever have the heart to tell them? He supposed they might have read the newspapers and already worked it out for themselves, but they weren't the type to believe the worst about people they trusted. Eyes shut, fingers in ears, 'La-la-la!'

But he would have to tell Gillian, whether she wanted to hear it or not. And the longer he left it, the worse it would get.

53

Frowning, Grace hung up the phone on her desk, wishing that she had been able to share with DCI Desai everything Ivo had told her about Adrian Starling, especially that he had been stalking her investigation right from the start. She beckoned Blake to join her in her cubicle.

'House-to-house at Ned Chesham's block has come up with someone who shared a ride up in the lift with Adrian Starling on the night of Chesham's murder,' she told him. 'Recognized him as an MP.'

'Starling killed Ned?' Blake was astonished.

'We don't know yet why he was there,' she said. 'He may have been innocently visiting someone else.'

'It's a hell of a coincidence though.'

'It is.'

'You told DCI Desai about our chat with Annabel?'

'Of course.' Grace felt increasingly ridiculous not trusting Blake with what else she knew about Starling, but disclosing information to a journalist was a sackable offence, and for Blake to withhold knowledge of her doing so would be equally serious. On the other hand, if Starling *was* a killer, what right did she have to remain silent?

'So are they picking him up?' Blake asked.

'They'll certainly want to know why he was there,' she said. 'The man who recognized him got out of the lift first and doesn't remember which floor Starling wanted but lives two floors below Chesham, so a visit to Chesham isn't ruled out. The man couldn't be specific about the time either, but it was within the possible timeframe for the murder.'

'Presumably Starling will turn up in one of the surveillance photos,' said Blake. 'That'll tie down the time.'

'Apparently not.'

'What? How could they miss him?' he asked. 'Too busy ordering pizza? Someone went for a pee? What?'

'I don't know. Meanwhile, Desai says the fact that Starling's daughter was once a patient isn't enough to arrest and interview him under caution.'

'I was checking through the files that St Botolph's sent over,' said Blake. 'I hadn't realized that Lucy Starling was a patient at the same time as Helen Fry.'

'Nor had I,' said Grace. 'Though it would pretty much confirm that Lucy wasn't a special girl.'

'Adrian Starling wouldn't know that.'

'No.'

'You think he might have gone to confront Chesham?' asked Blake. 'Threatened him with a kitchen knife and ended up killing him?'

'I've been hoping all along that it wouldn't turn out to be a distraught parent,' she said. 'Although with the wreck Chesham made of some of these girls' lives, I wouldn't blame their families for wanting him dead.'

Blake shuffled his feet. 'There's one other piece of information from the hospital records that might weigh against Starling,' he said. 'Lucy and Helen were both patients when Keith Stalgood looked into Trudie Bevan's allegation.'

Grace's blood ran cold. 'You mean, if Keith had managed to put a stop to him then, Helen would have been rescued, and Tim Merrick would still be alive.'

'Remember what Eileen Hendrick said, about Chesham telling her he had friends who knew how to make problems go away? Starling's an MP. Maybe he got wind of some kind of cover-up back when his daughter was a patient and wanted to get the truth out of Ned?'

'Keith would never have gone along with a cover-up!'

'I'm not saying he did. More than likely that kind of influence would have operated way above his level at the time anyway.'

'I'll ask him,' she said. 'I know he didn't agree with the CPS advice not to proceed, but he never raised any other kind of concern.'

'Is it worth passing all this along to DCI Desai?' Blake asked. 'Starling lost his daughter, his marriage and his career. If he suspected that Ned had got away with it once and was about to do so again, maybe he did decide to take the law into his own hands.'

She nodded. 'I'll email Desai.' As she spoke, Grace knew that similar arguments applied to Duncan, who had also been in the block of flats when Chesham was killed. It was not up to her to offer the benefit of the doubt to Duncan but not Starling. Indeed, by advancing the case against one possible suspect over another, she might even be contributing to a miscarriage of justice.

She caught Blake looking at her. It was a slightly odd, questioning glance that reminded her of how astute he'd proved to be at guessing her thoughts. She realized with a pang how much she wanted to protect what they'd started and how much it mattered not to let him sense that she was being evasive.

She checked the office behind him to make sure they could not be overhead, ready to suggest that they go somewhere for lunch where they could have a private word. She was certain he could be trusted with Duncan's secret, and it would be a relief to ask his advice, but her attention was caught by a man and a woman, both in formal suits, entering the MIT office. The woman spoke to someone sitting near the door, who pointed in Grace's direction, and the two visitors made their way over.

'DI Grace Fisher?' The man did not smile.

'Yes.'

He displayed his warrant. 'I'm DI Brian Colne and this is DC Suzie Wade from Essex Police Professional Standards Department. An allegation has been made that you may have breached standards of professional behaviour and we are conducting an investigation in accordance with police regulations. Can you come with us, please?'

Grace looked at Blake. Did they know about Ivo? Did they know that she had leaked information to him about Operation Mayfly? If so, it would amount to gross misconduct. She would be suspended. They could even search her house, treat her like a criminal. And it would be the end of her career.

'What's it about?' Blake asked the question for her, moving to take up a protective stance between them.

'We'll explain it to DI Fisher in due course.'

So this is what it's like, she thought, *that moment when your entire life swerves off the road.*

DI Colne nodded to his colleague, who turned to face Grace.

'While you do not have to say anything,' DC Wade began, 'it may harm your case if you do not mention when interviewed something which you later rely on in any misconduct or appeal proceedings.'

How could they know? She was gripped, unable to move even her facial muscles. *How could anyone possibly have found out?* And then it came to her: DAC Marx *had* placed her under surveillance!

'We have a room allocated to us downstairs,' said DI Colne, holding out a hand to usher her away. 'If you don't mind.'

Grace had no choice but to let herself be walked out of her cubicle and across the MIT office. Most of her team tactfully kept their heads down, eyes on their computer screens, although she could feel an intense frisson of curiosity electrify the room. Duncan gave her a covert little thumbs up as she passed. She noticed that the blinds to Colin Pitman's office had all been closed. *Coward*, she thought, raising her chin determinedly. Whatever was coming, she'd face it head on.

54

So now, thought Grace, it was her turn to experience sitting on the other side of the table. She couldn't remember when she had last been so scared. Her face felt hot and her hands were frozen. *Don't give them anything,* she told herself. *Don't say one word more than you have to.*

She had declined the services of a representative from the Police Federation and didn't want an official 'police friend' to hear what might be said. She sat opposite DI Colne and DC Wade as the younger officer took a couple of sheets of paper stapled together from a file on the table and handed them to her.

'This is the formal notice of your alleged breach of the standards of professional behaviour.'

Grace accepted the papers, still furiously wondering whether DAC Marx had sent a surveillance team to follow her to the superstore where she met Ivo. If they had, and they had photographs, perhaps even a covert recording of her conversation, then this was her last day in the Job.

'I'd like to remind you again that you have the right to seek advice from your staff association or to be accompanied by a member of the police service,' DC Wade continued, 'and you have ten days in which to provide any relevant documents.'

Grace nodded, looking down at the first page of the notice on which the details of her offence were given. She read the type-written words but they made no sense. There was nothing about Ivo or Operation Mayfly; instead it seemed to be about her house in Wivenhoe.

She looked up. 'I don't understand.'

'You purchased a house in Wivenhoe in September last year,' said DI Colne.

'Yes.'

'Did you enter that transaction on the Professional Standards Department register of gifts and hospitality?'

'No.' Her heart leaped with hope.

'From whom did you buy the property?'

Only half-listening, she flicked her eyes to the bottom of the printed form where there were four boxes to be ticked: the two on the right – for gross misconduct and a full hearing – were blank. Whatever she was facing, it was a lesser charge of misconduct which, at worst, might only amount to a written warning. As fear receded, anger took over.

'I bought the house from Pavel Zawodny,' she said, trying to keep her voice steady. 'It had been a buy-to-let for students, but he was selling up to return to Poland.'

'How did you come to meet Pavel Zawodny?'

'I bought the house on the open market through an estate agent and paid the market price.'

'Can you please answer the question.'

'I first met him when he was a suspect in a murder inquiry.'

'And one of the victims of that murder inquiry had lived in the house?'

'Correct. Zawodny was her landlord, which is what brought

him to our attention. Someone else entirely unconnected to him subsequently confessed to that murder and is now serving a life sentence. That individual confessed and was charged before the house was put up for sale. At the point I became interested in buying it, Zawodny had been de-arrested and was no longer of any interest to the police.'

'We are not alleging that the fact you purchased a house from someone who had previously been a murder suspect had any direct bearing or undue influence on the outcome of the inquiry,' said DI Colne. 'This is an issue of police honesty and integrity. The public rightly expect the highest professional standards from their police officers, and having received a complaint, it is important that we take action to ensure standards are adhered to in order to maintain confidence in policing.'

She longed to ask where the complaint had come from but knew she would never be told. 'I've done nothing wrong,' she said.

'You failed to record the transaction on the PSD register of gifts and hospitality. Given the circumstances of your prior relationship to the vendor, it might have been wise to have done so.'

'Obviously,' she said. 'If only because had I done so, I wouldn't be sitting here now.'

'So you accept that a need for transparency is one of the responsibilities that come with the uniform?'

'With hindsight in this matter, yes.'

DI Colne closed the file. 'Very well. The finding on whether your conduct fell below the accepted standards in relation to honesty and integrity according to the conduct regulations will be confirmed to you in writing. Do you have any questions you'd like to put to us?'

'No, thank you.'

'Very well. You're free to go.'

Grace made her way upstairs marvelling at how swiftly ice-cold fear could transmute into red-hot fury. *The bastards!* she said to herself. *The Yard has an active terrorist threat to deal with, internet fraud on an industrial scale, knife crime, drugs, murder and mayhem, and they prioritize precious time and resources on going after me over buying a house?*

Duncan and Blake were watching out for her return.

'Boss?' Duncan's eyes were full of concern.

'Are you OK?' asked Blake. 'What on earth was that about?'

She shook her head, not trusting herself to speak, but they followed her to her cubicle and stood waiting for her to explain.

'It was nothing,' she said, sinking into her chair. 'They more or less had to admit it themselves. I should have put my house purchase on the PSD register, that's all.'

'Someone must have put in a complaint though,' said Duncan.

'And it's pretty heavy-handed to send in the storm troopers in front of everyone like that,' said Blake.

'I know. I've obviously ruffled a few too many feathers at Scotland Yard.'

Blake lowered his voice. 'What if it's only a warning shot?'

'Then we'll have to wait and see.' Looking up, Grace saw the sympathy on the two men's faces and smiled. At least it was clear on whose support she could rely and whose she couldn't, and she could safely bat away that old and horrible feeling of having no refuge and no one to turn to. 'Thanks, guys,' she said. 'Don't worry about me. It'll be a slap on the wrist. I'll survive.'

Duncan nodded and went back to his desk. Blake took a step

closer. 'You went absolutely white back then when they said they were PSD.' He paused. 'Is there anything you want to tell me?'

'No, of course not.' She saw immediately that he knew it was a lie.

'Is it about us?' he said. 'You're my senior officer. They could choose to make that into a disciplinary matter if they're really out to get you.'

'It's not about us, I promise.'

'But there is something?'

She forced herself to smile. 'Just old ghosts,' she said. 'I'll explain another time over a glass of wine.'

She could see that he didn't believe this either, and his reaction hurt more than expected. The Met could play as dirty as they liked with her professionally, but she was damned if she'd allow them to mess with what felt like the start of something so good. She had to be prepared to fight back. She had to find out what was really going on.

55

Sam Villiers lived on a quiet road in one of those north London suburbs that Grace knew only as a name near the edge of the Tube map. She found him mowing a handkerchief-sized lawn, one of the few that had not been paved over in front of the row of seventies town houses. The up-and-over door to the garage that occupied most of the ground floor stood open, revealing a jumble of teenage bikes and dusty sports equipment. He was expecting her and, unplugging the mower, fetched two folding chairs from the garage and set them up beside the front door.

'I'll bring us out some cold drinks,' he said. 'The kids and the missus are indoors so we're less likely to be disturbed out here.'

He went inside, leaving her to sit facing the row of first-floor picture windows of the identical houses opposite. It was early evening when most families were likely to be at home, and she felt oddly exposed. She supposed Villiers had got used to living in such a goldfish bowl, but somehow it seemed an odd choice for a private investigator.

He returned quickly with a tray with two glasses, a carton of fruit juice and a bottle of mineral water. As he managed the business of choosing and pouring, he talked nervously.

'I was a bit surprised to hear from you, I must say,' he said.

'Thought you would have wanted to talk to me when Operation Mayfly was up and running rather than now it's over. So to what do I owe the honour?'

'Adrian Starling.' Grace had no intention of beating about the bush, even if it meant gambling with her future. The moment she asked about Starling, she tacitly gave away that Ivo had tipped her off, for how else could she possibly know that Starling had hired Villiers? 'His name is probably enough to account for why I was reluctant to speak to you before.'

'No idea what you're talking about.'

It was a poor lie, and she ignored it. 'Adrian Starling was seen entering Ned Chesham's block of flats around the time he was killed last Sunday evening,' she said. Observing Villiers' reaction, she was fairly certain this was news to him, and not welcome news either. 'We know that his daughter, Lucy, had been one of Professor Chesham's patients,' she continued. 'What the senior investigating officer, DCI Harry Desai, doesn't know is that Adrian Starling had been taking a close personal interest in both Operation Mayfly and my subsequent inquiries.'

'What's that got to do with me?' He obviously saw from her look that his bluff was a waste of time. 'OK,' he conceded, 'but if you already know that, what you want from me?'

'I want you to tell DCI Desai.'

Villiers remained silent, his body language giving nothing away. Grace took a better look at him, speculating which way he'd jump. He wore a flashy watch, his knee-length shorts had a designer logo, and his bronzed skin was deeper than an English summer could have achieved. He had been in the Job for over twenty years, but what kind of cop had he been?

'I'll have to think pretty carefully about that,' he said at last.

'But you don't deny that Starling's connection to Chesham was ongoing?'

'You already seem to know that.'

'Was Starling afraid that Chesham had sexually abused his daughter?'

Villiers' eyes sought hers. Was there a hint of amusement in them?

'Could that fear have made him crazy enough to kill Chesham?' she pressed. 'The murder weapon was a knife from Chesham's kitchen, which makes it possible his killing was spontaneous rather than planned.'

He looked down at his hands, adjusted his heavy gold signet ring, flicked a bit of cut grass off his shorts. 'If he did kill Ned Chesham,' he said with an edge of irony in his voice, 'then that will be useful for an alibi of provocation or self-defence.'

Grace mentally took a step back. 'Why? What other reason would Starling have to kill him?'

'I don't know, but nor do I buy into this whole concerned-father shtick.

'Why? Is he a paedophile?'

'Not that I ever heard,' said Villiers, 'and you get at least a sniff of most things if you rattle around Westminster for long enough.'

'So what did he want?' she asked. 'I'm assuming your services don't come cheap. Why would Starling want Operation Mayfly leaked if not to force the issue so he could find out about his daughter?'

'Dunno.'

'Did you know that Lucy Starling was a patient at the same time that you and Keith Stalgood were investigating Trudie Bevan's allegation against Chesham?'

Villiers swallowed hard. 'No, I didn't.' He pushed a hand through his hair. 'So that's why he came to me even though I was barely up and running. I wondered why he didn't pick a more experienced PI.'

'So you admit you were working for him?'

Villiers nodded. 'To be honest, I didn't see a problem. Far as I was aware, you weren't about to dig up any skeletons.'

Grace felt a flash of contempt. 'Yet you were still prepared to go ahead and let Starling destroy Chesham's reputation by making Mayfly public?'

He had the grace to look uncomfortable. 'Yeah, well.'

'Is that what Starling wanted? To destroy Chesham?'

'Look, I don't know. He's a client. You get used to clients being tight-lipped about their motives.'

It wasn't making any sense. Perhaps, after all, Starling's reasons for visiting the building where Chesham lived had absolutely nothing to do with his murder. But that reminded her about the lack of surveillance photographs of Starling entering or leaving. 'Is he being protected by someone at Scotland Yard?'

'He's an MP,' said Villiers. 'If he was, it would hardly be the first time.' He must have seen her alarm and rediscovered his conscience. 'You probably ought to watch your back, though.'

'Why? What do you know?'

Villiers wriggled a bit in his chair. 'He also paid me to pull the full works on you.'

'What!'

'I handed over what little I could find. You should expect a visit any day now from Professional Standards.'

'Too late,' she said, shivering at the memory of her terror as she'd accompanied DI Colne and DC Wade downstairs to the interview room. 'They're quicker off the mark than you give them credit for. They interviewed me this morning.'

'Yeah, well, sorry about that.'

Grace didn't know whether to be relieved that it wasn't, after all, someone at the Met who had tried to shaft her or furious that she had once felt sorry for the man who had ordered Villiers to set the dogs on her. Why? What did Starling hope to achieve? She recalled Annabel's avowal that she wanted to stop hating her ex-husband and wondered anew what it was that had made Annabel hold him responsible for Lucy's death.

'You're not in the clear yet, though,' Villiers said. 'Starling mentioned he might want me to start another hare running and inform DAC Marx that it was you who leaked the Operation Mayfly story to the *Courier*. It's rubbish, of course,' he added quickly, not meeting her eye, 'because you obviously know it was me. Cash in hand. Ivo Sweatman will back me up.'

'But why does Starling want to harm me?' Grace was furious. 'What threat do I pose?'

'Dunno. He told me it was all about scoring points off Scotland Yard. I just do what I'm told.'

'So why have you changed your mind?'

'I didn't sign up to be an accessory to murder.'

'So you'll speak to DCI Desai?' she asked.

'I'll have to think about that,' he repeated. He tipped his head back towards his house. 'I got a family to consider, a new business to get off the ground. If so minded, a man like Starling can do a lot of damage.'

'Not if he's in jail,' she said.

'Like I say, I'll have to think about it.'

Villiers walked her to her car. Before she started the engine she watched him return to his house. How far could she trust him? Not very far at all, was her guess. Even though he'd given her information he could have kept back, that wouldn't prevent him continuing to carry out Starling's orders, or at the very least reporting back on her visit. If he told Starling that the investigation into Chesham's murder was homing in on him, then the MP was only going to become more desperate to control events. And a desperate man backed into a corner was likely to be even more dangerous.

56

As soon as she was safely out of sight, Grace stopped to phone Keith to ask if she could drop in to see him on her way back to Colchester. Starling's interventions had no discernible logic to them. What reason would he have to kill Ned Chesham other than because he believed the professor had abused Lucy? The only person who might know was his ex-wife. Grace made good time on the journey and was able to pull up a couple of streets short of Keith's road and call her. It didn't take much persuasion for Annabel to explain why she held her ex-husband responsible for Lucy's unhappiness and eventual suicide.

Although Starling – and his party – had spun it that he'd relinquished his leadership ambitions for family reasons, the reality, Annabel told Grace bitterly, was that there had been a scandal – another one – and the party's price for hushing this one up had been that he stand aside.

Adrian, she said, had always had a penchant for low-end prostitutes and crack cocaine, and the higher he rose, the more he seemed to invite the risk of getting caught. Two earlier scrapes had failed to deter him, and, in covering them up, the whips had logged his misdemeanours as useful assets in case the party ever needed to count on his support. This time, however, the woman involved had died of a heroin overdose in his hotel room, and the manager – albeit discreetly – had called the police. Annabel had no idea how it had been done, but Starling's name had been kept out of everything.

For Annabel, however, it had been the final straw, and she had demanded a divorce. Starling, full of self-pity and still hoping to cling on to some of his ambitions, had rushed to Lucy and begged her to persuade her mother to change her mind and pose for the obligatory stand-by-her-man photo opportunity. Lucy, already fragile, hanged herself the following day.

Grace didn't ask why Annabel hadn't left him years before. Not only had Grace encountered plenty of psychologically abused women in the course of her work, she could also vividly remember how, when recovering from her own ex-husband's vicious physical assault, she'd gone on craving the sound of his voice and the feel of his arms around her. She wasn't about to judge another woman for loving the wrong man.

Thanking her for her help, Grace ended the call and drove the last few hundred yards to park beside Keith's driveway. As she got out of the car she looked up at the sky. The sun was about to set, promising a cloudless night. Nearer the sea, in Wivenhoe, she'd be able to see the stars, and she was stabbed by a sudden wish to be at home, pouring a glass of wine with Blake. Did she really need to make Starling her business? Ned Chesham's murder was DCI Desai's investigation; Ned's special girls faced no further harm; she'd done all she could and should let this go rather than risk provoking Starling into carrying out his threat to end her career.

On the other hand, if Starling had already got someone other than Villiers to tip off Professional Standards about her relationship with Ivo Sweatman, and the PSD had been keeping a beady eye on her, then she was bang to rights anyway and it wouldn't matter what she did next. She might as well carry on.

Keith welcomed her in. As she reached down to stroke his elderly spaniel, she heard a door close upstairs – his wife, she assumed, whom she had never met. If Keith minded the late intrusion, he hid it well. He led her into the comfortable lounge, where they seated themselves beside the open French windows, glad of a breath of evening air. The spaniel settled himself at Keith's feet, from where he could keep a wary eye on the intruder.

'So how can I help?' Keith asked.

'Have you heard of an MP called Adrian Starling?'

'Only that he's an MP.'

'His daughter Lucy was receiving treatment from Ned Chesham at the time of your investigation,' she said. 'You didn't come across him then?'

Keith shook his head and dragged a hand across his face. 'Another of the children I let down?'

'No,' Grace said decisively. 'That's not what this is about. Starling is a potential suspect for Chesham's murder.'

'Because of his daughter?'

'That's what I'd assumed,' she said, 'but now I'm hearing suggestions that it may not be.'

'What then?'

'He's been stalking my inquiries,' she said. 'He hired Sam Villiers to leak Operation Mayfly to the *Courier.*'

Keith did not seem particularly surprised. 'Never did take much to Sam.'

'Starling also has plenty of old scandals of his own to keep buried. Nothing that suggests any involvement with underage girls, but no shortage of sleaze, all of which has so far been kept safely under wraps. When you were with the Met, some time after the 2010 general election, did you hear any rumours of an MP being mixed up with a sex worker dying of an overdose in a London hotel?'

'No, nothing.'

'Shows how successfully Starling's name was kept out of it, even within the Met.'

'But if you're saying he knew something about Ned Chesham,' said Keith, 'why didn't he use his clout to expose him?'

'That's what I want to find out,' she said. 'Sam Villiers also told me that Starling paid him to cause trouble for me with Professional Standards.'

'Are you going to be OK?' Keith asked.

Grace was grateful. 'I think so, thanks. But I'd like a better idea of what I'm dealing with, and why. You told me that the CPS decision for you not to proceed against Chesham didn't feel right, that you argued it with the CPS lawyer.'

'That's true, but I don't see how Ned Chesham could have managed to influence the CPS.'

'Not Chesham,' she said. 'Starling. He was solicitor general at the time, second in command to the attorney general, who oversees the Crown Prosecution Service. Not too difficult for him to have had a word in the ear of a junior lawyer.'

'But why?' Keith looked horrified. 'And how would he know that Chesham was raping young girls? And if he did know, what about his own daughter?'

'Do you think someone could have interfered with your investigation?' she asked.

'It's always possible.'

'According to one of Chesham's victims, he threatened her when she was a kid that he had friends who knew how to make problems go away.'

'But I still don't see why Starling would protect Chesham when his own child was a patient.'

'I was trying to work that out on the drive over here,' she said. 'Family therapy is a big part of the treatment. And Lucy wasn't the only child of high-profile parents that Chesham treated. Maybe he wasn't above leveraging a few embarrassing family secrets if he found himself in a tight spot.'

'But we never interviewed Chesham. How would he know we were investigating?'

'He explained that himself,' she said ruefully. 'Trudie Bevan's mother told him.'

'So you think he blackmailed Starling into making sure my inquiry went away?'

'Maybe it wasn't Starling,' said Grace. 'But you have to admit it would be the perfect stand-off.'

'Except for all the victims who came afterwards,' said Keith bitterly.

She nodded her regret. 'One last question.'

'Go ahead.'

'Starling's ex-wife gave me the impression that party minders squared it with someone at the Met to scrub his name off the books after the poor woman's death in the hotel,' she said. 'Do you have any idea who that might have been?'

'Just after the 2010 election, you say?'

'Yes.'

Keith thought for a moment but then shook his head. 'Could have been a lot of people.'

'What were DAC Marx's responsibilities then?'

'I think she would have been an area commander. I suppose someone could have approached her. It's hardly unknown for the Met to do that kind of thing, or try to anyway, unless the press gets hold of the full story first. But it's no big conspiracy, Grace, just a way of keeping the wheels on the bus. And if the death of the woman in Starling's hotel was an accident or misadventure – and I can't see them getting the coroner to keep quiet – then, unless the Met could prove that Starling supplied the drugs, him being there wasn't a criminal matter.'

'Maybe not,' she said, trying not to be too squeamish about Keith's pragmatism, 'but if DAC Marx did do a favour for Starling seventeen years ago, it might explain why she wanted Mayfly cut short. Also, she had Chesham's block of flats under surveillance at the time he was killed, yet—'

'So the Met *was* continuing to investigate Chesham?'

'So it would seem,' she said. 'Yet there are no images of Starling entering or leaving. Why not? Is someone still looking out for him?'

Keith didn't seem to be listening. She had a plunging moment of sudden doubt. Was she just conjuring up a ludicrous cloud of suspicion and conspiracy in order not to have to confront the evidence of Duncan's potential involvement in Chesham's murder?

'The CPS lawyer who advised me not to proceed,' Keith said with a frown. 'Geraint Pryce. You say that Starling was solicitor general at the time?'

'Yes.'

'Only I seem to remember that soon afterwards Pryce joined the Government Legal Service. Quite a plum job.'

'So everyone gets to keep their careers and reputations intact,' she said, 'and not one of them could care less about the young girls who have to go on being abused, girls who are already ill and vulnerable.'

'That's about the size of it,' Keith agreed. 'But you'll have a damned hard time proving any of it. They'll think you're crazy, especially now Chesham's dead.'

It was a long time since Grace had felt so dispirited. There was nothing more for them to say, and she still had over an hour's drive home, so she thanked him and rose to say her farewells.

On the front step he called her back. 'How's Duncan, by the way?'

She turned and, seeing her former boss silhouetted against the homely gush of light from the hallway, yearned to unburden herself not only of all her dubious decisions but also the overriding sense that she had let Duncan down. But it was late and Keith looked weary. He had retired from the Job and had his own doubts and regrets to contend with. Her anxieties weren't his problem.

'You were right about Duncan,' she said. 'This investigation did get under his skin. You know, it would probably do him a lot of good to meet up with you for a jar some time.'

'I'll give him a call,' said Keith. 'He might like to come over for a barbecue this weekend if the weather holds.'

She smiled, wondering if Keith would take it amiss if she gave him a hug. But, in her mind anyway, a part of him remained her senior officer and she decided against it. 'You did the best you could to investigate Trudie Bevan's allegation.' She put as much force into her words as possible. 'Whatever has happened since, you are not responsible.'

'It's kind of you to say so,' said Keith, 'but it doesn't work that way.'

Not for a man of principle, she thought. 'Goodnight, boss.'

He smiled, said goodbye and closed the door.

Driving home, she thought about all the other people in addition to the victims themselves whose lives had been affected by Ned Chesham's abuse: young Tim Merrick's life cut short, Toby and Minnie Thomas's betrayed trust, Keith's guilt at his missed opportunity, and no doubt deep unease among many of Ned's medical colleagues too. He might be dead, but the stain of both his crimes and the failure to prevent them would continue to spread wide and deep for a long time to come.

She was relieved to reach the sleeping streets of Wivenhoe and, locking her car, looked up and saw the stars pulsing in a velvety sky. She was well aware that few places were immune to bad things happening, but for tonight this little town was her haven.

57

In the office the following morning Grace marvelled at how DCI Desai managed to keep his voice on the phone so deadpan. 'They were overlooked,' he said without a hint of irony. 'An admin error. But we now have two surveillance photographs showing Adrian Starling leaving Chesham's block of flats. They give us a precise time that fits comfortably with the sighting of him on his way up in the lift. I'm emailing them to you now. If you have any thoughts, I'd be glad to hear them.'

'Let me take a look, sir,' she told him, eager for his email to show up on her screen.

'One other item of interest,' he said. 'The plastic bag you'll see him carrying is from a local grocery store. We're finding out if anyone there remembers Starling making a purchase that evening, but similar bags were found in a kitchen drawer in Chesham's flat, and the resident who travelled up in the lift with Starling has no recollection of him carrying anything.'

Desai's incoming email pinged. Grace opened the attachments and studied them. 'The shirt he's wearing looks a bit tight,' she said.

'That's what I thought,' he said. 'The jeans too.'

'Every time I met Professor Chesham he was wearing a shirt in the same shade of blue. It was like his signature colour.'

'There's evidence that the perpetrator washed off blood in Chesham's bathroom.'

'So he could have changed into some of Chesham's clothes and carried his own bloody ones away in that bag?'

'Except his shoes, probably,' said Desai. 'Starling's bigger and taller than Chesham. He's probably got rid of everything by now, but we'll see what a search turns up.'

'You're going arrest him?'

'Right away. We've also got a couple of partial fingerprints from the flat. Given that Chesham had so few visitors, we might get lucky.'

If they had fingerprint evidence, thought Grace, then it was hardly surprising that DAC Marx had so fortuitously 'found' the missing surveillance photographs. She must have finally realized there was no point tying her fortunes to a sinking ship. Grace had no idea whether Harry Desai knew about her visitors yesterday from Essex PSD. If he had, his manner didn't betray any concern. It would be nice to think that Starling's arrest for murder would put paid to the MP's attempts to discredit her and also encourage Sam Villiers to place what he knew on the record. She gave a sigh of relief that maybe everything was, after all, coming together.

Desai rang off, promising to keep her in the loop. She stared at the photographs of Adrian Starling. In both of them he was expressionless: if he *had* very recently stabbed a man to death and then cleaned himself up, there was no sign of panic or fear in his bearing. He didn't hug the plastic bag guiltily to his chest or look around furtively; he held the bag quite normally, head high, shoulders back, stepping confidently out into the street. If he were to be found guilty at trial, she thought, then this would be the image of him that would be wired around the world.

'Penny for them.'

She looked up. Blake stood in the entrance to her cubicle, smiling at her.

'Come and look at these.'

He came to stand behind her, lowering his head until it almost touched hers. He turned slightly, as if dropping a kiss into her hair, and she felt herself blush, acutely aware of all the eyes in the office that could turn their way.

'It's Adrian Starling,' she said.

'So the photos turned up after all?'

'Admin error.'

'Of course.' He laughed. 'What else?'

What else, indeed? Grace felt sick at how easy it was to laugh off such blatant obstructions and evasions. Each minuscule and unchallenged act might not in itself be enough to pervert the course of justice, but add them all together into a culture of entitlement and mutual favours and they stank.

While she'd waited earlier that morning for her breakfast coffee to brew, she had googled Geraint Pryce, the CPS lawyer who seventeen years ago had advised Keith Stalgood that there was insufficient evidence to pursue a case against Ned Chesham. She learned that his name had recently been put forward for appointment as the next treasury solicitor, which would make him head of the Government Legal Service and, according to the article, one of the most highly paid people in the public sector.

She wondered if Geraint Pryce had ever suffered a single sleepless night worrying about his decision and whatever inducements Adrian Starling might have offered him to make it. And, if not, what the hell she could do to change that.

'Is it enough to arrest Starling?' Blake's question cut into her thoughts.

'Yes, they're picking him up now.'

'It's a good result,' he said. 'So why the frown?'

She made an effort to lighten up. 'Not sure I can explain.'

'Can't or won't?'

There was an edge to his tone that made her turn to meet his eyes. 'Won't,' she said. 'For your sake. Not yet, anyway.'

'I'm a big boy,' he said. 'I can look after myself.'

She shook her head. 'Sorry, no.'

He drew back. 'Is it about the visit from Professional Standards?'

'No.' She hoped a half-truth would satisfy him. 'That was about my house.'

He scrutinized her face. 'Suit yourself.'

He walked back around her desk and was about to return to his own when she called his name. He turned reluctantly, remaining far enough away that she had to mouth the words so that no one in the office beyond would hear. *Drink tonight?*

He hesitated and then his face softened. 'Sure.'

Her relief made her feel like a schoolgirl. She watched Blake sit back down at his desk, and felt her body thrum at the memory of him. She wanted this! It was good to feel so warmed – unfrozen – by his kindness, by her sense of how ready he was to care for her. She wanted a private life which this time would not be pushed off the rails by her work. It was time to let go of this case. What did it matter any more what had happened seventeen years ago?

And then she looked across at Duncan and knew she could never add her silence to the rest.

58

Clive promised himself that once he had spoken to Gillian, he would call an estate agent and put the house on the market. Either that or raze it to the ground with the three of them in it. He couldn't see how they could go on living here after the things that had been said and done in these rooms. He wasn't sure they could go on living at all. He had failed to protect his family and could see no prospect of helping them towards a brighter future. Perhaps they would all be better off dead. Maybe it was the kindest thing he could do for them now that he no longer knew how to take care of them.

He'd begun to work out how he might do it. It would have to be once Gillian and Meghan were both asleep. Maybe he could buy some kind of over-the-counter sedative at the chemist to make them drowsy so that they wouldn't fight back too much when he held a pillow over their faces. How long did it take for someone to suffocate? How would he know that they really were dead? He couldn't risk Meghan waking up and wandering in to find him trying to smother her mother. Or, later, seeing the blood after he'd slit his wrists in the bath. He'd have to be sure.

He'd need to alert the emergency services to come and find them afterwards. He supposed he could send a letter that wouldn't arrive until the next day. He could put in a spare door key. That would mean, once he'd posted it, he'd have to go through with it. But also that he'd never need to tell Gillian anything.

Why make her suffer unnecessarily by hearing the truth not just about Meghan but all the terrible things Helen had done, and the warped reasons why? If he did tell her, he would first have to persuade Gillian to believe him. And then endless discussions would follow, unpicking every word and look and action. What had they missed? Could they have prevented it? And even if they got through all of that, Meghan would still be underweight and not eating.

He wished he could take his parents-in-law with them so they wouldn't be left facing the realization that the first link in the chain leading to this final catastrophe was their failure to see what Professor Ned had done to Helen when she was a child. Maybe he could invite them to stay? Could he kill four people and then himself? He wasn't sure. But what else could he do?

Gillian had mentioned something about her parents wanting to come up for Professor Ned's funeral or memorial service. They were still holding fast to the idea that he was innocent and had been wrongly accused by the police. Funny that they hadn't talked about coming up to visit Helen in prison – maybe Gillian had dissuaded them – but it would be easy enough to fabricate a reason why they should stay for a few days.

His in-laws were in their early sixties, looking towards retirement, and lived a quiet life down in Devon. They'd moved there years ago to give Helen a fresh start once she'd regained enough weight to return to school. What life were they going to have with one daughter serving a life sentence and the other's family destroyed? Better for them all to die together, knowing nothing more than they already knew.

He acknowledged that if he included them, it would leave Helen facing prison alone. He had no wish to be cruel and understood that she was ill, irreparably damaged by her unnatural attachment to a monster, but no doubt she'd simply go on maintaining the utter ruthlessness with which she defended her delusions. She'd be all right. Look what she'd done to her family, right down to the nasty, jealous little digs at Meghan; she was even prepared to face poor Dr Merrick's parents in court and call their son a pervert rather than admit the truth. Clive could never say it to Gillian, but frankly he no longer gave a toss what happened to Helen; his job was to take care of his own.

One part of his mind kept sticking up a hand, trying to warn him that this plan was equally deranged, also a reaction to unbearable events, a kind of post-traumatic stress disorder, that there had to be another way, that maybe he ought to seek help before it was too late. But then he'd have to tell his wife that he had opened their front door to evil, an evil that she, Gillian, had picked up the phone to summon, and that together he and she had watched that evil walk up the stairs to their daughter's bedroom and close the door while they had lain down on their own bed and slept.

He couldn't tell her that. He couldn't. There had to be another way. Maybe he'd take a walk down to the chemist's later and see what they had to offer.

59

Grace leaned forward, concentrating on the video feed on the screen before her. She'd been pleasantly surprised when DCI Desai invited her to observe his interview with Adrian Starling and curious to see the man who had been scheming against her. She was aware of having watched him on television in various late-night discussion programmes before his fall from favour, but it was his fluency and forcefulness rather than his physical presence that she remembered. Looking at him now, sitting next to his solicitor, who radiated confidence and expertise, he looked drab and understandably exhausted.

Starling must realize that, with the cast-iron evidence DCI Desai had gathered, he was now enmeshed in a criminal justice system that no minders, political or otherwise, could subvert. However well a killer tried to cover his tracks, stabbing was a messy business that inevitably left an abundance of forensic evidence. A search of Starling's clothes, his house, his rubbish bins, plus fingerprints, DNA and other trace evidence at the scene of crime was going to produce enough to charge and convict him. Even if he offered a compelling enough account of mitigating circumstances to get away with a reduced charge of manslaughter, he must know he was looking at a prison sentence.

As Starling's solicitor read out a prepared statement admitting her client's presence in Ned Chesham's flat, Grace's thoughts strayed to Duncan. She was ashamed of her mismanagement. Knowing she had allowed her indecision to come between them right when he most needed a friend, she resolved to do better.

She shifted her attention back to the screen. Starling's story, according to his solicitor, was that he'd gone to Chesham's flat at the professor's request. Chesham had said he was in trouble and thought Starling might be able to pull some strings. Starling had refused. Ned had threatened him with a knife from the kitchen and, in the ensuing struggle, had been fatally injured. In a state of shock – he had never been a violent man – Starling had failed to call the emergency services and instead had simply gone home. It was a grave error of judgement not to have come forward, but he had been traumatized, out of his mind, not thinking clearly.

Harry Desai then began his questioning, courteously probing Starling's account of Chesham's initial call and the conversation that took place before the knife was produced. Grace was jubilant when Starling stressed that the call, from a number he hadn't recognized, had come out of the blue, and that he hadn't spoken to or given much thought to Ned Chesham since he'd treated his daughter for an eating disorder nearly two decades earlier. As soon as Sam Villiers came forward, she reflected, he would be able to give the lie to that, and with that first untruth exposed, Starling's self-justifications would swiftly unravel.

Desai encouraged Starling to talk about his shock at learning from the media about the allegations made against Chesham. It was clear to Grace that Starling's solicitor must have warned him against expressing any outrage he felt too strongly in case it suggested a motive for him to murder Chesham, and he was careful to downplay any fear he might have had that his daughter could have been abused. Nonetheless, Desai's sustained deference had the desired effect, and Starling slowly began to relax his guard, confident that his appeal for understanding would receive a sympathetic hearing.

'You can imagine how sorry I am,' said Starling. 'I can't believe it's happened. I've been told that's what happens with shock. I just don't remember anything after he came back out of the kitchen and started waving the knife around, or if I do, it's like a dream, like it happened to someone else. But you can see that I never meant to harm anyone.'

When Desai probed into how he had washed and then helped himself to clean clothes out of Chesham's wardrobe, Starling interrupted to insist that he just didn't remember.

'How long would you say you spent washing and changing your clothes?' Desai asked the question as if this were merely the kind of pointless detail demanded by some faceless official. 'Ten, twenty minutes, more than that?'

'I wish I knew. All that blood. It was . . .' He sighed and shook his head, robbed of speech.

'But you were sure, all that time, that Professor Chesham was actually dead?' asked Desai.

Watching Starling's reaction, Grace saw a flash of annoyance that reminded her of one of her young nephews when caught out over something he was sure he'd been clever enough to get away with.

'I was so frightened,' Starling said. 'I ran to the bathroom, locked the door in case he could somehow still come after me.'

'Did you have your phone with you? Did you think to call for help?'

'It was all so dreadful.' He raised his hands to look at the palms. 'All I could think was that I had to get the blood off.'

'Where was the knife at this point?"

Starling dropped his hands and looked at his solicitor, who gave a tiny nod. 'I don't remember.'

'It had been washed and wiped of fingerprints before being placed on the floor beside the body,' said Desai. 'Do you recall how it came to be there?'

'I was in shock. I've never experienced anything like that before. He was trying to kill me.' Starling's voice rose slightly, again reminding Grace of her nephews when they became tired and whiney.

'We can corroborate that you walked from the body to the bathroom,' said Desai. 'We have traces of blood from your foot-prints. However, there are no shoe prints leading from the bathroom to the bedroom, from where you took a shirt and a pair of jeans, or to the kitchen, where you found a plastic carrier bag in a drawer. Did you take your shoes off and leave them in the bathroom?'

Starling let out a laugh of disbelief and put a hand to his fore-head. 'I was the intended victim here. He came at me with a huge knife and I defended myself. Anything I did or didn't do afterwards was due to the shock of it all. You must realize how incapable I am of deliberately harming another human being.'

'You say that Ned Chesham called you that evening to ask for help,' said Desai, 'even though it had been years since you'd had any contact. Can you explain why you agreed to go to his flat?'

'I have devoted my life to representing people who need my help. The only reason I knew Ned in the first place was because I'd wanted to do my best for my daughter, a very troubled soul. I didn't know what to make of the stories about him in the press, but I felt I owed it to him to give him the benefit of the doubt. I'd like to think that poor Lucy wasn't made even more fragile by anything he did or said during her treatment with him.'

'Why do you think Chesham called you?' asked Desai.

This was the question Grace had been waiting for. As soon as she'd heard that Starling's fingerprints had been found in Ned's flat, she had somewhat recklessly called his ex-wife to ask if, during her marriage, she had ever met or heard her husband talk about Geraint Pryce. Annabel had recognized the name and said that she and Adrian had known him socially, if not particularly well. As soon as Grace was finished here, she would call Sam Villiers and push him to make a statement. If he refused, she'd ask Keith to work on him.

She watched on the video monitor as Starling drew himself up to become the former junior government minister she remembered from television.

'Ned seemed to think that, as a former solicitor general, I would be in a position to influence the judicial process,' he said. 'It was when I told him it was out of the question that he went to arm himself with the knife. I deeply regret what happened next, and always will. It was a confused and tragic event, not an easy thing to live with, I can tell you. But I acted purely in self-defence. I was his intended victim. I am in no way to blame.'

Grace supposed that the art of being a politician was to believe the thing you were saying at the moment you were saying it. Whatever had happened in Ned Chesham's flat that evening, this was the version that Adrian Starling had now convinced himself was true: he could not be held responsible for anything.

60

The letter was addressed to Grace at Colchester police HQ and marked 'Urgent and Personal' even though it bore a second-class stamp. According to the postmark it had been sent before the weekend. She thumbed the white envelope carefully before opening it in case it contained some kind of unpleasant surprise and then drew out a single page, neatly handwritten on both sides. Turning it over, she recognized the name printed in capitals beneath the signature: CLIVE GOODWIN.

Dear DI Fisher,

By the time you receive this letter, the local police will have found us. I think you will understand my actions when I tell you that Ned Chesham has betrayed two generations of my family.

There is one thing I cannot leave undone. I want you to give this letter to the judge when my sister-in-law Helen Fry comes to court. I know that hearsay evidence from someone who has died is admissible in a murder trial, and what I have to say is important.

The reality suggested by the letter's opening sentence – a reality that Grace had unconsciously brushed aside – became chillingly present. She read on, hardly daring to breathe.

> Helen killed Dr Merrick because he told her that he saw Professor Ned Chesham sexually abusing my daughter, Meghan. Helen killed Dr Merrick rather than have to believe it.
>
> I know what Dr Merrick saw because Meghan told me. She didn't tell you when you interviewed her because she was too afraid of what might happen to us.
>
> Helen is guilty of murder, but she was abused by Professor Ned as a child when she was his patient and has remained in thrall to him ever since. She won't admit this, but it is true, and the judge needs to know it when he passes sentence.
>
> Please tell Helen I am sorry, but it was impossible to share the truth with my family, and I could see only one way to protect them.

Grace's hands shook as she typed Clive Goodwin's name into the search field of the police database. It was flagged up immediately: a newly opened investigation into four suspected murders and a suspected suicide, currently assumed to be a family annihilation by the suicide, Clive Goodwin.

Grace wasn't aware of crying out, only of the members of her team turning to look in her direction. Duncan was the first to get to his feet and rush towards her.

'Get me in to see Helen Fry,' she said. 'Now!'

Duncan hurried back to his desk, passing Blake with a mystified shake of his head.

Blake arrived at her side. 'What's happened?'

She pointed at the screen and hid her face in her hands. As she began to cry, Blake put a comforting hand on her shoulder and leaned forward to look at the screen.

'Oh my God,' he said. Noticing the letter, he picked it up and read it. 'Oh no. Sweet Jesus, no.'

'It's my fault,' wept Grace. 'It's all my fault.'

'No, no, it's not.' He crouched down beside her chair and took hold of her hands. 'How can it be your fault? You did everything you could. Ned Chesham would be at the palace getting his knighthood if it wasn't for you.'

'You don't understand,' she said.

'Come with me.'

Blake pulled her to her feet, and she let him shepherd her out of the office and along to the end of the corridor, the only available private space. She leaned her forehead against the glass of a window that looked out over a road junction and closed her eyes.

'The whole family,' she said. 'Meghan and her mother and both her grandparents. What must he have been going through to do that?'

'That's on him,' said Blake firmly. 'His decision. Nothing to do with you.'

'But you don't know it all,' she said, the sobs threatening to return. 'It could have been stopped. Those bastards. Those *bastards*!'

'Hush now,' Blake said. 'I know it's bad – it doesn't get much worse – but you're not responsible.'

'That's what they all fucking say! Been saying for years!'

Blake tried to take hold of her, to hug her to him, but she fought him off. 'You don't understand!'

'Boss?' Duncan stood a few feet away. His face was pale with shock. 'I spoke to the prison. Helen Fry's already been informed. They don't know if she'll agree to see you or not, but they'll accommodate a visit whenever you want.'

'This can't be allowed to happen,' she said. 'This has to stop. It has to stop somewhere.'

'Do you want me to drive you home?' asked Duncan.

Grace turned, hardly conscious of what she was doing or saying. 'Oh Duncan, what do I do? You know what this stuff does to people. What do I do?'

Duncan glanced at Blake and then at the floor. 'I spoke to my mother on Sunday,' he said. 'I'm going to go and visit her once I've fixed some leave.'

Grace abandoned all attempts not to weep.

'It's all right, boss, it's all right,' said Duncan. 'She said the guy slung his hook years ago, but she didn't know how to find me. And now he's dead. See, it doesn't have to end as badly as this. It can be OK. It can come good in the end if you let it.'

'I'm so glad.' Grace reached out to squeeze his arm. 'Thank you.' She took a deep breath and tried to let it out slowly, shuddering with the effort. 'Sorry, guys.' She managed a smile. 'I'll be OK in a minute.'

'Take your time,' said Blake.

'I'll leave you to it,' said Duncan.

'Would you like to go home?' Blake asked again, as Duncan returned to the MIT office.

'I must go and see Helen Fry.'

'Shall I come with you?'

'Please.'

'Is Duncan OK?'

She managed a smile. 'I think so.'

Blake checked back along the corridor to make sure it was empty and then put his arms around her, pulling her tight and kissing her hair where her head lay against his shoulder. 'You're not responsible. You did a fantastic job,' he whispered. 'Bloody fantastic.'

She raised her head to look into his eyes and then kissed him. What she didn't say – couldn't say – was that she was far from finished with this case.

61

Grace sat with her hip just touching Blake's. She wasn't sure she could have endured this visit without that human connection. She'd never spent much time in women's prisons and was finding the dense atmosphere of psychological disturbance more desperate than in a male prison. Or maybe she'd brought those feelings in here herself – she wasn't sure.

Before they set out Grace had learned from the local CID who were dealing with the Goodwin deaths that they too had received a brief letter from Clive that morning. This contained a front-door key and a warning as to what they would find at the house. Grace had then sent them a copy of her letter, preserving the original in an evidence bag for the coroner.

It was too early for post-mortem examinations to have been carried out, but it was thought that the deaths had taken place on Saturday night. CID had already discovered that Clive had gone to his GP on Friday afternoon complaining of acute stress and lack of sleep and been prescribed a short course of sleeping pills. The empty bottle was found in the kitchen bin. His wife, daughter and mother-in-law had been smothered in their beds. His father-in-law was sitting in a chair in the living room, an empty glass of whisky beside him and a plastic bag over his head; the handles had been tied tightly at the back of his neck. Clive had climbed fully clothed into a full bath, where he had cut his wrists. A nearly empty whisky bottle was on the floor beside him.

Clive's statement in his letter that Tim Merrick had seen Ned Chesham sexually abusing Meghan was the last piece of the jigsaw in the case against Helen Fry – and, as Clive had hoped, the manner of her reaction to it could be crucial to her defence. Blake had therefore brought recording equipment for an interview under caution.

A prison officer brought Helen into the room. She was wearing her own clothes – jeans and a baggy pale blue Gap hoodie. She had lost weight, and her hair, tied back in a single plait, looked lank and unwashed, but her eyes were bright with anger. She didn't wait for Grace to speak. 'Did Clive kill Ned?' she demanded. 'Is that why he's done this?'

'I'm very sorry for your loss,' said Grace, taken aback by the intensity of Helen's fury. 'But no, the Metropolitan Police have already charged someone with the murder of Professor Chesham. Meanwhile, I need to remind you that you're still under caution. Anything you say—'

'Who is it?' Helen interrupted.

'Do you understand that you remain under caution?'

'Yes. Just tell me what happened.'

'Do you remember a girl called Lucy Starling? She was a patient at the same time as you.'

'I thought she killed herself?'

'She did,' said Grace. 'It's her father who has been charged.'

'Why? Why would he want to hurt Ned?'

'Helen, we're here to talk about your family.'

'I don't care about them! I don't care about any kind of life without Ned!'

Grace looked at Blake, who gave a tiny shrug, equally thrown by Helen's perverse response.

'What's going to be done to him?' asked Helen. 'To Lucy's father? I hope he rots in hell!'

Grace had to remind herself that Helen was a specialist psychiatric nurse: surely some tiny bubble in her mind must retain the knowledge that her lack of reaction to the violent deaths of her entire family lay far out on the edge of sanity? Grace decided it might be best to begin by playing along with Helen's unreasoning preoccupation. 'You loved Ned?'

'He loved me.'

'So why didn't you marry, have a life together?'

'We couldn't. I'd been his patient. He'd be struck off. I could never let him give up his work.'

'So you were lovers?'

'Of course.'

'Recently?'

Helen shook her head. 'It wasn't possible. And he said it wasn't fair. He was older, and I should find someone else, have a life. He only ever wanted what was best for me.'

'What about him?' asked Grace. 'Did he pursue other relationships?'

'No. I was all he wanted.'

'He told you that?'

She smiled. 'He didn't have to.'

Grace simultaneously felt her flesh creep and experienced a deep pity. She was finally beginning to gain some insight into the precise nature of the delusion Helen had been so desperate to protect. 'What about your niece, Meghan?'

'What about her?' Helen almost spat out the words.

'What sort of attention did Ned pay to her?'

'None. She was nothing.'

'Helen, do you have any understanding of why your family are dead? Your sister, your parents, your niece.'

She looked confused for a moment. 'I thought Clive had killed Ned, so I thought . . . No, I don't know.'

'What did Tim Merrick say to you when he called from Wryford Hall that night?'

'I told you, he needed advice.'

'About what?'

'About stuff he was feeling.'

'About Ned?'

'No.'

'Did he tell you he'd seen Ned with Meghan?'

Helen laughed. 'No.'

'Meghan told her father that Tim Merrick had seen Ned sexually assaulting her. Is that what Tim told you?'

'Ned wasn't interested in Meghan!'

'Why not?' asked Grace.

'Why would he be?'

'The same reason he was interested in you at that age.'

'He loved me. We fell in love. It was different. Special.'

'And you were terrified that he'd fallen in love with Meghan? Your niece, a girl who reminded him of you at that age?'

'No.'

'That job in Newcastle he wanted you to take.' Grace could hardly bear to inflict such cruelty, but Helen's fantasy wasn't harmless: too many people were dead because of it. 'He was trying to get rid of you, wasn't he?'

'No!'

'The love affair was over. He'd found another special girl to replace you.'

'Not her!' she shouted. 'She was just a stupid kid. She thought she could lead him on, take my place, but she couldn't. I was the only one who understood him, who could support his work. He knew that, he always knew that. It all started with me. He needed me. I was the one he loved, only me!'

'But that's not what Tim Merrick said that night, is it?' asked Grace. 'Tim wanted you to believe what he'd seen, that Meghan had replaced you.'

'He was a liar, a filthy liar.'

'So you shut him up. Hit his mouth with a rock.'

'It wasn't true. I couldn't let him say those things.'

'You weren't the first, or the last. You must have realized over the years that he chose a new girl every summer.'

'No! That's not true. You're lying. Ned loved me. There was never anyone else. Never. He only loved me, and now he's dead and I have nothing.'

Helen laid her arms on the table in the bleak prison room, bowed her head and wept. Grace could only hope that somewhere amid her grief Helen might find some compassion for her own younger self, for the healthy childish emotions so irretrievably bent and twisted out of shape.

62

It was a while since Ivo had been required to put the serious frighteners on anyone, and even though he'd never been the kind of schoolboy that liked pulling the wings off flies, he had to admit he was looking forward to his encounter with Geraint Pryce.

Grace Fisher had telephoned from a public call box the day before, sounding uncharacteristically angry and upset. She'd asked outright if he'd do her a favour, clarifying that she'd do the job herself except, coming from him, she hoped it would pack a bigger punch. Once she'd explained the full background to her request, he'd readily assured her it would be a pleasure to put in an appearance as the stuff of Geraint Pryce's worst nightmares.

Ivo hadn't let on about the dent to his professional pride once he'd understood how he'd let himself be conned – and by a bloody politician, for fuck's sake! He realized now how his own guilt as a father had swept him into an unquestioning accept-ance of Adrian Starling's protestations of parental grief and regret. That hurt. A chief crime correspondent was supposed to be smart enough to sniff out the phoney, and most especially the deliberately misleading, but then he supposed it just proved how easy it was to be taken in when you asked someone to believe what they already wanted to believe.

Which, if you thought about it, was more or less why he was here. If Geraint Pryce had comfortably forgotten his past actions or was too inclined to overlook their consequences, then he was in for a rude awakening.

It had been easy to discover that Pryce lived with his family in a big house on Wandsworth Common, where he kept regular hours. Ivo had decided to intercept him as he took his dog, one of those hybrid mutts with a silly name, out for its morning walk, aiming to enhance the pressure of being doorstepped by a tabloid journalist by adding the possibility that Pryce would miss the 08.17 to Victoria and be late for work.

Ivo arrived in good time to position himself beside the Pryces' front hedge, ready to cut off any retreat into the house and to obstruct Pryce's usual route across to the common. The house faced a busy road, tricky to cross at rush hour without using the zebra crossing. He doubted Pryce would be prepared to man-handle a reporter out of his way, and fully expected him to cringe at his exposure to all those gossipy neighbours setting off on the school run. To which end Ivo had selected a particularly scruffy and stained old trench coat and brought along a shorthand notebook and pen, ready to look the part.

Pryce appeared bang on time, and Ivo stepped into position. 'Mr Pryce?'

'Yes.'

'Ivo Sweatman, chief crime correspondent on the *Daily Courier*. May I have a word?'

'What about?' Pryce, a small, wiry man with sharp, quick movements, tugged impatiently at the lead to hold back the dog.

Ivo smiled. It was always sweeter when they started out with total confidence in their authority – all the further to fall. 'It's about your connection to Adrian Starling MP and the late Professor Sir Edward Chesham.'

'I don't have a connection. Now, if you'll excuse me—'

'We're running a big splash, and I'm offering you the opportunity to put your side of the story.'

Pryce tried to step around him, but Ivo, smiling, blocked his path, pen poised as if to take shorthand notes.

'Would you care to comment on the decision you made when you were a CPS lawyer not to proceed with an earlier complaint against Ned Chesham?'

'Get out of my way!'

'You must have seen yesterday's news,' said Ivo, 'about the tragic murder-suicide at the weekend. Three generations of the same family. Did you?'

'Yes.'

'Would you care to comment?'

'It's got nothing to do with me.'

'Ah, but that's where you're wrong,' said Ivo. 'You see, those five people who died were all related to the underage girl Ned Chesham was abusing seventeen years ago when, against the express wishes of the detective in charge, you closed down a police inquiry into what Chesham was up to. That girl, now aged thirty, is herself facing a possible life sentence for the murder of a blameless young doctor. Six deaths that could have been prevented if you had only done the right thing. Are you sure you wouldn't like to comment?'

'Edward Chesham was solely responsible for his own actions. Now please get out of my way before I call the police.'

'Go ahead and call,' said Ivo pleasantly. 'I'm sure they'll be very interested in the conversations that took place between you and Adrian Starling prior to your decision not to proceed, as well as the timing of your first appointment to the Government Legal Service.'

'This is all nonsense.'

'Your hat's in the ring for the position of treasury solicitor, isn't it? And I believe a decision is imminent. As I say, this is your chance to put the record straight.'

Ivo was thoroughly enjoying himself, and happy to see that the same could not be said of Pryce, who yanked again at the dog lead as the poor animal strained to reach the open spaces of the common across the road. It would just have to find relief later in the back garden. Pryce turned, attempting to escape back to his front door, but with Ivo keeping a tight hand on the garden gate was too scared to attempt physical force. He looked – and, Ivo hoped, felt – pretty foolish.

'When you were a lowly CPS drone,' Ivo continued, 'Adrian Starling asked you to stall on Keith Stalgood's investigation, and you did his bidding. Maybe you were embarrassed or too gutless to refuse, maybe it was vanity at being approached by a junior minister, or maybe it was sheer self-interest. Certainly your climb up the greasy pole since then has been remarkably smooth. But now Starling's going down for murder, and all that dirty washing' – Ivo raised his voice as a mother walked past with a baby buggy – 'all that dirty washing is going to come tumbling out of the basket.'

Pryce's face was red. 'Starling's case is *sub judice*,' he said. 'You can't publish anything linked to him.'

'We can run the story immediately after the trial verdict.'

'What is it you want?'

'I want you to face up to what you did.'

'I did nothing wrong.'

'Ned Chesham was sexually abusing children,' said Ivo, 'and you deliberately put the kibosh on an active police investigation.'

'I gave the correct advice,' said Pryce, trying to recoup some dignity. 'If I remember correctly, there was no realistic prospect of conviction.'

'Certainly not once you had barred the detectives from approaching the hospital authorities or any of the patients' families.'

'There was a man's reputation to consider,' Pryce blustered.

'Is that why you think British justice exists?' asked Ivo. 'To advance a man's professional career? I thought it was to protect people. Did you even bother to ask yourself why Starling wanted you to interfere in a police inquiry?'

'He was the solicitor general!'

'How do you know he wasn't a raging paedophile?'

Pryce blinked.

'You don't know, do you?' Ivo demanded. 'But you went ahead and did what he asked anyway.'

'Are you trying to blackmail me? Is that what this is about?'

'No, this is sheer spite. What I want is for you to spend the rest of your life looking over your shoulder, remembering what you did and worrying about the moment when all those nice important people you invite to dinner or take to the opera are going to find out.'

'I have no idea what you're talking about! Find out what?'

'That you brown-nosed your way into a better job and never once looked back to see how many people paid the price. So, to help you focus on what I want, I'm warning you now that I'm going to dig into your whole family – your wife, son, daughter, siblings, parents, cousins, in-laws, godchildren. I promise that if ever anyone you remotely care about slips up, it's going to be smeared over the front page of the *Courier*.'

'That's not fair. My family have done nothing.'

'Nor had Dr Tim Merrick, Clive Goodwin and his family – all dead – or dozens of sexually abused young girls, some of whom went on to kill themselves. Yet they're the legacy of your casual decision to suck up to your boss. You need to find a way to put things right.'

Pryce stared at Ivo in disbelief, as if this truly was a nightmare from which he would at any moment awake.

'First of all,' said Ivo, 'the *Courier* is going to make sure that the right sort of rumour and gossip reaches the ears of the nomination committee scrutinizing the appointment of the new treasury solicitor.' Seeing from Pryce's expression that his threats were finally hitting home, Ivo felt a satisfying glow spread through him. 'But what I *really* want,' he said, getting right in the man's face, 'is for you never to sleep well again. Do you think you can do that for me?'

Pryce scrabbled to get a hand on the gate. Ivo waited long enough to relish the man's naked panic before stepping aside. Pryce ran to his front door, fumbled for his key and then dropped it. Managing to retrieve it, he tried to fit it into the lock while also pressing the bell repeatedly. When he looked over his shoulder to check if his tormentor was following him, Ivo gave him a mock salute and walked away. Job done.

63

Grace sat across from Blake in a booth in the Colchester bar where they had drunk cocktails together a fortnight before. It was already busy with the early Friday evening crowd, and with the promise of a hot and sunny weekend ahead, the mood was cheerful and upbeat.

Since the visit to Helen Fry, although they had seen each other in the office every day, they had otherwise spent the time apart. During the drive back from the prison Grace's strengthening determination not to let Geraint Pryce off the hook had made her itch with impatience to call Ivo and enlist his help. To do so she'd needed to be alone. Afterwards, on tenterhooks to hear how Pryce had reacted, she'd had, albeit unwillingly, to fob Blake off – and he hadn't tried to disguise how he felt about that. At work no one else could have detected any change in him, but after she'd sent him home alone on Monday and then dodged his suggestion of dinner on Tuesday, he hadn't approached her again.

The drinks now on the table in front of them had been her idea, and she'd been hugely relieved when he'd accepted her invitation. She would have preferred an outdoor table at the quayside pub in Wivenhoe, but the steely hint of irony in his glance had suggested that such proximity to her home – and bed – might be premature.

Anyone looking at him now would see a man in his early thirties, fit, strong and calm, but Grace had learned to see the vulnerability beneath his outward confidence, a vulnerability that had little to do with weakness and much to do with his willingness to be open and generous. She longed to tell him everything, to describe the history of her unorthodox relationship with Ivo Sweatman and to defend her reasons for trusting a tabloid journalist, but something held her back. She was unsure whether it was her own deep-seated lack of trust, pragmatic insurance against how messily some relationships could end, or a genuine wish to protect Blake from ever having to lie for her. Maybe it was a tangle of all three. Or even some perverse loyalty to Ivo himself, a recognition that the privacy and exclusivity of their bond mattered to him, and she should honour it. Even – and the realization surprised her – that the irregular nature of their friendship meant something to her too.

'Do you know where Duncan's gone tonight?' Blake's voice cut into her reflections.

'No, where?'

'Out for a meal.' His eyes danced with amusement. 'With Joan!'

'That's wonderful!'

'I hadn't realized there'd been a sweepstake in the office. No winner, apparently.'

'No, probably not, given how long it's taken for him to ask her.' She laughed. 'That is such good news!'

'And we're here,' he said, angling his head to turn it into a question.

'We are,' she said, taking a deep breath. 'I wanted to say sorry. It's been a difficult few weeks, and I know I've been ... a bit slippery.'

'Go on.' He tipped his glass to hers and took a sip of his Tom Collins.

'I can't explain – won't explain,' she corrected herself, recalling his earlier words. 'Won't because it could put you in a difficult position professionally. That's all I'm going to say, but it's got nothing to do with us.'

'Apart from you not telling me what's going on, you mean.'

'It was a situation that's unlikely to arise again.'

'To do with DAC Marx and Scotland Yard?'

'No.'

'Does Superintendent Pitman know?'

'Blake, I'm not going to play twenty questions!'

'I thought you hated political intrigue.'

'I do,' she said. 'That's why I have to keep this stuff to myself.'

His eyes searched hers. She leaned forward to take his hand, longing for the simplicity and directness of the first evening they'd come here, of the way they'd danced together afterwards and kissed on the way home. She knew now how much she wanted to be with him, to have the chance to know him better, know him best. But he gently withdrew his hand, shaking his head.

'Not good enough, I'm afraid.'

'Please.' She reached out again to touch him. 'Give it a chance. We could have something really good here.'

'I know. But a house built on shifting sand and all that. I'm not a control freak. I'm not saying we have to tell each other everything or that I have to know where you are every moment of the day, but whatever this is about, it's important to you, isn't it?'

'Yes.' Grace reviewed her two most recent conversations with Ivo. She hadn't sought him out merely because he could operate in areas from which the police were barred, it was also because his sense of injustice chimed so precisely with hers. She never needed to spell things out and yet always felt secure that, despite his journalistic instinct to exaggerate and denounce, he would calibrate his actions according to her wishes. She marvelled that until now she'd never seriously felt the need to review their encounters. But what would Blake's judgement of her behaviour be? Would he understand and truly support her or decide that she had been reckless or even corrupt?

And even if he were sympathetic, and she could tell him all the things Ivo had done for her, she would still have to give up any future association. It wouldn't be fair to risk Blake's career as well as her own.

'I haven't always been able to trust the institution of the police,' she said. 'And when that's happened, this thing I'm talking about is like my safe room. It's important to me. And I won't and can't tell you any more than that.'

He squeezed her hand and let it go, his eyes on the candle flickering in its holder of orange glass. 'Then, whatever we might become, there's always going to be a crack in it, isn't there?' He looked up at her, his mouth crooked in a sad smile. 'And don't tell me it's how the light gets in, because I don't think that's how it works in real life.'

Grace felt paralysed. Was she really going to give Blake up for Ivo? Not that it was Ivo the man; it was their shared fight to put things right. After everything that had happened to her, what she'd seen done to others, she couldn't give up that fight.

'This case started with Tim Merrick's murder,' she said, 'and has finished up with carnage. The real responsibility lies with people who'll never be punished, never believe they did anything wrong, who will stay invisible. Everyone from Toby Thomas's mother, who never made it her business to get to the bottom of why she mistrusted Chesham, to James Gibson, the surgeon who automatically accepted the word of a medical colleague. Or, in a different situation back in Maidstone, Colin Pitman, the senior officer who turned a blind eye when a beat copper was seriously out of control. That's what this is about for me. That's why I want you to let me keep my secret. It's part of who I am.'

'I know,' said Blake. 'And I admire you, I really do. And I'll be right at your shoulder fighting the baddies until we're the last two left standing. I promise you that. The rest, I'm not sure.' He swallowed the remains of his drink and shifted along the banquette, ready to get up. 'Have a good weekend, Grace.'

Every bit of her wanted to run after him, except that deep down she knew he was right, that he'd seen in her the sliver of ice that had entered her heart when she'd left Maidstone magistrates' court after her ex-husband's conviction for assault and had had to run the gauntlet of her jeering police colleagues. She realized now how much she'd hoped that Blake might help to melt that shard of anger and outrage, but it wasn't to be. It had become part of her. Maybe in time, she comforted herself, he'd discover that it could also be the thing that drew them more tightly together. She'd just have to wait and see.

ACKNOWLEDGEMENTS

I did a great deal of research on the subject of child sex abuse within the entertainment industry, the church, music schools and American college and university sports teams, reading numerous press reports, articles, official reports and grand jury transcripts, and watching television documentaries. What all these cases had in common was that the abuse took place within prestigious institutions with cherished reputations.

My understanding was particularly enhanced by *Our Guys: The Glen Ridge Rape and the Secret Life of the American Suburb* by Bernard Lefkowitz (University of California Press 1997), *In Plain Sight: the Life and Lies of Jimmy Savile* by Dan Davies (Quercus 2014) and the 2015 Oscar-winning movie *Spotlight*.

For taking time to share knowledge and answer questions I would like to thank John Cameron OBE at the NSPCC, Caroline Kerr, Professor Anthony Bateman and Jackie Malton. And for sharing the exploration of my characters, my thanks to Jo Strevens. All errors are my own.

As ever, big thanks to the wonderful team at Quercus – Jane Wood, Therese Keating, Hannah Robinson and Hugh Davis – and to my amazing agent Sheila Crowley and her assistant Abbie Greaves at Curtis Brown.